M000113172

Hooked on You

Jenn Matthews

Dedication

As this is my first novel, of course, I must dedicate it to my wonderful wife. She continues to support me through everything. I think she's more excited than I am about having my book published!

My parents have also been a driving force, always encouraging me to be creative and strive for success in whatever I am passionate about. Paul and Ann, thank you.

And finally, to my granddad Matthews, who died in 2008. He was a significant support to me in my early days of writing.

Prologue

Chalk & Silence

"Sami." Ollie ignored the smell of burning rubbish that, as usual, hung in the air. She held up her hand to the dark grey, scratched wall behind her. Who needed a blackboard when the walls themselves were just fine? "Can you complete these sums?"

Sami rounded his desk, grinning at his friends. He rubbed his hands together.

Ollie swept her arm outwards across the wall, as if the sums were a grand painting that Sami was allowed to add to. The rest of the children whooped as he arrived in front of the numbers and saluted Ollie, who returned the gesture.

She was glad she was able to treat the children with such enthusiasm—Iraq wasn't the most peaceful place, and she hoped she could bring some joy to their lives, even if it was just during school hours. The dwindling number of children each week made it difficult to retain her sunny attitude some days though—the boys collected into gangs as soon as they could hold a rifle, the girls lost to marriage to a man twice their age.

Why can't I do more? They deserve to be taught everything. Ollie supposed she would have to stick to maths and English as the British Army had prescribed. Some small dribbles of science where it didn't interfere with their beliefs. *I wish I could take them all home.* The collection of children, from the ages of five to twelve, all learned the same things at the same time. Sometimes, teaching such a mixture of ages was difficult, but it worked well. Ollie made sure she gave each child work they were able to do, and she encouraged the older children to help the younger ones in a sort of buddy scheme. The older kids got to express what they had learned, and the little ones had one-to-one tuition, something they usually would not be able to afford.

One of the oldest pupils, Sami stuck his tongue out of the side of his mouth and completed the maths problems on the wall. When he finished, all the children clapped, a response Ollie had encouraged from the first day, and something she made sure each child got in an equal measure, a collective appreciation of anyone who made an effort.

"Very good job," Ollie said, giving them all her widest smile. As inadequate as their curriculum was, they at least took joy from what little she was giving them.

Sami skipped back to his seat.

All her children looked at her with curious eyes, eager to learn. She explained the results Sami had chalked up and then looked across the class. A field of confident faces shone back at her.

I did that.

When the lesson was complete, Ollie sent all the children outside to play and dig up worms from the dusty ground. Their next lesson would be to study them and see who could find the longest one. Using things they could find in nature was a good way to get something simple like using a ruler into a lesson. She stood in her classroom, taking in her surroundings anew: a cement building with no glass in the windows and no doors in the frames. The sky out the window was cloudy today, and the hills in the distance were more grey than green. The little town of tents, old caravans, and makeshift huts sprawled across the valley, power lines stretching overhead.

Ollie startled at the sight of Zoe hanging around just outside the classroom doorway.

She entered the classroom and strode up to where Ollie stood trying not to smile too brightly. Her heart thudded in her ears, louder than the tatty football the kids were bouncing against the exterior wall of her classroom.

Zoe wore beige linen trousers and a plain white polo shirt. Her sturdy boots, the colour of the sand floor, had frayed laces. There was a smudge of mud on her face. Her hair was scraped back into a ponytail, a few wisps of it tickling her face.

Ollie kept her distance and relaxed a little as she realised Zoe was doing the same. She reached out, wanting to rub the mud from Zoe's face, but they were too far apart.

Zoe tilted her head to one side, her eyes shining.

We can't. Ollie dropped her hand.

"Great lesson." Zoe leaned against one of the more sturdy-looking desks. "They really respond so well to you."

A shy look passed between them.

"I know." Ollie flicked her hair back.

"Mad isn't it? You a PE teacher and now look at you." Zoe's eyes shone. "Teaching maths and spelling."

Ollie shrugged. "They don't need to learn the finer rules of netball or how to run to a bleep test. They need the basics."

In the moment of quiet, Ollie continued to wish she could take them all away—Zoe, Sami, all the kids outside on the concrete somehow finding a way to still be kids in a place like this—to somewhere where 2 a.m. raids didn't happen.

Zoe shook her head. It was as if she knew where Ollie's thoughts were. "The radio said there was an airstrike this morning. Not far away." Her face was tight.

Ollie's gaze travelled down her body. Zoe's knuckles were white as she gripped the desk. It made her reach automatically for Zoe again. Huffing to herself, Ollie dropped her hand. "It's all right. Fadhil said they won't go near the schools. Not the new ones, anyway. Some kind of unspoken rule, apparently."

"I know." But she folded her arms over her chest.

Silence spread between them. Ollie leant against the opposite desk.

The loud, exuberant voices of a group of children playing on the concrete courtyard caught her attention. They had no need for unbroken toys, or mobile phones, not like Kieran and Helen, who had always wanted the next new thing growing up and who now relied on tablets and smartphones to entertain themselves. They seemed overly privileged compared to the children here.

Zoe shuffled closer until the side of her boot touched Ollie's. Ollie dropped her head and looked at her own boots—army issue and the only part of her uniform she wore while in her teaching role. When she looked up again, Zoe's eyes were dark.

"Tonight?"

Ollie's mouth opened but no sound came out.

"I've missed you." Zoe chewed her lip.

"I've…" Ollie toed the floor. "I've missed you too." Then she shook her head and stared straight at her. "But it's… I shouldn't."

Zoe pressed her lips together and closed her eyes for a beat. "I feel like the bubble's bursting around us. Snapshots of your husband and family keep breaking through."

Ollie winced and nodded. She didn't trust herself to speak.

"It's not the same for me. I know it isn't. I don't have a spouse or kids or…" Exhaling, Zoe gestured in the dusty air "And I've never cheated on anyone. Not in my whole life. But I can imagine, at least."

"I love our bubble." Ollie's voice was thin, breathy, as if she had no energy to push it out of her. "But you're right. Things keep getting through." She pushed her fringe back out of her eyes. "Every time I think of my kids…" Tears squeezed her throat.

"I'm sorry. I'm sorry we got into this mess. But I can't help the way I feel about you."

"I can't help the way I feel about you." She felt stronger these days, like Zoe's presence was building her up, brick by brick.

It's wrong, though. All this lying. All this deceit. But she makes me feel like I'm actually alive. I've never felt like this at home. Ollie studied the woman across the space between them. *Maybe I'm at home when I'm with her.*

"All right," she said in the end, tremors washing over her as she felt sick for a heartbeat. She gripped the side of the desk and closed her eyes. "Tonight."

The old football thumped against the wall. Kids laughed.

"Those textbooks will be here tomorrow," Zoe's tone brightened.

I feel better, too, knowing we'll be together tonight. "That's fan—fantastic. The kids will be so excited."

"They will. Tota was telling me yesterday that she's never held a new book—always old, scrappy ones with half the pages missing." Zoe rubbed the rubber sole of her boot against Ollie's.

They couldn't. Not here. Ollie was about to speak, but her thoughts were interrupted by a low moan.

"What is…?" She lifted her head.

The noise was continuous and getting louder. The walls began to shake, the floor too, and they both stood properly. This was all too familiar.

It felt like slow motion, the missile hitting the town the school nestled inside. The noise that erupted and then the screams. And then such silence.

I'm looking down at the sky. Something hurts.

Then there was only blackness. Then, a bit later maybe, the feeling of being carried. She heard the unmistakeable whirring of army helicopter blades. *What time is it? Why don't I hear the kids anymore? Where am I?*

Ollie felt herself being turned sideways, hands skimming her spine from top to bottom. Her eyes focused finally. The school was no longer there. In its place concrete pieces blocking the view of the grey hills. *Where am I?*

She was turned onto her back once more. A warm, soft hand held hers and pressed her fingers against a wet cheek as they rose into the air, heading for safety.

Chapter 1

Chain Stitch (ch)

Five years later

Anna pulled into the driveway and smoothed her hair down against the back of her head. *A good day at school. And perhaps a lovely meal out tonight.* Her heart beat quickly and she checked her make-up in the rear-view mirror. *Twenty minutes until dinner. Just enough time to get those less-than-hardy begonias into the greenhouse.*

As she swung into the house, Bethany appeared from the living room. "Mum, seriously, Timothy's gonna do his nut in. You're ten minutes late."

"Oh shush, will you?" Anna hung up her coat and exchanged her work shoes for her gardening shoes. "It'll be ready in a few minutes. So long as his fish and chips are on the table at six, he won't 'do his nut in', as you put it."

Bethany scowled and shuffled into the garden with her mother, her mousy-brown long hair catching the fading sunlight. "Gardening? Again?"

Chuckling, Anna set about lugging the hefty pots with various plants in them over the lawn to the greenhouse, moving them one by one inside. "Darling, I like to garden. And these little sweeties won't survive unless they're somewhere a bit warmer."

"You literally just finished book club. Can't you sit down for five minutes?" Bethany had her arms folded. She scuffed a concrete paving slab with her slippered toe.

"Things to do, plants to move." Anna groaned, and her back ached as she pulled a particularly heavy pot over the threshold.

Bethany made no move to help her. "Why don't you go out? Call some of your friends? Don't you have any friends? What about Jack? Or Patricia? Meet up with one of them."

"Jack will be happily at home on his backside with a beer. And Patricia is busy, and too far away for any kind of impromptu get-together." She thought about her best friend, living so far away these days. And then Jack, her gentle colleague, with fondness. *Actually I had better text him and remind him about tomorrow's staff meeting.*

"You're as bad as one another." Bethany tilted her head to one side, and her long hair dropped forward over her shoulder. "And Liam?" Her nostrils flared.

"Liam is on training, away for the week." Anna looked up and brushed her hands together to rid them of the dust she'd collected. "I told you that."

"Oh. Right." Bethany looked out over the garden. "I must have forgotten." When she turned back to Anna, her gaze had softened. "I usually zone out when you talk about him."

Anna pretended to smack her around the back of the head as she passed her on the garden path, and they grinned at one another.

"So, fish and chips, and then what?"

"More Agatha Christie tonight, I think."

Bethany rolled her eyes. "I'm going to go out on a limb and reckon you've read whatever book it is at least…" her hand flew through the air as if in search of something, "…eight times?"

"Nine." Anna poked her tongue out.

Bethany returned the gesture. "You really need to get a life."

"I don't." Anna continued into the house and went to the kitchen to turn on the oven. She stooped down for a moment. Her knees needed a heartbeat or two to gather themselves. She rose with a half-grimace.

Precisely ten minutes before teatime, Timothy arrived in the kitchen to set the table. He did this every night they ate together. It was his way.

"Anna," he said, "you look happy. Did you have a nice time at the book club?"

"I did, thank you, Timothy." Her hand hovered by his shoulder waiting for permission, which he gave with a nod. Their silent language. She squeezed his shoulder and then moved away.

"What books are the kids reading at the moment?"

She smiled more broadly. *He's making small talk. How very polite of him.* "Some C.S. Lewis. We started where you're supposed to, and that is, of course, the first book he wrote, not the first in the series."

"*The Lion, the Witch, and the Wardrobe.*" Timothy placed the mats, cutlery, and glasses on the table with pinpoint accuracy. *I never had such a neat table before he moved in.*

"That's right."

"You really do need to get a life." Bethany still had her arms folded.

Anna tipped chips and fish onto two trays and slid them into the oven. She checked the temperature quickly, then leaned against the work surface. "My life is just fine."

"Aren't you bored?" Some of the derision had faded from her eyes. She seemed genuinely curious.

Anna pulled at her bottom lip. She sighed deeply. "Maybe. I don't know. I just have so much on, what with the book clubs and work and the garden..."

"Get a man in. And Jack could do half the book clubs. He's English, too, you know. He does know books."

"I don't know." Anna pushed her fingers through her short hair. *It would take hours to explain how I run my things. I might as well simply carry on doing them myself.*

"At least think about actually leaving the house and going to do something that involves people your own age."

Anna narrowed her eyes at her daughter, only half-jokingly.

"You know what I mean." Bethany threw up her hands. "Or at least... maybe learn something new? Go do a craft or...buy a kit." Their eyes locked. A standoff. Bethany stepped into Anna's arms and wrapped her own around her. "Please, Mum. Just...find something that isn't work."

With her nose buried in her daughter's hair, Anna allowed the familiar scent of hair dye and hairspray to flow through her. When she pulled back, she plastered her best serious-mother look onto her face. "You've been on about this for weeks. If I say yes, will you be quiet about it?"

"I will." Bethany squeezed her triumphantly.

"I'll try, okay?" *Perhaps I do need something new. Something to instil a sparkle of something exciting into my life again. It's been nicely quiet, but it does feel like things have been dragging the last few years.*

When Anna properly pulled back, Timothy was seated at the table, turning from one to the other with a quizzical look. "It's seven minutes to six and you haven't poured your wine yet."

She smiled fondly at him and went to the cupboard for a bottle. She could practically hear Bethany's eyes rolling behind her.

The hedgehog key ring Ollie was constructing stared up at her with large friendly eyes. She plumped it up and attached the key ring finding to the small hoop she'd made in the top. *Some kid is going to love this.*

With a sigh, she looked around her shop. For over two hours no one had come in. *I suppose no one has extra money at the end of the month.*

The bell over the door tinkled.

Maybe if it was one of her regulars she could engage in some kind of conversation. Ollie looked up. Nope, nobody she knew. She relaxed back in her chair. *No one wants to be bothered the minute they come in.* The shop was a little overwhelming to some people. *I'll offer my assistance if she looks lost.*

The redheaded customer was standing stock-still with her chin in her hand, gazing around the floor-to-ceiling shelves, looking like she'd stepped into Aladdin's cave. Ollie reckoned the woman was about her height, perhaps an inch or so shorter. She looked curvy under her big red coat, and her hair was short but neat. Cinnamon-coloured freckles dusted her cheeks and her neck. Ollie blinked when her gaze trailed lower, and she stared out of the window for a moment to gather herself.

The shop was small, but Ollie tried to keep it well stocked with colourful things stacked high. She had a collection of regular customers who wanted a whole variety of activities, usually involving yarn. She was not going to call it "wool" as most of her products didn't contain ingredients from a sheep. Acrylic and nylon were easy to wash and cheap to purchase; cotton and mohair were more luxurious, but a little more expensive. Ollie had even heard of yarn being made from ostrich feathers, but had never been inclined to buy any.

She went back to watching the woman, who seemed to be about Ollie's age, as she looked around the shop. Ollie smiled at the curiosity that seemed to have ignited.

The woman turned full circle and caught Ollie's eye. Ollie widened her smile and tried to appear approachable until it got awkward and she broke the woman's gaze and attached a price tag to the hedgehog. When she looked back up, the woman was still standing there, one eyebrow cocked at the hedgehog.

"The kids go nuts for these." She stood, her hands flat on the desk. Time ticked by, and the woman still didn't speak. *Come on. I haven't got all day.* She tapped her finger against the desk. "What can I help you with?"

"I wanted some wool."

Ollie pushed away a grimace at the word. "Hundred percent or a blend?"

The woman blinked.

"What's it for?"

"Knitting," the woman said. "I want to make a present for someone."

"Okay." She rounded the counter and stopped next to her. While they both looked up at the shelves, Ollie snuck another glance at the woman and noted her tense stance. "Colour? Project?" she asked with growing curiosity. *Why does choosing yarn make her stressed?*

"Red," the woman said. "Maybe a scarf. Would that be easy?"

"Have you knitted before?"

The woman shook her head. "Figured it can't be that difficult. Was just going to find a how-to on YouTube."

Ollie held back her opinion on that idea "I prefer crochet myself. Bit more flexible."

"Is it easier?" The woman started to play with her fingers.

"I think it is, but I'm biased."

The woman eyed the hedgehog amid the collection of various other small animals with key rings sticking out of their heads. "Maybe I'll do that, then." She fingered a ball of yarn at eye level.

Ollie nodded. "That one would work for a scarf," she said. "Hooks?"

"Excuse me?" The corners of her mouth pulled upwards.

"D'you have a set of hooks? You'd need a five, maybe a five-and-a-half, for that thickness."

"No. I don't have hooks."

"This just going to be a one-project event, or are you planning on making a hobby out of it?"

The woman shrugged but took the ball of yarn and squished it with her fingers. "Not sure. My daughter is trying to push me into developing a hobby. She said crafty things are very *in* at the moment." She smiled. "I'm not sure I'm that bothered about what's *in* exactly."

Ollie snorted and shrugged. "Me neither. I just do things I enjoy."

"Well apparently I don't have too many of those. I like to garden, read books. Wine. I like wine. But a woman cannot live on wine alone." She continued to squish the ball. "Bethany says I need a hobby, something I can do when I'm not guzzling Merlot. Or perhaps instead of."

"Sounds good to me," Ollie said. "Crochet, then?"

"Okay." She took another ball in the same colour from the little cubbyhole shelf and brought them to the till. "These, then. You think?"

"Great choice," Ollie replied. "Hooks, though?"

"Hmm. Suppose I'd better."

"Any trouble using your hands? Arthritis?"

Her arms folded with an indignant air.

"I have a regular customer in her thirties that uses padded hooks because her knuckle joints are painful."

"Oh. Well, in that case, no."

"I'd be out of a job if I couldn't use my hands." Ollie held out the pack of crochet hooks.

The woman took out her purse.

She rang through the items and put them in a paper bag. Money was exchanged. "What do you do?" Ollie asked.

"English teacher. Reams of marking and lesson planning. Book clubs after school."

"Ah. Yes, I can't imagine having arthritis with that career."

"No."

"YouTube, though?" Ollie's lips squished into a tight O shape.

The woman nodded.

"No good. You should learn properly. Face-to-face lessons."

"Are you offering?" Her eyebrows flicked up.

Olli smiled at the obvious tease. *Is she flirting with me?* No, she couldn't be. "Well, I run a couple of classes. Tuesdays and Thursdays. Only a fiver a pop, and you get free cups of tea."

The woman tilted her head to one side.

"No need to decide now," Ollie said, grabbing one of her business cards from the counter. "Give me a ring if you're interested."

The woman took the card and looked at it for a moment. "I'll have a go with YouTube first. If I need you, I'll call."

Ollie held a finger to her forehead in a tiny salute. "Speak to you soon, then."

The woman pursed her lips but then smiled as she took her bag to the door.

Ollie allowed the grin she was holding back to spread.

Anna put the paper bag beside the sofa and opened the box containing her dinner. The aroma set her mouth watering.

Chicken chow mein. How naughty. Her stomach made an impolite noise as she plated the food up and put Timothy's portion in the microwave for later. She sat at her large oak table to eat, a glass of red wine set close by as she stared into space. *That woman is wrong; I'll be fine with YouTube.* The Internet was an endless resource for things like crochet, how to re-grout the bathroom, how to wire a plug…

The first finished, she poured herself another glass and brought it into her cosy living room. Timothy was out at chess club and Bethany was out with friends—who knew what time that one would be home? Arthur was curled up in the other chair, his eyes closed in a content sort of way, his bushy tail twisted around his feet. On occasion, his pointy ears swivelled at some noise or other that she couldn't hear.

Peace and quiet for once. Anna sighed deeply, fired up her laptop, and tapped *how to crochet* into the search bar on the YouTube website. While it loaded, she took out her ball of wool and fingered the softness.

Arthur lifted his head and wandered over. She scratched his ears as he purred. "Don't even think about chasing my wool, mister."

He purred some more.

She got out a hook and held it like a pen. "Right. Here goes."

An hour later, she was about to throw the wool, hook, and laptop across the room. "What? What do you mean?" she shouted at the American woman on the screen. "Do what with *what*?"

Arthur was hunkered down with his backside in the air, his back legs ready. He sprang, but she managed to pull the wool and hook away just in time. She swept the back of her hand into his face. He hopped backwards. "No," she said firmly.

His eyes were wide, as if he were admonishing her, not the other way around.

"This is not yours."

He sat down, but his gaze snapped back to her wool. She huffed and closed the computer window. So far she had managed to make a very sloppy-looking knot in the soft red yarn. *Well, that's no good.*

With his tail primly around his paws again, Arthur lifted one of them and patted Anna's hand.

She pushed him away, then spent a while trying to unpick the mess on her hook before tying it tightly into a ball before snapping the end off and then throwing it to the floor. "Fine. Here."

He chased the knot for a moment, then, when it didn't move by itself, sloped indignantly back to his armchair.

"There's just no pleasing some people."

The woman on YouTube made it look so easy. *Why can't my brain communicate the information to my fingers?* Anna couldn't even keep the yarn straight, and she kept dropping the strand.

She drank a large amount from her glass, then plopped it down on the coffee table. Her handbag was calling to her. The business card was still inside. Darn That Yarn. She got the card out and placed it on the table. Did everyone feel like this when they started to learn?

Arrogant woman. She opened another window on her computer, searching for the same thing, but this time in Google. *Maybe written instructions will be easier.*

They weren't.

She picked up her phone and found the number she wanted.

Liam answered. "Hi, Anna."

"Do you happen to know of anyone who knows how to crochet?" she asked without preamble. "Or knit, for that matter?"

He chuckled. "I don't think so. Odd question, though. How are you?"

"Frustrated. Annoyed. Trying to teach myself to crochet but failing miserably."

He hummed, which made her smile. "Want me to come over? I have a bottle that is just begging to be drunk."

"Tempting offer." She snuggled into the cushions of her sofa. "But I do have marking to do. And Timothy will be back in a while. Just needed to offload. Sorry."

"No probs. Always here for you if you need me."

"Thanks. So, how's your day been?"

They chatted for a while until he said he had to go: the football was about to begin. Her stomach felt warm at that—he would have missed it for her had he come over. *He would have enjoyed a visit with me much more than football.* Maybe she should have just invited him. An orgasm always made her feel less frustrated.

She put the TV on. A period drama was running but couldn't really hold her interest. What was it with most TV shows being so boring nowadays? She put her wine down and snuggled deeper into the sofa.

The next thing she was aware of was a noise waking her up. When she opened her eyes, Timothy was staring down at her. *Wow, must have fallen asleep.*

"Are you ill?"

Anna shook her head. "No, I'm just tired."

"Why aren't you in bed, then?"

She smiled up at him. "I was trying to learn to crochet. But I suppose it's simply not going to happen."

"Why not?"

Arthur meowed, so Timothy went over to stroke his back.

"Maybe I don't have a crochet brain. Or something."

"What's that?" He pointed at the card on the coffee table.

"The lady at the wool shop does classes," she said. "It's her card."

"Are you going?"

"No."

"Is it too expensive?"

"No."

"Will you be working on the day it is scheduled?"

"No. She does them in the evening. Thursdays. No book clubs on Thursdays."

"You should go to a class, then."

Not for the first time, Timothy's way of seeing the world made her think more clearly. She nodded and sighed. *I really did want to prove the woman in the shop wrong. Damn.* "Okay."

He went into the kitchen, and the sliding noise of the bread bin opening carried through into the living room.

She took out her phone and stared at it for a while before dialling the number on the card.

"Hello?" said the woman on the other end, the last vowel drawn out.

Her shoulders relaxed somewhat. "Hi. My name's Anna. I'm… I came into the shop? Today?"

"Ah, yes." There was a pause. "Have you given up with YouTube, then?"

Anna laughed a bit and nodded even though the other woman couldn't see her. "I have. Could I book in for this Thursday coming?"

"Of course." The noise of shuffling and the click of a pen echoed in the background. "So you're Anna?"

"Anna Rose. Like the flower."

"Right. Okay. I'm Ollie, by the way. Williams. The class starts at seven. Well it's more a group, really. Some people bring in their own stuff to do. Most do actually."

Ollie sounded more friendly than arrogant now.

"And we're hoping to make a huge throw for the church hall. Everyone's started bringing in squares to contribute. We have a new project each week on top of that. But don't worry about that, not when you're a new starter. You'll be my only beginner, so I'll have plenty of time to go through everything."

"Great. Thanks." Anna touched the end of her chin with her finger. *I'd better be a good pupil.*

The greasy-spoon café was somewhere simple and neutral to meet. It didn't serve alcohol. *No need to make them think I have more problems than I already do.* She tapped her fingers against the table. *Could do with a beer, though, to settle my nerves.* She shook her head vigorously until her brain felt like it was waggling around in her skull. *No. I just need to be calm, collected, and honest.*

When Helen and Kieran entered, Ollie sat up straight and then started to stand. Kieran laid a hand on her shoulder. "It's fine, Mum. Stay sitting down."

Ollie's chest tightened, and she hesitated but stood anyway. "No, that's okay." She stepped up to Kieran and held one arm open for him. "I was hoping for a hug. That too much?"

Kieran glanced at his sister with worry in his eyes but stepped into Ollie's arms despite Helen's hard look. "'Course not."

At her son's clean and familiar scent, Ollie's whole body surged. *It's been so long since I've held him this close. Since he was a kid, really. He never let me hug him when he was a teenager, and then all the business with the divorce.* She sank into him and tried not to cry when his long arms enclosed her.

Patting her back, he chuckled and moved away. "All right, no need to overdo it." Ollie was glad he was nervous, because she felt like she was going to vibrate out of her boots any minute.

"It's wonderful to see you both, really it is." Her mouth clamped shut, and she inwardly rolled her eyes. *Calm and collected.*

Helen eyed her with a blank expression. She was an adult now, and Ollie could barely believe it. Apart from passing greetings, she'd last properly spoken to her daughter when she was fifteen. Ollie's stomach clenched as she remembered the summer holiday she'd tried to take them both on three years ago. Images of Helen folding her arms and turning her back on her still haunted her every now and then.

I can't believe they're both here.

Ollie held out a hand to Helen, realising that a hug was too much to ask. Helen stared at her for a moment but then rolled her eyes and gripped Ollie's hand firmly. They shook hands like business acquaintances.

Better than enemies, I suppose.

The kids sat, and Ollie went to the counter to get them cups of tea. She splashed out on a slice of cake for each of her children and a granola bar for herself.

Back at the table, she sat with her back like a plank of wood. Her hands stayed clasped on the table. "So…h-how are you both?"

Kieran, always the more talkative of the two, dived right into a story about his work. Then he complained about his new flat and how much his father had had to fix. *Things I could have fixed for him.* Ollie bit her lip and chose not to comment. Her ex-husband deserved the privilege of being able to help their son. He hadn't caused all the mess—she had.

A stone of cool expression, Helen sat silently until the waitress arrived. Ollie watched her nervously as the waitress slid the chocolate cake in front of her. Helen looked down at it, and something resembling warmth passed across her face.

Ollie took a slow breath. "You always liked chocolate."

It took a long moment, but Helen's eyes lifted to her own. She said nothing, however.

"Aren't you going to speak to me?" Ollie asked, the pressure in her throat making the words sound like a plea.

Helen's shoulders sagged. "I am. I just…" She picked up her fork, her gaze intently on her cake. "I'm just not sure what to say."

She hates me. "I'm sorry about everything," Ollie whispered and blinked back the tears that gathered.

"You've said it a hundred times, Mum." Helen shook her head. "I just don't think it's worth saying it anymore. I know you're sorry. It doesn't mean anything yet."

"I know. I know." Ollie picked up her teacup, if only for something to do that didn't involve crying. She felt like she was breaking. *This isn't going to work. I'm never going to be the kind of mum I've always wanted to be, not now.* "I wish it would just all go away."

"What I don't understand," Helen said slowly, "is why you stayed with Dad for twenty years if you didn't love him."

"I did, sweetheart." Ollie sighed. "I did love him, whatever anyone thinks. I certainly did in the beginning."

"But then you fell in love with someone else?" Kieran asked carefully.

Ollie nodded. "It was over, romantically, with your father, before that. But yes."

Helen's head rocked from side to side, and her eyes darted about the space between her nose and her cake, as if Ollie's words were too much to process. "Why did you stay with him, though?"

"It was easy." Ollie decided to be honest. *There have been too many lies.* "I was away so much, it didn't seem to matter. When we were together, we were great, weren't we? Like a happy family."

Kieran smiled at her and placed his big hand over hers. She smiled back, and he squeezed her fingers.

"Reasonably." Helen was still staring at her cake. She hadn't taken a bite yet.

"I wanted to be home, but I wanted to be at work too. You know what my job meant to me."

"You were always there, though. Never with us." Helen picked up her fork and stabbed at the cake as if it might be alive.

"I know. Well, now I'm here, and I'm available. So long as I'm not teaching, or in the shop… You should come see the shop. I'd hope you'd like it." She directed her words at Helen. "You always liked art, didn't you? Not like Mister Monkey here." She grinned at her son, who blushed modestly. Images of him up a tree with muck all over his face flashed in front of her eyes. The tears hiding on the brink receded just a bit.

"True." Helen bit her lip and then took a forkful of cake. She hesitated, her gaze flicking up to Ollie before she ate it. Her face relaxed, even, and her mouth turned up ever so slightly at the corners.

Everything seemed to flop into a mess of relief in Ollie's body. *Progress, indeed.* "We have card-making supplies, and little kits to make fabric animals. If you like one, you'll definitely get a family discount."

"I don't want any handouts from you." Helen's fork clattered to her plate. She sat back in her chair. "It's not going to make up for it. Any of it."

"I just meant…" Ollie reached out to her, but Helen was out of her chair in a heartbeat.

"No, Mum. You can't buy me off with promises of pretty things like I'm still ten years old. It doesn't work like that." Her hair bounced about her shoulders as she left the café.

Ollie slumped on one hand, her fingers sinking into her hair. A tear dripped down her wrist and into the shirtsleeve she had rolled up to her elbow.

A warm hand on her back made her relax somewhat. *At least my boy is still here.* She turned her head to one side on her hand and smiled sadly at him.

His hand smoothed up and down her spine. "You just need to give her time."

"Where's my little girl gone? The one that used to jump up and down when I came home from work? That terrific little girl that hung onto my legs when I was leaving on assignment?" She leaned heavily towards her son, and his arm circled her shoulders.

"She'll come round, I promise. Just you see."

"Kieran, I can't do any more to make it right." She sat up then, away from his embrace. "I didn't mean to offend her. The family discount; I'd give it to any of our relatives if they'd just talk to me, or visit."

Kieran nodded, his dark eyes soft. He looked so much like his father, who was a good man despite all he had been through. *All I've put him through.* Ollie swallowed and shook the tears away.

"Eat your cake, drink your tea." She eyed Helen's cake and pushed it into the middle of the table. "If she comes back, she can continue with hers."

Kieran sipped his tea and started to munch on his cake. It made her stomach unclench just a bit as she watched him.

One down, perhaps. One to go.

Red and orange leaves blew around Anna's feet as she strode up the street towards the shop. She had arrived early with a crisp new five-pound note ready. The yarn she had bought and all her shiny new hooks were tied with an elastic band and stuffed in an old fabric shopping bag. The front door to the shop was locked, so she found a door to the side, with a sign on it reading: *Crochet Groups.*

A man in his late twenties let her in. He had sandy-coloured hair and a large grin. "Evening. You must be Anna."

"Yes." She blinked. "How did you know?"

"I come every week, been coming since it started. I'm practically Ollie's right-hand man." His grin widened. "She told me you would be joining us. And she described you."

"Described me?" Anna looked at him in confusion, then settled her face into a more relaxed expression. She followed him into a dark corridor. "All good, I hope?"

"Oh, definitely. Very much so." The man pursed his lips as if holding back more.

"Let me guess. She told you about my foray into the world of online crochet, did she?"

There was a pause while he looked at her, his gaze steady. Then his face relaxed, and he held a hand out, showed her into a large airy room with tables and chairs. "Yes, that's it. Oh," he said chuckling, "my name is Matthew."

"Nice to meet you. Anna Rose."

They shook hands, and he left her standing in the classroom.

She put her cloth bag atop one of the tables. The room was covered on two sides with shelves full of patterns, books and materials. Handmade items hung all over the walls, and a stereo stood in one corner. In another corner was a countertop with a sink, a kettle, and a mini fridge. When Ollie came in, Anna turned to give her a smile.

"Hi, Anna," Ollie said. "Welcome. It's nice to have a fresh face joining us."

"I'll need a lot of help." Anna rolled her eyes.

"It's okay. We'll get you there." They locked gazes for a moment.

There was a warmth in Ollie's eyes that Anna liked. She sat down, her cloth bag on the table in front of her.

More people filed into the classroom. They seemed like a good mix of ages and genders—mostly women, but Anna had expected that. A couple of teenagers were whispering between themselves. An old man shuffled inside in what looked like an old pair of leather slippers.

Ollie greeted every person with a pat or a hug. Some people handed her crocheted squares in a variety of colours. Ollie placed them into a shallow wicker basket on the counter. She held on to the old man's elbow as he took his seat. She smiled at everyone who smiled at her.

Everyone likes her. Anna watched people pull out their projects. One older lady had a huge blanket that would probably cover a king-sized bed. It flowed down her knees and onto the floor. Ollie approached and said something quietly to her. The lady wrapped her arms around Ollie, patted her cheek, and then kissed it. Ollie seemed to shine with affection. Anna thought she saw them exchange a knowing smile, as if they shared a secret.

A teenage girl took out the striped head, legs, and tail of something that resembled a cat.

It looks like Arthur.

Matthew came to sit next to her and laid his pieces out on the table. He aligned everything together on the smooth surface and smiled at Anna as she peered at his work. He gestured to the pieces before him. "What do you think?" he asked, his eyebrows knitting together.

They were pale blue, flecked with navy. Neat stitches with little bubbles across in a pattern. "Um. It's lovely." She looked up at him. "What is it?"

He frowned. "A cardigan. Can't you tell?" His hand went over his mouth, and she took another look.

"Of course I can." She touched his arm. "I was thrown by the lack of buttons. Very nice."

"Spent a fortune on the yarn." He sighed. "It's for my mum. She's lovely." He shrugged. "Dippy, but lovely."

"I'm sure she'll love it," Anna said.

He beamed at her. "Usually I don't try anything so difficult. More of a quick-and-easy kind of guy. I'm never making anything like this again; it's been an absolute nightmare." He looked Anna up and down. "I expect you're not as lazy as me."

"I don't know yet," Anna replied. "I've never done anything like this before."

"Right, everyone," Ollie said, standing up at the front and clasping a bunch of papers. "We'll be making chickens today."

"Chickens?" Anna hissed. She pressed her lips together obediently as Matthew flapped his hand at her.

"The head and body are made in one, the legs are one row of doubles, and the beak is just a cone. Who'd like one?"

A few people put their hands up.

Ollie handed the patterns out. When she passed Anna's table, she leant down, her loose blond curls swinging by her eyes. "Don't worry, I'll sit down with you in a minute." She placed a pattern on the desk. "Take one, though. For when you've learned enough."

"Okay," Anna said.

When Ollie offered him a pattern, Matthew held up his hand. "No thanks. Looks too complicated." He indicated his cardigan.

Ollie looked carefully at his work before giving him a thumbs up. She turned on the stereo, a popular channel but at a low volume. "And keep those squares coming, guys. The Women's Institute is rather lacking in crocheters, and Sandra is continually telling me how awfully grateful she is about the project. That back wall has been empty for months."

So far, there were quite a few squares in the wicker basket. Anna wondered how big the wall hanging was going to be in the end. She unwound the elastic band from her hooks and arranged them by size on the table. The cloth bag got stuffed into her handbag. She stared at her hooks, then looked around. Everyone was getting to work.

Matthew had a hook and ball of wool and was continuing with what looked like a sleeve. His attention seemed to be repeatedly drawn towards someone behind them. Finally, she followed his gaze.

A dark, curly-haired man sat next to the teenager with the cat-shaped item. Anna looked back at Matthew and cleared her throat.

He feigned sudden concentrated interest in the pattern he had laid out, but underneath his bowed head, she saw a small smile.

Anna peered at the curly-haired man and his teenaged companion. *Interesting.* But before she could contemplate this discovery more, Ollie passed her to fill the kettle and collected together some mugs.

"Teas?" she asked.

Anna put up her hand.

"Coffees?"

Anna sat with her hands clasped, listening to the quiet murmurs and occasional chuckles that filled the rom. The kettle rumbled on the counter as it boiled.

Once everyone had a drink, Ollie brought Anna's over and slid into the seat next to her. "Right, then," she said. "Let's start with how to hold your hook and yarn."

Anna felt all fingers and thumbs as Ollie demonstrated making a slip knot, then showed her how to maintain the correct tension. She copied her successfully, but had put the hook down onto the table. "I'm sorry. Show me again how to hold it?"

Ollie was obviously used to showing beginners how it was done. "Don't worry, you'll get it. Here, let's try a chain stitch."

Anna felt like there was yarn coming out of about six places on her hand, but after gentle coaxing and carefully placed encouragement, she shakily made her first chain. She let out a stuttering laugh.

"You'll get it, I promise," Ollie said.

"Thank you for being so patient."

"You're welcome."

It felt strange being the object of Ollie's kind and sparkly eyes. *She's very pretty.*

Anna swallowed hard. *Where did that come from?* She made herself focus back on her slightly trembling hands. Ollie sat and watched her continue to work but didn't interrupt.

Anna let out a slow breath, set her shoulders and finished another chain stitch. That earned her one of Ollie's kind smiles.

"See? You're doing it."

They sat in silence for a couple of minutes. Anna continued to make a string of stitches around a foot long. As she worked and got used to how the stitches felt and she relaxed further. The stitches were getting neater and more uniform.

Anna reached for her tea and took a sip. "Mmm, perfect," she said. "So…how long have you been crocheting for?"

"Five years," Ollie said.

"Oh! I would have thought longer."

"I started crocheting after I was in an accident." Ollie sipped her coffee. "I was bored. My children pushed me to go do *something*. Anything to stop me watching daytime TV in my pyjamas. Had a neighbour who sat with me and showed me the ropes." She smirked. "So to speak."

"My daughter convinced me as well."

"Yes, you said."

Anna held out her chain. "So, what now?"

"Depends how much of a perfectionist you are." Ollie smiled.

Anna rolled her eyes. "Um…am I that obvious?"

"If you want them really neat, you can undo them and start again." Ollie made a sweeping gesture with her arm.

Anna pulled the end of her chain and the whole thing unravelled in small pops. The now-unused wool spread back and forth across the table.

"Try to make them about twice the thickness of the hook you're using," Ollie said.

Carefully, Anna remade the slip knot.

Ollie gave her a thumbs up. "Brill." She looked around. "Mind if I leave you to it?"

"Not at all," Anna said, though that was a complete lie. She missed Ollie's presence already.

"Let me know when you're confident with the chains, then we'll learn some doubles."

She found herself suddenly determined to get confident with chains as quickly as possible.

As Ollie rounded the table and walked amongst the group, Anna noticed a slight limp on her right side. Perhaps from her accident. She peered at her for a moment more, before turning her attention back to her chain. *Why can't she spend more time with me?* Anna blinked rapidly. *Because she's here for everyone, you idiot.*

Around half of the group periodically called Ollie over to ask for help, and she moved between them with an energy that bubbled around her. Despite her determination to succeed at single chains, Anna was more than once caught up in watching Ollie help people. *She's a born teacher.*

Matthew paid alternating attention to the man across the room and his own pattern. Anna wondered how he could focus on two things like that, but asking would make him lose his place.

She nodded towards the curly-haired man. "Who's that?"

His cheeks reddened. "Um. Just someone that came in a few weeks ago."

Matthew reminded her of the girls in her form when a new, rather attractive male teacher had started at the beginning of term. "And you're interested in him because…?"

Matthew swallowed, but then grinned sheepishly and shrugged. "Oh, I'm really not. He's just…" He looked carefully over his shoulder. "He's nice to look at."

"Right." She tried not to smile. It was sweet, really, watching someone with such obvious confidence get shy over another human being. "Why not go over to him?"

"I thought about it. Usually I'm not one to shy away from introducing myself, but…" His gaze lingered on Ollie, who was helping out somebody close to Curly Locks.

"Have you been warned off?" *Is he spoken for? Are Curly Locks and Ollie an item?* But she hadn't seen her spend any inordinate amount of time with the man, no more than with Anna. Maybe even a bit less. And they didn't seem to have that flirting spark a couple usually had.

"Of a fashion." He huffed and went back to his sleeve. "Nothing like Mother Hen reminding me that if I do with Harry what I usually do with men, I'll then have to see him every week afterwards. And Ollie wouldn't forgive me for tainting such a lovely atmosphere with the *consequences* of my escapades."

"Ah." Anna tried not to laugh. *Not an item, then.* "So you're the fancy-free type, hmm?"

"That's me." He waggled his eyebrows suggestively at her and she giggled. No wonder he was so devoted to his mother. Anna bet she had let him get away with murder as a child.

"So, you obviously enjoy coming here." Anna returned her gaze to her doubles.

"I do." His voice was silky, affectionate and settled, as if he were enclosed in a big fluffy blanket someone had tucked around his shoulders as they stirred the sugar into his cup of tea for him.

"What is it about the group that you like?"

"I like that I'm part of something. Something fairly normal. If you can call crochet normal, I don't know. I like the people. And Ollie's a friend." He snorted. "If I didn't come to her classes, I probably wouldn't see her sober."

"Sounds like you two are close."

He sighed. "Best mates."

She concentrated on her chain, on making each stitch exactly the same size with the exact same tension in her yarn. The room seemed to grow quiet around her, and her shoulders slowly dropped. When she looked up, Ollie was leaning against the sideboard watching her.

"Knew you'd want to make them all perfect," she said.

Anna suppressed the urge to beam. "Well, if you're going to do something, might as well get it right," she said modestly.

"Ready to learn some doubles?"

"Goodness yes."

Ollie immediately slid back into the chair beside her, like she'd just been waiting for an excuse. "Okay. So we stick the hook into the chain just there…" Ollie pointed with her little finger. "Then yarn over." She plucked Anna's yarn gently and pulled it over her hook. "Pull a loop through."

Anna pulled the loop through the chain stitch herself.

"Yarn over again, then pull a loop through both hoops."

"Right."

Ollie's blond hair fell forward as she leaned closer. A small waft of chlorine and lavender tickled Anna's nose.

By the time Anna looked at the stitch again, Ollie's instructions had disappeared from her memory.

But Ollie just smiled and went over it four more times with her. "Keep going across. When you get to the end, give me a shout." She stood to put the kettle on again.

That top looks so nice on her. It was grey and well worn. Anna wished she could wear something so casual to work, but it wouldn't be appropriate at school.

Matthew nudged her and held out his sleeve. "Nearly done," he sang.

"So quick! It's a very nice colour. May I?" At his nod, she ran her fingertips along a row of stitches. "Lovely and soft. Your mum's going to love that. Perfect for winter."

"I've been working on it for ages," Matthew said. "I didn't think I'd get it finished in time." He paused. "Or at all."

"How long have you got left?"

"Two weeks until her birthday. At least she only turns sixty once. I won't have to make anything this extravagant for at least ten years." He pointed to the neck. "Just the edging here to do, and to sew it together."

"Wonderful." Anna gestured at her dozen stitches. "This, I feel, will take a lot longer." She looked at her work again, and her heart sank. "Damn. I've already completely forgotten how to do it."

"Hook in the chain," Matthew said. "Yarn over, pull through, yarn over, pull through."

"Thanks," Anna replied, her nose almost touching her hands as she continued. She got to the end of the row just as people were starting to pack up.

Ollie came over and indicated the second untouched cup of tea she'd made for Anna, who stared at the cold drink and winced.

"Sorry."

"I've never seen anyone so focused."

Anna huffed and held out the row. "It's gone all curly."

"That's okay." Ollie pulled on the curl gently, like a spring, and her smile broadened as it bounced into the air. "That means your tension is okay."

"It does?"

"Once you've finished one row, you do a chain stitch, and that counts as the first double for the next row."

People were leaving, putting their five pounds into a box at the door. Matthew smiled at Harry but didn't speak to him. She probably shouldn't keep Ollie. She and Matthew probably had plans for the evening. She gazed over at her cloth bag.

"It's fine," Ollie said. "Stay until you've done another few stitches."

"So I go back and forth?" Anna did a careful chain stitch before turning the piece and slipping her hook into the next stitch. *I like Ollie, and she doesn't seem to dislike me. Maybe she'd like to go for a drink.*

"Yep."

Anna nodded, but decided against making the invitation. *She barely knows me, and this is a business arrangement.* Ollie and Matthew saw one another socially, but butterflies crumpled Anna's stomach when she considered asking her herself. She wasn't sure why she felt awkward about it. She wasn't usually so nervous with other people.

Ollie had gathered several cups onto one table and was moving them, one in each hand at a time, to the sink. Matthew walked past and didn't offer to help. As he held a hand up, Anna mirrored his gesture as a goodbye. *So, no plans, then.*

"I don't want to keep you," Anna said.

"It's fine. I've got to wash up anyway." Ollie moved the last couple of cups to the sink. They clattered noisily.

Anna looked up. "So, how long have you worked here?" she asked as the room emptied.

"Actually I own it. Two years now." Ollie ran the tap and filled the bowl. "Bought it with some inheritance. And a divorce settlement."

"Ah. Part of the angry ex-wives club too?"

A quick breath of air huffed from Ollie as she wiped round the inside of a mug. "Something like that."

"It's nice. The shop."

"I never thought it would do well but…I suppose your daughter is right. Crafts are the *in* thing."

Anna chuckled. "Yes. Sometimes my darling daughter is right."

"Teenager?"

"Absolutely."

"I've got one of those." Ollie turned her full attention onto Anna.

"How old?" The sudden focus on her was surprising, though it was nice; but it was also a bit disconcerting somehow. She looked back down at her doubles.

"Eighteen."

"Mine's twenty."

"Technically, twenty years old isn't a teenager." Ollie's voice had a teasing lilt.

Anna found the flow of her fingers and the tightened wool was a little more fluid and less disjointed. Her retort was deliberately tinged with amusement. "Yes, well, she often acts like one. What about yours? Uni?"

"Chemistry. Yours?"

"Italian and politics."

"*Molto bene.*"

That lilt again in her voice captured Anna's attention, and she found Ollie's smile waiting for her.

"Just the one daughter?" Anna asked a bit shakily.

"I have a son too—Kieran. Grown-up but can't tie his own shoelaces."

"Hmmm," Anna replied, relieved to be on more familiar ground. She fell easily into the comfort of grousing with another mother. "Even when they've left home and moved on they still want you to look after them, don't they?"

"At some point he's going to have to learn how to look after himself. I remember when he went away to university, I told him it wasn't up to anyone else to cook his meals or wash his clothes."

"I have an adopted son too. He has autism, lives with Bethany and I. He was a pupil of mine, very bright, desperate to be welcomed into society. His mum died a few years ago. He's tried living in a few shared flats but… they've never worked out for him. So I suggested he move in with us."

"That's kind." Ollie started placing the clean cups in the drainer.

"He was always so lovely at school. And I couldn't let him carry on living like that."

"How's it working out?" Ollie asked as she dried her hands. She sloshed bubbly water out of the bowl.

"Okay. I think the fact that he's a boy is stranger than his diagnosis."

"He and your daughter get on?"

"Fairly well. They have their moments." She got to the end of her next row, laid her crochet down on the table, and pushed up from her seat. "All right. I've kept you long enough."

It took a moment longer than normal for Ollie to answer. "Been nice to get to know you."

Anna nodded, pushed her yarn and hook into her bag, gathered up the remaining hooks, and stretched the elastic round them. She took out the five-pound note from her purse and held it out.

Ollie shook her head. "First class is free."

Anna folded her arms and regarded Ollie with amusement. She pursed her lips and narrowed her eyes, her usual instinct to flirt taking over. "What's your game?"

"I'm not playing a game." Ollie put up her hands as if Anna were pointing a gun at her. "Just want you to come back next week."

Anna paused. *Why am I flirting with her? At least she doesn't seem too uncomfortable with it.* Her arms dropped to her sides. "Okay, then." She put the note back and snapped her purse closed. "I'll have to come back, make sure your efforts aren't all for nothing."

"Practice makes permanent."

"Isn't it 'perfect'?"

"Only if you practise correctly. If you practise something wrong, it won't be perfect."

"Good point."

Ollie lowered her gaze.

She looks sad. Maybe I should ask if she's okay. Or perhaps out for a drink? But, no, she was still too intimidated by that idea for some reason.

"See if you can make it a square," Ollie said before Anna could speak, pointing to the cloth bag.

"Okay." She was relieved to see that the sadness had disappeared. She followed Ollie into the dark corridor and moved past her onto the street when Ollie held the door open for her.

"See you next week, Anna."

Anna nodded and walked away, her cloth bag firmly under her arm.

Chapter 2

Double Crochet (dc)

The attempted square mocked Anna as she held it up before her. Her throat tightened, and her jaw ached from grinding her teeth. "Damn. How have I managed that?"

Bethany's raised eyebrow nearly gained the power of speech from across the room. "How would I know?" she said. "You're the one that went to the class." She promptly went back to her magazine.

Anna huffed and stared at the neat row of double crochet stitches she had begun with. "I don't understand." She frowned and started again. Ten minutes later, she found herself in the same situation. She sighed, put the almost-triangular piece onto her lap, and folded her hands on top of it.

Timothy wandered in with his laptop and sat in the armchair. "Dinner was an eight out of ten," he said. "As good as last night, but not as nice as the pie you made on Monday."

"Thank you, Timothy," Anna said.

He smiled at her. "What's the matter? You're frowning."

"I'm having yet more trouble with crochet." She pouted at her work.

Bethany sighed loudly and rolled her eyes.

"Hey, miss," Anna said. "You're the one who decided I needed a new hobby."

"Yeah, to meet people and get you out of the house," Bethany said. "Not to be all moody and ask *me* how it's done when you've got some new friend who should be teaching you." She shrugged and rolled her eyes again. "Ask her tomorrow."

"I'm not sure I could show my face in there with a square like this." She held the piece so it dangled from her hook.

Arthur rolled onto his back and looked up at her from the carpet. He stretched his white-socked legs out and purred. His gaze moved to the mess in her hands.

"You are not having it," Anna said. "I don't care how awful it looks."

"Why do you call it a square? That's not a square shape," Timothy said.

"No." Anna wiped at the tears of frustration that had gathered in her eyes. "It's not, is it?"

"You must be making fewer stitches at the end than at the beginning."

She stared at him. "How do you figure that?"

"If you start with twenty stitches, for example," he said, "and you accidentally do one less stitch each row, you will end up with a very neat, if unintentional, triangle. Like you have there."

"Timothy." Her eyes were suddenly alight, and she sat up a little straighter. "You're a genius."

"No, I'm not. Just remarkably intelligent, statistically speaking." He pointed at her work. "You should count the stitches for each row you do. Maybe you are missing one each time."

She followed his finger, then undid the same rows she had done incorrectly and began again, mouthing the numbers to herself as she went and making sure she had the same amount of stitches on each row. Timothy was right. She had been missing out the last stitch of each row. She exhaled into the quiet room.

Bethany was engrossed in her magazine.

Timothy had his headphones on, watching something on his laptop.

The tension dropped from Anna's stomach. She could do this.

Arthur continued to purr.

Ollie picked up another key ring to attach to the tiny unicorn she was making. She shook her head at the yellow-and-green toy and looked over at the cluster of unicorns on the desk. It simply didn't look as cute as the pink, purple, and sparkly baby-blue ones. *So much for non-gender-binary toys.*

The bell jingled and she glanced up. Matthew was sauntering towards her.

"All right?" she said.

"I've finished my cardigan," he announced. "Which means I'm allowed to go out for a drink. What do you say?"

She looked at her watch. "I say: 'an hour left until I close'."

"Not too long, then." He perched on the arm of the sofa and fingered the handmade rainbow throw slung over the back. "So, looking forward to tomorrow?"

Why were his eyes glinting? She turned her attention back to her unicorn. "What's happening tomorrow?"

He smirked. "Crochet class. With the lovely Anna."

That deserved a snort. A snort and a pointed look. "There are other people at the class, you know."

"And?" He continued to examine her.

She tilted her head. "And it'll be nice to see her again, yes."

"You did plenty of *seeing* her last week." Matthew threw his head to one side. "I'm surprised she didn't notice."

"She was too engrossed in crocheting. She barely noticed me."

He just gave her a smile and shook his head.

"Anyway, what about you and your eternal passive interest in Harry?"

He twisted his lips and clutched at a fistful of the throw. "Just a passing fancy."

"Is it?"

"Very much so." He turned back to her. "Anyway. Anna."

She cut him off before he could go there. "She's divorced. Blatantly straight."

"You're divorced. You're not straight."

"Hmm."

A moment of silence passed. Matthew bounced from the sofa and squeezed her arm. "The Cock and Duck?" he asked. "Just for one, perhaps?"

"When we close." She batted his hand away. "And it will be just one. Some of us have a shop to run."

"'Course," he said with a bright look.

"I've got some boxes to move into the storeroom."

"All right, then. I'll be back in an hour to whisk you away from this drudgery, m'lady."

She rolled her eyes as he promenaded out the door.

Anna had a free period on Thursday afternoon, so she got home early, applied a tad more make-up than usual, and waited for the sound of her doorbell. It rang at four o'clock sharp.

Liam's smiling face emerged as she opened the door. He hadn't changed out of his 'school clothes', but then, neither had she. "Evening," he said.

"Not quite," she said, looking at her watch. "But near enough." She took her handbag from the hook and followed him to his car.

Her stomach fluttered as they drove into town, but when they pulled into the car park of the same old pub they'd been to countless times before, her heart sank just a touch. *Never mind. One day, when we have more time together, or something to celebrate, he'll take me somewhere a bit more posh.* He parked carefully, and she did admire the way he made sure his car was just perfect in the space.

I don't know why he and Timothy don't get on. They both care so much about detail. She was glad he had driven. Her parking wasn't dangerous, but he always commented if she was an inch this way or that. It made her grit her teeth.

His hand felt heavy against the small of her back as he steered them into the pub and guided her towards a small table by the window. She sat and gave him a grateful smile. He was being chivalrous, and there was nothing wrong with that. She liked being treated as if she was special. As if she was someone to be worshipped. It made her stomach tingle.

"Thank you." She took the menu from its holder. "Just a red wine, please?"

He stood with a scrape of his chair and went to the bar. She took in the roundness of his backside in his dress trousers as he left, and then leant forward over the menu to peruse her options.

Their dinner was pleasant enough. A bundle of kids raced around the pub, and she watched them with joy. They looked about ten or eleven. Soon, they would be coming to her school, fresh-faced and hopefully eager to learn. She loved that look, the bright and huge eyes, the quick wit and the pureness the eleven-year-olds brought on that first day. *Next year. A whole year away, in fact.* Returning her attention to Liam, she noticed his hard gaze on the children.

"You watch. One of them will fall, running around like that in an enclosed space. Don't their parents know how to control them?"

She sighed. "I expect they're just letting off some steam from a boring day at juniors."

"Well, they should sit down and be quiet. Especially at a place like this—somewhere so nice. I don't pay good money to have kids running all around me screaming. Get enough of that at work."

She held back from rolling her eyes and instead chose to take his hand. She squeezed until he looked at her, and then she sent him a warm smile. "There are places we could go where the atmosphere is a little more... romantic." She tried to keep her tone light, but the swirling annoyance in her stomach made it a bit hard.

He seemed not to notice, thankfully. "Next time we go out, when we have a proper night off together, we'll go to the theatre, hmm?"

A flash of Liam in a suave suit, holding his arm out to her as they ascended the steps into the local theatre made her smile. Hope shone from his eyes, and she felt her whole body soften. "That sounds marvellous."

As they ate, she watched the precise movements of his knife and fork. He really was quite handsome, and he did scrub up well. His job, as boring as it probably sounded to everyone else, sometimes fascinated her. What he didn't know about health and safety, policies and procedures, was nobody's business. She liked hearing the stories about scrapes he'd had to clear up when he was just starting out in the job, and the way he spoke about some of the managers he had worked with sometimes made her howl with laughter.

"How are the kids?" Liam took a perfectly cut sliver of steak from his fork and chewed it with precise movements.

"They're okay. Bethany seems to be doing well at uni. She's not asked me for help, not that I have the time. But she seems happy. Pleased that I'm broadening my horizons when it comes to non-work-related activities."

They exchanged a smile.

"And Timothy?"

"He's well. Enjoyed the recent stock take they did at the shop. He really is exceptionally good at counting things. He'd do it all day if they let him."

He swallowed. "I can imagine. He wouldn't get far, though, would he? If he wasn't diagnosed as retarded?"

Anna's stomach twisted at that word. She narrowed her eyes at him. "Please, Liam."

"Please *what*?" Liam shrugged and put his knife down perpendicular to his plate and then picked up his glass. "It isn't as if it isn't true." He took a sip. "Or am I using the *wrong word* again?"

Anna continued to stare at him, her hands curling into fists. If she spoke she'd say something she would later regret.

"Oh, it is that? Okay. I clearly need to write some kind of list and carry it around with me. 'Words I'm Not Allowed to Use to Describe Timothy' or something." Liam sighed. "He's not even here to catch me. What difference does it make?"

"Why call him anything but Timothy?" Anna bit her lip and considered her plate, unsure whether she was hungry anymore. "Why use adjectives that might make me annoyed with you? You know how I feel about it."

Liam huffed and rubbed the back of his cropped hair. "I just don't know the right language to use."

"I know." *It doesn't make it any less annoying.* She sighed deeply and chose to let it drop. *What's the point? He's been making mistakes like these since we started dating. It's not like I'm going to change him and I suppose he doesn't do it maliciously.* She was thankful Liam and Timothy had barely interacted back at the house.

Their main courses were over. She placed a hand on her belly and pondered having a dessert. *I have crochet at seven. And I could do with refraining from anything too fattening, especially as I'll probably indulge hugely when it comes to Christmas.* She didn't much like her tummy, which protruded a bit more than she cared for and made her feel shy when she undressed in front of Liam.

By the time the waiter arrived and handed them each a dessert menu, Anna lifted a hand in a definite "no" gesture.

Liam smiled at her and pushed her hand back to the table. "We'll both have a crème caramel each." He nodded reassuringly at Anna and sipped from his glass of water. "We always have the crème caramel. You love it."

She pushed away a pout and stared at her napkin for a moment. It took a measured moment before she could lift her head to return the smile. "That's true. It is nice." *He doesn't mind, I suppose, if I carry a bit of extra weight. And it is nice to have a treat now and then.*

On the way from the pub to Ollie's shop, she glanced towards the cloth bag in the footwell of the passenger's seat, pleased with the three squares she had managed to crochet during the last two days. She'd had to Google how to fasten off, and it had taken Timothy's help to figure it out, but still.

"Who'd have thought you'd enjoy crocheting so much?" Liam said with a wide smile. He placed his hand on her thigh as he drove.

Anna nodded. "You're right in your assumption that I really didn't think much of the whole craft-hobby idea at first. I've surprised myself."

"Glad you've found something you like—and maybe some new friends in the group?"

She nodded. "Matthew seems sweet, and Ollie, the woman that's teaching me, she's really very lovely." Anna closed her mouth tightly. *The crochet group is my thing, nothing to do with you.* She'd never had anything that was just for her alone.

"Brilliant." Liam pulled up outside the shop and leant over to kiss her. She smiled against his lips, the rough of his stubble against her face, his hand under her chin. His aftershave filled her nostrils.

"I'll see you," he said with a wink.

"See you."

He let her get out before giving her a little finger wave that she returned.

Her stomach felt a little fluttery. It wasn't from the kiss. What then, she wondered? It was probably because she was excited about learning a new skill and meeting new people.

She knocked. When the door opened, Ollie was standing there.

Anna grinned. "Hi."

"Hello." Ollie stepped back to let her in.

They stood in front of one another for a moment. Anna fumbled in her cloth bag. "Oh, I have things to show you."

They moved into the corridor, then further into the classroom. The room was half-full already, and most people looked up from their conversations to wave at her.

Anna waved back. The young woman with the soft toys was there, as were the older lady with the huge blanket and the old man with his leather slippers.

"Don't tell me, you've made a filigree blanket all by yourself and you no longer need lessons."

"Oh no. I do still need you. But look." She put her bag atop the table and pulled out three squares.

"Well done." Ollie smiled at her. "You must have worked hard."

Anna shrugged and looked at the floor for a moment. "Many slip-ups along the way. But I got it sorted in the end."

Ollie held up the squares, one on top of the other. "You could easily make a scarf out of these. Maybe do six more? Sew them together."

"Ah." Warmth flowed into Anna's stomach, settling down the fluttering feeling. "A little sewing I can do."

"Good."

"What's this week's project?"

Ollie handed back the squares and pointed at a seat for Anna.

"Granny-square coasters," Ollie replied. "Don't worry, though, if you want to continue with your scarf."

"I think I will. Might as well finish a project before I start a new one."

"Good thinking," Matthew said as Anna took the seat next to him. "The number of unfinished bits and pieces I have at home…"

"Yes, you really do need to finish some of them." Ollie pointed a finger towards him. Her eyes crinkled in the corners.

"I know. Now I'm done with Mum's cardigan, I thought…" He fished out something white, green and yellow.

Ollie snorted. Anna peered between them at an unfinished rectangular project in Matthew's lap. "How old is the baby that blanket was intended for, Matthew?"

He lowered his head slightly. "Four?"

"Months?" Anna asked.

"Years," he replied on a moan.

"I'm sure he'll like it still," Anna said.

At another knock, Ollie moved away to answer the door.

"Or maybe you could find someone else that would like it?" Anna added.

"Maybe." Matthew sighed and folded his arms. "Or maybe I will just keep it for myself. I could make it bigger and perhaps keep it for cold nights in."

"I think that's a great idea. I don't know about you, but I don't treat myself as often as I should." She indicated her squares. "I'm making this scarf for myself," she announced and cuddled one of the squares to her neck. "And I rather think I'm going to like it."

As the last of the group wandered in, Ollie stood at the head of the table and waved around the new patterns. "Coasters. You'll need some Aran or cotton yarn in two colours and a four-millimetre hook. I've translated it back to British; the original was in American. And we all know how annoying that is."

Everyone tittered except for Anna, who frowned in slight confusion.

Ollie handed Matthew the pile of patterns and he gaped at her, then studied the copies in his hands. "I don't understand. What am I supposed to do with these?"

It was a struggle for Anna to hold in her laughter. He sounded genuinely befuddled. *Yep, his mum must have spoiled him rotten.*

"What else? Hand them out for me while I get the kettle boiling."

He wasn't quite ready to leave behind the gaping. But then he stood and obliged her. Meanwhile, everyone proceeded to the main area of the shop to choose yarn. Anna watched them go, then took out her significantly decreased ball and started with a row of chain stitches. She looked up towards the counter.

Ollie leant there, arms folded loosely, watching her from behind her floppy fringe.

Anna made careful and slow double crochet stitches, her fingers a little clumsy at being watched.

For another long while, the radio quietly played popular songs Anna recognised but couldn't name. The light chatter around them continued. Someone scraped their chair back and moaned as they stretched.

When Anna looked up again, Ollie was looking down at her right knee, her hand rubbing the side of it. Her other fist was clenched and her shoulders were tense. Dark brown eyes eventually looked her way, and Anna smiled. With a smile, Ollie stepped towards Anna's table, dropping to one knee to inspect her row of stitches.

Anna willingly held out her work, eyes bright and hopeful.

"I can't believe you've picked it up so quickly," Ollie said. "Very neat."

"Thank you." Anna felt herself beam this time, then instantly felt a bit silly about it and made herself glance to her side, where she caught a glimpse of Matthew next to her, his head bowed over his blanket.

Someone guffawed from across the room, and everyone turned to see. The old man closed his mouth immediately and looked wide-eyed before everyone settled back down to their conversations and crochet. The joke seemed to have been in his own head.

Ollie's fingertip smoothed along each stitch of the neat row of doubles as if she were reading Braille. Her hand stopped at the end of the row, a millimetre away from Anna's. She took it away. "Have the coaster pattern, though." Her voice seemed a bit wobbly.

"Okay."

Ollie gripped the table edge to haul herself up and went to the front to collect a pattern.

"I feel I'm going to create quite a collection," Anna said.

After she laid the pattern on the table, Ollie moved back to the front of the room.

Matthew was, as usual, splitting his attention between his baby blanket and Harry, who seemed deep in conversation with the woman with the big blanket. The woman was rubbing his back and leaning close to him, and Anna thought there was something grandmotherly about her. She thought back to the way the lady had been affectionate with Ollie the week before. Harry rested his cheek on her shoulder for a brief moment, then smiled and continued crocheting.

She nudged Matthew. "Come on, spill," she said quietly. "What is it with him?"

Shaking his head, Matthew stared down at his hands. "I've seen him out. He was with a whole group of friends at The Cock and Duck. Current feeling is that he's at least interested in guys but perhaps not interested in me."

She carefully watched the man from over her shoulder. "Hmm. Why don't you strike up a conversation? I know Ollie's told you not to go in for the kill, as it were, but at least you have something in common. Just talk to him."

He fiddled with his hook. "I don't know. Not sure I want to be disappointed."

"Ah. I understand. So it's more fun to watch him from afar than to actually see whether he's interested."

Matthew sat up straight. "It's fine. Not like there aren't plenty more out there who are interested. It's fine. I'm sure he's lovely, but probably not what I'm looking for."

"What are you looking for?"

"I'm far too young to be settling down. And he seems like the stay-at-home-with-a-cocoa type. Might as well leave him to it." There was a deep spark in his eyes, though.

She decided to leave it and continued with her doubles. Various people asked Ollie for help, but otherwise, she leant against the counter at the front, her gaze drifting around the room, as though she were a teacher watching her students complete an exercise, keeping an eye out for the confused or distressed.

I hope she can spend more time with me this week. But then she scolded herself. *She's not my personal tutor. I haven't even paid for her services yet.* Anna tried to focus on her squares, rather than lifting her gaze to Ollie's quite so often. However, once Anna had finished one square, she gave herself permission to look up.

Ollie blinked rapidly. Her gaze flashed away, then someone close by Ollie caught her attention and pointed to the kettle. She looked startled, but pushed herself up from leaning against the counter and immediately grabbed the kettle to fill it and set it to boil. Standing with her back turned, she laid her hands on the counter in front of her.

Anna watched her.

As steam rose from the spout and the kettle clicked off, Ollie got twelve mugs from the cupboard above the counter and everyone put in their orders. Ollie made the drinks, still with her back turned.

When Ollie brought her cup over, Anna sighed as she took a sip. *Nothing like a good cup of tea.*

Ollie handed out the remaining drinks, saying something encouraging to each person about their work. She was so gentle and kind with everyone.

Halfway through the session, Amy—the young girl with the soft toys—called Ollie over, her voice frantic. "I can't get the hook in the stitch here!"

Ollie was by her side in a moment and knelt down. "Let me see, soldier. It's okay." The lady sitting next to Amy was touching her forehead in frustration.

"Ah, I see what you've done, Amy. You need to slacken off a bit, and remember those chain stitches in the corners, yeah? You've chosen a really thick cotton, so I'm not surprised you're having trouble."

Amy's face fell.

"It's all right, you'll be fine. I might suggest you use a six, though, rather than a four. That's Aran you've got there."

They sorted it out together, with the young girl visibly calming under Ollie's instruction. Anna turned back to chat with Matthew and worked through her squares.

"Other than that," Ollie said, "you've done really well. Keep at it, soldier. You'll get it."

"D'you reckon?"

"Of course." A chuckle. "Have I ever been wrong?"

Amy laughed. Ollie appeared in front of them again. Matthew suddenly showed a suspicious amount of concentration on his work. Not that Anna minded.

Ollie smiled. "You're doing all right, then?" she asked, her voice quiet.

Anna nodded and drained the tea from her mug. She had laid her squares out on the table in a long row. "What do you think? Three more squares?"

"I reckon so."

"Okay." Anna settled back into her doubles, but looked round when she noticed Ollie sliding into the seat next to her. *Where did we get to when we spoke before? Ah yes.* "So, you've been here two years?" Anna's gaze was trained back on her crochet.

"That's right."

"What did you do before running a shop?"

"I was in the army."

Anna's head popped up.

Ollie snorted. "What?"

"Nothing. You don't seem the sort."

Ollie said nothing.

Anna froze and then laughed. "Not that I suppose there is a sort of person that *should* be in the army. Or could. I don't know why I said that."

"It's okay, I get that a lot."

"Big jump—army to crochet."

"Well, it wasn't really in my master plan." Ollie's eyes glazed over for half a heartbeat. "My accident happened while I was in Iraq."

Anna placed unfinished square onto the table. This conversation should have her full attention. "What happened?"

"The building I was working in was bombed." Ollie fiddled with her fingers and looked down at her knees.

Anna winced. Her hand hovered for a while, right near Ollie's fingers. *I barely know her.* It dropped to her lap. "Injuries?"

"Cuts and abrasions, mostly. They thought I'd broken my back, but turned out my knee was worse. Didn't notice that until they got me to a hospital."

"Blimey." Anna nodded. "That's bad luck, Private Williams."

"Sergeant." Ollie blushed and cleared her throat. "Although I haven't been called that in… I'm a teacher. Was."

"Oh." *That explains an awful lot.* Anna relaxed at the revelation. "You didn't say."

"I know." Ollie tucked her hair behind her ear, then set her jaw and lifted her gaze to Anna's. "Sorry. It feels weird to say, just because it's been nearly six years."

"Subject?"

Her shoulders softened. "Physical education. Running around sport halls and fields. Got my teacher training through the army; worked in a few schools over here but owed the army some time, so ended up in Iraq teaching kids to read and write. That's what I was doing when…" Ollie's hand moved in a pattern through the air.

"Medical discharge?"

She gave Anna a short, sharp nod.

"That must have been hard." *I can't even imagine. One's entire life changing so much, in such a short space of time.* Anna leaned a little closer and accidentally knocked her foot against Ollie's.

Ollie moved her foot away. Her shoulders had gone tense again.

She lifted her hand again and moved it towards Ollie's hands, clasped on the table. Before she could touch her, however, Amy called out for help and Ollie pushed back the chair with a scrape and stood.

An overwhelming feeling of sadness about Ollie's past gripped Anna's insides. She grasped her hook and felt the cool of the metal against her fingertips. Matthew shifted next to her and leant close as Ollie went to help Amy. He put his hand over hers and squeezed her fingers.

"She doesn't like to talk about her army days," he said.

Anna's gaze drifted back to her half-finished square. "No, I can imagine she doesn't."

"And she wouldn't talk about them unless she really wanted to."

Anna turned and looked at him. "She wouldn't?"

He smiled, squeezed her hands again, and then went back to his blanket.

Anna stared at the table. She pushed away the ache in her stomach and picked up her square.

By the end of the session, the sadness had cleared enough so she could chat with Matthew again. She found him an easy person to talk to—a little sarcastic but otherwise kind and thoughtful. And very funny. He had many stories about previous members of the crochet group. She found herself drifting back into humour and enjoyment.

Ollie didn't come back over apart from to set another cup of tea on the table in front of her, so Anna hung around as everyone else packed up, pretending she had tea to finish off, which wasn't strictly a lie—her cup had sat neglected while she finished the squares. She folded the crocheted pieces up and settled them neatly in her cloth bag, ready to be sewn together at home.

Amy passed her with an awkward teenaged grin. "Hi."

"Hi. Amy, right?"

"Yes, Miss."

Anna squinted at her. "Oh, you're in Mr Jones's Year 11 class, aren't you?"

She nodded.

Thank goodness she's not in one of my classes. "Well, you don't need to call me 'Miss' here. 'Anna' is fine." She indicated the cat head clutched in Amy's hand. "He's looking marvellous."

"Thanks, Mi—um. I mean, Anna."

"You been coming long?"

Amy shrugged. "Couple of years. My mum used to come but she's ill so…I look after her. But she can manage a couple of hours on her own in the evening, once a week."

"You're a young carer?" Despite Anna's insistence on informality between them, the teacher in her pushed through.

"Yeah."

Anna nodded. "That's a very grown-up thing to do."

"Anna, can I ask you something?" Amy's cheeks reddened at using Anna's first name.

"So long as it isn't advice about crochet, of course."

Amy giggled. "Do you think everyone should go to university?"

"Hmm. Good question." Anna tilted her head. "I think it depends what you want out of life, doesn't it? If going to uni means you'll get the degree you want, so you can do the job you want to do, then yes. But if you're dream is to work as something that doesn't require going to university, I think there's really no need." She smiled at Amy. "What do you think?"

Amy perched on the edge of Anna's table.

"I agree. I think some people should and some people shouldn't." She bit her lip. "My dad thinks I should. But Mum says I should do whatever makes me happy."

"I think doing things that make you happy are very important."

"Me too. But what if I don't go to uni and then I miss out? Like, with a degree, you have more choices, don't you?"

"You can go later. There's nothing stopping you from seeing some of the world for a while first."

"I can't afford to have a gap year."

"I don't mean travelling," Anna said gently. "If you're not sure what job you'd like to do, you could try a few, see what floats your boat."

Amy brightened. "That's a good idea."

"You doing A levels?"

She nodded.

"I expect you've chosen your subjects."

Another nod. Amy swung her legs back and forth a bit.

"You have so much time to decide. I remember being your age and trying to figure out what to do. When I was young, you either became a secretary or a teacher. Guess which I chose?"

Amy's eyes sparkled. "A secretary?"

"Indeed." Anna laughed.

"You like it, though?"

"I do. Very much."

Amy pushed her shoulders up happily and then slipped from the table. She went back to her own table and sent Anna sparkly little smiles from her seat. Anna returned them. *I hope she has enough support with her mum.*

She seems happy enough. She made a mental note to ask Mr Jones about her, make sure he knew about the young-carer thing.

Busy with her hands in the sink washing up, Ollie didn't seem to notice Anna's lingering presence until Matthew swept past her and touched her arm. Ollie glanced over but finished washing up before turning around.

"Nowhere to be?" Her voice was light and amused.

"Not tonight. Timothy is at his girlfriend's house and Bethany is, as usual, out." Anna brought her mug over. "You didn't have a drink." She lifted Ollie's mug—a brightly coloured thing with a rainbow across it—and held it out so Ollie could look inside.

The mug was clean, and a dry tea bag sat at the bottom of it. Ollie frowned. "Um, it's okay."

Anna put the mug down. *It's now or never.* "Maybe I could buy you a coffee." She lowered her lashes, one hand held out towards the door. "I'm sure that little greasy-spoon place round the corner is still open."

"I don't think it ever closes, does it?" Ollie's eyes seemed to be searching Anna's.

That wasn't a rejection. Good. "Come on, then. I'll wait for you to do whatever you need to do here."

"That would be…that would be great."

Anna waited outside while Ollie did the necessary routines to lock up the shop. When she came out, Anna was holding up a five-pound note. "And this time, you have to take it," she said.

Ollie stuffed it into her jeans pocket. "Fine. Twist my arm."

They walked down the darkened side street the shop stood on, crossed the road, and turned left onto the main street of shops.

"I finished my squares," Anna said.

"Great." Ollie smiled at her.

A few people were hanging around outside the local pub or smoking outside their flats. The town was bustling, the halfway pleasant early evening coaxing people outside to chat.

"Is there something you'd like to make next?"

Anna paused and thought. "I liked the blanket Matthew was making. I'm not saying I could even attempt anything as complicated as that but…"

"I'll make you up the pattern." As they approached the café, she held the door open, allowing Anna to go in first. "It's simple enough. I've done it a few times, and it's sort of tattooed onto my brain."

Anna found them a table. Once Ollie was seated, she sat across from her and clasped her hands tightly in her lap. What to say? She wanted to ask Ollie more about her past, but how to do it gracefully?

The waitress took their orders and offered them free slices of cake, which Anna accepted but Ollie declined.

"I try not to eat too late," she explained. "Gives me a stomach ache." She rested her forearms on the tabletop.

Anna fished a napkin gingerly out of the holder and took a fork from the little pot. She lay them down carefully in front of her. She watched the cake being sliced and listened to the coffee machine whirring. Two men dressed in high-vis jackets and cement-smeared trousers made their way to the counter, paid, and left.

Only a young couple remained in the café, behind their table. Their joined hands and lowered voices made it obvious what they were. *They look like they're on a date.*

She turned back to Ollie and kept her voice low when she spoke. "So, tell me about your family. Are you in touch with your children's father or…?"

Ollie's lips pursed for a moment. "We communicate. Usually amicably. But we've been separated for nearly five years. Divorced for three."

They both leaned backwards as the waitress brought their drinks over.

Once she was out of earshot, Anna asked, "Rough divorce?"

With a glance at the couple behind them, Ollie replied, "Yes. Quite rough." She sipped her coffee.

Anna nodded. "You ended it?"

"No. He did." She sighed, then smiled weakly up at Anna. "You don't want to know all the ins and outs…"

"I do if you want to tell me."

The young couple giggled behind them. Anna shot them an annoyed look over her shoulder, wishing they were alone.

As if they'd noticed, the couple gathered their things. They paid and walked out hand in hand. The waitress moved out the back, and the sound of cupboards opening and clinking china drifted through.

"It's part of the club." Anna poked her Victoria sponge with her fork. "Angry ex-wives. Nothing you say leaves the room."

"Okay." Ollie's gaze swung away though.

Perhaps she needs the distance.

"I had been offered another ten years in the army, teaching in one of the new schools in Iraq. My ex wasn't happy. Wanted me home. Kids missed me."

"Seems a little unfair. Was he not supportive of your career?"

Ollie slid her hands around her coffee cup, looking into its depths. "After twenty years, you'd think he would have been. There was more, though. I was seriously hurt in the explosion. Lots of recovery time at home. I wasn't happy. And I'd…" Ollie sighed sadly and looked up at Anna. "I had done something very…awful. While I was in Iraq."

"What did you do?" Anna's fingers twitched on the table.

"There was…someone else. Someone I taught with. We got… We became intimate."

Anna ate some more cake but didn't break eye contact with Ollie.

Ollie looked away. "One of our mutual friends found out. He was working with us in Iraq and…he must have seen us. Sent my ex a letter, explaining my shortfalls. Awful, really."

"Were you in love?" Anna's voice was close to a whisper.

"At the time?" Ollie shrugged, but then, after a long moment, she nodded.

"Well, usually I would say cheating was a definite no-no." Anna's fingertips touched Ollie's knuckles where they wrapped around her coffee cup. She spoke slowly. "But I can tell from your expression it wasn't something you did lightly, or without thought. Am I right?"

Ollie nodded again. Her hand loosened from the mug.

"Not like what my ex did to me," Anna continued. "Any young TA that took his fancy. The pupils all knew. He never hid it." She shook her head.

"Canoodling at work?" Ollie's knuckles tightened around her mug again.

"Yep."

"What a tosser."

"Tell me about it." Anna put her fingertips to her temple. "And the worst thing was my colleagues all told me he was playing away from home. I just shrugged it off. Then he royally buggered up, got caught by the Head shagging the cleaner in the storage room—clichéd, I know. Embarrassed me in front of everyone. I nearly killed him." Her eyes burned at the memory.

"If you still want to, I could probably find a guy." Ollie's lips were curling upwards.

With a loud laugh, Anna squeezed her fingers, then removed her hand from Ollie's. "That's very sweet of you, but he's my daughter's father. They still see one another."

"At least my ex-husband was reasonably civil during the whole thing. Well, you know, considering. He was angry and hurt, of course."

"Of course." She sipped her coffee. *Why do I feel sorry for her?* Ollie had cheated on her husband. That was usually on Anna's list of unforgivable offences.

"You've been practising hard."

She frowned in confusion. "Hmm?"

"Crochet." Ollie pointed at Anna's forefinger where it curled around her mug. "You have a sore line here. You're pulling the yarn over it too tightly."

Anna took her hand from her cup and looked at her forefinger. "Ah. Is that where I'm going wrong?"

"I got the same thing when I first started. I remember feeling like I was going to drop everything if I didn't hold on tight to it."

"Sounds familiar." Anna rubbed her finger and grimaced.

Ollie bent down to fumble in her bag. "I'm sure you have your own hand cream, but… Here. Try this."

Anna read the label on the small bottle. It seemed to contain nothing she was allergic to. She opened the cap and sniffed. Herb scents filled her nose and she felt the hairs standing up on the back of her neck. "That's rather nice."

"Keep it."

"Oh no, I couldn't." Anna tried to give it back.

"I buy in bulk. The chlorine in the water at the baths makes my skin sore. I teach swimming to kids. So I have about twenty bottles at home."

"I'm sure I can find some…"

"Honestly, its fine. It's good stuff, I promise."

Anna still held out the bottle, her gaze steady. Ollie took a deep breath and then grasped Anna's fingers, pushing the bottle away.

Her chivalry about it made Anna smile despite herself. "Fine. Thank you, Ollie."

"It's got…rosemary and mint. Or something." Ollie slotted her fingers together on the table again.

After decanting some into her palm, Anna rubbed it in. "Thank you." She slipped the bottle into her handbag.

They sipped their coffees and Anna realised she didn't have much of her cake left. When there was just a mouthful remaining, she took a clean fork from the pot and held it out, handle first, to Ollie. "It's lovely cake. And I'm sure one mouthful won't hurt."

Ollie looked at her for a few heartbeats. *Was the cake question really that big a deal?* But then she took the fork from Anna and scooped up the last piece. She pushed up her shoulders and hummed in pleasure.

Suddenly aware of Ollie's mouth, more specifically the way her tongue darted over her lips to lick away a stray crumb, Anna felt her stomach go fluttery—similar to when Liam kissed her but a lot more intense. Startled, she stared into her coffee mug and watched a small bubble float across the surface. She drank the remainder, before sighing as the warm liquid heated up her stomach and relaxed her.

By the time she managed to look up again, she realised they'd both finished their coffees. *So I suppose we'll be leaving soon. Damn.*

"So, how's the love life?" Strangely, it took a while for Ollie to look at her after saying that.

"I'm currently dating a lovely health and safety officer called Liam," she replied. "You?"

There was a pause. "Free and single currently," she said eventually.

Anna waited for some kind of embellishment, but none came.

"So 'dating', hmm?" Ollie continued, again not meeting Anna's eye. "Serious? Or…" She made a vague waving gesture with her hand as if to fill the space of that sentence.

"So far reasonably casual. I'm sure he'd like more though."

Ollie seemed to relax a touch. "I bet. Attractive woman with a great mind too." She winked. "What's not to like?"

Anna's smile broadened and she shuttered her eyes. She felt quite breathless for a moment. "There's just one problem."

"Oh?"

"A stupid one, really." Anna rolled her eyes and leant an elbow on the table, her fingers combing through her own hair.

"Do tell."

"Timothy. Liam isn't comfortable with him."

"Your adopted son? Why not?" Ollie sat back in her chair, her arms folded across her chest and her eyebrows furrowed.

Anna looked up from under her own wrist. "Liam is easily irritated by him. Timothy's odd, he says odd things, does odd things. Liam can't handle that."

"How long have you been together?"

"Six…seven months."

"And he's not suggested he'd like it to become more serious?" Ollie leant her head to one side.

"Oh, he has. I'm the one who's reluctant. What we have is comfortable and fun, and anything more wouldn't work."

"Because of Timothy?"

"Liam doesn't stay over if Timothy's at home. Which he usually is. And he complains when I have to leave early to make Timothy's supper or… Timothy has a very strict routine and can't deal with even the smallest change. He's my priority—he and Bethany."

Ollie's gaze on Anna was steady. "Do you think Liam would make you choose—between him and Timothy—if he wanted it to become more serious?"

"He's kind, kind to me at least. I don't think he'd ask that sort of thing, which is a shame, actually." Anna laughed. "If he did force me to choose, at least then I would know my answer."

Ollie nodded and looked into her empty coffee cup. She cleared her throat and poked the cup away from herself with her fingertips. She seemed unsure what to say next.

"Until things change, casual is fine," Anna said more to fill the silence than because she thought it needed saying. "I don't mind getting some of my needs met at the sacrifice of the rest." She blinked and realised how her words had sounded.

Ollie leant forward, chin in her hand. "He's all right in the sack, then."

It wasn't a question. Anna laid her palm against her hot face, and her gaze slid away from Ollie's. She rubbed at the back of her neck.

"There's nothing wrong with fun," Ollie said. "I suppose it depends what you're looking for."

"I suppose it does."

"Are you looking for anything more?"

"I have no idea." Anna lifted her eyes to Ollie's again.

"Well, anyway." Ollie stood and moved towards the counter. "I'll get this."

"No, don't be silly. It was my idea." She grabbed her purse from her bag and joined Ollie.

"It's fine."

She was so kind and gentle with the crochet class. Who knew she had this stubborn streak? "Honestly, Ollie."

"All right, then. How about we split it?"

It wasn't how she'd intended this to go. But it was a compromise she could live with, she supposed. "Okay."

The waitress arrived, and they tumbled identical coins onto the countertop.

Anna pulled her coat close around her middle as they left. "Where do you live?" she asked as they weaved around groups of people outside the nearby pub. Music thrummed from inside, the orange glow from the electric lights spilling out onto the street.

"I have a flat above the shop. You?"

"Parson Street. Liam dropped me off, so I'm getting a taxi home."

"Ah."

The shop was on the way to the taxi rank, and it was early enough that Anna didn't think she'd have any trouble just flagging one down. Ollie stopped when they reached the side door.

Anna held her hand out to Ollie. She felt very aware of the cold breeze brushing her fingers. Ollie grasped Anna's hand in her own.

"Same time next week?" Ollie asked.

"You don't get rid of me that easily."

A group of people passing behind them forced Anna to step up close enough to Ollie that the fronts of their coats brushed. Ollie reached for her waist as the group passed them. It made Anna warm all over, despite the early winter chill.

When the group of people were clear, Anna did not move away. The single inch difference in their heights seemed huge. She held her breath as Ollie gazed down at her. She wasn't sure, but she thought she saw Ollie's gaze flick down to her lips, then back up. Suddenly feeling shivery, she swallowed and stepped back.

Ollie let her go and fumbled in her pocket for her flat keys. "See you next week then." She smiled at Anna over her shoulder, then turned back to her door.

Anna smiled back, then realised Ollie wasn't looking at her anymore. "Don't forget the pattern," she said to get her attention back.

"I won't." Ollie glanced back at her but then pushed her door open with her body, before quickly closing it behind her.

For a moment, Anna stood staring at Ollie's door, but wasn't sure why. She gathered her coat around herself, pulled her cloth bag and handbag onto her shoulder more firmly, and made for the taxis.

Chapter 3

Treble Crochet (tr)

With a bounce in her stride and a smile on her face, Anna arrived at work on Friday right on time. She sauntered into the staff room, flicking the newly-sewn-together scarf over her shoulder.

Tally smiled up at her.

A whistle sounded from the far end of the staff room, where Jack was making a coffee. Warmth blossomed in Anna's stomach as she sat. "Well, what do you think?"

"Monsoon?" Tally asked.

"No. Guess again," Anna replied.

"Looks posh," Tally gestured with a pile of papers. "I give up."

"You give up far too easily, Tally." Anna laughed. "Okay. I'll make a confession. This scarf is part of a new hobby I've begun. Although I'm pleased to know you think it was professionally made."

Jack moved closer, putting his coffee down. "You actually made that yourself?"

"Don't seem so flabbergasted, young Jack." Anna leaned back in her chair cheerfully. "I'm reasonably good with my hands, you know."

"It's gorgeous." Tally touched the scarf with careful fingers. She pressed the end of it against her face and gave a little giggle.

Anna snuggled her cheek into the part around her neck. "I *am* rather pleased with myself."

Tally's fellow teaching assistant approached with a cup of tea and spent time fingering the scarf as well. "Aw, Ms Rose. Where did you learn to knit?"

"It's not knitted actually, lovely Rachael. It is very much crocheted."

"Is there a difference?"

"One hook versus two needles, I believe." Anna relished in the attention as Rachael nodded. "I've started crochet lessons."

They all complimented her work, and Anna felt like a teenager getting praise from a teacher for an essay. "I'm sure I'll learn more stitches on Thursday." She grimaced at the slip of her tongue. *Damn. Too much information.* They'd ask her about it the minute she got into work on Friday morning. Not that she was embarrassed about it. It was just something she would like to keep to herself for the moment.

She went into her classroom and then draped her coat on the back of her chair, the scarf joining it. Jack followed her, shutting the door behind him. He looked at her for a moment.

The smile fell from her. "You're making me paranoid, Mr Holmes. Why the scrutiny?"

"I'm curious." He perched on the edge of her desk. "I get that the crocheting is fun. I get that you're probably meeting new folk and enjoying yourself. But I haven't seen you quite so..."

"Yes?" Anna asked, voice lower. *Don't patronise me. I'm two decades older than you.*

"Jovial?" He grimaced apologetically.

She put one hand on her hip.

"Giggly?"

Her jaw dropped. "Giggly?"

"Sorry." He shrugged. "Just something I've noticed."

"I am perfectly at liberty to be excited about a new hobby and a new friend...group of friends."

He pounced on that. "Friend, eh?"

"There are other people at the group. They come and go each week, from what I can see." Anna closed her eyes for a moment. Did she really have to explain herself to Jack? "And they all seem very nice."

"But you have your eye set on one 'friend', hmm?"

She sighed. "Jack."

"Come on," he teased. "Give me something."

"We're just friends. *Absolutely* just friends."

"What's his name?"

She paused and then swallowed. "Ollie?" She tried to gauge his reaction.

"Modern name," he said, pressing his lips forward and nodding. "Bet he's younger than you. I'm told having a toy boy is *in* these days."

She laughed. "Ollie and I are the same age. I think."

"Want me to take on some of the book clubs?" Jack's face softened, and she relaxed too. He'd stop teasing now. "Doing five a week is a lot, you know. I only do one."

"I know. But you have a department to run."

Jack shrugged. "I know how hard you work." Something akin to concern shone from his eyes.

"I'm fine." She patted his arm. "I enjoy doing them. The kids love them, and I'd miss it."

"Even though I've seen you rush your lunch on at least ten occasions. You'll do some damage to your stomach, you know. Lunchtime is supposed to be for relaxation." He touched her hand where it now lay on his shoulder. His hand was warm, his face lined.

Do I look tired? Is that why he's so concerned? "What can I say? I'm a stickler for work."

Jack scrutinised her for a beat or two and then sighed. "Well, the offer remains. You need to relinquish some extracurricular, I'm here, and I have time. I don't have a family to run. Just an English department."

They exchanged another smile.

"So, this Ollie, hmm?" Jack's teasing grin had returned. "Your delightful new friend."

"What about Ollie?"

"What happened to Liam?"

She took a breath. "Liam's still in the picture. What? I'm not allowed to have other friends?"

"Hope this Ollie is something to look at." He headed towards the door, the bell for the beginning of registration ringing above his head.

"I suppose so," Anna said to herself.

Actually, Ollie is rather beautiful. She pressed her lips together and tried to smile as he left the classroom and her form began to filter in, pushing at each other in that way they had at the end of term.

"Okay, guys, come on. Usual drill."

Everyone smiled at her, even the difficult pupils. She smiled right back, and everyone settled. She called the register, and, despite some of the form joking around with it, they got through it quickly.

"Couple of notices. The quad is being repaired, so please be careful at break and lunch. Don't go into the cordoned-off areas." She looked up from the piece of paper from which she was reading and caught one teenager's eye. "Yes, Dave, that means you. It means everyone. I doubt the school nurse would appreciate a load of my form arriving at her office with feet coated in concrete because they couldn't follow simple instructions."

"What about that fit building guy, though, Miss?" one of the girls piped up. Her eyes twinkled with something between innocent reverie and naughty sexuality.

Anna pulled a stern look onto her face "You keep your hands off the workmen, Charlotte. They don't need your advances while they're working."

Charlotte smiled and nodded. "Okay, Miss."

"He is well fit, though," her friend interjected.

"How 'well fit' one of our workmen is, is absolutely nothing to do with you." Anna pointed a finger at the table where both girls sat. "Sexual harassment is illegal, especially when someone's at work." She regarded the whole class. "Come on, guys, you know this."

Murmurs of agreement came from the whole room. Anna felt pleased. Her form was good, on the whole. One last look around settled her worries, and she continued with the monotony of announcements on the paper in front of her.

Ollie turned the television to something easy, a nature documentary. A glass of wine sat in her free hand as she leant back into her sofa cushions. It had been a busy Monday in the shop: All the kids on October half-term had been eager to spend their pocket money, hankering after a cute and *awesome* key ring. She'd completely sold out of the hedgehogs, and the unicorns too. And then there was her swim class of hyperactive ten-year-olds. Her brain was half thinking up other animals to make for tomorrow, half watching the meerkats on the screen jumping all over each other.

Takeaway packets stacked by the sink awaited a spark of renewed energy tomorrow morning. Her belly was full, and her body was tired after a whole day of selling and interacting with children and their parents. She didn't mind the holidays so much; at least she turned a good profit.

Her eyes closed, tiredness taking over her mind until she had very little control over where her thoughts led her. She thought about a pair of green eyes, followed by freckled cheekbones, short red hair, and careful hands cupping a mug of hot tea. Full lips smiled at her and then laughed.

Ollie put her wine glass on the coffee table and relaxed back into her sofa, stretching her legs out. The sound of Anna's voice filled her mind, and she sighed, her hands stationary on her stomach.

She hadn't allowed herself the pleasure or freedom to think about anyone this deeply for a few years. Since Zoe, really. Actually, she hadn't thought about a *man* since way before that. She hadn't thought about anyone, male or female. Had she ever fancied a man? Had she even fancied her ex-husband, with whom she had spent twenty years?

The kids needed some sense of normality with me away so much.

She must have fancied him at one point. She married him, didn't she? But it was so long ago, she couldn't remember the feeling anymore. She was only attracted to women these days.

Mostly passing fancies, though: her first physiotherapist, the nurse who had changed her IV once when she got an infection in the wound in her knee. She'd considered them briefly, but her fantasies never went beyond a quick visualisation, something to get things going before blankness invaded her thoughts. Her hand was all she needed to find that type of release—until the niggling stab of guilt afterwards. How many months of psychological therapy had it taken for her to finally believe that she could fantasise about whomever she liked?

But she could, so she lay back and thought about Anna—although her hands stayed put—and she drifted off on her comfortable and reliable sofa with Anna's voice and those soft eyes playing like a movie in her thoughts.

When she awoke several hours later, the television was replaying BBC 2 trailers. She rolled off the sofa and went off to potter through her bedtime routine. In bed, she lay in her underwear, her exposed skin a little tingly against her cotton sheets.

She decided against any form of relief. She couldn't think about Anna while she did that, and if she touched herself, her brain would inevitably stray in that direction. She hoped they were becoming friends, especially after their little trip to the greasy-spoon café and the warm look in Anna's eyes when she stayed so close outside Ollie's front door.

No. Friends didn't do *that* while they thought about each other. Definitely not.

She fell asleep a little achy and frustrated.

Dinner was in the oven, and Bethany sat expectantly at the kitchen table, waiting for the timer to ping.

Anna sat across from her, nursing a lovely hot cup of tea. "Timothy will be home in about twenty minutes," she explained, her fingertip tracing idly along the handle of her mug. "He knows I'm going out, so there shouldn't be much hassle."

"Okay." Bethany lifted her own cup to her lips. "I love lasagne."

An affectionate chuckle rumbled through Anna. "Well, I thought I'd get you something nice, considering I'm abandoning you tonight."

Beth waited for a moment before reacting, as though she had to think about how she should do so. "That's okay. You go out, have fun." Her gaze flicked towards the front door.

Something similar to lead collected in Anna's stomach, and she looked more closely at her daughter. "I'm hoping Liam takes me somewhere romantic. Somewhere with candles, maybe. Nice music."

"That'd be awesome."

The doorbell rang, and Anna stood slowly, draining her mug. "My date has arrived," she announced in a whisper.

Bethany grinned and shook her head.

The way Liam shifted from foot to foot in his smart suit and tie was unusual for him. "Anna. So nice to see you." He leant in to kiss her cheek.

A flush tingled through Anna's body, but she eyed him cautiously. "Why the eager demeanour? What have you done?"

Liam's gaze bounced from side to side. It settled through the door and into Anna's house. With a flick up of his eyebrows, he indicated he wanted to come in.

She stepped back and closed the door behind him. *He doesn't usually come in.* "What is it?"

A long mane of brown hair swished across Anna's field of vision as Bethany stepped into the hallway. She seemed to be pretending to have some kind of task to do. She rifled through the pockets of her own hung-up coat. Anna knew better—she was eavesdropping.

The neat creases in Liam's suit skewed as he shifted his feet. "Well... unfortunately my mother has had to come along tonight."

Anna stepped back. "You've brought your mother on our date?"

A snort from Bethany.

"She...she wasn't feeling well. She has a touch of vertigo and is worried about staying home alone. Especially since Dad died, she..." His large eyes were wet.

Emotions prickled through Anna, but she put them aside and settled on compassion. She stepped towards him and rubbed his arm. "Well, I suppose the romance will have to be put on hold for tonight, then. Your mother and I get on, don't we?" She patted him. "Stop looking so terribly forlorn."

He relaxed and nodded. "All right. Good."

When Anna turned to glance at Bethany, she found her stock-still, eyes like saucers, and with one eyebrow raised. "Really?" Bethany said, the word drawn out. "You're asking if your mum can be there on your date?"

"It's exceptional circumstances." His shoulders had hardened again.

Bethany scoffed. "Ace. Have a great time." Sarcasm dripped from her.

Anna collected her things and they headed out. Liam's hand planted itself at the small of her back. Anna's insides quivered, but not in a good way. *What a pain. I thought our evening would be just the two of us.*

"What a twat." Bethany's voice drifted through the closing door. Anna admitted she was thinking the same thing.

But, no. Liam hadn't caused his mother's health issues, and it was nice he cared enough to put her needs before his own. It would be nice for him to put Anna's needs before his own, sometimes, however.

Margaret was in the back of the car, looking significantly uncomfortable.

Anna turned in her seat once they'd pulled away from the kerb. "I'm so sorry you're feeling poorly."

"And I'm sorry I'm about to spoil your dinner."

"Don't worry about it, Mum. Anna's happy you're here."

Anna's stomach twisted again, and she had to close her eyes and turn back to the front to stop her true feelings from spilling into the car. "Of course I am." She let out a slow breath and nodded.

It was a shame they were accompanied. The restaurant was all sweet smells and soft music, a perfect place to take a romantic partner. Not so great a place to take your mother, unless she needed cheering up. Liam's mother really did seem to need cheering up, however. The way her eyes softened in the quiet, comfortable atmosphere of the restaurant made Anna feel bad about wishing they were alone. When Margaret wobbled a bit sitting down in her chair, Anna steadied her with a hand to her shoulder.

She allowed Liam to focus the conversation. He knew his mother much better, and she trusted him to guide the talk into areas where Margaret could contribute. Anna found she wanted Margaret to have a good time, and to see her as someone her son should be with. She found she cared what Margaret thought when it came to their relationship.

I suppose everyone feels that about their in-laws. Not that Liam and I are married...or really that serious. Perhaps I hope Margaret thinks we're serious.

Why is that? She considered her predicament. They weren't serious; they were just dating, weren't they? *What if Margaret thinks I'm stringing him along? I don't want her thinking that.* She tried not to slink down in her chair under the occasional glances from the older woman.

The conversation mostly consisted of Liam complaining about work, as usual. "I don't understand why people can't just follow policy. It's written out in black and white. I've made it as simple as it could ever be."

Margaret hummed sympathetically and took a sip of water. "Oh dear. It does sound like a quandary for you, Lee-lee."

Anna bit back a giggle. She'd never heard Liam's mother call him that. "I suppose people just don't have the time to read policies. Not that I can speak for anyone, really. I, of course, have read everything in the folder you have ever written." She fluttered her eyelashes at him and he smiled back. It was true: as his girlfriend, she'd felt obliged to set a good example and read the folder from cover to cover. It hadn't exactly got her heart beating, not like a good mystery novel, but she'd felt all the better for it. The look on his face afterwards had been glorious, as had the two orgasms he'd managed to give her the evening after.

The space between her legs fluttered just a tad. She felt her cheeks turning red. She was eternally grateful Margaret was not a mind reader.

"It's the most important thing they can do," Liam continued. "Really. Honestly. Nothing is more important than following the set of rules that depicts exactly how things should be done. All other things should follow on after." He swirled the ice in his glass round thoughtfully. "I might bring it up, you know, at the next staff meeting. I've been thinking about it for a while: getting the new members of staff to start off with an induction week. They'd read the folder, then answer questions on it." He grinned and chuckled. "I reckon it'd be a fun beginning to their teaching career."

Even Margaret seemed to be hiding her disbelief. Anna felt better about her own amusement. She squeezed Liam's hand and exchanged an eyebrow raise with his mother.

"That daughter of yours had an attitude this evening." The change in subject made Anna look over.

She let out a slow breath. "Hmm. Yes. Isn't it lovely that my twenty-year-old is able to express herself so freely?"

When she glanced at Margaret, she found her unreadable.

Liam drummed his fingers on the table. "Well, she seemed outright rude, if you ask me. Disrespecting me and how I do things."

"She was just upset that we..." She glanced at Margaret apologetically. "Bethany was pleased we were having a nice meal out together. She worries about me. I think she had this image of a romantic date in her head and... she was disappointed we'd be a three, rather than a two."

"I'm sorry I've ruined your evening." Margaret looked at the napkin in her lap.

"Like I said, it's absolutely fine. Your health is far more important than Liam and I having time alone. And it's been lovely, it truly has." She was overdoing it with the gushing, but she didn't care. Margaret didn't deserve to feel bad.

Margaret looked up, and the edges of her mouth pulled upwards. "So long as you make sure you plan another time, when I'm not feeling so awful?"

"Oh, don't worry, Mum. I plan on wining and dining Anna until I die." He swooped in and kissed Anna full on the lips.

Anna pulled back, but he closed the space again. She forced herself to accept the kiss, even while her stomach churned at his words. *We've never discussed the concept of forever. We also never discussed him snogging me in full view of his mother.*

Swishing through the water, Ollie grinned at the toddler splashing towards her. "That's right, little one. Kick those legs."

The mother holding the child smiled as well. "She's doing ever so well. Look at her."

"I know. Absolutely brilliant. She'll be ready for the Olympics soon." Ollie preferred the children's pool—it was warmer and cuddled her injured knee comfortably. She always had to take painkillers before she went into the adult pool.

Another parent came over with their child, who was wearing a bright pink tutu attached to her costume. The mother had a halter-neck tankini that showed off her curves.

Ollie often wondered about how people chose their costumes. She liked the simplicity of her usual black one-piece and a pair of board shorts over the top that nearly hid her knee and brushed over her scar so that most people didn't see it. It made her feel comfortable and staved off too many questions from her pupils and their parents.

"How long have you been teaching swimming?" the mother asked. Ollie couldn't remember her name, but it didn't matter.

"Two years."

"Do you need qualifications or…?" The woman seemed genuinely interested, but wary. Perhaps she felt Ollie wouldn't want to talk about herself.

Ollie didn't mind. "Yes, you need your Level One and your Level Two. I thought about doing my Three, but I don't need it to teach classes. I have enough."

"Oh. And do you do anything else?"

"I own a shop," Ollie said, holding out her hands until the little girl squealed and grabbed them. Her mum let her go, and Ollie pulled the child around in the water. "I sell crafty things. In the day, obviously. I do this as an extra thing." She laughed as the little girl shouted and splashed, then let her hands go. The kid kicked wildly in glee and the mother looked on in delight.

"So, how many classes a week do you do?"

"I do three in the week and one on a Saturday morning. I also teach crochet two evenings a week."

"Full week," the mother said and then laughed. "Don't you have a life?"

Something hardened in the pit of Ollie's stomach. Her jaw ached. "I like to be busy."

"Really? When do you relax?"

Ollie felt the pull of the water behind her, or was it her own need to swim away from the woman? "I like what I do." She tried very hard to remain professional. Somehow, a little of the bitterness she felt towards the woman seeped through. "I mean…" She concentrated on the delighted face of the little girl, who was poking a bubble in the water with a huge amount of focus. She took hold of the girl's feet and tickled them. The giggling that brought forth dissolved some of the tension as if into the water around her. "It's a real pleasure to be able to help kids have fun."

Uncertainty still trickled from the mum. *Please don't ask me anymore.* "I wouldn't manage constantly working. Got to get some feet-up-gin-in-hand time at least once an evening."

She decided to let that one slide. How much gin the mum consumed of an evening was as much Ollie's business as the hours she worked were the mum's. With a flutter of relief, Ollie noticed the time. "Okay, guys. Time to get out and dry. Great work today." In her changing cubicle, her stomach still churned as she rubbed at her skin roughly with her towel. *Do I work too much?*

Thursday came around rather slowly for Anna. Timothy and Bethany were constantly at one another's throats. Bethany was irritated by Timothy's inability to change his schedule so she could watch some show where a bride relinquished all control of the wedding to her groom, and then the ultimate fallout was televised. Timothy had declared her tastes childish. Bethany replied she thought his were too.

Four days of this and I'm ready to smack their heads together.

But they were both adults, more or less, and needed to work it out themselves. Thank goodness the today had been quieter once Bethany had shut herself in her bedroom with university work. Arthur had taken to sitting on Anna's lap, meowing and nuzzling her hands, so she gave him plenty of treats and cuddles. She knew that the kids would sort it out soon, but in the meantime, home life wasn't as picturesque as she would like. She felt rather naïve for wishing for perfection, but there it was.

It was a relief to leave work at four o'clock. She would have plenty of time to go home, mow the lawn, have a shower, and make her dinner before the crochet class at seven. She had decided on the colours for her blanket—burgundy, of course, navy blue, and cream. She'd seen the combination in a furniture shop once and had never forgotten it. The trio would match her living room well.

Her house phone rang and Anna huffed, wondering why she even had a house phone when her mobile worked just as well and wasn't always halfway across the house. She hauled herself to her feet, her knees cracking.

"Hello?" She looked at her watch, hoping it wasn't something that would take too long.

"Anna, it's Patricia."

A comfortable feeling enveloped her stomach at the voice of her best friend. "Why, hello. How are you?"

"Great." Patricia sounded her usual bright self. "Never better."

"Can't talk long," Anna said. "Places to be."

"Ah, yes, your crochet thing. How's that going?"

"Wonderful. Well, I've a lot to learn." Anna leant against the telephone table. "But it's fun. And it's nice to be filling my time with making things, rather than just pages and pages of poetry chosen by the national curriculum."

The easy friendship they'd developed and maintained since college carried the conversation fluidly, but after ten minutes Anna hastily looked at her watch. "I'm awfully sorry. I have to go."

"Hot date with some wool?"

"Something like that."

"You must be making something sexy. Can you make a cock ring out of crochet?"

Anna stifled a giggle. "Speak soon," she sang.

"Love you, babes."

She drove to the shop early, hoping to catch Ollie for a few minutes before the class started. That way she could get herself settled with the pattern. She parked and strode to Darn That Yarn.

I wonder whether Ollie chose the name herself. She could just imagine Ollie getting frustrated with a project and proclaiming the new name of her shop to the world.

Anna had managed to arrive twenty minutes early and stood by the side door, wondering whether Ollie would even be downstairs yet. She paused before she finally knocked.

A blond mop of hair stuck itself out of a window open right above the side door. "Anna." Ollie's face was alight. "Hi." Her mouth was full of food.

Anna's heart fell. "Sorry." She squinted upwards. "I wanted to...I suppose I thought if I was early we could sort out the new pattern."

Ollie threw her a hand gesture, as if she were physically waving away Anna's apology. "It's fine. Just one minute." She disappeared from the window.

I should have just arrived at seven like everyone else.

The side door opened, and Ollie ushered her in but fanned her hand towards another door. "Go on up."

"To your flat?" Anna eyed the staircase in front of her with curiosity.

"Yep. Go on."

Anna ascended the narrow staircase, and when she reached the top, she found herself in a sparse but comfortable flat, the open doors hinting at a bedroom, bathroom, and office. A large living space took over most of the flat, with kitchen things on one side and sofas on the other. It was decorated in soft greys, blues, and greens. A warmth settled over Anna as she looked over the flat. Various crocheted items adorned the furniture.

"That looks great," Ollie said, pointing to Anna's scarf before going to the counter in the kitchen.

"Thank you. I love it, actually." Anna stroked the softness of the scarf with her fingers.

"You worked very hard on it. Quick drink before we join our fellow crafters?" She finished off her sandwich and leant against the counter. "Tea?"

"All right. Thank you."

The dining chair made a scraping noise as Ollie dragged it out from under the table for her. Ollie made tea for them and then sat across from her, leaning backwards in her wooden chair. Anna sat with her bags in her lap.

"So, how has your week been?" Ollie asked.

"Fine, thank you." Anna grimaced.

Ollie shot her a long look. "You don't look sure."

"Well…" Anna let out a slow breath. "Okay, kids arguing."

"Ah." Ollie sipped at her tea and gestured for Anna to do the same.

Her bags went onto the tiled floor and she pulled her chair in a little more. Her fingertip circled the rim of the china mug, and she took in the pretty flowers wrapped around it. The mug was warm against her palm as she slipped two fingers into the handle.

"Something specific or just a personality clash?"

"Television rows. Personal comments. I'm trying to let them sort themselves out but—"

"But at some point you'll be locking them in a room together and not letting them out until they've kissed and made up?"

"Pretty much." Anna chuckled. "Honestly, they're in their twenties. And I know Timothy's a special case, but, really, you'd think I had a couple of ten-year-olds under my roof."

"Kieran and Helen still fight like cats and dogs. Not as much as they used to, though. Probably because they no longer live together."

"If only they'd communicate like sensible human beings."

"Might be a bit much to ask."

"Ugh," Anna said, putting her fingers to her forehead. "I just wish I could have a night off sometimes."

"Then welcome," Ollie said, "to an evening of treble crochet stitches and making new friends." Her eyes were soft as they looked at Anna over her mug.

Anna smiled back, closed her eyes, and breathed in the steam from the tea. Ollie's flat smelled like herbs, a soft scent that made her think of the hand cream she'd given her. "It's nice here, anyway." Anna swept her chin in a circle to indicate the flat.

"Thanks." Ollie sat back and crossed her legs. She tapped her forefinger against her mug. "Came with the shop. Almost identical to my old place, actually. Furnished too. Made moving in pretty hassle-free."

"You couldn't get something more substantial in the divorce?"

"Nope. Didn't get a whole lot from that. And I don't need anything bigger," Ollie said. "This does perfectly for now. Perfect for one."

"Fair enough."

Ollie looked at her watch. "We'd better go open up the classroom. And you"—she pointed a finger at Anna—"had better choose some DK for your blanket." She stood and picked up her keys, a large bunch with a simple green heart on a key ring.

"DK?" Anna stood, too, and gathered her bags.

"Double knit. Sorry. Keep forgetting you aren't familiar with the lingo." They headed downstairs.

The noise of things being moved around drifted through from the classroom.

"Have you decided on colours?" Ollie moved to stand close to Anna.

"Actually, that's as far as I've got. Navy, burgundy, and cream."

"Lovely." Ollie grabbed a set of steps from against the wall, opened them out, and climbed up. She leant forward to take two balls from their little cubby holes. She held the navy and cream balls out, her head tilted and her eyebrows raised in question.

Anna stuffed the wool under her arm and grabbed the ladder, flashes of Ollie tumbling from the top making her shiver. *She probably does this all the time.* She was dating a health and safety officer; it was only natural she would want to keep Ollie safe. As she allowed her gaze to trail up Ollie's long legs, she realised Ollie's backside was right at her eye level. She swallowed. It wiggled a bit as Ollie fumbled to move some balls around. Anna couldn't tear her gaze away. It was a very nice bottom, hugged perfectly in a black pair of jeans and brushed by the bottom edge of her white long-sleeve top.

Another one of Anna's rules was that she didn't ogle bottoms. She was far too set in her feminist ways. She didn't approve of men doing so, and therefore she didn't do it herself.

What is the matter with me?

Gripping the ladder more firmly, she forced her gaze back to Ollie's boots. Her insides relaxed a little as Ollie finally clambered down.

Ollie's fringe was hanging in front of her eyes, and she pushed it back, holding out a ball of burgundy wool. Anna's expression must have displayed her pleasure, because Ollie beamed at her.

"Perfect?"

"Yes." As she took the ball from Ollie, their fingers brushed.

They looked at one another. The earth seemed to stop spinning. Everything was quiet.

A loud knock on the side door broke the moment.

Anna pulled her lip into her mouth while Ollie went to open the door. Clutching three balls of yarn tightly to her chest, she wasn't sure she had the ability to move without dropping one of them. She steeled herself, set her fingers tight around them, and breathed deeply for a few minutes. Then she walked towards the classroom.

Six or seven people had arrived already. Anna was instructed to sit next to Christian, a tall, broad-shouldered man about her age, with a toothy smile and kind eyes.

"You came last week," he said after introductions had been made.

"And the week before." Anna shook his hand. "I'm afraid I'm still a bit of a novice."

"Well, we've all got to start somewhere." He took out a huge cardboard box from under the table.

She peered inside. It contained four cones of some kind of thick material made into thread. "What on earth is that?"

"T-shirt yarn."

"Made from...T-shirts?" Anna couldn't help staring at him.

"Essentially, yes."

"What do you make with it?"

"Well, you can make lots of things. I'm making some toy baskets for the grandkids." He held up a ratty-looking piece of paper with a pattern for a large basket with handles on it and an owl face on the front.

"How clever." Anna reached into the box to pick up an end. She frowned at him. "What size hook would you need for that?"

He moved slowly, his eyes gleaming, and produced a wooden hook as wide as Anna's thumb.

Anna tried not to swear in shock. She failed.

As Ollie shot her a look from the other side of the room, Christian laughed.

"You know we have minors here tonight, right?" Ollie grumbled.

A hand clamped over her mouth, Anna still sniggered through her fingers.

Christian waved the hook as if it were a magic wand, and that just made her laugh harder.

When Anna looked back over, Ollie just shook her head and shrugged and then began handing out the pattern for some his-and-hers slippers.

Matthew and a couple of the others scoffed at it.

"I know, I know," she said. "Heteronormative pattern. But there are so many good ones." She smirked at Matthew. "You can rename yours 'his-and-his' if you like."

Matthew was quite camp in the way he spoke and the way he behaved. He winked at Ollie, which made Ollie blush and look at the floor for a moment. Why would Ollie blush at that? Did she have a problem with Matthew being gay?

Christian's starting colour was a lovely bright peacock-blue. Anna watched his large hands for a moment. It looked like difficult work, and not just the stitches. *My hands would ache within minutes.* She looked down at her own collection, and the balls looked so small in comparison.

A hand-typed pattern was slipped onto her desk. Ollie was smiling down at her.

"Mad, isn't he?" Ollie glanced towards Christian.

"A bit." Anna's brow furrowed at all the abbreviations and acronyms in the pattern. Then she noticed a hand-drawn red box on the side of the paper. "You made me a key."

"You only need trebles and chains and slip stitches for this pattern. Reckon you can handle that?"

"I already know chains," Anna said. "What's a slip stitch?"

"Like a double, but without the extra yarn-over-hook and pull through."

Anna just stared blankly up at her.

Ollie smiled and perched on the side of the table and showed her until Anna nodded. "And then trebles."

A treble, it turned out, was simply a longer version of a double, and Anna got the technique pretty quickly.

"Were you as good at teaching in the field as you are at teaching crochet?" she asked.

Ollie averted her gaze, and Anna immediately regretted the question. But after a moment, and a deep breath, Ollie nodded. "Better," she replied with a wink.

With a sense of relief, Anna took out the correctly sized hook and leant her elbows on the table by Ollie's hip.

"A small row of chains, and a slip stitch to form a ring," Ollie said slowly, allowing Anna to follow on the pattern with her finger. "Chain three, two trebles into the ring, chain two, three trebles..."

Anna's gaze darted from an abbreviation to the key and back. She continued reciting the pattern herself. "Chain two, three trebles, chain two again—there are a lot of these, aren't there? Three trebles, chain two and join with a slip stitch into the...the third chain."

"Easier than Shakespeare?" Ollie teased.

"It does look like a completely different language, to be honest. That is, until you look at this handy little key." Anna eyed her. "I can tell you wrote this yourself. I hope it was a copy-and-paste thing."

Her lips twisted, and Ollie glanced away, flicking her hair away from her eyes.

"You're not telling me you typed this out from scratch?" Anna rolled her crochet hook between her fingers. "Oh, Ollie. You shouldn't have."

"Just wanted it to be right." Ollie tapped the side of her head. "Got it up here, the whole pattern."

"How long did it take you?" Anna asked.

Ollie scratched the side of a finger. "Not long."

"Ollie." Anna pointed towards her with her hook, ready to give her a royal telling-off for going to so much trouble.

Amy called out, needing help beginning the slippers, and Ollie smiled briefly before hopping down from her perch.

Christian was making something disc-shaped—perhaps the base of the basket for his grandchildren. It was getting bigger and bigger as he turned it like the steering wheel of a car, adding stitches in a spiral.

Anna made a slipknot and began, following the pattern slowly and carefully. Realising she'd made a mistake, she undid the piece and then started again. Her stomach warmed as she felt her confidence grow. *I like trebles. They're huge.*

Once she'd finished the first four clusters of trebles, she joined them up and held them out, scrutinising the tiny, messy bundle of wool. Her hands shook a little with unease. She looked over at Ollie, but she was deep in discussion with Amy and the lad sitting next to her, so Anna turned to Christian.

"Doesn't look right to me," she said, holding the work out at him like an offering.

He took it from her and teased the tiny piece into a square shape with holes at each corner. "It's fine, don't worry." He gave her an encouraging smile.

She tilted her head to one side and reconsidered the square. "That's... that's okay, then?" She glanced towards Ollie again, who seemed miles away. *I wish she'd come over.*

"Yes."

"Okay." She sighed and allowed her shoulders to drop. With a single nod, she bowed her head towards the pattern and continued. Similar to Christian, she worked round in a circle, making sure she remembered the two chain stitches in each corner.

As she finished the second row, her phone rang. She dropped her crochet hook with a metal clang on the floor and bent down to grab it while simultaneously answering her phone.

It was Timothy, and the moment she picked up the phone she knew something was wrong from his panicked tone.

"Anna. It broke. I didn't mean to. It's smoky and..." His voice was muffled, as though he had put the phone on speaker. All she could hear were smacking sounds—his hands against the sides of his face, she could easily imagine.

"Don't panic." She stuffed everything into her cloth bag. "Timothy, I'll be right there."

She was half aware of Ollie's eyes watching her as she left.

When Anna arrived home, having possibly ever so slightly broken the speed limit several times, Timothy was waiting for her by the front door.

He point-blank refused to go into the kitchen and had sensibly closed the door after accidentally setting the toaster alight with a teacake.

She stroked his upper arm. "It's all right. You've done the right thing by calling me." She looked around. "Where on earth is Bethany?" There was a growl in her voice.

"She's in her bedroom," he said, starting to pat the sides of his head. She held his hands to his face and he stilled under her touch. He stood in front of her, shoulders slack. "I didn't know what else to do." His breathing was shallow and his face was beetroot.

"I'm home now, Timothy."

"I knocked and knocked but she wouldn't open the door." His voice was a little muffled from between two sets of hands.

She took his hand in her own. "This is what we'll do," she said. "You go sit in the living room. I will look in the kitchen and assess the damage."

"What if the fire isn't out? What if the whole kitchen is ablaze?"

"We'd know, wouldn't we? It'd be very hot in here"—she gestured towards the kitchen door—"and there'd be smoke, wouldn't there?"

He nodded.

"Once I've had a look, I will go up to Bethany's bedroom and give her a piece of my mind."

Apparently having decided this was acceptable, he went into the living room.

Anna held her breath and closed her eyes tight before opening the kitchen door. Her entire body relaxed on an exhale. Apart from a slight blackening to the wall behind the toaster, the only harm seemed to have been to the actual appliance. She figured she could do with a new one anyway—that one was at least ten years old. She tumbled the toaster straight into the bin and cleaned the area around where it had been. Then she trudged upstairs to confront her delightful daughter.

Ten minutes of shouting from Bethany—and stern words from Anna, resulted in Bethany shuffling downstairs to apologise to her brother. They gathered in the kitchen, and for a second or two, Timothy eyed the place where the toaster had been.

"It's okay," Timothy replied. "However, the rule remains that I am not to come into your bedroom."

This made Bethany's mouth fall open.

"Which is why after knocking for a long time, I had no option but to phone Anna."

"Maybe we should—maybe we should change the rule, then." Bethany's voice was tentative. "So long as changing it is…is okay with you, Timothy?"

"I will need a detailed and specific list," Timothy said, clasping his hands in a businesslike gesture, "itemising each individual situation in which I am permitted to enter your bedroom."

Even though Bethany grimaced and rolled her eyes, Anna stayed quiet. They had to sort this out themselves.

"How about…" Bethany looked at the floor, eyebrows furrowed. "What if the rule changed to…you knock on my door. If after three knocks you don't get an answer, you can open it?"

"Am I allowed to come in?"

"No." Bethany's voice was sharp, but she softened as she looked at her brother. Then she smiled and shrugged. "Unless you think I'm dead."

"Right, kids." Anna strode to the counter to open a bottle of wine. "Let's watch a silly movie and eat popcorn. What do you say?"

With a nod from Timothy and a shrug from Bethany, it was decided.

"How was your crochet group?" Timothy asked once they were all sat down.

"Until it was *rudely* interrupted by a misbehaving toaster, lovely, thank you." Anna patted her cloth bag.

"Meet anyone new?" Bethany tilted her glass of wine at her mother, and her tone was overly flippant, like she didn't want to seem interested but actually couldn't wait to hear the answer.

"A man called Christian. He was making the strangest thing. A basket out of something called *T-shirt yarn*—can you believe?"

Bethany pursed her lips for a moment. "Actually, that sounds kind of cool." She slid her gaze towards Anna and narrowed her eyes. "But you *are* going to have to give me more information. What's he like?"

"Tall. Blue eyes, I think." Anna sipped from her glass and shrugged, using her other hand on the remote to find a movie to watch. "I didn't look that closely."

"Nice-looking?" Bethany asked, the embodiment of pure innocence.

"Okay, I suppose." She glanced at Bethany, who couldn't hide the intensity in her expression. "Ah, I see. No. Not in any way my type, Beth."

"Shame." Bethany twirled her glass and grinned with a conspiratorial air in Timothy's direction. Timothy just grinned back but didn't comment. *Have they been discussing my love life?* "Could do with someone interesting in your life."

"Uh, excuse me? What about Liam?"

"What about him?" Bethany shrugged. "He's such a bore, Mum."

"Oh, you just don't know him very well yet."

"You've been going out what…" Bethany counted silently on her fingers. "Like, seven months? And he never stays here. And you never drive him anywhere; he always drives. And he talks about nothing but his work and how crap it is."

"I don't like him," Timothy said.

"I know you don't, love." Anna sighed and shot Timothy a smile, hoping for one in return. He stared at her, his expression remaining sombre.

"He was nasty to me when you brought him home," Timothy said.

"He wasn't *nasty* exactly." Anna scratched her jaw and grimaced.

"He used the *R word*, and I don't like the *R word*. It's a word that is used to negatively describe someone with learning difficulties."

"He did *not*." Bethany eyes were large, and her hand flew to her throat. "Mum. Seriously, that's not cool. Get rid."

Anna held out her hands as if they were searching for an explanation. "He just…he simply didn't have the right word in his vocabulary and…" She shrugged dejectedly. "I did pull him up on it." She eyed Timothy. "He *did* apologise, didn't he?"

"Not very sincerely." Timothy's gaze remained downcast.

He shouldn't have to deal with that. Anna's heart ached. Timothy should never feel that being ridiculed was normal. Her glass of wine held no answers as she stared down into its rich red. She sighed.

"I'm sorry, Timothy. I'll have another word."

"No need." He shrugged. "He probably won't get it."

Tears stung her eyes. She closed them against the intensifying ache in her chest.

They all quietened in front of the television. The action noises filled the room: guns crashing, cars screeching, and characters shouting at one another.

Timothy munched his popcorn.

This evening could have been so much worse. What if he had set fire to the kitchen? I'll have to go through some safety information with him at some point. Anna sipped her wine, barely tasting it. She knew logically that all was well, but she couldn't help worrying.

The light from the television flicked across the surface of her glass, turning into a fiery red as it hit her wine. Her stomach burned with the non-existent memory of her kitchen on fire. *Pull yourself together.*

Her mobile rang for a second time that evening and she stared down at it as though yet another catastrophe was imminent. She saw a number she didn't recognise.

"Hello?"

"Anna?" The voice was female.

The burning sensation eased, as if Ollie's voice were an icy presence that quenched it. "Ollie, hello." She sat up straighter on the sofa. "How did you get my number?"

Ollie laughed. "Oh sorry. I may have…um…saved it when you called me that…that first time."

The remote control was passed on to Timothy, and she carried her wine glass into the kitchen. She noticed Bethany's raised eyebrow watching her leave.

"Hope that's okay?"

"'Course." Anna said.

"I was phoning because…because I was…honestly, I was worried. You left in such a hurry. Christian said it was something about Timothy?"

"All sorted now." Anna slid into a chair and placed her glass on the oak table. "He refereed an argument between a teacake and our toaster. Set fire to them both. No harm done." She smiled. "Sweet of you to worry, though."

"Oh…well…"

Anna gave her a moment, sipping at her wine and rolling it around in her mouth. It suddenly tasted scrummy.

"Glad it's all okay," Ollie eventually said. Her voice seemed stronger. "Is Timothy all right?"

"He's fine. Think he was more concerned he'd set the kitchen on fire, to be honest." Anna leant her elbow against the cool wood of the table. "Very small fire, mainly located inside the actual toaster."

"Good."

Anna leant her phone against her shoulder and fingered the stem of her wine glass. She scrambled for something more to say. "So, hope the rest of the group went well."

"Yeah, fine. Thanks. Amy is such a clumsy kid, though. Her yarn went flying across the room, nearly hit Matthew on the head." Ollie snorted.

Laughter bubbled up Anna's throat. "Oh dear. Perhaps she could do with a sling for it, or something. Like a kangaroo's pouch."

"Oh my God, that's a great idea. You design it; I'll get the patent sorted."

They laughed some more before quietening.

"Crumbs, I'm sorry. I just realised I didn't pay you for the lesson."

Ollie's chuckle made the ache in her stomach completely dissipate.

"Don't worry. I won't let you off that easily. You can pay it next week."

"All right," Anna said. "You do have a knack for convincing me to return, don't you?"

"I'm the best."

Anna stared down at the wood of the table, traced a finger around one of the knots. *I wonder if Ollie's settling down for the evening too. I wonder what she's wearing.* She stared at her wine and then pushed it away. It was obviously loosening her mind, making her think things she wouldn't usually. *First I stare at her backside, and now I'm wondering what she's wearing.*

"Anyway," Ollie said on a sigh. "I suppose it's nearly bedtime for me. You working tomorrow?"

"Nope, the wonders of October half-term. You?"

"Well, I'm sort of by myself. No one to actually run the shop if I have a day off. And what with the swimming lessons I teach, I don't have much time to sit around. So, Sunday is my only day of rest."

"You should get an assistant," Anna said. "What does Matthew do? He told me when I first met him that he was your right-hand man."

"He probably meant when it came to picking up…" Ollie cleared her throat. "Picking up potential dates."

"Ah right, a wingman, is he?" Anna sipped at her wine. "Although I'm sure the places he goes to find potential partners are a little different from the places you would go."

Ollie muttered something that sounded like agreement. "Anyway. I'll let you go," Anna said. She was surprised how deflated she felt about the prospect.

"Been nice to talk to you." Ollie's words came out in a rush.

They made Anna feel tingly all over. "You too. Um. Text me if you get bored. I might not answer straightaway but…it's half-term. All I have to do is housework. And a bit of marking."

"A-ha. I remember it well."

"I can't have my phone set to ring when I'm teaching, but if I'm at home, it's usually close by."

"Well, I'm the boss. I operate under a very strict mobile-phones-allowed policy at my place of work."

"Ha! Okay, I'll see you next Thursday, Ollie."

"Yes, you will."

"Bye, then."

"Goodbye, Anna."

The line went silent, and Anna and sat back in her chair. She smiled, rubbed her upper arms, and reached across the table to finger her wine glass. Ollie's voice was warm, and it was natural and easy to listen to.

When she turned around, she found Bethany leaning against the door frame leading into the hallway.

"Everything okay?" Anna asked.

Bethany had her eyebrows pushed downwards, but the corners of her lips were curled up. "Yes. Can I have another glass?"

"Do you have uni tomorrow?"

"I do not." Bethany tossed her hair back.

"In that case, my dear, feel free to finish the bottle." Anna smacked her thighs with her palms, drained her glass, and stood. "I am off to bed."

Chapter 4

Granny Squares

"How does Lady Macbeth persuade her husband to do what he does?" Anna looked around her Year 10 class and smiled encouragingly at them.

Callum raised his hand. "She calls him a coward."

"She does indeed. What else?"

Another hand, attached to Amelia, who sat right at the back of the room. "She says he isn't a man if he doesn't go through with it."

"Great answer. If we look at this passage here"—she pointed to the projector and clicked through until she found the one she wanted—"she says, 'Art thou afeard to be the same in thine own act and valour as thou art in desire?' She's saying he should *act* rather than just *want* to act. I suppose she's saying actions speak louder than words, isn't she?"

Invigorated scribbling spread through the classroom. She stood back and allowed the class to write, to take in the things they had decided upon. At times like these she truly loved teaching, when it inspired her and made her glad she had decided to do it all those years ago.

The bell rang for the end of the lesson. The scraping of chairs and collecting of possessions made thinking difficult, but then her world quietened as the class moved out into the corridor. It was almost time for the book club, and today it was the turn of the Year 7 group, who wanted to learn about Colin Dann and his animal books.

She left the classroom and rounded the corner towards the staffroom, intending on a quick bite of her sandwich before the club. She gave Liam a wave as he emerged from the staffroom door. He waved back and then approached her.

"Hello, gorgeous." He held out his arms and caught her waist.

She stiffened and allowed him to peck her cheek before stepping away. Looking hesitantly around the corridor, she took in the kids raising their eyebrows at them. "Not at work, Liam, please."

"Sorry." But he was grinning smugly.

"Anna, you should have your lunch." Timothy had arrived, his arms full of boxes— presumably of stationary. His eyebrows were pressed downwards in an expression she recognised as concern.

"I was just about to," Anna said and tried to move towards the staffroom through the bustling of children.

Liam stepped into her path. "Perhaps one real kiss, just for me?" He flicked his eyebrows up once. "To keep an old man going until the end of the day?" He reached for her again, and her gaze flicked up and down the corridor. *Does he really need this to feel like a man? Can't he do that without pestering me at school? What if the Head sees?*

"Anna doesn't look comfortable with giving you a kiss," Timothy said, his stare at them penetrating. "Her back is tense and her shoulders are up. That indicates she is uncomfortable with the situation."

Liam gave him a withering look. "I don't think you know what you're talking about, son."

"I do," Timothy argued. "I've researched extensively my adoptive mother's behaviour so that I don't misunderstand how she is feeling. I do that with people I have the most interactions with." He stepped back and frowned at Liam. "I don't know how you are feeling because I haven't done any research."

"You strange boy," Liam said, laughing. "And you really think Anna would be uncomfortable giving me a kiss? Of course she doesn't mind." He leant in and puckered up.

Anna stepped away. "No, Liam. Timothy's right. It's inappropriate. And I do feel uncomfortable." She sent Timothy a smile. "We're at work, and we are not alone. Usually you're such a stickler for policy."

"I'm on my official break. Contractually, my time is my own." He looked from Anna to Timothy, huffed, and spread his arms wide, nearly smacking a Year 8 around the face with his hand. The pupil ducked and murmured something Anna was sure was a swear word, but she ignored it.

Liam walked away, weaving between the remaining children as they all fled towards the canteen for their food.

Continuing to smile at Timothy, Anna beckoned for him to come closer.

He shook his head. "I have to get these set out for when the kids finish their lunch." He lifted a finger from the bottom of one box. "And you have lunch to eat."

"I appreciate you standing up for me, Timothy."

"You're welcome. I always will. I don't like it when you're uncomfortable."

"My hero," she sighed, putting her head to one side. "And in the future, I'll stand up for you a lot more, okay?"

He grinned toothily. "You agreed with me just now. I consider that 'standing up for me'." He waved with the fingers not gripping his box, then moved away, towards where his shop was, and Anna turned into the staffroom to eat her lunch.

Ollie held back from texting Anna; didn't want to seem too eager.

How long should I leave it? Two days? Three?

At some point, Anna would find out about her sexuality, and Ollie wanted to have been as casual and as careful as she could before that happened, while still being a good friend. She supposed they could be defined as friends now.

She rolled her shoulders a few times, enjoying her glass of wine after a vigorous morning in the swimming pool and a long Saturday afternoon at the shop. The Cock and Duck was thrumming with people, thumping music at a level just quiet enough to be able to talk, so long as one raised one's voice.

Matthew lounged across from her with his vodka and Coke.

She side-eyed the straw in his glass, a bright shade of pink.

He lifted an eyebrow back at her in defiance. "Coke is bad for your teeth," he said. "I'm just giving my pearly whites a chance."

She nodded distractedly, her hand tracing the outline of her phone in her pocket, wondering if she should just take it out and use it, rather than hoping it would buzz with a text from Anna.

She wrinkled her nose. The Cock and Duck still smelled of cigarettes so many years after the smoking ban had come into effect, which made Ollie wonder whether they'd properly cleaned it in ten years.

Matthew was following a dark-haired young man with his eyes. He picked up his drink and stared at the man over the rim. After a moment, he took the straw out and pointed it at him. Ollie slowly glanced over her shoulder. The man seemed a little older than Matthew but had nice eyes and stood confidently with his drink in his hand, his elbow on the bar. She didn't recognise him, but that barely meant anything these days. She didn't look at people all that much. She focused mostly on Matthew while they were out. *No one is ever interested in me, so why bother?* She snorted.

Matthew pursed his lips around a smile.

She rolled her eyes. "Are you going for it, or shall I go get him for you?" Ollie pushed back her chair.

Matthew flew a hand out and grabbed her arm. "Subtle, Ollie," he whined, eyes wide. "Just...wait a minute."

"No point in seeming too eager?" Her lips curled.

"I wouldn't hesitate to agree."

She smiled and shook her head in defeat.

"It works, though," he continued, the ice in his drink tinkling as he poked his straw around. "You should try it."

"There's no one here I'm interested in." Her shoulders rose defensively.

"I don't mean here. God, some of these girls are young enough to be your—"

"Yes, daughters. I am aware."

"No." Matthew laid a hand on her shoulder.

She shrugged the hand away.

He leant closer. "I meant, you know, try it with Anna."

"Straight." Ollie lifted her glass to her lips.

"How do you know?"

She sighed. "The indications are all pointing to it. Divorced."

"Irrelevant," he said around his straw.

"Has children." She counted the items of evidence on her fingers.

"Meh."

"Has a boyfriend."

"Inconclusive."

"Oh, honestly," she said without raising her voice. "Matthew. She would have said something if she were…you know."

She didn't like saying the word. It made her shudder with something that should have been long lost, something that five years of actually allowing herself to look at other women should have blotted out of her.

"*You* haven't told *her* you're gay." Matthew tilted his head in accusation.

"Well, yes, but that's different, isn't it?"

"Why?"

"What am I s-supposed to say?" Ollie said, fingers splayed in the air. "Hi, Anna. Oh, by the way I'm…" She sighed and shook her head.

"Why on earth not? You need to start practising saying it in front of the mirror, Ollie." He stared at her and then his face softened. "It's just a word. It shouldn't be that scary."

She scratched at her head and rolled it on her neck. "I know."

He took her hand and she looked down at their fingers all knotted together. Letting out a long breath, she squeezed his fingers tightly.

"So, when you called her, did she sound pleased to hear your voice?" he asked.

Ollie tried to remember Anna's tone of voice amid the beating of her own heart. She swallowed. "A bit."

"And she said she would see you next week."

Can you read my mind? "She did." Ollie inhaled quickly at a sudden thought. "Oh, but she hadn't paid for this week just gone, so she probably feels obliged."

"Have some faith. It's obvious she likes you." He chewed his lip. "But in what capacity? That's the million-dollar question."

"She suggested I text her," Ollie said. "If I'm bored."

"And it's been two whole days? And you *haven't*?"

A whine escaped her. "I don't want to seem too eager. Or something."

"But she *told you to*?"

"Maybe." Ollie drained her glass with a large gulp.

"Text her." His eyes were wide as he pulled his hand from hers.

Ollie took her phone out and looked at it. She sighed and shook her head. "What do I put?"

"Am I actually going to have to talk you through this?"

She shook her head quickly. "No. No, of course not." She started typing, her hands ever so slightly shaking.

"You should invite her here," Matthew said, his gaze on the ceiling.

As Ollie sent the text, a pleasant feeling blossomed in her stomach. The minute she processed what he had said, however, she folded her arms. "No. Not going to happen, Matthew."

He laughed.

With a flush, she realised he was joking. She smacked his arm, and he pushed his eyebrows down, recoiling into his chair, even though she knew she hadn't smacked him hard enough to cause any pain. "You be careful, soldier. You carry on and I'll have to do something about Harry and you." She grinned. "I've seen you staring at him across my classroom."

He looked absolutely appalled. "You wouldn't."

"Try me." She indicated their empty glasses. "Another?"

He nodded, his gaze returning to the young man he had eyes for out at the bar. "I'll get them."

Ollie rolled her eyes.

As she retrieved her phone from her bag on the way up to clean her teeth, Anna noticed Ollie had sent her a text. *Typical—the one time I leave my phone in my handbag, I get a text from her.*

She rested one ankle on top of the other and leant back against the headboard. She curled her toes inside her bedsocks before wiggling her shoulders into the pillows and opening the message.

Hi. It's Ollie. Hope your evening is going okay?

The familiar warmth began in her stomach, similar to when they had spoken on the phone the week before. *Why does the fact that a friend has texted me make me feel like a teenager?* Grown-ups were allowed to receive texts, surely?

And that was such an alien word for her. *Friend.* Did she actually have any? Patricia, whom she spoke to on the phone as often as she could with their conflicting schedules, but they lived so far away from one another these days it was difficult to actually meet up face-to-face. Most of the female staff at school were younger than she was.

Ollie was about the same age. Perhaps a bit younger. Anna wasn't sure.

How should I reply? I'm going to need something to help me think. She pulled off her weekend clothes and put on her pyjamas. The brushed cotton felt soft and comfortable against her skin. She carried her phone back downstairs and went to the kitchen cupboard, found her bottle of red, and poured herself a glass. Once she was settled on the sofa, she reread the message from Ollie and typed out a response.

> *Hi Ollie. My evening is going okay, just having a glass of red! What are you up to?*

Her insides squealing childishly, Anna sipped at her wine and picked up her book from the arm of the sofa, hoping to distract herself. She opened it to where the bookmark rested. She read one line. Her phone pinged and she snapped the book shut again.

> *Helping Matthew pick up potential partners. Save me!*

Anna chuckled and shook her head.

> *That does not sound fun. I've had a day of dusting and detailing the oven. I'm reading Jane Austen for the eightieth time. All my perishable plants are inside for the winter, cosy in my greenhouse. Perhaps I'll do some more of my blanket.*

Another message reached her phone, and she kept it in her hand. Her book forgotten for the moment, she laid it on the arm of the sofa.

> *Heaven. And well deserved after such a busy day. How is the blanket going? x*

Anna's stomach fluttered as she gazed at her phone.

Arthur trotted over from the armchair, meowing. He jumped up beside her on the sofa and she allowed him to settle down, his head curled by her hip. He stretched out a paw across her belly, his eyes shuttering in a human-like smile.

She texted Ollie back while trying not to move too much and disturb the cat.

Not too badly—I'm on my fifth row. I might change colours. X

She tapped a fingertip against the side of her phone. *Do friends use a kiss at the end of a text?* She squinted and checked back. Ollie had used a kiss; she hadn't imagined it. Maybe it was like punctuation. She put her fingers to her forehead but grinned. *My old English teacher would have my guts for garters.*

Her phone pinged.

Good going, Anna. Cream or navy next? X

Anna's breath caught. Ollie remembered which colours she had chosen.

Navy, I think. X

She rested her cheek against the back of the sofa and closed her eyes. Both kids were in their rooms; she could hear Timothy's television muffled by the ceiling. Harmony had descended over her little house, and she was glad. Sucking her bottom lip into her mouth, she sighed.

She set her wine glass on the coffee table and reached for her cloth bag. Arthur meowed in irritation at the disturbance. She retrieved the next colour and found the end. *How on earth do I join one colour to another?*

The Internet was fruitful with crochet advice when she searched on her phone. She didn't want to bother Ollie every single time she needed help. All the tips seemed far too complicated for a wine-accompanied evening, however. She tied the ends together into a knot and leaned back to look at it. That seemed neat enough.

Good choice. Be great to see how big it's getting on Thursday. Hope you have a lovely evening. X

Anna grasped her hook and blanket in one hand, typed out a quick reply with the other.

Why thank you. I still expect the whole thing to unravel before my very eyes, but we shall see. See you Thursday. X

She settled down for the evening, her mind too awake to go to bed just yet.

Ollie waited, leaning against the counter by the classroom kettle and glancing at the big clock on the wall. She tapped her fingertips against the underside of the counter. *I hope she's early again.*

People filtered in one by one, greeting her with hugs and smiles. There wasn't a single person she didn't love to see at her classes, and there wasn't a single person who didn't want to be there. Ollie had been in so many places she didn't want to be in her life.

Luckily, as the morose thought entered her mind, Anna walked through the door, beaming. She said hello to Christian and Matthew, who both hugged her.

Ollie hung back. She waited for their eyes to lock. They didn't say a word to one another, just glances for a while. Nerves overtook her, however, and she dipped her head, letting her hair fall to hide her eyes.

Anna sat by Christian and started to talk with him. Her expression brightened as he produced his final product: a blue basket with handles and an owl's face. She rubbed his arm in glee and her eyes shone with delight.

A battle prickled inside Ollie for a moment. She enjoyed Anna making new friends, but yet wanted Anna all to herself. Ollie shoved the turmoil away. *Of course she can have friends other than me. How selfish is that?* She took a big breath and forced her insides to settle.

Beside them sat Sarah. She was a short woman with wavy hair in a ponytail. Ollie remembered her wearing it up in a beautiful, intricate French braid when Ollie attended her fortieth birthday party a few months ago. Her large hazel eyes spent most of their time stealing glances at Christian.

Watching their introductions, Ollie felt a twist in her stomach. *She's barely said hi to me.* She screwed her eyes tightly shut. At least with Anna occupied, Ollie would have a chance to focus on the rest of the group anyway. And it would maybe stop Matthew being such a nag about her attraction towards Anna.

She handed out a pattern to make button-up cuffs—quite a feminine article, but good as a Christmas present. "You'll need a six for these and any yarn you fancy. I've made some with a sparkle in, which works well."

A few people went out to choose yarn.

When she stepped up towards Sarah, Christian, and Anna with patterns in hand, Anna smiled up at her. Warmth seeped into Ollie's bones as their gazes locked.

"I always seem to have a project of my own to make, don't I?" Anna asked. "One day I will make one of your patterns, I promise."

"So long as you're enjoying yourself, it's fine. When you're out of ideas, you can help us make the hanging for the Women's Institute in the church hall."

"Yes, that sounds like an exciting project. How did it come about?"

Ollie's stomach tingled as she glanced towards the ever-increasing number of squares in her wicker basket. "Sandra, the head woman—or whatever you call them—of the WI, approached me, wondered if we could make something for the hall. Apparently some big mural they used to have hung up there ended up with rain damage from a leak in the ceiling. Bits started dropping off it and it went mouldy. Anyway, they had the leak fixed so it wouldn't happen again, so I said sure, figured people have enough odds and ends lying around that they're doing nothing with."

"How big is it going to be?"

"As big as we can get it. The wall it's going on is three metres high and seven wide, but I doubt we'll fill the whole space."

"Big ask." Anna's gaze flicked towards the squares. "Lovely idea, though. Something we can do together." She tapped her hook against her chin. "Once I've finished this, I'll help out."

"That'd be amazing." Too much enthusiasm had slipped out. *Oh well. I'm supposed to be excited about it, I suppose.*

Anna nodded. "Well, look—nearly run out of wool." She held up her blanket.

"Have you done that all this week?"

"I have. Not bad for an amateur, hmm?" Anna winked at her.

The warmth in Ollie's limbs flooded to the rest of her body.

"Fast learner, obviously," Sarah said, smiling first at Anna, then Ollie.

"Reckon you'll be finished tonight?" Christian asked.

"Oh no, I doubt it." A blush crept across Anna's cheeks. "Probably not tonight."

"You might." Ollie went to put the kettle on, then grabbed the mugs from the cupboard.

Anna went back to talking with Sarah and Christian. Eventually they all became engrossed in their own projects, heads bent and conversation petering out.

The kettle clicked off. Ollie turned to make everyone drinks, the steam billowing into her face as she leant over to collect teabags and sugar.

Matthew sat in the middle of the room. He was inching closer and closer to Harry, who usually sat at the back. Harry, with his large brown eyes and handsome curly hair, changed where he sat each week. He seemed to want to interact with every one of the menagerie of people who came. He had a slow and gentle way of crocheting, a kindness that seeped from him in sunny waves. He'd made so many squares for the project, each one detailed and beautiful, and she was very grateful. She hadn't spoken to Harry extensively, but she wished Matthew would stop staring at him, or else make a damn move to be friends.

It's like an MI5 agent crossed themselves with a droopy-eyed golden retriever.

Ollie felt like she'd barely seen Anna, and by the end of the class, she wished the clock could have slowed down. *I should have offered her some help.* As she watched Anna pack up, she noted the blanket was nearly finished.

As Matthew stood, Ollie hopped around the table and pushed him towards where Harry was collecting together his yarn. Matthew made a grunting noise of protest, but she shot him a hard look. He rolled his eyes.

"Would you just go and say hi? It's getting silly now."

Matthew dropped his shoulders. A long moment later, he shuffled towards Harry.

When Ollie remembered to turn back and check on them, Matthew was standing before Harry, saying something too low for her to hear. Harry's mouth pulled into a wide smile that made his eyes shine.

Finally.

Everyone else trailed out of the room and into the night. Matthew and Harry left together, still talking—albeit awkwardly.

Only Anna remained. She wound her yarn into a small ball before replacing it in her bag. Ollie took her time placing the mugs back in the cupboard, hoping the thudding of her heart would quieten. She tapped her fingertip in a staccato rhythm on the handle of the cupboard after closing it.

Come on, she'll be out of the door before you turn round at this rate. Remember what Matthew said: just go for it.

Going over to her turned out to be the easy part.

"Um..." Ollie played with the sleeve of her top. As she shifted her weight from her right hip to her left, the familiar ache in her leg twinged. *I wish I didn't feel so awkward around her.*

Anna stood there, gazing up at her, her bag slung over her shoulder, a ten-pound note held out in front of her. Her expression that accompanied the offering made Ollie remember the time one of her friends at junior school gave her a Malteser, announcing it was the last one and that meant they were married.

Sometimes I wonder why I didn't realise my attraction to women earlier.

"My fees for today and the week before," Anna said.

She stuffed the note into the envelope with the others. "How a-about we go for a drink?"

"Greasy spoon?" Anna's tone was level. "Although they may not have free cake again."

"I was thinking...you like Merlot." Ollie shrugged. "I mean, if you'd like to...you know." She swallowed and looked around herself, then back at Anna. "Go for a proper drink?"

"Sure." The corners of Anna's eyes crinkled. "Would it be weird, though," she continued, her fingers playing with the strap of her cloth bag, "if I crocheted? I'm so close to finishing and...do people do that in the pub? I've never thought to look."

Ollie held a finger up, trotted into the main shop, and returned a moment later with a cylindrical bag with a wide handle. "People do now," she said. "I can help you if you get stuck."

Anna nodded and stopped fidgeting. "Well that sounds... That would be lovely."

With a bounce in her step, Ollie locked up the shop, and then they walked out into the cold air. Ollie led Anna to her local, a small establishment with quiet music and a few old blokes drinking cider in the back. They took a small table, and Ollie went to order them a drink.

Anna hummed as a glass of wine appeared in front of her.

The chair was reasonably comfortable as Ollie slid in beside her; their backs were to the window, and Ollie tried not to think about people walking past, seeing her with a woman and making assumptions. She tried to calm her fluttering nerves by focusing on Anna as she lifted her glass to her lips.

The burgundy liquid reflected onto Anna's freckles as she took a sip and closed her eyes.

Ollie gazed at Anna's lips for a moment and almost shook her head. She reached down to the floor where her bag sat and took out the small oblong she'd already made, unclipped the peg that stopped the piece from unravelling, and wound the yarn over her finger.

She began to crochet the brightly coloured yarn in short rows, glancing up after a few stitches. Anna was still looking at her.

Those green eyes were wide. "What're you making?"

"Lego blanket," Ollie replied. She tore her gaze away from Anna's face to concentrate on the first few stitches.

When she looked up again, she caught Anna scanning around, to the far side of Ollie's lap, then down at her bag. "Pattern?" she asked.

"Hmmm. No." Her cheeks flushed. She wished she'd brought something a little more defined, indeed, something with a pattern. "A friend of a friend—their kid loves Lego. She saw this on Pinterest and…" Ollie cleared her throat. "She's paying me so…" Ollie made a popcorn stitch—a round bobble that poked out—and turned her head to grin at Anna, not needing to keep her gaze on her fingers for every stitch.

Anna watched her.

Ollie pointed at the large blanket, still bundled in the cloth bag by Anna's feet, with her hook tip. "Come on. Idle hands and all that."

Anna gathered up her blanket. She started crocheting trebles, but then wobbled and huffed to herself. Ollie looked up from her work again: Anna's neat trebles were falling prey to small fumbles.

The desire to help at every opportunity fought against Ollie's teacher training, which told her she should let Anna figure out how to correct her own mistakes. *I'll leave her, she'll be okay. No need to highlight that she feels nervous.* She paused inwardly. *Why does she feel nervous?*

The sound of Anna sipping her wine and sliding the glass carefully onto a beer mat made her look up again. Anna's shining eyes were staring at her.

"You're amazing," she told Ollie.

Ollie fumbled mid-stitch as she relished in the look of wonder in Anna's eyes. "Five years of practice," she said. "I can pretty much work out anything for myself so long as there's a good enough picture of the thing I want."

"That's because you're clever," Anna said with quiet certainty, then returned her gaze to her blanket. Her fingers worked smoothly and steadily now.

Sunshine seemed to dissolve through Ollie's skin, a feeling that was growing more and more familiar the more time she spent with Anna. "Um, you don't need help with that, either, do you?" Ollie eyed the blanket, reaching for her own wine glass. It was easier to focus on the red liquid than to look up at Anna and confirm whether or not she was imagining things.

"Maybe not. But it *is* nice to have company."

The sunshine feeling intensified, and a soaring sensation took over. She shivered, overwhelmed. She concentrated on her Lego pieces, and her whole body relaxed into the low murmur of the pub, which was just rickety and old-fashioned enough that no one stared at them for their strange activities. The smell of spilt beer, old fags, and sweat tickled Ollie's nose and reminded her of days long past, of being allowed a packet of crisps and a lemonade while out with her parents. The memory grounded her even further and reminded her that she was safe, and that her feelings were valid, even if they weren't reciprocated.

"I do find it therapeutic," Ollie said. "Even five years later."

Anna stopped to take a sip of her wine.

"Is that what it was? Therapy for you?" Her green eyes were steady on Ollie's.

She should have felt worried about disclosing that part of her history. But Ollie returned the gaze with an unfamiliar feeling of strength. "Not really—at least not at first. I just needed something to do. Slowly, though…" Ollie shrugged. "Once you get good at something—get so good you don't much have to think about it but you're making something, creating something with your own hands—it starts to mean your life is actually worth it again."

Those eyes were trained on her glass. "Better than sitting on your backside all day, I suppose."

"I'm not sure I would have managed without the crochet, without at least something to take my mind off everything."

"Recovery and divorce, both at the same time?" Anna winced. "I can't imagine."

"I used to go for a run when I was stressed, before I was blown up. But when you're stuck in a wheelchair and then reliant on crutches for months on end…" Ollie sighed. Her fluttering fringe tickled her forehead. She grimaced. "I know I was lucky."

"What luck that the old lady who lived next door had the time to teach you."

It was as if a snake had coiled around Ollie's stomach and squeezed it.

A frown slipped across Anna's face and she touched the back of Ollie's hand, just for a moment. "Hey, I'd miss her too."

Ollie nodded. "Maggie died shortly after I found my feet again." She shook her head and then made herself sit up straight. "She left me some money. She didn't have children."

"She must have been terribly proud of you."

Tears threatened to fall. "She told me if I didn't put it to good use she'd come back and haunt me." It was a relief to remember something that broke the sombre mood. Anna laughed, and it made Ollie break into a snigger.

"To Maggie," Anna said, raising her glass.

Ollie clinked their glasses together. "To the woman who stopped me going insane."

"What did you do with the money? Did you a take a holiday or something once you were recovered?"

"Nothing quite that glamorous. I bought the shop," Ollie said. "And I put some of it towards taking my swimming instructor courses. Those things aren't cheap."

"I think she'd be happy with that."

"I hope so. At least I'm using some of my teacher training." Her attention shifted back to the tiny blue oblong hanging from her hook.

They worked in silence for a little longer. Ollie heard a huff from Anna's side of the table.

She looked up to see Anna pulling the end of the yarn through the loop on her hook and tugged it tight. "Done." Her hook tinkled as she placed it on the small table. After sliding out and standing tall, she held the blanket out with both hands.

Ollie beamed up at her.

"Not bad work, hmm?"

"Absolutely, not bad." Ollie grinned at the eyes peeping over the top of the blanket, which was heavy enough to bow in the middle between Anna's hands. "I love the colours you chose."

Anna dropped back into the chair, before folding the blanket into quarters, stuffing it into her cloth bag.

"Just weave in the ends and you're done." Ollie looked at her own hook and then continued to crochet.

Anna reached for her wine and sat back with a sigh. She swallowed the last of it and pushed up her shoulders with a wide smile. Another wordless but pleased noise escaped her. "Another?" Anna started to stand, reaching for her purse.

"I'd love one…but…"

"You have work in the morning."

"Yeah."

"So do I." The purse went back into Anna's bag.

I suppose it's for the best. Ollie wasn't sure if she could manage another glass of wine. Her limp always became more pronounced when she drank too much.

Ollie packed her bits and pieces away and got up to use the toilet, indicating with a pointed finger where she was headed. She limped off to the Ladies'. Her step faltered just in the moment she hoped Anna wasn't watching her walk. She felt exposed, hated to be watched when she walked. The disabled toilet loomed invitingly in front of her, but she skirted past it. *I'm not using a disabled toilet in front of her.*

Once she had clambered from the toilet, she scrubbed at her hands. The circular mirror above the sink held her reflection. The small smile on her face felt stuck in place. It had been so nice to spend time with Anna outside the classroom again—but the evening was very nearly over. Her reflection blinked and she gripped the side of the sink in dismay. *Oh damn.* Her own eyes stared judgingly back at her. *I've talked about myself for the entire evening.* She decided she would ask Anna more about herself next time they met.

She left the bathroom to join a smiling Anna before they left the pub.

It was cold. Ollie wanted to offer Anna her arm, to walk close with her and claim it was about sharing a little body heat. However, Anna had her scarf and coat gathered around her, so that excuse wouldn't work.

"Did you manage to get a new toaster?" she asked instead, her breath swirling around her in the winter air as she walked beside Anna.

Anna laughed throatily. *Rather a sexy noise.* "Yes, I did, thank you. A nice shiny one, in red, if you must know."

"Very nice. So, basically, it matches everything in your house."

Anna shook her head. "I do branch out into other colours sometimes, you know."

"Are you telling me that your house is not one big burgundy paradise?"

"Not quite. Just the toaster, and a few other bits."

"I hope the kids are happy with it."

"They don't get a say in the matter." Anna held her head high.

"I like a woman who can take control of toaster-choosing operations."

Anna playfully bumped Ollie's shoulder with her own. Her shoulders relaxing, Ollie lifted her head to smile back at her. They arrived at the car park close to Ollie's flat.

"This was a nice evening." Anna turned to stand in front of Ollie as they stopped by her car. "Thanks for inviting me."

"I'm glad you said yes."

Car keys jingled as Anna pulled them from her pocket, but she made no move to unlock her car. She fidgeted with the strap of her cloth bag. "We should do it again sometime," she said, eyes big and green and shining in the street lights.

Some of Ollie's reserve floated away and her gaze drifted down to Anna's lips. Anna shifted her feet in a restless gesture, but then suddenly tilted her chin up.

A jolt of surprise coursed through Ollie that she had to work to tamp down. *I'm reading too much into this.* So Ollie just squeezed Anna's shoulder and stepped back, stuffing her hands into her jacket pockets. "Definitely."

Still smiling, Anna pressed the button on her key. The beep of the car unlocking sounded like a child's screech in the deserted car park.

Ollie stepped further away, dipping her head to one side.

Curvy hips settled themselves into the driver's seat. Anna gave her a little wave through the side window.

Contemplating a salute but dismissing the idea before she could follow through, Ollie waved back, her bag swinging from its long strap. She stopped abruptly when it banged into her body. *Smooth, Ollie.*

The engine roared into life, and a moment later, Anna drove away.

Her knee was starting to ache, and Ollie's gait was slow on the way back to her flat. She trudged up the stairs. As soon as she entered the flat, her bag thudded onto the living room carpet. Her body was buzzing, full of nervous energy—alive.

She's so pretty. I want to kiss her. She flopped onto the sofa, her head dropping immediately into her hand.

Friends was fine. It would have to be.

Chapter 5

The Scarf

It feels like the weather has been ghastly forever. The rain pattered noisily against Anna's kitchen window before she left for work. She reached for her scarf and found it not in its usual place on the coat rack. Looking about her, she checked everywhere she could think of. Where on earth had she put it?

Had she left it at school? Once there, she searched the staffroom and her classroom. She hoped it wasn't gone for good. Her heart hammered as her anxiety increased.

I love that scarf. It's the first thing I ever made. Oh, goodness, what is Ollie going to think when I tell her it's gone missing?

When Anna got home, the scarf was back on the rack, but over Bethany's coat. Anna pouted and stomped into the living room. "Did you borrow my scarf?"

"Yeah." Bethany turned away from a music television-channel to look at her. "What? It's cool."

"I made it for *me*, Beth."

"But I like it, Mum."

Anna rolled her eyes.

"Can I have it? I already told Kathy you made it. She was really impressed."

With her clasped hands in front of her, Anna thought about it for a long moment. "Okay. But maybe ask next time you want to borrow my things?" She stepped round the sofa to sit next to her daughter. "I was worried I'd left it somewhere."

"You're not that batty." Bethany leaned against Anna's side as Anna put her arm around her back. "I mean, there was that month where you kept putting your purse in the fridge, but that was menopause-related. I wasn't too worried."

"Oi!"

Bethany just laid her head against Anna's shoulder. "And how was the evening of movies with your father?" She kept her tone kind, affectionate. An extensive list of books on the subject of divorce and its effect on kids had convinced her that being civil was the right thing to do, no matter how she felt privately about him.

To her surprise, Bethany made a disdainful noise in her throat. Anna grinned despite herself, buried her nose in Bethany's hair, and inhaled the hairspray and lingering hair-dye smell.

"All right," Bethany said. "He's an arrogant sod, isn't he?"

"Well..."

She snuggled against her mother and turned the television over to a documentary. "Honestly, Mum. Don't know what you ever saw in him."

Anna pulled her feet up underneath her, grabbed the throw that now sat permanently on the back of the sofa, and pulled it around them both. Bethany buried a lot further into her side, and they watched television for a while.

When Timothy came in from work at five, he was scowling and patting his hands over his thighs. This was not a good sign. Anna immediately got up and went to him, put her hand out to touch him, but let it hang in the air between them. She waited for his breathing to slow and his expression to drop.

"What's happened?" she asked.

He sat on the chair by the door to take his shoes off, shaking his head. "Work... Don't understand...something."

"What don't you understand?" Anna squatted in front of him to get to his eye level.

Bethany came into the hallway, frowning.

"People. Sometimes." He looked up at her, eyebrows furrowed. "Good evening, Anna."

"Good evening, Timothy." She kept her gaze soft so as to not make him more uncomfortable than he already was. "Talk to me about what happened today."

He nodded and pulled her up from the floor by the hand. Hand in hand, they walked into the living room. He slumped in the armchair across from the sofa. Bethany followed them. She turned the television off.

Good girl.

"They wanted to talk to David and me today. They said that some things had been stored unsafely in the main stationery cupboard; you know that we don't even go in there because we have our own supplies." He folded his hands in his lap. "It was..." He cleared his throat. "Liam."

"My Liam?" Anna asked. "Health and safety Liam?"

He nodded. "He sat David and me in one of the little rooms and asked lots of questions, but I wasn't sure what kind of answers he wanted. So I asked him what he meant, and he shouted. Said I was trying to be difficult. David said I wasn't. I like David. He's kind to me."

Anna's heart sank. "What happened then?"

"He used the *R* word again. I didn't know what to do. David took me outside. We hadn't done anything wrong. We didn't have to stay in the room."

"You're right. David is nice," Anna said, half to herself.

"David went to get our boss, Mr Trenchard, who runs the charity we donate some of our profit to. Mr Trenchard went and spoke to Liam, and Liam left. Mr Trenchard said he would talk to me tomorrow and that I didn't need to worry. He said Liam wouldn't talk to me again while I was at work."

"That's *so* not on," Bethany said, her hand against the side of her head as she leaned her elbow against the sofa. "Mum."

"I'll talk to him." Anna patted her thighs, looking around for her phone. "I'll phone him now and tell him he's not to speak to you like that again. If he wants to stay in my good books—"

"No, Mum," Bethany interrupted. "You need to get rid. He's obviously an arsehole."

Closing her mouth, Anna looked for a long time at her daughter, her stomach clenching. Then she looked at Timothy. *He's so perfect.* Tears sprang to her eyes.

Timothy's gaze was trained on his knees, his lashes lowered. "It's probably my fault," he said, letting out a huge sigh. "I just don't understand. When people shout, it confuses me. I don't deserve to be shouted at, do I?"

In a second, Anna was kneeling by his feet. She put her hands on his arms and squeezed. "No," she told him, tears streaming down her face. She rubbed at them. "You are a wonderful human being, and no one should ever shout at you."

His eyes were round when he looked up at her.

She smiled at him through her tears. "I'm so sorry, love." She turned to her daughter, groaning as she stood from the floor. "I think we all need a cup of tea, don't you?"

Nodding, Bethany caught her mother's eye. There was an affectionate note in her expression that made her want to cry all over again. Bethany stood too, and went to put the kettle on.

Anna took her phone out from her handbag and walked with it into the downstairs study. She closed the door behind her, Arthur making it in just before the door shut on him. He meowed around her legs as she sat in her comfortable office chair and found Liam's number.

"Hello?" He sounded as he usually did, which made Anna's strength grow. Suddenly he sounded disgustingly cocky. *How dare he just say hello, like nothing has happened.*

"Liam."

"Anna. Nice to hear from you."

Of course you know it's me, I've rung your mobile. She grasped the arm of the chair before speaking, gathering strength. "Listen. What happened today—"

"With Tim?"

Anna gritted her teeth. "Timothy. Yes."

"I hope you haven't given him too hard a time." His voice held something that sounded like humour. "I'm sure he won't be fired, but—"

"Actually, I was under the impression that he did nothing wrong and that…" *Didn't this Mr Trenchard talk to him? Was he that oblivious?* She closed her eyes and rested her head back against the chair. "That you called him a simply inexcusable word."

"Did I?" Liam laughed.

Her jaw tensed further. "Yes. Timothy told me you called him a…a retard."

"I may have." She could practically hear him shrugging.

"That's not okay."

"Oh, come on, Anna." His voice was breathy and his words drawn out, whining almost. "It's just a word."

Anna sat up straight, her elbow planting onto the desk. "No, it's not. You, as an employee of the school and as an *adult* cannot use such language." Bile rose in her throat. *Why is he being so calm about it all?* "You've done something seriously wrong."

"Is that what he said?"

"No, it's what I'm saying. And as a consequence, I'm afraid we can no longer see one another."

"Look, I know you're annoyed at me. But you should have been there. The way he acted, anyone would have done the same—"

"No." Anna used the simplest term she knew to get her message across. "No more, Liam. You've said these things before about him, and I'm not having it."

"Anna—"

"No. Timothy is sweet and wonderful and talented and gentle, and finding his way. No one I spend time with will ever use *that word.* It's non-negotiable."

"But…" He seemed to have run out of words.

Good. "We're over. Or whatever the term is these days. Broken up. Dumped."

"Dumped?" Liam laughed, but the shock remained in his voice.

"That's right. Don't call me again. I'm deleting your number from my phone."

Ten minutes later, she returned to the living room to find Bethany sitting next to Timothy on the sofa, both of them grinning as she swiped back and forth on her phone. They looked up when she came to sit by them. Bethany raised a single eyebrow.

A relieved and tired sigh escaped Anna's lips. "I've, as you would say, got rid."

Bethany beamed and shifted closer to hug her.

She directed her gaze onto Timothy. "I am your mother, Timothy, whatever the law may say, and you're both my children, and we don't need anyone ruining our wonderful family."

The next morning, Anna went straight to the head teacher's office and explained the situation. The Head looked gravely at her as she spoke and assured her it would be sorted by the end of the day. Suffice to say, later, Anna saw Liam heading out with a box full of his things and flames in his eyes. Her chest tightened as she thought about him going home by himself and stewing in a mess of his own creation.

She set her jaw. *My family is the most important thing to me. And what if he treats another kid with learning difficulties like that? What if the next kid is someone who doesn't have anyone to stand up for them?*

She sat for a moment in her car, watching the rain patter on her windscreen. Then she turned the ignition and drove home. She had done the right thing, of that she was sure. From now on, family came first.

Thursday continued to be a wet one, and Anna rushed from her car under her umbrella. She banged hard on the side door of Darn That Yarn.

Ollie's smiling face immediately fell as she looked Anna up and down. "Come in, come here. Let me take your coat."

Anna shrugged off the soaked garment and shook herself in Ollie's hallway, her skin prickling with goosebumps as the rainwater dripped down her back. "My God, it's cats and dogs out there."

"Something to be said about working in the same building in which you live." Ollie shook out Anna's coat and then hung it over a small radiator. "I've not been out at all today."

"Lucky you." Anna wrapped her arms around herself.

"Heating's on full blast." Ollie looked at her watch. "Come on through."

Anna followed her into the classroom and found a radiator to stand and shiver against.

Ollie pouted at her, then turned to get cups ready and to fill the kettle. "How has your week been?"

Anna looked at the floor. "It's been…hectic. Pretty difficult, actually."

Before she could formulate a more detailed response, however, there was a knock at the door and Ollie went to answer it. Soggy people arrived one by one.

Anna moved away from the radiator, going to sit with Matthew again.

He set the little case containing his hooks on the table in front of him. "I've finally completed all my works in progress and have come to class today refreshed and eager to learn something new."

The stress of the last few days fell from her shoulders as she took in his bright blue eyes. "I've relinquished ownership of my scarf to my daughter." She pushed her bottom lip out in jest

"Begrudgingly?"

"Somewhat."

"Make another," he suggested with a shrug. When Harry entered, Matthew sat up a bit straighter and smiled. Harry smiled back.

"That's progress," Anna said quietly.

Matthew turned his smile towards her. "I know. We chatted a bit last week."

"I watched you. And what did you talk about?"

"Nothing deep. Crochet, mostly. Did you know it takes him like an hour to make each square he brings in for the church hall? Insane, hmm?"

Anna chuckled. "Maybe he's the slow-and-steady type. 'Harry' sounds like a slow-and-steady sort of name, doesn't it?"

"Do you think so? Well, it works for Prince Harry." Matthew seemed rather smug about the fact.

"Ah. So you're dating royalty?"

"We're not dating." Matthew looked aghast. "We literally just said hi. And he showed me his horse on his phone."

Anna's eyes nearly fell out of her head.

Matthew frowned and then laughed. "Oh no. He has an actual horse. It's a rescue. Sounds like he spent ages reading up on horse care. And I think he really likes it. Her. She's a girl horse."

"A mare," Anna agreed. "What colour is she?"

"Chestnut. And she has a…" He pointed up and down his nose. "White stripy thing."

"She sounds lovely. Maybe he'll ride her here one day. Whisk you away on horseback at end of class."

He snorted, but the redness of his cheeks suggested perhaps that was not an unappealing image.

Everyone had gathered, and Ollie leant against the counter in her usual arms-folded pose.

"I've got a pattern for a bunch of roses. Anyone interested?"

Anna didn't put her hand up.

As Ollie handed out the patterns, Anna placed her hands on the table in an emphatic gesture.

"You know," she said to Matthew, "I think I *shall* make another." She strode into the main shop with a few of the group to look at yarn.

Ollie came up behind her and touched her arm.

"Hey," she said. "Have you dried off a bit?"

"Yes, thank you." Anna smiled at the way Ollie hid behind her fringe again. *Someone could do with a haircut.* "I need a new scarf. My daughter stole mine."

"Well, that's no good. Maybe this time around you'd like to try something a little more...complicated?"

"Not too complicated, please," Anna replied, a finger raised.

With a chuckle, Ollie went back to the classroom and returned a moment later with a pattern. "What d'you think?" Bobbing on the balls of her feet, she held it up for Anna to see.

When Anna gripped it by its side, she came close enough that she could smell lavender, perhaps Ollie's shampoo or perfume. It was nice, but she tried not to breathe too deeply, lest Ollie notice what she was doing. She also tried not to let her eyes wander to the long dark eyelashes resting low as Ollie looked down at the pattern.

"Baby alpaca?"

Ollie nodded. "It's quite a fine yarn, but really soft. Small hook too. You've not used a three before, have you?"

Anna shook her head.

"I think you'll be fine."

"Looks like a lot of counting," Anna said.

People milled around them, taking balls of yarn from the little cubby holes and carrying them back to the classroom. Matthew slid past them, paused, and then moved on.

"Are you telling me an accomplished secondary-school teacher such as yourself can't count to..." Ollie checked the pattern. "Fifty-two?"

"That's more than my age," Anna pouted. "Only one more, but still."

As her mouth opened, Ollie's eyebrows rose. "Me too," she said.

Anna beamed. "Oh, well, there you go."

They smiled at one another for a while. *Too long really*, Anna thought.

She became ultra-aware that she was practically leaning into Ollie's personal space. Ollie let go of the pattern, so Anna stepped back.

"The alpaca yarn is over here," Ollie said, holding her hand out towards the left side of the shop. "Colour?"

"Grey, I think."

"Not burgundy?"

"No," Anna replied. "I'm aware I rather like burgundy. But I wear a lot of it and...grey would go with more of my clothes."

"Good thinking."

Anna chose a light grey and sunk her fingertips into it, relishing how soft it was.

The smell of Old Spice wafted around her as the old man she'd seen at the group every week moved beside her.

"Hello." Anna held out her hand.

The old man gripped her fingers gently and shook them. "Anna, isn't it?"

"That's right. How are you today?"

"Joints are terrible." But he smiled all the same. "Thought those flowers were a good idea."

"Oh yes." She watched him look through the wool in the little cubbyholes. "I expect they'll look lovely on your kitchen windowsill."

A twinkle shone in his eye. "Oh, they're not for me, dear."

He chuckled to himself and chose some wool. She didn't think it appropriate to ask any further; she suddenly got the image of this doddery old man springing into some nursing home to present a wrinkly old lady with pearls in her ears and a blue rinse with a bunch of perfectly crocheted flowers. The thought made a giggle bubble upwards, but she pressed it down so she didn't embarrass herself.

She felt a lot better as she sat next to Matthew, who had chosen some pink and purple DK for his roses. Anna placed the pattern onto the table in front of her and bent over it, her fingertips against her chin. After taking her three-millimetre hook from her little collection, she made a slipknot and put it onto her hook. *God, it feels miniscule.* She looked around the classroom.

The young girl who had been having so much trouble during the previous weeks was chatting and crocheting happily away with her friend. The older lady with the huge blanket was beginning something else in a deep green. The old man had chosen yellow and orange and had a twinkle in his eye. The radio played softly, something old. It lulled her and made her think of warmer weather.

Christian and Sarah were sitting together. She was grinning, then blushed and lowered her head towards him.

"I think Sarah and Christian have something going on," Anna told Matthew, her mouth behind her hand.

Matthew leant to look at the couple across the room.

"All right, don't make it obvious."

He turned back around. "I have staring rights. I introduced them." He tossed his head back with a panache that made her laugh.

"Good instincts."

"Why, thank you. I've been waiting nearly a year for them to get together. I was on the pinnacle of getting them both drunk and surreptitiously giving Christian Viagra."

Anna snorted and shook her head.

He glanced over at the counter. "You and Ollie seem to be getting on okay."

"She's lovely. Awfully skilled."

He nodded.

"Does she not have many friends?" She kept her eye on Ollie, who was now preparing their drinks.

"Not too many. Since the divorce, she's sort of…thrown herself into this place."

"It's a wonderful shop." *But still, a shame.* "I can imagine she's a very good friend."

His eyes seemed glassy as he looked over at Ollie. Small lines appeared between his eyebrows, then disappeared. "She is."

The pattern was more complicated than she thought it might be, but the picture on the front looked so beautiful that Anna found herself immersed in trying to get it right. The yarn was so skinny, and her fingers felt like sausages. After a while and several mistakes, the pattern started to click in her brain, and she finished the first row.

Ollie brought over a cup of tea for her when she had completed row three. Anna's stomach felt warm and tingly. She smiled up at Ollie and held up her work.

The beam she got in return settled an infinitely comfortable feeling over Anna. Ollie simply nodded and allowed her to continue without a word.

For the remainder of the class, Anna could feel the smile on her lips as she got twelve rows done. When everyone started to pack up, she was so happily engrossed in her work, the sounds of scraping chairs and clinking metal hooks startled her into attention. Her neck cracked as she stretched it one way and then the other. She pushed her arms in front of her and yawned. As she packed up her own things, she watched Ollie collect her mug and take it to the sink to wash.

Feeling too tired to socialise, and too achy to hang around, Anna dropped five pound coins into the envelope and lifted her now-dry coat from the radiator. She felt cocooned by the warmth, pulling the collar up against the wind as she left.

She turned back to glance at the shop as she walked down the street and saw Ollie leaning out of the door, frowning. She waved at her with the hand not currently attempting to control her umbrella.

Ollie hesitated before waving back and then disappeared inside.

The coat was soaked again by the time Anna had walked to her car and driven home. She bade the kids goodnight before dragging her cold self upstairs to run a hot bath. She left her phone by the bath playing a little soft music and climbed into the steamy bubbles.

She nearly fell asleep—in fact she probably would have if it hadn't been for her phone buzzing and attempting to escape into the water. After quickly drying her hands on the bath towel hanging above her head, she picked up the phone.

Hope you got home safely and aren't too wet from the rain. You alright? You seemed sad when you left. X

Sorry I left in a hurry, absolutely knackered! Long day and my new pattern has made my head spin a bit. How has your week been? x

She pressed Send and kept her hands out of the water while she waited for a reply. The music on her phone continued to lull her into a state of comfort. Her bones began to heat up as the swirling water chased away the chill.

My week has been okay, thanks. Quiet at the shop with the kids back at school. Many kids splashing about at the baths, though. If you need help with the scarf, just call or pop in. Always happy to help. Keeps me out of trouble too. X

Sitting up a little straighter in the bath, Anna gazed at her phone with a heat in her belly that definitely wasn't due to the bathwater. She couldn't resist: she phoned Ollie.

Who picked up immediately. "Hey." Her tone was bright. "You all right?"

"Tired," Anna replied. "Just having a bath."

There was silence on the end of the phone.

Anna frowned. "Ollie?"

"Oh. Yes, I'm still here." Another pause followed. "Sorry. I can call you back later, if you like."

"I called you. It's fine." Anna settled a little further down in the warm water, her hand resting on her sternum. "So, it's been a quiet week over there?"

"Boring. Finished that Lego blanket, though. The mum picked it up yesterday. She loves it."

"Good."

"Done anything nice? You know. Other than teach?"

Anna pursed her lips momentarily. "Are you implying I enjoy going to work?"

"I would hope so."

It must be hard for her. She used to teach, too, and now she can't. "I do enjoy work, of course I do. Sorry."

"S'all right."

"I've not done anything nice, actually. Just hung out with the kids." Anna's stomach fell as she remembered her weekend. Something rose up in her throat like bile. She swallowed it down and sighed.

"Are you sure you're okay?" Ollie said after a beat or two.

"Actually…I broke up with Liam."

Another pause.

"I'm sorry," Ollie said. "Are you…" She cleared her throat. "Are you all right?"

"I should be." Anna's voice felt stronger. "No, I am."

"Did he do something?"

She sounds tense. "You remember I said he and Timothy really don't get on?"

"Yep."

"Well." Anna sighed. "There was an incident at school. Timothy runs a little shop after school time, selling sweets and stationery. The kids absolutely love it, and they love him. And Liam was questioning him and his colleague David about… Anyway, he wasn't very nice to him. Timothy's colleague had to intervene, their boss got involved. Timothy came home in such a state."

"He's all right now?"

Anna smiled. "How sweet you are. Yes, he's fine."

"Good."

"Liam was fired."

"Good."

Anna chuckled at Ollie's simple response. "I went to the Head, explained what had happened. And now Liam is without a job." She sighed. "I feel quite responsible."

"Don't. He sounds like a complete arse."

"Ha. Well. That seems to be the opinion of most of the women in my life." Anna swished the water around by her hip, watching the dwindling bubbles whirlpool.

"Sounds like a good decision on your part, anyway." Anna heard a few crackles before there was silence again. "Sorry. Just sat down with a cuppa."

"I should have brought one upstairs with me. Or perhaps something stronger."

"Mmm," Ollie sighed. "A bath and a glass of wine. Perfect combination."

"Next time."

"Oh. I have news," Ollie said, her voice bright. "Christian and Sarah got together." Silence for a moment. "Sorry. Bad choice of topic, after your week. I'm sure you don't want to hear—"

"No, please. Do tell. I saw them together this evening and thought something was going on."

"Apparently he asked her out after the group last week." Ollie made a humming noise. "All rather sweet."

"Sounds it."

"Honestly, who would have thought my little group would induce such romance?"

"Oh, I don't know." Anna felt all sleepy and very fond of her friend. "I think crochet has a wonderful ability to bring people together."

"It's obviously worked for them."

She caught what sounded like sadness in Ollie's voice. "Now, come on. I'm sure you know you're really quite a catch."

"If only the rest of the British public would recognise that," Ollie said, laughing.

"I could set you up with someone if you like," *She's been so kind. It's the least I could do.* "I know a few single men; some of them are even nice-looking."

"No, thank you," Ollie snapped.

Anna paused. "Oh. Uh, all right."

"Sorry." She sounded calmer. "I just… I'm not really interested in…in dating at the moment."

"I'm sorry," Anna said. "Of course that's fine."

"Who has the time to date, anyway?" she joked.

Thank goodness I haven't upset or offended her. "I know. And it's such a faff meeting new people." They laughed together. The water was starting to get cold. "Anyway, I need to get out and into bed. "I'm up early in the morning. Need my beauty sleep."

"No, you don't."

"Oh, shush." Anna sat up in the bath, brushing bubbles from her bare knee, which was shiny from the bathwater. "See you next week."

"See you."

Anna ended the call and placed her phone on the side. After climbing out of the bath, she wrapped her towel around her, and then went to sit on her bed. Her clean towel was squishy against her skin. She pulled on her pyjamas, which smelled like the new fabric softener she'd purchased just that week. *This is luxury.*

Her phone buzzed. She smiled at the text and snuggled under the covers, her head on her soft pillow.

Sorry about Liam. He doesn't deserve you. Goodnight. X

Anna hummed contentedly, rubbed her cheek against her pillow, and then typed out a quick reply.

He really doesn't. I need to trust my daughter's instincts, I think. She never liked him. Night. X

She fell asleep thinking about how her life was already so much better.

Chapter 6

Loose Ends (A Pencil Pot)

Tuesday afternoon was busy for Ollie, even with her usual crochet class cancelled. Schools had for some reason let out early, and children were flocking into the shop, looking for crafty things to make Christmassy gifts out of. Her handmade reindeers had already sold out, and it wasn't even December yet.

By five, Ollie was nearly pulling her hair out. Why were there so many people with so many requests for things she did not stock?

The busyness of the shop had left her feeling a tad shaky. She knelt on her good knee, surrounded by sheets of discarded paper in every colour under the sun.

The tinkle of the bell yielded two familiar voices that carried across the shop.

When Ollie looked up, Sarah and Christian approached with matching smiles, hands joined between them.

Ollie gave them a smile back. "Hello," she said, her eyes closing on a sigh as they stared at the carnage that enveloped her. "Don't ask."

"Kids?" Sarah asked.

"Yep." Ollie clambered up, grimacing as her knee screamed at her. She grabbed on to one of the shelves. Christian put his hand out to her, but she batted it away. "What can I do for you?" She had to push away the temptation to roll her eyes at the way they turned and grinned at one another before answering.

"We're thinking about making some matching wrist warmers," Christian said, his eyes never leaving Sarah's.

"D'you have a pattern already?"

"Yes," Sarah replied.

Ollie relented. The love between them *was* brightening up the rest of the shop. But it made her miss looking into a beautiful woman's eyes, touching a soft cheek, kissing gentle lips, knowing the other person was for her and her alone. Looking at the two of them so in love, she missed being gathered up into someone, no one else mattering.

She moved towards the rainbow of yarn and then stretched up above her head. "What d'you need?"

The couple finally broke their gaze and returned to look at her.

"Right," Christian said. "Hundred percent cotton. Reasonably thin…" His eyes returned to Sarah.

Ollie shook her head. "Focus, dear Christian," she said, and he laughed, which made Sarah laugh too.

"Blue and cream," he said.

Ollie left them to their staring, grabbed a couple of skeins to their specifications, and placed them on the desk by the till. They paid and left, whispering into one another's ears. Ollie wiped her hands down her face and stood for a moment, then slumped into her chair behind the desk. Her ribs expanded and released on a loud huff, unheard by anyone else in the empty shop.

Her phone was in her hand before the idea had truly formed in her brain.

No crochet class tonight. Drinks?

Matthew replied fairly quickly in the affirmative.

Ollie closed up. After running upstairs, she dragged a brush through her hair, applied some make-up, and found her favourite leather jacket.

Ten minutes later, they were sitting in The Cock and Duck, drinking beers out of bottles and checking out the other customers.

"Anything happen with that bloke from the other week?" Ollie asked.

He let out a snort. "Apart from a fumble in the toilets on Saturday night, which was brief and ended rather unsatisfactorily…?"

"Thanks for that." Ollie drained her beer quickly, hoping the delicious taste would push away any nausea. "And Harry?"

"Just friends."

Ollie sighed. "Seriously."

"I don't want anything boring. I'm young." Matthew squinted accusingly at her. "I need to be out there, having fun and being free."

She just shook her head. "Whatever. Another?"

"Thought you didn't drink on a school night?"

"I'm breaking my rule."

He put up his hands in an "I'm not complaining" kind of way. She smirked at him before taking their empties to the bar and ordering them two more.

Their night turned out rather well. Matthew managed to grab three numbers from guys he'd made eyes at, and a couple of women had actually noticed Ollie, shooting her smiles across the bar. She had returned the smiles but hadn't delved any further; she hadn't really been attracted to any of them. They were all so young. *Short skirts and low-cut tops are not really my thing.*

They were deciding their fifth drink would be their last when Matthew's eyebrows lifted and he nodded towards the bar. "Girl checking you out."

An eye roll seemed appropriate, but when Ollie turned around, she discovered "girl" wasn't really that accurate. Mid-forties, if not a little older, brown hair in a low ponytail, simple jeans and a baggy T-shirt. Dark eyes and a smile that brightened at Ollie's focused attention.

Ollie turned back around. "That's more like it," she muttered. "I'm, for once, not old enough to be her mother."

"Grandmother," Matthew said and earned himself a kick and a very rude word. "Hey," he complained wryly, "that's not very grandmotherly language."

She would have kicked him again, but the woman came over and held out a hand.

"Hi, I'm Tracy."

Ollie stood awkwardly from her armchair and grasped her hand. *Confident, I like it.*

She invited Tracy to sit with them, as she didn't appear to be with a particular group of friends. As they chatted about this and that, Ollie's stomach fluttered at the attention, something she was reasonably unused to.

Matthew left when the clock hit eleven, reminding Ollie she had to work in the morning.

Ollie rolled her eyes, which made Tracy laugh, and then hugged him goodbye.

Tracy touched the tiny silver pendant at her sternum and looked at Ollie through lowered lashes.

They chatted some more, then Ollie realised she really should stop drinking and go home—and perhaps get the woman's number. She felt so unused to the dating thing, the "getting to know a woman so you can be romantic at some point" thing. She stumbled slightly as she stood.

Holding a hand out towards her, Tracy downed her drink. "I might walk you home."

Ollie didn't argue. They walked side by side, shooting one another little smiles, until they reached Ollie's door.

"You live above a shop?" Tracy asked.

"It's my shop." She held out a hand in a half-shrug.

Tracy nodded. "Craft stuff, hmm. I'm not really into all that."

Ollie's head dropped forward nervously as she stepped back towards her door.

Tracy stepped up with her, right into her personal space. The gentle scent of wine drifted close from her breath. "Never mind, though, hmm?" she whispered.

Ollie tensed as Tracy's hand touched her cheek, cupping her face. She inhaled deeply as their lips met. *Sod it.* She slipped her hands around Tracy's waist and returned the kiss, which had no intention of being chaste or friendly. One or both of them made a noise between a gasp and a moan, and Ollie turned them, pressing Tracy up against the wall beside her front door. She sneaked her fingertips into Tracy's belt loops and held her steady.

Their tongues battled, and Tracy pushed back. Their teeth knocked together, they were so hungry for one another. Tracy's fingers dug into her scalp. Ollie shivered, but not with the cold. As soon as she broke the kiss, she took a breath. She was about to dive back in but blinked as Tracy looked behind them. Ollie kept her hands on Tracy's belt loops, but turned and caught sight of a short-haired redhead lingering in the doorway of a pub across the street, her eyes wide. It was dark, but Ollie's stomach fell as Anna took off down a side street at a hurried pace. Ollie stepped back and let Tracy go.

"Who's that?" Tracy looked from Ollie to the street behind her.

"Someone…no one."

"Bollocks." Tracy grimaced. "Ex?"

"No, no." Ollie looked at the pavement and toed the concrete with her shoe. "Just someone…someone I'm friends with. I think."

"Did I just out you?" Tracy asked, leaning against the wall. "Sorry."

She shook her head. "It's okay."

Tracy eyed her. "Maybe I should go. You should try and catch her up."

"No, I don't want you to go," Ollie said, thankful for the beer that was loosening her tongue. Tracy was pretty and appeared reasonably clever. She shouldn't throw away a potentially fulfilling relationship for a woman she would probably never have, should she?

"That's sweet. But your friend deserves an explanation and… Are you in the closet?"

"No. Not as such." Ollie grimaced and sighed, looking out towards where Anna had legged it.

"Good. Can't stand girls in the closet. Waste of time."

Ollie's face tightened. She was feeling regret and guilt and a whole ream of other emotions, most of them telling her to leave this woman she barely knew and run after the woman she actually did want to get to know. But fear twisted her gut like a boa constrictor with its prey. She didn't want to face Anna, to see the rejection and discomfort on that beautiful face. She'd seen that before—in her children's eyes and in the eyes of her ex-husband—five years ago. Her parents. Her brothers.

She sighed deeply. She would have to face Anna. Otherwise Anna would feel so uncomfortable that she would never grace the shop with her presence again.

"I'll see you." Tracy touched Ollie's arm. She indicated the side street with a tilt of her head.

Ollie watched Tracy's retreating back and shoved her keys back into her jacket pocket, then ran, her boots clumping on the pavement. She wished she were fitter, wished her knee didn't throb with every step, wished her steps were even, that she didn't limp all the time.

She found Anna hanging about on the corner to the main road into town, the smell of an Indian restaurant wafting around her. The bright lights illuminating the Taj Mahal made her hair glow more red than usual.

Anna turned to greet her with a look of surprise. "Hello. You're out late."

Ollie stopped next to her. "Anna," she said breathily, her heart pounding with more than her run. Her gut hurt, along with her throbbing knee.

"Just waiting for a taxi," Anna explained, her arms folded over her coat, her knuckles pale.

"Out with friends?" Ollie asked, staring across the road at a couple walking their dog.

"Just a friend from work. Jack. He fancied a drink." They both shifted their feet. "Reckon I've convinced him to join a football team."

"Enforcing hobbies onto everyone now, are we?" Ollie was hoping for a smile, a flicker of anything that meant they were still okay.

"Seems like you have hobbies I didn't know about," Anna said and her gaze immediately flicked up to Ollie's.

Ollie looked at the ground, closed her eyes and folded her arms. "If you're referring to…my romantic preference…" Ollie huffed out a breath and set her jaw. "I never said I was straight."

"You never said otherwise," Anna replied, her words like knives, but then lowered her gaze again. "Sorry. That was uncalled for. I suppose I shouldn't have just assumed."

"It's not your fault."

"Of course. It's up to you who you…who you…"

"Snog?" Ollie's mouth twisted into a lopsided grin. She was relieved as a similar expression played on Anna's face. It broadened when she continued. "Kiss? Smooch? Make out with…?"

"I can't believe I was offering to set you up with one of my male acquaintances, though." Anna was smiling, and Ollie didn't care about anything else. "You should have said something at the time. I feel like a total prat."

"I'm not used to saying it out loud." Ollie leant sideways against a lamp post and shifted her weight to her good leg. "It's a new thing, actually, my a-attraction to women." Ollie squinted steadily at her and waited for a reaction.

Anna simply smiled. "Do you think it was always there or…or did something change?"

"I don't know." She shrugged. "Maybe it was always there."

An ambulance went by, blue lights whirling, and they both watched it go. "Your, um…your a-affair," Anna began. "Was the teacher…?"

"A woman?"

Someone walked past, talking on his phone. They both looked away and shifted their feet until the man had passed.

"She was, yes."

Anna nodded. "Right."

"I'm sorry I didn't tell you." Ollie's eyes searched Anna's.

Anna looked back, her eyes shining in the street light. Then she shook herself. "Oh, hey," she said in a light tone. She reached out and rubbed Ollie's upper arm. "It's fine." She smiled properly, fully. But her gaze drifted across the road, so Ollie followed it—a taxi had pulled up. A flicker of something passed Anna's eyes. *Was that disappointment?* "Are we still friends?"

"Of course."

Ollie offered her hand for Anna to shake, but apparently Anna had other ideas. She wrapped her arms around Ollie's shoulders and pulled her into a hug.

Unsure of what to do, Ollie patted her back, her heart smacking against her ribs. She sighed happily and rested her chin on Anna's shoulder, laying her hands tentatively against the back of Anna's coat. Anna made a noise deep in her throat, and Ollie pressed closer. Perfume drifted up into Ollie's nostrils. She shivered and tried to pull back but found Anna squeezing her tight.

"No more secrets, hmm?" Anna said as she held her.

Do hugs usually last this long? She swallowed thickly and realised Anna had asked her a question.

"All right."

They broke apart then, and Anna nodded towards the taxi.

"I should go," Anna said, but sighed and looked at the ground.

I should ask her back to mine. Ollie blinked. What would they do at eleven thirty at night? She shivered again, this time in arousal, as flashes of things they could do floated through her brain. She pushed them away. *Stop it.*

"You're cold, you should get inside," Anna said.

Ollie's cheeks felt hot, and the rest of her felt anything but cold. "Okay. See you Thursday."

Anna squeezed her upper arm again, then turned on her heel and trotted across the road to the taxi.

Ollie stood for what seemed like an hour after it pulled away. She stuffed her hands into her pockets and then trudged back with an exaggerated limp. *Any physical pain is worth what just happened. Despite how terribly it could have gone, I'm so glad she knows.* Her stomach twisted with fears about what would happen next with Anna, but Ollie forced herself to be brave, and to hope that their lack of secrets would mean a better friendship between them.

Anna found she kept forgetting things the next day. Thoughts of Ollie's revelation plagued her like a swarm of locusts, poking at her mind whenever there was a lull in her classes. Lunchtime rolled around, and Anna was seriously considering two spoonfuls of coffee rather than her usual one, if only to break through the daze she seemed to be in.

As Jack stepped closer to her, she acknowledged his presence with an apologetic smile. "You got my text, I hope?" she asked and he nodded. "Sorry about leaving in such a hurry. I suddenly felt a bit queasy."

Jack gave her a disbelieving but kind look, and she avoided him by stabbing her salad with her fork and munching steadily.

He sat beside her and dropped his head to the side. "Come on," he insisted, his voice low so no one else could hear. "What really happened?"

"I was simply… I felt unwell."

"Nope. Sorry, Anna. I don't buy it. You were fine up until the moment you took off on me."

She was ready to give him an earful about minding his own business, but then his face was so full of lines that she relented. The staffroom was full of too many teachers and assistants, however, with potentially prying ears.

"My classroom?" she pleaded and stood, bringing her lunch with her.

She perched on the side of her own desk in her own, familiar classroom, and he slid up beside her. They faced the blackboard, and Anna's gaze passed over the half-scrubbed-out chalk. "Right. Okay. You know my new friend?"

"Ollie?" Jack said.

"Well…" Anna looked up at him, then took a deep breath before using the correct pronoun. "*She*…was outside the pub. With a female friend. They were kissing. And I freaked out… No, that's not the right word… Anyway, I didn't handle it all that well and…"

"Are you attracted to her?" Jack's eyebrows had risen. He sounded less surprised than he looked.

"What? No. Of course not I…I was just a bit shocked at seeing her with… I mean, she hadn't told me she liked… It just caught me off guard, I suppose." She grimaced at how she sounded and covered her face with her hand.

"So you buggered off and left me with half a glass of wine?"

"I'm sorry." Anna groaned through her fingers. "I'm a terrible friend. And I seem to be saying that an awful lot this week."

"Don't worry. You can owe me a drink."

She sighed.

"So you talked about…her like she was a potential…you know." He nudged her with his shoulder.

"Well, she's not." She looked away from him, at the blackboard, her refuge from the expectant expression she knew was there, but somehow she couldn't focus on the words in chalk written across it. "She is beautiful," she said. "I'm sure she could have any woman she wanted."

"So what about the class tonight? Is it going to be weird?"

"Oh, no, she caught me up after my little… Well, anyway. She apologised for not telling me, and I apologised for freaking out when I saw her. To be honest they were practically snogging one another's faces off. It was a bit full on."

A knock at the classroom door interrupted his laughter. Tally stuck her head round it.

"Natalie Scunthorpe and Chelsea Summers have had an altercation," she said. "Chelsea's asking for you."

Annoyance gripped Anna's middle. "Be right there."

The door closed behind Tally.

Anna sighed. "It should be fine. We apologised, made up, had a hug. Everything's okay now." She frowned and pouted. "I'm not sure why I reacted like that, if I'm honest. It wasn't like I've not seen two women… I mean, I haven't lived my entire life in a cave."

A noise of agreement vibrated from Jack's throat before he pushed back from the desk and went to the door. He turned to give her a pleased smile.

She smiled tightly at him as he left and then sprang up when she remembered she was needed to dismantle an argument between two adolescents.

That evening, Matthew answered the side door when Anna knocked, and although he greeted her warmly with a hug, she couldn't help feeling a little disappointed. Trying not to dwell on that, she focused instead on showing him her new scarf.

He lifted the end from her front and squinted critically. "Lovely. Although," he said, closing the door against the wind behind her, "Ollie's going to kill you."

"What for?" Anna asked, her eyes wide. *Oh God, she's told him how I reacted the other night!*

Matthew pointed to her bosom.

Anna's eyes widened even more. "What?"

"How you tie in your ends." He leant close to her, at the same time eyeing Ollie, who was in the shop area showing a new member of the group the various yarns. "You can't just tie a knot to keep it all from unravelling."

"How are you supposed to tie in the ends, then?"

"I'd show you, but you're paying Ollie to teach you these things. It's her job, really." He scooted away from Anna as Ollie came in.

Anna placed an innocent palm over the end of her scarf to hide her misdemeanour. They had barely gotten their hellos out before Matthew blew her cover.

He pursed his lips and pointed at Anna. "She's a knot-tier."

Anna's mouth fell open. She let her hand fall away from her chest with a sigh.

"You are not," Ollie said.

Anna threw Matthew an accusatory look before shrugging at Ollie.

Ollie flapped her hand to indicate she should go into the classroom, but her jaw was tense. "We'll talk later."

Anna felt a bit flustered at her deadly serious tone.

Only six people were at the group that evening—Sarah and Christian had obviously made other plans, probably together. Harry was there, with about six different colours of yarn, working slowly on a detailed square. His face was furrowed, and he seemed irritated with whatever he was doing. He kept undoing his work and then redoing it.

Matthew was throwing some surreptitious glances at him from the back row, where he slid into the seat next to Anna.

"Tonight we'll be making…crocheted bikini sets," Ollie said. Everyone laughed and Ollie's eyes gleamed. "Only kidding. Little in-joke there for those who have been coming for a while. You *can* actually get a pattern for a rather flattering bikini, but I can't imagine swimming in it would be the best idea." Again, tittering flooded the room. "Cuddly caterpillars this week." She handed out patterns to everyone.

Harry ran a hand through his shiny locks and then held it in the air, indicating he wanted help.

Matthew started to stand, but at Ollie's stern look and the wiggle of the end of one forefinger, he sat back down and huffed as his arms folded.

Anna smirked at him. "Remember, you said Ollie was the one who should be teaching?"

He narrowed his eyes at her. "I was just planning on saying hi again, not putting her out of a job."

"Maybe give him a minute to get settled with whatever he's having trouble with before you pounce?" Anna suggested.

"Make up your mind. Go talk to him, don't go talk to him. Christ." Matthew sighed and indicated her scarf. "Other than the hideous knots, that's lovely."

She ducked her head, warmth flowing through her body. "Thank you. So, cuddly caterpillars for you this evening or something of your own choosing?"

He held up the pattern, waggling it so the colourful cartoon-like faces of the two caterpillars pictured appeared to move comically. "These seem good. I'll have a go."

She grinned. "For once, I think I'll join you."

They walked together into the main area of the shop and chose some simple DK, both of them wanting to stray from the pastel colours in the picture to something much brighter.

"I'm going to force this little guy on Bethany for Christmas," Anna mused wickedly. "And she likes green, so I think I'll use three different shades." She grinned, picking up an almost fluorescent ball and laughing at Matthew's grimace.

"What about your adopted son? Timothy, is it?"

"Ah, yes, he is feeling very sad this week as he managed to break a pencil pot his late mother knitted him years ago."

Matthew frowned and then stared into space for a moment. He picked up purple, orange, and green yarn, carried the balls out of the shop area, and followed Anna back to their table.

"Pencil pot?" he asked.

"Yeah. I'll have to find him an identical one. He won't be happy with anything less."

"Ollie's made pencil pots before."

"Crocheted?"

"Yeah. You should ask her for the pattern."

"Oh, I'm sure she's very busy with Harry and all…" She fiddled with the balls of wool as she glanced over at Ollie.

She was bending over Harry's table, her fingertip resting on the pattern in front of him. He was nodding. Whatever Ollie was saying was obviously clicking with him.

"I can distract him if you like," Matthew said, but Anna knew he wouldn't dare after the look Ollie had given him.

"No, that's quite all right," Anna replied and moved her gaze away as Ollie stood and looked about the room.

Matthew put up his hand. Anna wanted to slip down in her chair as Ollie came over.

"Yep?" she asked, her voice strong. She gave Anna a single glance but focused on Matthew.

He blanched. "Um, so…" He looked down at the pattern. His mouth hung open like he'd been knocked on the head.

Ollie folded her arms. "Make a loop, six doubles in the loop. Increase as usual for a circle." She regarded him with glinting eyes. "Come on, Matthew, this is your bread and butter." She grinned at Anna.

Returning the smile, Anna felt warmth in her stomach as the laughing gaze trained on her own.

"Anna wants to make a pencil pot for Timothy," Matthew blurted out.

"Don't worry," Anna said, lowering her head a little, the amusement in her belly replaced with nervousness. "It's fine. I'm good with the caterpillar."

Ollie reached forward to gently squeeze one of the balls, her thumb sweeping slowly over the yarn.

That's an odd thing to do. I'm sure she knows what her wool feels like.

"I have a pattern for some pots, different sizes, so you can choose one or make a set."

Her embarrassment faded.

"But," Ollie said, her gaze suddenly stern and her arms folded, "we need to do something about your inability to tie in your ends."

Heat crept into Anna's cheeks. "You never told me any different." She caught the echo of the previous night in her own words.

Ollie's cheeks were tinged with pink as she cleared her throat. "I'll show you how to do it properly," she said, her voice much quieter.

"Okay."

Standing and shifting his things to one side on the table, Matthew pointed across the room. "Just using your loo." Anna didn't quite believe it, but he practically dashed out of their space, taking the opportunity to greet the new man at the front of the room with a friendly face and handshake.

Anna watched him go and then discovered Ollie had replaced him in his seat.

"Pass me your scarf." She held out a flat palm.

Anna took the scarf from the back of her chair and pulled the chair close to the table. Ollie rested her elbows on the table, the scarf between her hands. "Right. We don't tie knots in our work."

"Right." *I feel like I'm being told off at school. Why is that a nice feeling?*

"What you do is, when you're done, you pull your thread through, leaving a tail of about ten, maybe twelve inches." She held her forefinger about that length away from the end of the scarf to demonstrate.

Anna watched her hand and then looked up at her face. They were very close; she could see the little mole on Ollie's right cheekbone.

"Then you take a thick needle, thread the tail onto it." Ollie pressed her forefinger to each of the neat stitches Anna had made across the end of the scarf. "You sew the tail under each stitch, through one way, about this far." Ollie traced her finger across about five inches. "Then you sew back again the same distance, obviously going over the stitch here." She pointed to the stitch where she'd indicated Anna should change direction. "Because otherwise you'd just unsew the entire thing."

"Oh," Anna breathed. "And it doesn't unravel if you do that?"

Their gazes locked.

Anna swallowed.

Ollie paused before she answered. "Shouldn't. If you've sewn far enough."

Anna nodded but didn't break Ollie's gaze. *What do I want right now?* Ollie's breath tickled her face. *She's so lovely. I want to look at her all day.*

Another voice screamed inside her head. *What on earth does that mean?*

Ollie was giving her a shuttered-eye look, the tips of her cheekbones still a little pink.

Because she didn't want her to feel embarrassed—goodness knows she'd caused enough embarrassment that week—Anna leant backwards, turned away from her, and reached for the dark green ball of yarn she'd chosen for her caterpillar.

"Thanks for your help," she said and then cleared her throat. "You do have a nice way of explaining things."

When she looked back at Ollie, she was smiling at her. "You're welcome." Ollie didn't move away.

Realising Ollie still had hold of her scarf, Anna reached for it, intending on divesting her of it. Her fingertips brushed the back of Ollie's hand. Tingling shot through them.

She has such soft skin. Anna had to swallow, to look away. She tucked the scarf behind her and then twisted back around to find Ollie pushing the chair back and standing.

Matthew had returned and was looking between them. "All sorted?" he asked.

"Anna is up to speed on how to tie in ends." Ollie gave Anna a wink.

Her hands suddenly became very interesting, but, no matter what, the grin on Anna's face wouldn't shift.

The end of the caterpillar-filled class rolled around quickly, and Matthew packed up his bits hastily, clearly so he could catch up with Harry before he left.

The two men greeted one another warmly.

He's usually so confident. What is it about Harry that makes Matthew fall over himself? She wondered whether it was something that accompanied the young these days. *Fun is easy. Serious takes some time.*

Ollie limped over and handed her a piece of paper. "The pencil pot pattern," she said.

Squinting, Anna looked down at it. "Oh, it starts the same as the caterpillars."

"That's right. Make a ring, six doubles. I'm sure you'll work it out."

A smile settled on Anna's face as Ollie collected hers and Matthew's mugs from the table.

Ollie watched Matthew and Harry leave. "He literally got three numbers last night."

"Impressive."

"I know. I don't think he really knows what he wants—something desperately passionate with no emotion, or something that involves cuddling up in front of the television." Ollie's gaze darted around, and she watched the door close behind the last person. "Look...about last night."

"You don't need to explain," Anna said, taking a five-pound note out of her purse and handing it to Ollie.

Ollie took it and smiled in acknowledgement. "I don't usually... It's not my thing...you know... The woman you saw me with..."

"It's fine."

"Actually"—Ollie's eyebrows slanted upwards—"I think I'd like to talk about it. To someone who isn't going to tease me forever about my atrocious taste in women."

Her gaze moving to the table in front of her, Anna thought for a moment.

"Cuppa tea?" Ollie asked.

Anna lifted her gaze, and Ollie pointed upstairs. The warm flat was appealing, and a cup of tea even more so.

Ollie closed up the classroom, leaving the mugs in the sink. When Ollie noticed Anna looking, she shrugged. "I'll do them tomorrow."

She led Anna up to her flat. In the kitchen area, she flicked the kettle on and got out two mugs, the stylish ones they'd drunk from a few weeks ago.

"Christian and Sarah came in yesterday afternoon," Ollie said, watching the kettle boil.

Anna leant next to her, against the counter.

Ollie closed her eyes for a moment and shook her head, her hands against the edge of the surface as she leant her weight forward against it. "They're very much in love, I think." She looked sideways at Anna and then flicked her eyes back to the kettle. "They weren't all over one another, or inappropriate or anything… It's just been a while. And to see two people that much into each other…" Ollie scuffed the linoleum floor with her boot.

"It made you think about what you were missing," Anna finished.

Ollie nodded. The kettle rumbled noisily and the light on the side faded away. Ollie poured their drinks and then bent to her fridge to get milk. She grimaced when she stood, a strangled sort of moan edging out of her mouth.

"You all right?" Anna asked, reaching out a hand.

"Knee's giving me jip. Since I did a spot of running last night."

"I'm sorry."

The smile Ollie gave her was understanding. The spoon tinkled as Ollie stirred their teas and then removed the teabags. "I think we need to stop apologising to one another."

Laughing, Anna took the tea from Ollie and followed her to sit in the living room. "So, you're lonely?" Anna asked.

Ollie opened her mouth on a smile. "Something like that."

"You should call the girl you were with," Anna suggested, wiggling her backside into Ollie's comfortable sofa. "You didn't seem to be having a terrible time last night."

Ollie looked up at Anna, her eyebrows ever so slightly furrowed.

God, her eyes are so beautiful. Anna suddenly felt a fraction dizzy. *Fluttery* might be a more accurate word. She kept her breathing calm and steady, but her stomach felt strange all of a sudden. Dropping her gaze to her own cup of tea, she took a sip, allowing the hot tea to almost burn her tongue and ground her.

"I think I was drunk," Ollie said.

"A little more fussy during the cold light of day, are we?" Anna asked, with an eyebrow cocked and a smirk.

"She wasn't into crafts…or anything, really. We didn't have a whole lot in common."

"That's a shame." Anna tilted her head and patted Ollie's knee. "And quite the deal-breaker, hmm?"

Ollie nodded.

"Well, I suppose you never know who you're going to meet."

"What about you? Anyone on the horizon?"

"I think I'm just going to focus on me for a while," Anna said. "After Liam… My children come first. And I need to have a serious think about any future choices I make."

Ollie nodded. "There's no law that says you *have* to be with someone. I've been single for a few years. It's not all that bad."

"Something nice about having someone to come home to though," Anna said, staring into her tea. She watched the tiny tendrils of steam rise from it. "A warm body to be next to at night."

"That's true."

They smiled at one another, gazes catching.

Ollie had turned on a lamp, and the room was cast in a soft glow. Her skin appeared golden, and her eyes were dark. They held the gaze for a while, before Ollie took a deep breath. "As terrible as my marriage was when it ended, it wasn't all that bad. Not in the beginning."

Anna smiled. "I suppose my own was bearable for maybe a day or so."

Ollie's chuckle broke the tension between them.

"Before he decided to stray. When Bethany was little, it was all right."

"Here's to better relationships," Ollie said, lifting her teacup.

Anna clinked them together and happily sipped.

The clock on Ollie's mantelpiece ticked in the silence. Cars drove by on occasion. An emergency vehicle, possibly an ambulance, flashed by, its sirens silent due to the late hour. Anna wondered who the ambulance was for, which poor soul was suffering.

"So, you're not going to call her?" Anna asked, taking a last sip and placing the cup on the coffee table.

Ollie shook her head.

Anna lifted a hand to finger the throw on the back of Ollie's sofa. Tiny bobbles of wool were flicked here and there, as if it had been washed several times. She felt oddly reassured.

"Probably best," Ollie said.

"You need someone who at least attempts to learn to crochet." She shifted forward on the sofa, and then stood, giving Ollie a little shrug. "I should get home," she said, her face splitting into a wide smile. She set about gathering up her coat and bags. "Timothy will be wondering where I am. And I have an absolute mountain of marking to do before tomorrow."

"Of course." Ollie grabbed Anna's mug and stood, too, her face twisting.

Anna touched her arm. "Ollie."

Ollie looked at her with a strained expression.

"Can I suggest you take some painkillers?"

A pout pulled at Ollie's mouth.

Anna skimmed her fingertips over Ollie's shoulder. "Please?"

After a sigh of deference, Ollie nodded. "As you asked so very nicely," she teased. She put the cups by the sink, walked her to the door, and led her down the stairs.

Slipping by her in the narrow corridor, Anna stepped out onto the street. Holding an arm open, she smiled up from where she stood, a step lower than Ollie.

Hesitation flickered across Ollie's features.

Anna shuffled close to the doorstep. She wrapped an arm around Ollie's hip, careful and mindful of her weak side as she pulled her in.

The warmth of Ollie's chin against the top of Anna's head was stabilising. Ollie's whole body went floppy as she exhaled. Her thumb smoothed back and forth against Anna's shoulder.

After pulling back, Anna left without a word, her hands shaking and her heart pounding. Her face was flushed and she had that fluttery feeling again, like she'd almost fallen, and couldn't catch her breath. She walked swiftly back to her car, back to the safety of Radio 4, and allowed the cool air to pass over her face from the blower before turning the heat up.

What is the matter with me?

After sitting for a moment or two, Anna drove home, utilising the time to calm her thudding heart.

Timothy was in the kitchen, pyjamas on and ready for bed. He waved goodnight to her and retreated upstairs with his cocoa.

She watched him go fondly, and then took off her coat and shoes, and put her bags away. After trudging up the stairs, she looked in on Bethany, who was typing at her desk in her bedroom.

Anna sat on her own bed and just breathed for a moment or two. *Perhaps the menopause is hitting me hard.* She couldn't understand why her body was confusing her. Hot one minute, jittery like a schoolgirl the next.

She sat and thought. The wind rustled the few remaining leaves still clinging to the branches outside her bedroom window. A tentative theory floated across her mind, tugging at the analytical part of her, the area of her brain she used to decipher Shakespeare, or tease apart a mind-boggling poem. Her head pulsed with the beginnings of a headache. She couldn't consider it now; it was all too much. After finishing all the marking she had to do, she would sleep on it and think about it in the morning.

Chapter 7

The Hat

On Saturday morning, Anna had put a wash on, cleaned the kitchen, and sorted out a shopping list for that afternoon. With Timothy not due back until later and Bethany out for coffee with her father, it was a small luxury to read on the sofa in complete quiet, Arthur curled up at the other end by her feet. She lay on her back, her head rested against the arm, her knees bent.

After a while, her book ended up on the floor. With her eyes closed, the thing she had been thinking about for the last day-and-a-half rattled around inside her brain much more easily: About how beautiful Ollie was. About how her eyes sparkled when she taught. Her hands were so skilful.

I'm attracted to her. The theory had stuck, and she needed to speak to someone about it, because she was having no joy on her own. The notion of talking with Bethany did not sit with her for long. And as logical and surprisingly accurate as Timothy could be, she needed someone with a little more relationship experience.

Anna stroked her socked foot over the cat's back, careful not to annoy him but wanting to connect with another living thing. "What do you reckon, little man?" she asked and he looked up at her. "What would you think of Ollie? Would you think she was pretty?" She smirked. "She has an entire shop full of wool, so I expect you'd be rather enamoured by her."

Under her foot, his purr intensified, and he rolled around until his paws curled into the air.

You're no use. Not since I took you to the vet for that "little operation". No desire whatsoever to bring a girl back to your cat bed.

As for talking with a work colleague, the moment she even hinted she might be attracted to a woman it would be all over the school, and she did so hate being the subject of gossip. It had been bad enough with Liam. She liked to believe Jack was discreet, but she'd already told him she wasn't attracted to Ollie. She popped him on a reserve list, in case she could think of no one else.

She tried to consider the whole thing rationally. She hadn't been attracted to a woman before. Was that what was making her stomach churn? *Is my identity shifting? Am I becoming someone I don't recognise when I look at her?*

There were plenty of attractive women in films and television and magazines, right? What if she was attracted to some of those women too? Maybe that would tell her something. She sat up and then padded over to the magazine rack.

She chose a shiny-paged edition that belonged Bethany. She flicked through and considered all the pictures she could find of women. They were all either in embarrassing situations or fashion-orientated poses, and she threw the magazine back into the rack.

Her mobile loomed at her from across the room. Hmm. YouTube. She opened the app and wondered what on earth she should search for. But once she had typed a few words into the search bar and had clicked Search, she nearly dropped the phone. She closed the app the second after the results flew onto her screen, her cheeks burning. *Nope.* She'd probably get arrested now if her search history was looked into.

There was a buzz in her hand. She stared at the phone in horror, as if it knew what she'd accidentally searched for and was currently judging her. But then a small smile tugged at her lips at the name on the screen.

I'm bored. How you doing? X

Her stomach blossomed with warmth. Ollie was sitting in her shop, thinking about her.

If only it wasn't Ollie whom she was attracted to. She sighed. *She'd know how to advise me, and I feel so safe talking with her.* Ollie was intelligent and reasonably in touch with her feelings. She had a sensitive nature and knew how to make her smile. *And she's gay.* Together they would probably have been able to figure it out.

Anna sighed again and tapped out a text she made sure was especially cheery, despite feeling anything but.

> *I'm okay thanks. Housework mostly! How fun. Shop not busy today? X*

She briefly thought about jumping in her car and just going to the shop to hang out there, but she knew deep down it would only put off the soul searching she really did need to do.

> *Not at all—very surprising. I'm busy making rabbits—found the most amazing pattern. Can you receive picture texts? X*

Anna's phone beeped before she could finish her reply. Rather than a no-nonsense picture of a bunny in Ollie's hand, or set on a desk, Ollie had chosen to take a photograph of her own face with the rabbit squished against her cheek. Her eyes glinted at her creation.

Goodness, even just the cheekiness of it made her feel tingly. Anna gazed at the picture for several minutes before realising she really ought to respond.

> *Who knew you could make something so adorable? I think I might put in an order for one. I'm sure I can find a young family member or friend's child to gift him to. Or perhaps I will just keep him for myself! X*

A longer than usual text, but she really felt the need to gush. The rabbit was beautiful, small as Ollie's hand, with a delicate nose and thin ears folded to create spoon-shapes. The creation was finished with tiny paws and feet, and the hint of a round, fluffy tail.

Her chest tightened at the expression on Ollie's face, the darkness of her eyes, the pursing of her lips, her beautiful cheekbones. *Oh Lord. I am in such trouble.*

After clicking away from the text message, she quickly found the number she needed.

"Hi, Anna. What can I do you for?"

"Patricia, hi. I know it's been ages since we really talked, but I'm having a bit of a crisis and I could use someone to mull it over with."

Arthur stalked up her body and stood on her chest, making her squirm.

"What's the matter?" Patricia's concerned tone was so different to her usual teasing self that Anna's stomach immediately clenched.

"I'm okay physically, don't worry. Like I said, I'm just having a bit of a personal crisis at the moment. With someone I know."

"Oooh, do tell." The familiar intrigued tone was back.

Anna stroked the cat's head gently as she tried to form what she wanted to say into a coherent sentence. "Okay. But before I start, I'd like you to promise you're not going to go all…well, forgive me, but…all *Patricia* on me."

Laughter reminded her why she and Patricia were such good friends. The woman really was difficult to insult.

"I'm going to assume your problem is relationship-related, then."

Anna let out an affirmative noise and noted Patricia hadn't promised not to tease, but her stomach felt less like it was a tight ball of wool.

"Start from the beginning."

So Anna did. She spoke about how close she and Ollie had become, how she felt safe with her, and how she wanted to spend time with her. How Ollie made her laugh and made her stomach warm when she looked at her. How she looked forward to attending the classes each week, and not just because of her newly acquired hobby.

"I just…I think…I think it's more than just friendship I feel. Which is ridiculous, when you think about it. God, have I ever been attracted to a woman, Patricia?" She was breathless and the tight ball in her stomach was back in full force.

There was a moment of silence on the other end. Anna started to worry that Patricia had put the phone down on her until she heard a large sigh whoosh against her ear.

"Sometimes it's difficult to tell with you, Anna. You flirt with a lot of people, and, unlike with me, there's rarely anything behind it."

Anna huffed. "That's not very helpful." She put a hand over her eyes.

"I do apologise," Patricia said. "Anna, you are usually so confident in how you feel. But the way you talk about Ollie is totally different. I'd say if you think you're attracted to her, you probably are. I must admit, it's refreshing to hear you talking about something other than work and that awful Liam. I've been meaning to say for a while: I don't think he's good for you. He's turned you into an indecisive wimp."

"I broke up with him."

"Good. Now let's look at this rationally."

"I've been trying to do that, but my brain just doesn't seem to be working."

"Of course it is. Turn it around. If it was me in this dilemma, what would you ask me?"

Anna scratched Arthur behind the ear. "I don't know."

"Yes, you do. Close your eyes and think."

"I'd probably ask you whether you…you would like to kiss her."

"Okay. What else?"

"Do you feel a spark between you when you're close? Every time you touch her, does it feel like electricity? Would you want to spend time with her alone?"

"And if I were attracted to this person, how would I answer?"

"I assume you'd want to kiss the person. You'd feel a…a spark. Definitely. If you were attracted to her. You'd want to take her out. You'd want to take her to bed, spend all night…just…you know."

"Is that how you feel?"

A long pause followed, but Patricia waited.

"Yes."

"Then I think you have your answer."

Anna sighed deeply. "What if it's just a phase?"

"Really?" She sounded mightily unconvinced.

"Could it not be?" Anna asked, feeling a little insulted.

"I don't think so, sweetie."

"Ugh." Anna moaned, smacking her fist down onto the sofa.

Arthur shot her a look and moved to sit down by her feet, regarding her with suspicion.

"It's just very… It's so complicated."

"Why? Does she not find women attractive?"

"I think it's a case of whether she finds *me* attractive."

"She's gay?" Patricia asked.

"Seems so."

"Well that simplifies things, doesn't it?"

Anna didn't answer.

"Look, sweetie, I think you need to leave it to good old Mother Nature to convince you how truly attracted you are to this Ollie."

Sitting up, Anna stretched her neck one way then the other. The cracks both sides made, made her wince. "What do you mean?"

"I think you should take some—well, let's say some time for yourself—and see what…or more importantly *who* pops into your head."

"Time for myself?" Anna swallowed. "Are you implying I…Patricia!"

Patricia laughed. "Look, don't tell me you don't; everyone does. If thinking about Ollie while you do it is…effective…then I think you have your answer."

"And this conversation is over," Anna said, allowing fondness and humour to shine through her tone. "Thank you for the chat."

"Good luck, sweetie," Patricia sang out.

A groan of resignation left Anna's lips as she put the phone down. She lay back again and closed her eyes. *Really? Pleasure myself?* Not that she hadn't done it plenty of times quite happily, but the idea of basically booking a time slot like that made her feel self-conscious, especially when she knew she would be trying to do it with Ollie in mind.

When she looked at the screen of her phone, she saw Ollie had replied to her earlier text.

Of course you can have one! What colour would you like? Let me guess…Burgundy? ;) x

Anna smiled but then rolled her eyes in frustration. Ollie had sent her a wink. *What does that mean?* Did it mean anything? She flicked back to the photo Ollie had sent. Dark eyes shone up at her. Her gaze trailed down. She imagined those smirking lips exploring her own.

Sucking her bottom lip into her mouth, Anna locked her phone, then opened it again. *Stupid.* She needed to reply.

How much are you charging for the rabbits? X

For you, the first one is free. X

She shook her head. *I need to get up off this bloody sofa and clean something else.* She thought back to Patricia's suggestion. Would doing *that* while thinking of Ollie make it obvious how she felt? Did she *want* to do that while thinking about her friend?

After another hour of cleaning, Anna decided to get some fresh air. Her head felt like it was swimming, and she needed to step out of the claustrophobic house. She grabbed her handbag, locked the door behind her, and strode up the road, hoping the crisp air would make her mind feel less like it was the inside of her vacuum cleaner.

She happened across a café; a new place with red and white paint outside and a window table that looked out onto the street. It was on the main road, and people hurried past, on their way to important places.

A hot chocolate was definitely in order. She was feeling a little shaky after her stress-infused walk and hoped the milk and sugar would balance her body.

Her head tipped to one side as she allowed the sweetness to roll around her mouth. She watched the people walking past. Resting her head in her hand, elbow on the table, she picked out one woman. *Do I find her attractive?* Another woman, a little younger than she was, trotted past, at least seven shopping bags slung over her arms, and her hair swiping against her face in the wind.

The next woman had long brown hair in a plait and big brown eyes. A small boy hung from her hand.

Her insides tingled as the boy asked his mother something and she beamed down at him and stroked his cheek.

I'm not being selective enough. I'm sure Ollie doesn't find every single woman attractive just because she's gay.

She shook her head to clear it and sipped from her still-warm hot chocolate.

A tall blonde walked across the road, wearing skinny blue jeans and a black jacket. She wasn't an exact match to Ollie, but she was close enough. Anna considered the woman, studied her eyes, the prominent cheekbones. Then she looked lower, areas she wouldn't usually allow her eyes to wander along. *I wonder what she looks like naked.*

Anna downed the remaining hot chocolate, gathered her coat around her, and left with her head lowered and her cheeks burning.

Everyone was safely tucked up in bed. Arthur was curled up asleep on the sofa in the living room, and Anna had forced herself to have a bath to ease some of the tension in her shoulders. She'd used her favourite bubble bath and a freshly laundered towel.

She sank into the deep mattress, naked except for the duvet, which was pulled up to her chin. After having consumed perhaps more wine than was strictly necessary, she could feel the drowsiness brushing over her skin in waves. Her mind wandered.

Sod it. It's not like anyone is ever going to find out.

She closed her eyes and brushed her fingertips against her neck, then her collarbone, allowing her brain to go where it fancied. The image of someone lying next to her swam across her mind, and she allowed that person to lack facial features for a moment. Her palm slipped downwards to cup her breast, and she turned slightly to the middle of the bed, towards her invisible companion. She imagined the hand was not her own.

She snuggled her cheek into the pillow as her hand steadily kneaded and smoothed against her own soft flesh. A sigh slipped past her lips and she stretched her back, allowing her legs to fall open under the duvet. As she rubbed a little harder at her breast, her thumb began sweeping in small circles, pebbling her flesh.

Usually, she didn't need quite so much foreplay—she was an expert at providing herself with pleasure. She knew the different ways she liked to be touched, and knew which way could be most effective, depending on her mood. But tonight she wanted to become completely immersed in her fantasy. She wanted to see who emerged into her evening daydream.

Her ribs expanded as her breathing deepened. She rubbed her thumb more insistently over her nipple, shivering at the tingly feelings that shot down between her legs. The maintained caress caused her skin to pucker, her sex to blossom and ache. She rolled her hips and relished in the responding arousal that sparkled through her. After lifting her free hand, she brushed her fingers over her other breast and gave its nipple the same attention.

She waited as long as she could before giving in, before allowing the person next to her in her fantasy to come into focus.

Oh damn.

A mop of blond hair, a small smile, and squinting dark eyes met hers. The hand that Dream Ollie used to touch her breast moved downwards and tickled her ribs.

Anna shifted closer to the middle of the bed, could practically feel Ollie's breath on her face. She rolled onto her side, before sliding her hand downwards even further. Her fingers tangled in her soft pubic hair and then curled between her legs.

A knock sounded at her door. *Of course.* Anna pulled her hand sharply away.

"Mum?"

Forcing away a growl, Anna grabbed her pyjama top and pulled it on before nestling her duvet securely around her ribs. "Come in."

Bethany's face emerged when the door opened. She was chewing her bottom lip, and her gaze was trained on the floor. "Sorry. I couldn't sleep and was going to make some hot chocolate. Would you like one?"

Anna cleared her throat, her heart pitter-pattering. "No, thank you. I've already brushed my teeth."

"Okay." Bethany blinked into the dark room. "You okay?"

Attempting a smile, Anna clutched the duvet a little more tightly. "Yes, darling."

Bethany backed out, closing the door behind her.

Inconvenient. Anna sighed heavily and flopped back into the pillows. Her phone buzzed on her bedside table. She let out a growl, but it was cut short when she saw who the text was from.

Thought I'd say goodnight. And let you know that the yarn I've used for your rabbit is so soft. X

Anna stroked the side of her phone, and her whole body calmed.

Goodnight. And I look forward to cuddling her when you've finished. X

Anna placed her phone back on her bedside table. She rested back into the pillows, her hands folded over her stomach, and closed her eyes.

What to do now? Would it be right to continue? The double interruption had brought her arousal down a few notches. She turned her head on the pillow and stared at the space where Dream Ollie had been. Now there was simply empty air. But her body was still squirming. Her sex twitched when it remembered what she had been about to do. *I'm not sure I'll sleep if I don't.*

Slowly, she trailed her fingertips down her now-pyjama-clad breasts, enjoying the way the cotton felt against her skin. She closed her eyes and slipped her fingers through her pubic hair, discovering that her sex was still slick. She imagined Dream Ollie uttering soft words to her, imagined they'd been together a while; neither of them were new to it all. There was no nervousness or fear, just comfortable understanding and desire. Dream Ollie knew how to touch her, how to stroke her clitoris just so, back and forth in slow sweeps. She rolled onto her side.

Her previous elongated foreplay had left her so very wet and swollen that soon she was pushing against Dream Ollie's fingers. She gasped quietly as waves of pleasure built within her. Her fingers slipped inside, and she pushed hard against her own hand, her other one clutching the side of her neck the way she imagined Dream Ollie would. She would stroke Anna's cheek as they lay so close together. She would whisper words of affection and encouragement, her voice low and gentle.

Anna toppled over the edge into burning pleasure and release, Dream Ollie's soft chuckle reverberating through her head.

When the pleasure seeped away and when she could finally think again, Anna removed her hand and rested the back of the other against her eyes. She took in a deep breath and let it out slowly. *I guess that answers that question.* She sighed. She slightly hated herself in those few moments afterwards. A feeling of sickness washed over her and brought tears to her eyes. *Ollie's my friend. She's so kind and pretty.* She wiped at her eyes and then rolled out of bed to wash her hands and use the toilet.

Once she returned to her bed, the sick feeling had dissipated. It all made sense now: her relief at Ollie not wanting to call the woman Anna had seen her kissing, her eagerness to receive a text from Ollie, her unwillingness to miss a week of the class. She felt so wonderfully warm when Ollie looked at her.

Does Ollie feel the same?

Wednesday morning rolled around, and Ollie hopped downstairs with a spring in her still-lopsided step. Those painkillers Anna suggested had been a good idea, she admitted begrudgingly. She felt much better for it. Her knee had behaved itself lately, and it helped that she hadn't done any more running, if only to stop Anna from being so concerned.

The visit to the physiotherapist on Monday night had resulted in a sheet full of the exercises Ollie really should have been doing all along to maintain the strength in her right leg. She did them religiously, as instructed.

She settled into a day of dribs and drabs of customers and, with a wave of hope, decided to text her children. She started off light, with the same text to each.

> *Hi, how's it going? Was hoping we could meet up soon for another coffee? Text me back and let me know. Mum x*

She tapped the side of the table and stared at her phone for a while. *I need to calm myself. They won't text back immediately. They have lives.* She looked around her empty shop and sighed deeply, forcing her happy mood back into place. *They'll text back when they have a moment, I'm sure.*

But after a few hours of no reply, and a slowly eaten lunch Ollie barely wanted, her good mood was dwindling. She stared back at her phone, the large numbers of the clock on it appearing to change every hour, not every minute. She placed her phone face down on the table.

The minute she did, it buzzed. Her heart leapt as she picked it up.

> *Hi Mum. I'm game for a coffee, but Helen's not keen. She told me she doesn't want you to text her, so I'd leave it up to her. Phone you later? Kx*

As it dropped back into her boots, Ollie's heart felt like lead. She left her phone on the table, tucked her hands under her thighs and stared at it.

At least I know. But I refuse to not try. Maybe if she knows I'm here she'll start to see I'm not a monster.

The rest of the afternoon seemed to drag, and Ollie found each tinkle of the bell announcing a customer a relief from her melancholy thoughts.

Her phone rang as she was turning off the till, and she picked it up hastily. "Matthew, you okay?" she asked, staring at her watch.

"You still okay to help me move?"

She could hear cars driving past. He was probably walking from work. She blanked for a moment, searched her brain for a conversation they must have had, and came up with nothing.

"Yeah, sure," she said, trying to sound bright and cheerful, and not the least bit confused or guilty. Her pause must have given her away, however.

"You forgot, didn't you?" he moaned.

She swallowed. "S-sorry?"

"Your mind is somewhere else," he said. "Perhaps with a certain redheaded schoolteacher?"

"Shut up," she replied, shifting her phone to her other ear and going to the door to lock and flip the sign. "D'you want my help or not?"

"Yes, please," he replied, his voice sickly sweet.

"What time?" She peered out into the street. *Is it going to rain?*

"Six-ish? After you've finished at the leisure centre? I know it'll be dark, but I'm working until five and then I have a meeting…"

"That's fine, mate." *It doesn't look like it will rain.*

"Just so you know," he added, "we did talk about it, and you definitely agreed to help."

"I'm sorry, Matthew," Ollie replied on a sigh. She shuffled back behind the counter, opening the till and sorting through the card receipts. A sigh escaped her at the dwindled amount. "Have you much to move?"

"I've got a van for the evening. Shouldn't be too much."

"Good." Ollie looked down at her leg and scowled, then tucked it under the chair. "See you later, then."

"Brill. Thanks, Ollie."

Kieran phoned her while she walked to Matthew's flat. "Hey, buddy." She pressed the mobile to her ear as she limped through the late finishers who mingled along the streets.

"Hey, Mum. Sorry about Helen."

"That's okay. Not your fault."

"I just…I don't know. Maybe she needs time."

"I'm not giving up," Ollie insisted. "She can be as harsh as she likes, but I refuse to be one of those mums that never sees her kids."

"Okay." There was a smile in Kieran's voice.

"Anyway," Ollie said, trying to come across as breezy. "How are things with you?"

"Good. Work's okay. Went on a date with this woman from Accounts. She's pretty cool."

"That's great, glad to hear it." Ollie crossed the road at the traffic lights, the beeping of the green man making it difficult to talk for a few seconds. "What's she like?"

"Really clever. She dances. Jive and stuff. Pretty cool."

"You going to go with her? Take her dancing?"

"Oh no. Two left feet, me."

"You get that from me," Ollie replied, chuckling. "You dad still remains a whiz on the dance floor."

"That's coz your knee's duff, not because you're clumsy."

"Bit of both."

"Anyway, your love life?" He sounded very tentative, as though he was expecting to have his head bitten off.

"Well it's sort of… It's quiet at the moment. I'm biding my time."

"So there is a…a woman?"

"Yes. Sort of." Ollie gestured into the evening air. "We've not—she's not… Anyway, I like her."

"What's her name?"

"Anna. I'm not sure if she's… But she's nice to me."

"So she might be…straight?"

"I'm assuming so. She hasn't told me any different, but you know how these things are."

"Ah. She just might not be interested in you."

"Nail on the head."

"So, just friends?"

"For the moment. If she makes a move or whatever I won't say no." Ollie sighed. "She comes to my crochet group."

"So you just see here there?"

"We've been out for a few drinks. She's very lovely. Pretty, clever, funny. She has great taste in wine."

"Mum," Kieran said, sighing until his breath made a fuzzy noise. "Be careful."

"I will be."

"Because you've been… I know Zoe hurt you."

Ollie stared at the pavement as she limped along it. "It won't be like that."

"But…what if this Anna is just like Zoe? You know, throwing you out once things get complicated?"

"Things are different now."

"How? You're still disabled."

She grimaced.

"You're still the same person you were. You sound head over heels with this woman even though she's, so far, given you nothing in return. A few drinks? With no—I'm assuming you haven't even spoken about a relationship or… Look, why don't you just go find someone else?"

"I like her, Kieran."

"You liked Zoe. And look what happened there. The first sign of trouble and she chucks you out. Bathwater situation. The letter and…and everything. Please be sure of what you're doing before you go heart and soul into something that might end badly."

Ollie stopped in front of Matthew's flat and folded her free arm over her chest. "Look, just let me do what I want to do. I'm being careful. I'm being sensible. But Anna's different. She's…she's very special. She makes me laugh and truly wants to spend time with me. We have some things in common too—she's a teacher as well."

"So was Zoe."

Ollie gripped her phone hard. "Oh, will you please leave it, Kieran? Not all women are the same. Not all teachers are the same. You're right. Zoe was a disaster, even without the explosion. She was a big, humiliating mistake which I have now learned from. So, please, just trust me to choose my own path in this pretty crappy life I lead, okay?" Her jaw hurt from gritting her teeth. Her shoulders ached from being hunched against the cold and the stress of the conversation.

Kieran sighed but otherwise was silent for a while.

Ollie scuffed her boot on the concrete, waited for some kind of response.

"I…I just worry. I'm sorry if it comes out like…like I'm interfering. But I worry, Mum."

Matthew's door opened and he leant out, waving at her.

"I know you do. I have to go. Please, next time you see Helen, just put in a good word. I'll give her space for now, but I refuse to give up. She's my daughter."

"Okay. Love you, Mum."

"Love you too, buddy."

Anna arrived intentionally early on Thursday, hoping to catch Ollie before the class. She knocked on the side door, her knuckles stinging.

The window opened above her head. Ollie appeared at it and smiled and waved before pulling back in without a word.

Anna waited a good minute or so before the door opened.

Ollie ushered her inside. "Cuppa?"

"Lovely. Thank you." She followed her up, noting the stiff and stilted way Ollie climbed the stairs.

When they entered the flat, Ollie's limp was more pronounced and she moved over to her kettle to flick it on. "Feel free to make yourself at home." When she turned around, though, she sucked in a hiss.

Anna was immediately beside her. "I thought you were supposed to be taking painkillers?" she said sternly.

"It's not my knee." Ollie grimaced, a hand at her own back, her head lowered.

"What have you done?" Anna reached for Ollie's shoulder.

Ollie leant into her hand and groaned. "I helped Matthew move into a new flat."

The muscle under Anna's hand felt hard as a pebble. "Achy back?"

Ollie nodded.

Letting out a small noise, Anna pointed towards the dining table, a silent order. "Let me make the tea. You sit down."

"I can't let you do—"

"Yes, you can. Sit down. Or I'll give you detention."

One of Ollie's eyebrows rose.

Anna just jerked her head towards the dining table. Ollie obeyed and moved over to one of the chairs. She sat slowly, her back ramrod straight and her hands on her hips. She leant carefully against the back of the chair and closed her eyes. Safely out of Ollie's line of vision, Anna pressed a hand to her sternum. She really didn't like to see Ollie in pain.

The teabags were thankfully easy to find, and the fridge was an obvious white appliance containing milk. Once she had brought the teas over, Anna pulled a chair up to sit beside her.

Ollie's nose wrinkled, then she looked down at the wooden tabletop. "Hefted his chest of drawers up three flights."

"You're a nightmare, you know." Anna scraped the wooden chair against the floor as she turned it towards Ollie. After a sip of her tea, she placed the mug onto the table. "Would you like me to have a look?"

Ollie's eyes went wide. "Um."

"It's alright. Biology A-Level, you know. I was a bit obsessed with the muscular-skeletal system, as well as the great Bard."

"I can't ask you to…"

"Perhaps," Anna said, smoothing her palm against Ollie's shoulder again, "you could stop being a pain in the bum and actually let someone help you for once." She caught Ollie's gaze.

A long beat passed. "That would be…that would be great, actually."

"All right, then." Anna stepped around Ollie to stand behind her.

Ollie shifted forward, her forearms against the tabletop. Her shoulders were still, as though she was holding her breath.

"You tell me if it's too much, okay?"

She started with a light touch, skimming across Ollie's back and then digging in a little. Her hands trembled as she brushed the ends of Ollie's hair where they rested just shy of her shoulders. The scent of lavender drifted upwards, and Anna closed her eyes for a moment. After a few gentle manipulations, the muscles under her hands became less like rocks.

A breath puffed from between Ollie's lips. Her head sagged forward to rest against her arms. Anna took that as her cue to move her fingers down Ollie's spine, stopping every now and then to concentrate gently on specific muscles to test the waters. When she reached the middle of her back, Ollie inhaled, and a short, sharp groan caught in her throat.

"Just there?" Anna asked.

The noise Ollie made sounded like a yes.

"I'll be careful, but try to relax." Her fingertips pressed, gently at first, then with more force as she felt Ollie's knots releasing and her shoulders slumping. Her whole body seemed to soften.

Anna's stomach stopped aching as Ollie sank with obvious relief against the table. She swept her palms up and down Ollie's back and then snuck them over her shoulders, fingertips brushing against her neck. She stroked the blond ends of Ollie's hair. They were like little curls of dried grass on a beach.

A shiver overtook Ollie, and she slowly lifted her head, a languid sigh on her lips. She blinked a few times as though she had just woken from a dream.

"You're welcome," Anna said.

Ollie smiled. "Where were you yesterday when I couldn't get into bed?"

"Oh dear. What a prat you are. With your injuries, you should not be helping to carry furniture up staircases."

"*Helping*?" She snorted. "I carried the bloody thing by myself."

"You're insane." She didn't feel annoyed, however, just warm. Her fingertips tingled from where she'd lingered on Ollie's shoulders.

"I know." Ollie cupped her mug with one hand, threading her fingers through the handle.

Anna looked at her watch. "Ten minutes to."

"Plenty of time to drink these." She paused. "But I definitely owe you a proper drink."

"Have to be another night. Timothy wants me to watch a documentary with him when I get home."

They gulped their tea. The comfortable silence between them was a blanket made with soft yarn where Anna could relax back and nearly fall asleep. The pad on Ollie's thumb rubbed against her forefinger. Anna noted how her foot was hopping about a bit under the table. *She seems nervous.*

The friendly banter had petered out, but Anna found she didn't mind. Their gazes locked on occasion over the slowly steaming mugs. Smiles were exchanged. Without a word between them, they eventually headed downstairs to the classroom.

Sarah and Christian were back, wearing matching wrist warmers and gazing into one another's eyes.

I can see why Ollie would be jealous of what they have. They seem very much in love.

Amy inched closer to her as Anna worked on arranging her pencil pots in size order on the table and sewed in the ends the way Ollie had shown her. "They for your classroom, Miss?"

Anna chuckled. "Actually, they're for Timothy. He broke the one he has at home, so I thought it would be nice to make him some new ones."

"Aw, bet he was really pissed... I mean really upset." Amy giggled. "They're well cool. I've got some stupid plastic ones at home, but the ones you've done are wicked."

"Thank you." Anna arranged them on the table and sat back, satisfied. "So, how're things?"

"Mum's not great." The space between Amy's eyebrows wrinkled for a split second before she seemed to catch herself.

"That's a shame. How are you doing?"

Amy yawned. "Okay."

Anna gave her a moment. "Anything you need, you know where my office is, don't you?"

"Yes, Miss." Amy rolled her eyes. "Can't I just call you 'Miss'? It feels weird calling you by your first name."

"If that's what you're comfortable with, of course you can."

"Okay." Amy yawned again and rubbed her eyes. "Sorry."

"That's okay. Why are you so tired?"

"Up with Mum most of the night." She shrugged. "It's fine."

"If you're struggling, you need to go to Pastoral Services. They'll show you who to phone."

Amy didn't look convinced.

"Tell me you will." She put on her best stern-but-affectionate face.

"Okay. Yes, Miss." Amy's smile broadened back to full beam again.

"Good girl. Always ask for help if you need it. Best to do it now than to get so tired that your marks suffer."

"Yes, Miss." Amy wrapped her arms around herself and let out a deep sigh. "Thanks, Miss."

"You're welcome. How're you doing planning your future?"

"Okay. Not sure I want to do uni and leave Mum. Dad won't help—they're divorced. He's sort of...wiped his hands of her."

"What's the matter with her?"

"She has MS. Has trouble walking around and carrying stuff. Can't make a cup of tea unless she drinks it actually at the kettle."

"That must be hard for her. But for you, too, watching her get worse."

Amy nodded.

"Go get some help. If you want me to come with you, you only have to ask."

"Yes, Miss." Amy seemed a bit brighter. She shuffled away.

I really should keep checking in with her. Young carers get such a crappy deal. It's great she can come to this group, though. She seems to love it.

Once everyone was settled, Ollie took her usual place. "Welcome. I have a pattern for a bobble hat." She looked around at the group and laughed at something behind Anna.

Anna looked over her shoulder and found Sarah and Christian had both thrust their hands up into the air. She turned back to roll her eyes at Ollie.

"Right, then." Ollie directed her words at the couple. "Please don't make matching ones, guys. It's really disgusting."

A dramatic pause later and Anna could almost see the couple blushing without having to turn to look.

"I'm kidding, of course," Ollie said. "You do what makes you happy."

A few members of the group, including Anna, held their hands out for a pattern.

"What a surprise," Ollie said as she handed one over to Anna.

"I thought I'd make a hat to go with my daughter's scarf," Anna explained. "The one she stole from me."

"Well, Merry Christmas, Bethany," Ollie said and followed Anna to the far wall where the balls of chunky wool sat.

Anna perused the pattern while Ollie moved away from her. *Gone are the days when she would help me at every moment.* But she concentrated on the pattern, reading it thoroughly, trying not to show how disappointed she was.

But Ollie was soon back at her side. Anna was still looking at the pattern.

"All right?"

"I don't know what this…this…" Anna peered at the paper. "*Front post*…something…is."

"I'll show you. Why don't you choose some yarn?"

At Ollie's confident smile, Anna relaxed a little and stepped up to the cubbyholes. She reached for a single deep-red ball and carried it back into the classroom with her chin high. Sitting at her table and with no one in the seat next to her, she continued to peruse the pattern.

Ollie was again accosted by various people all wanting help, and it was a good twenty minutes before she was able to sit beside Anna. She had grabbed a hook from the little pot on the sideboard, as well as a half-used ball of wool. Pretending to crack her knuckles, which made Anna laugh, she shot Anna a grin.

"Hi." Anna held up her hook, the ribbed band around the bottom of the hat already a few centimetres wide.

"Oh, well done." Ollie touched the neat rows of slip stitches.

"Figured there was just one thing 'in back loops only' could mean." At Ollie's impressed look, Anna looked down. *Am I blushing again?* "But show me these new back...post thingies."

Ollie shifted close to her and did a quick row of chain stitches with the yarn she had brought to the table. Then she worked a speedy row of treble stitches. "Right. You want to do your first row of trebles, then join them with a slip stitch, okay?"

"Okay." Anna peered at her working with her head close to Ollie's.

"So, then when you start the next row, it's: yarn over hook, then you go round the back..." She turned her hand back on itself, twisting the yarn around. "Pop your hook in from left to right, like this." She did so. "Yarn over while it's in the post, draw it through the two loops, yarn over again, draw it through." She looked up from her hands.

Anna inhaled quickly at how close they were. An inch or so more and she'd be close enough to kiss her. *Well, no time like the present.* Anna parted her lips ever so slightly. Swallowing, she dropped her gaze to Ollie's lips. *Subtle.* She flicked her gaze back up to Ollie's. "I think I understand." She licked her lips. "Maybe...just show me one more time?"

Ollie blinked at her for a moment and then did so, explaining each step slowly. As her careful, long fingers made the stitches, a shiver ran through Anna at the false memory of those fingers touching her a few nights before.

That was just a fantasy. Stop getting distracted.

"How's that?" Ollie asked, then cleared her throat. Her voice had gone hoarse.

Anna held her gaze in silence, uncertain of her own voice at the moment. "And the…the front post stitch?" she finally asked. Her own words were breathy. She could swear Ollie's eyes had lowered to look at her lips.

Quit stalling. Kiss her already.

"The same." Ollie sat back in her chair. "Just round the front."

"Okay." *That's all you can come up with to say? Brilliant, Anna.*

"And…and when you get to decrease, you don't do it as usual, I think…" Ollie lowered her head towards the pattern, a slight stutter in her delivery. "Yes, you just skip the stitches."

"Okay," Anna said again. She probably wasn't going to remember a single thing she was being told right now, damn it.

Ollie smiled at her and tilted her head to one side as if asking a question. "She'll like it, I think," she said. "Your daughter."

"Bethany." Anna said her daughter's name slowly, as if learning it for the first time. Her face was starting to hurt with the amount of smiling she was doing. And then came the inevitable awkward pause.

Might as well have another go. She tried again, touching Ollie's shoulder blade gingerly. "How's the back?"

"Better." Her lips pursed for just a moment. "Thank you."

Harry had sat beside Anna while Ollie had been showing her the new stitches, and now he looked at the pattern in front of her. "I made one a bit like this a few years ago. I love the bobble."

She found herself irrationally annoyed at his sudden presence but then told herself she was being ridiculous. This was a crochet class, not a pickup bar.

Already Ollie was at the kettle, the familiar clinking of mugs ringing across the room. She leant against the counter, hands against its edge, and cast her gaze downwards.

Anna took the high road and smiled at him. It wasn't his fault Anna couldn't find the nerve to make her move.

"I'm Harry," he said, and Anna realised they hadn't ever been properly introduced.

"Anna. Nice to meet you."

She settled lazily into Harry's company and worked on the rim of the hat while they chatted about their projects. "So, your granny squares are amazing," she said.

He picked up one of the three he'd brought with him, an almost 3-D shape with a huge bobbled flower in the centre and little flecks of green around it. "Thank you," he said. "They are for the wall hanging."

"I gathered." Anna squished the flower shape. It had a pleasing texture. "I suppose I need to start making some as well." She pushed up her shoulders. "Ought to do my bit."

"They take me a long time, but they're really worth it. I like making things for a good cause."

Harry's gaze drifted over to Matthew, who was in deep conversation with Christian. She took a deep breath and added a deliberate element of innocence into her voice. "Matthew said you have a horse."

He turned back to her and pulled his mobile from his pocket. "Yep. She was a performing horse, in films and stuff, you know? Very sweet natured, but getting old now, and the company that owned her was going to put her in an animal shelter. I heard about it and went to see her and immediately fell in love."

Anna looked down at the photos Harry was showing her on his mobile. "Oh, she's beautiful. What's her name?"

"Florence." He grinned at her. "It really suits her."

"A lot of work, though, having a horse."

"Oh, I know. I read up on it all before I... I'd actually been thinking about getting a horse for a while but...it was just a bit too scary. Frivolous, perhaps. You know?"

Anna nodded.

He put his phone away. "But when I heard about Florence...I just couldn't let her go to a shelter." He shook his head, and his eyes shone with emotion. "I took the plunge."

"You ride her?"

He nodded. "Yep, every weekend. She's in stables, of course. I found a really good one, with fields, and they take the horses out every day. She even gets to work with kids sometimes."

"That's fantastic. It sounds like you've provided her with a wonderful life."

A mug of tea appeared in front of her, and another joined it as Matthew crouched in front of her. Anna cocked an eyebrow.

Matthew looked up at Harry, however, and smiled at him. "Nice to see you again," he said.

Anna tried not to show her amusement, contenting herself with a knowing look at Ollie, who shot one back, her hand in front of her mouth.

"Hello," Harry replied, smiling too. "Anna was just telling me she's making a hat for her daughter."

Matthew politely smiled at Anna, and swept his thumb over the yarn she was using, but his eyes were firmly locked with Harry's. It was obvious his behaviour was all for Harry's benefit. "You're accommodating, Anna," he said. "She already stole your scarf."

"Well, this is to match," Anna said.

"I think it's a lovely gesture," Harry said, smiling genuinely.

Matthew nodded. "Oh. 'Course. Me too."

If she looked at Ollie right now, Anna knew she'd see Ollie's amusement and they'd both laugh. She didn't want to be cruel. Matthew was obviously changing his mind about Harry, and one never knew; maybe they would end up together.

Matthew turned his attention to the fluffy granny squares Harry had brought for the throw project. "And these are just, well, they really are something."

A wide grin crossed Harry's face in a way that Anna found promising. "Thank you."

"They must take you ages."

"They do. But I love making them."

Matthew looked through the three squares Harry had made. "I just… get one done in like…twenty minutes." He seemed forlorn. Anna wanted to hug him.

"I could lend you some…some patterns if you like?" Harry suggested, pulling out a couple of papers from his bag. "Um…these are pretty quick, but they look nice too, if you're not into really detailed things."

Their gazes locked, and Matthew relaxed a bit.

"That'd be nice. Suppose it's quality rather than quantity, right?"

Harry didn't nod or shake his head, and Anna wondered if he was trying not to upset Matthew. "We probably need a load of plain ones anyway," he explained. "Otherwise the whole thing will look a bit..."

"Busy?" Matthew's face brightened.

"That's it," Harry agreed, also relieved.

By the end of the class, it appeared as if Harry and Matthew were finally getting to know one another properly. They dropped their fivers into the envelope and left together. Sarah and Christian left, too, hand in hand, already wearing their matching hats. Anna hadn't been close enough to Ollie to flirt again. She was beginning to wonder if it would ever happen.

She lifted her finished hat into the air for inspection. The ends were sewn neatly in and the pompom was a perfect sphere attached securely.

Ollie came over, already smiling as she fingered the edge of the hat. "Fantastic," she said, and then went back to wash up the mugs in the sink.

Drifting over to stand next to her, Anna took a tea towel from where it hung on a hook. She made a conscious effort to trail her gaze down to Ollie's lips. *Surely she's noticed by now?*

"Now they both have a present each," she said, taking each mug from Ollie to dry it and set it on the side.

"That'll stop them bickering."

"It will." As they handed a mug between them, their fingers brushed and Anna didn't move away. Neither did Ollie. They looked down at their hands.

Anna let out a slow breath, before moving the mug away to place on the counter. "Thanks for the pattern." Her voice felt thin, like her smallest crochet hook.

"You're welcome."

Once the last mug was dried, Anna hung the soggy tea towel back on the hook. She pulled her coat around herself snugly, ready to make her way out into the winter air. An involuntary shiver passed through her as she imagined how it would feel when she stepped out. "I gave Bethany the caterpillar," she said, suddenly remembering

Ollie raised her eyebrows. "And?"

"Weirdly, she really liked it. Said it was cute."

They smiled at one another for a minute, gazes locked. Anna was unsure of what to do or say next, but unwilling to end the evening just yet. *Is something going to happen?*

"Oh!" Ollie said, making Anna jump. She limped out into the shop. Anna followed her, curious.

After rounding the till, Ollie bent on one knee and seized something from behind her chair. "Here," she said, producing a small dark red rabbit with tiny beady eyes and cream inner ears and tummy. "I finished him."

Anna's heart stuttered. "Oh, Ollie. He's gorgeous." She took the rabbit and held him carefully, turning him one way, and then the other. "He'll be sitting by my bed," she said, her lashes lowered.

They were standing close together again.

Smiling broadly, Ollie stepped away and put some distance between them.

Anna followed her, however, wrapping her arms around Ollie's shoulders, the rabbit in her hand against Ollie's neck. "Thank you."

"No problem," Ollie said. She sank her face into the side of Anna's neck.

Anna shivered as Ollie's cold nose touched her warm skin. She tried not to inhale deeply, but Ollie's scent filled her lungs again. Anna squeezed her hard, closed her eyes for a moment, then pulled away and kissed her on the cheek.

Ollie's face flushed, which made Anna smile. *It's not quite a full-on snog, but things are looking positive.* Ollie chewed her lip and looked away.

Tonight's mission accomplished, Anna gave her a moment. "Well." She dropped her gaze to the floor as well, her whole body tingling. "It's late. I've got a programme to watch. And you should go rest your back."

"I'll take some ibuprofen before I go to bed," Ollie promised before Anna could even suggest it.

"Sensible," she said with a warmth in her stomach she knew she would cherish the whole way home. "Take care." She left Ollie standing stock-still for a moment, but then footsteps followed Anna, and a hand on her shoulder stopped her before she reached the door.

"Oh," Ollie croaked. Her gaze flicked to the ground.

Anna squinted at her. *You're like a complicated crochet pattern, aren't you?*

"We should… I mean, if you like." Ollie cleared her throat. "We could go for a drink?"

Anna smiled. "Okay, that would be nice. When are you free?"

"Saturday night? Evening, I mean." Ollie was fiddling with her fingers.

"Perfect. How about dinner?"

Ollie's smile grew. "All right."

"Say…six thirty?"

"I'll pick you up," Ollie said. "Text me your address."

"I will." Anna pulled her scarf more securely round her neck. "And… feel free to text me whenever you're bored." She stroked the soft ears of the rabbit before slipping it into her cloth bag. "Bye, Ollie."

"Bye. See you Saturday."

Anna disappeared into the night, the wind blowing her coat around her knees. She got halfway down the street before she turned and deliberately looked back, right at Ollie.

She was still there, hanging out of her door.

Anna just wiggled her fingers at her before she turned the corner towards the car park, a huge smile plastered on her face.

Chapter 8

Tiny Stars

Anna looked at herself in the full-length mirror stuck on the inside of the wardrobe door. She only used it when she really wasn't sure about an outfit. Her hair was neat—nothing new there—and her make-up light but enough. Usually by the time six thirty rolled around, she'd rubbed off any lipstick she'd applied at the beginning of the day. So the bright red colour currently neat across her lips would be a change at least.

Next, she considered her clothes: a purple wrap-around top that hugged her curves and highlighted the dip of her waist, and a pair of grey trousers. Flat shoes but pretty, she hoped. She really didn't have the patience for heels these days, and it wasn't like she was terribly short. She wasn't sure if Ollie would wear heels. She didn't want to be taller than Ollie, because she knew there was an inch between them and she sort of liked it.

Was she reading too much into it? She didn't mind looking nice, but it wouldn't do to arrive with too much cleavage on display or too much leg on show. She had a feeling she'd probably just make Ollie run a mile. As far as Ollie knew, Anna was straight as an arrow. But she was going to rectify that tonight.

How on earth am I going to do that? I can't just blurt it out. Anna was so engrossed in her own self-critique that she jumped at the knock to her bedroom door.

"Mum?"

"Yep," she called out before her daughter slowly pushed it open a crack.

"Tell me you have clothes on," Bethany said. "Because you naked is not a sight I want to see."

"No bits and pieces on show tonight, darling."

The door opened some more and Bethany stepped in. She blinked at the sight of her mother facing her, a smile threatening to push past her post-adolescent derision. "You look okay," she said.

Amusement and relief flooded through Anna.

Bethany relented and smiled back. "Yeah, okay, Mum. You look great."

"Reckon?" Anna brushed her palms against her waist, conscious of how fitted the top was. "I don't look pudgy or…"

"Are you kidding?" She rested her chin on her mother's shoulder and crushed her in a hug. "If I didn't know better I'd say you were on a date."

Shrugging out of the embrace, Anna regarded Bethany with narrowed eyes.

Bethany pursed her lips. "Are you on a date?" Her head dropped towards her shoulder. "Timothy says you are."

"How would Timothy know?" Anna tried to keep her tone light.

"He's very perceptive. And quite a bit more direct, or haven't you noticed by now? He says you smile every time you come back from crochet, more than when you used to go out with Liam, even, and that you seem more energetic on the whole." Bethany smirked. "He has a spreadsheet to prove it."

"Oh Lord." Anna's face burned. She looked at her shoes for a moment.

"It's okay if you are. I'm not going to go all weird on you. You totally didn't bring me up to be a homophobe, Mum."

"I would think not." It encouraged her to lift her gaze back up.

Bethany sighed. "It's fine. As long as we get to actually meet her at some point. I'm not having you dating someone like…you know, Liam."

"We're not dating." Anna sat on the end of her bed and clasped her hands. Her foot bounced up and down.

"Your outfit screams 'date'." Bethany's hand was positioned firmly on her hip.

Anna hid her face in her fingers. "Does it?"

"She's clueless, isn't she?"

When Anna took her hand away, she found Bethany had a glint in her eye. "We've not…" Anna searched for words to explain. *Bloody English teacher and I can't speak the language.* "...exactly had the conversation about...*preferences* and, well, we have, but...anyway..." Anna hid her face again and let out an almighty sigh. *And now I'm waffling.*

Bethany touched her shoulder.

"Yes, she's clueless." Anna stood and paced a little back and forth.

Turning her head one way, then the other, Bethany watched her.

"Hell, so was I until a few days ago."

"Mum." Bethany caught her arm, stopping her from wearing the carpet raw. "Mum. It's all right."

Their gazes locked.

Shaking the tension out of her shoulders, Anna placed her palm carefully atop her daughter's.

Bethany's hand squeezed her. "It's perfect, actually. Your outfit."

"Do you...do you really think so?"

"Yeah. It's lovely." She fingered the neat bow at Anna's hip that held the wrap-around top securely in place. "The colour suits you. Makes your eyes look super green."

Bethany squeezed her arm again before she left the room. Anna turned back to the mirror, tucked a little wisp of her hair behind her ear, and grabbed her handbag.

Ollie pulled on her boots and tied the laces with fumbling fingers. "Dammit." She jumped up, felt her knee creak, and rubbed it. "Dammit." She hopped past the mirror in her tiny hallway, then stepped back in front of it. She looked in horror at her reflection. "Dammit."

A tissue. She needed a tissue. Ollie scrubbed at the smear of eyeliner she *definitely* had not intentionally graced her cheek with. She looked at her watch, grabbed her keys, and swung out the door.

She swung back in. "Oh, for goodness sake." Her purse was still on the little windowsill by her front door, and she nearly dropped it as she stuffed it into her pocket. Wobbly legs descended the stairs two at a time. She managed to get out the side door and into the taxi without falling over her bootlaces.

The driver entered Anna's address into his device as Ollie fastened her seat belt and leant against the backrest, groaning. Usually a Saturday evening was filled with cleaning and vacuuming.

To calm her nervous, restless energy, she went over the list in her mind: She'd managed to clean the bathrooms—both the small toilet in the shop and her main one in her flat—and both kitchens. The vacuum had skimmed through all her rooms, and she'd stripped and remade her bed with fresh sheets. *Not that I'm expecting anything.* Not bad, she thought, considering the fact she wasn't often out of the flat before eight to meet Matthew and that her hurried cleaning tonight had caused a terrible amount of sweat, resulting in an unplanned shower, resulting in her being late for the taxi. She would still make it on time.

When the taxi pulled up to a nice terraced house—the front garden neat but showing the signs of winter—Ollie knew they were at the correct address. She asked the driver to wait and forced herself to walk slowly up Anna's path to her front door. No need to seem too eager, or as if she'd run the entire way.

A young woman answered the door.

Ollie smiled at how similar Bethany was to her mother in appearance, down to the striking green eyes. "Hi," Ollie said after a beat, inwardly shaking herself and trying to smile in a way that didn't look terrified. *Or terrifying.* "I'm..." She swallowed. "I'm Ollie."

"I'd never have guessed." Bethany stepped back. "Suppose you can come in."

"Thanks." Ollie stepped into the hallway, so big compared to her own digs and wonderfully warm. She could see a dark-coloured telephone seat next to the coat rack and a stylish number of prints hung on various walls.

Bethany shouted for her mother and then stood, arms folded. "Where are you taking her?"

"Um...to..." Ollie's gaze darted up and down, looking through doors and searching for Anna. She felt as if she were having her barracks inspected and as if she should stand up straight and salute. *She's scarier than my old sergeant major.* "To Dulcie's. That little Italian—"

"Satisfactory."

Ollie shrank under her critical gaze.

"But don't let her have too much wine."

Wow. "Uh, I won't."

"And what time will you be back?"

This is like a teenager being interrogated by the parent of someone she's taking out.

"Um…I'm not sure."

"Make sure she texts me when she knows. I don't want to have to stay up if you're going to be out really late."

"I'll try."

Luckily for Ollie, Anna arrived in a cloud of subtle perfume. She grabbed her coat, her eyes glinting at her daughter.

Ollie caught a peek of a very flattering top before Anna's coat hid the garment and her curves.

"I hope you're not interrogating my friend, Beth?"

"Me?" Bethany made a valiant effort to look shocked. "Would I?"

Anna smiled at her daughter and pulled her close, kissing her cheek. "Of course you would."

Bethany's face spread into a smile.

"I'm to make sure you let Bethany know when you'll be home," Ollie said. *Must get into the daughter's good books.*

Anna raised her eyebrows at Bethany.

"What?" Bethany said. "I have work to do tomorrow. Don't want to be waiting up until whatever time you decide to *stagger* in."

"Fine," Anna said, sliding her handbag over her shoulder, her coat already pulled tight and her scarf tucked securely under the collar. "I'll let you know as soon as I know."

"Much appreciated." Bethany gave Ollie one last look up and down before sauntering out of the hallway.

Ollie relaxed a little.

"Come on, then, show me your wheels," Anna said, pushing her house keys into her handbag and then reaching for the door handle.

"Actually, I haven't driven here," Ollie said as they stepped out into the night.

"Oh," Anna said, frowning. "I distinctly remember you offering me a lift to wherever you'd chosen for dinner."

"Dulcie's…and I came in a taxi," Ollie said, walking ahead of Anna towards the gate. "Sorry if that's presumptuous of me, but I do envisage wine featuring quite heavily in the festivities." *Bethany just said not* too *much wine.*

Anna barked out a single laugh and touched Ollie's arm. "Sound like a good plan."

They sat next to one another in the back seat. Ollie instructed the driver where to go. It was only a few miles to the restaurant.

It was dark already, being nearly the beginning of December, and Ollie caught Anna glancing at her too. A couple of times Anna lifted her hand, but each time she plopped it back down in her lap.

Ollie's heart raced. *Chill out. We're just in a taxi on the way to dinner.*

When they arrived at the restaurant, they got out on either side. Anna rummaged in her handbag as if to get out some money, but the taxi sped away. Confusion flashed through her expression.

Ollie put a hand to her wrist. "Credit card, prepaid." She enjoyed the O shape Anna made with her lips.

But then someone shouted Anna's name behind them, and they both spun around.

A man with an older lady on his arm walked slowly up the pavement towards them. They were dressed in posh clothes. The smile on the man's face looked hard and maybe even cruel.

Ollie was immediately on alert and gripped Anna's wrist where she still held it.

The man looked between Anna and Ollie and then stuck a hand out to Ollie, his grin widening. "I'm Liam. Nice to meet you." He made it sound anything but.

Ollie looked at him and then looked at his hand. *So this is the famous tosser, Liam.*

Anna relinquished her wrist from Ollie's grip and stepped towards Liam, her arms folded. "I'm busy, Liam, and as far as I can remember, I told you not to call me anymore." Her voice turned into a hiss.

"You were quick," he snarled, looking Ollie up and down. "She's on the rebound, you know."

Ollie set her jaw and glanced at Anna, whose face was as red as her coat. Ollie cursed inwardly at the way Anna was looking at the ground. "Doesn't bother me. Just out for a nice dinner." She tilted her chin upwards.

Liam swayed, and Ollie wondered if he'd been drinking. "Shame you never got to say goodbye properly to my mother." He pushed his companion forward and held out his hand. "No time like the present. Perhaps now would be a good time to explain why you cost me my job?"

Anna and Liam's mother stared at one another. Ollie felt an almost overwhelming urge to laugh.

This is surreal.

"Margaret," Anna said, lowering her head.

"Anna, dear." Liam's mother gave him a look, her stance becoming more upright and assertive. "The play won't wait for us," she said and grabbed his arm with a white-knuckled hand, pulling him back the way they had come.

Incredulous, Ollie watched them go until she realised Anna was shivering a bit. She took a chance and rubbed Anna's arm.

"I'm so sorry," Anna said, shaking her head slowly.

"Not your fault." She stilled her hand but left it there. The wool of Anna's coat was scratchy against her palm but she didn't mind. "I have met dickheads before."

Anna huffed out a laugh and then smiled up at her. Ollie's stomach felt warm as Anna's hand slipped into the crook of her elbow, steering them across the wide pavement and towards the entrance to the restaurant. She let go as they went in through the door, and an Italian front-of-house staffer greeted them, took their coats, and led them to a table.

Heart still thumping with adrenaline, Ollie realised she would have forcibly removed him into a taxi if Liam had tried anything. Her brain concocted a scene where she'd kick him in the gut and sweep Anna up into her arms to carry her away, both of them laughing.

Nice idea, but with my broken body, entirely impractical. She sighed. *Also cruel as hell. The guy probably doesn't deserve actual physical violence, however nasty he's been to Anna's son.*

Ollie bit her lip as they approached a small table to one side that held a single rose in a tiny vase, cloth napkins, and shiny silverware. Was it too romantic?

The smile Anna sent her as they took their seats made Ollie relax. She pointed to Anna when the man offered them the wine menu.

An amused but pleased look shone from across the table. Once the man had left them with their menus, Anna caught Ollie's eye. "This is beautiful," she said.

Ollie shrugged. "Seems silly to go somewhere substandard when neither of us has very many days off."

"Yes, with all the lesson planning and marking I have to do, and the book clubs, and you working six days a week, I'm amazed we managed it."

Ollie studied Anna across the table. The encounter with Beth before they had left Anna's house hadn't worried her—of course Anna's daughter would feel protective of her mother. *They've been a family unit for years.*

The tosser ex-boyfriend was a different matter. The things he'd said had unnerved her, especially his comments regarding Anna being on the rebound. *Is she? Am I just someone to latch on to after the unhappy end of a relationship?*

But that didn't sound right. She felt comfortable with Anna—they were two adults sharing a meal, plain and simple. None of the nerves she would expect if she really believed Liam's views were present. Her opinion of Anna hadn't wavered. *I still think she's fantastic.*

And I really must stop thinking like that. Friends. Maybe. Hopefully.

Emerald eyes gleamed in the soft light of the restaurant, and one of Anna's forefingers ever so slightly caressed the thick, shiny card the wine list was printed on.

The waiter came over then and leant between them to light the candle beside the rose.

Anna dove into the wine list.

The shiny fork by her hand felt terribly interesting to Ollie for a while. She shifted it back and forth with her fingertip. "What looks good to you?" she asked, glad Anna was in charge of that particular decision. *I need to do some research into wine if I'm ever going to have a proper conversation with her about it.*

"Hmmm. They have a good Merlot on offer. Always a plus." One eyebrow rose in query.

Ollie nodded. "Whatever you like, comrade."

"I'm not drinking the whole bottle," Anna said with a giggle. "Want to share?"

Ollie pursed her lips, pretending to think about the issue. Then she nodded.

"Excellent." Anna sat back and gestured to the waiter. She ordered them a bottle of her preferred Merlot and a jug of water.

When he came back with their wine, he poured a little into Anna's glass, having apparently cottoned on to the fact she was the one in charge.

The taste of it made her smile. After he filled both their glasses, she patted the table to indicate he could leave the bottle. "So"—she turned to Ollie—"it was busy today at the shop?"

"Fairly," Ollie replied, sipping her own wine. "Oh that's really lovely. You have good taste." She swallowed. Was that flirty? Did she care if it was? "I know literally zilch about wine, I'm afraid."

"I'm well aware," Anna replied with a chuckle.

She changed the subject, noting the slight pinking of Anna's cheeks. *I'll have to compliment her more often, if it causes that reaction.* "People are starting to think about making things for Christmas now." She pushed a curl of hair that had escaped her tiny ponytail around her ear. "One lady was intent on making some sort of…necklace thing. Out of these *huge* beads she'd purchased on eBay and lots of bright pink DK."

"Sounds delightful."

"I'm still not sure what she meant." Ollie held her wine glass and her free hand up in a shrug. "I just gave her what she wanted and didn't ask too many questions."

Laughter sprang from Anna's mouth.

Ollie frowned, unsure why Anna was laughing, but then her eyes widened and she nearly choked on her wine as the double meaning occurred to her. "'Gave her what she wanted.' Goodness, you have a dirty mind." Ollie held her temple with her hand and tried not to end up a nervous red-faced wreck.

As their chuckles quietened, their starters arrived. Anna took her first mouthful, and Ollie watched her, enthralled. Anna moaned very quietly, the dip she'd sunk the squid ring into still clinging to her fork.

A shiver ran through Ollie. Instead of staring at Anna's lips, she pushed a piece of smoked salmon onto the small piece of bruschetta, dripped some of the lemony dressing on top, and popped the whole thing into her mouth.

The taste slid over her tongue, making her groan. She was pleased with herself for her choice of dinner establishment. The food was fantastic.

She was even more pleased about the look on Anna's face. *Is that what desire looks like on her?* Perhaps, at least her desire for good food and wine. The small flick of an eyebrow upwards made Ollie smile more.

Well, here goes. Her fingers shaky, Ollie repeated the move: salmon on bread, drizzled with sauce. Then she held it out to Anna, expecting her to grab it herself with her hand. But she didn't.

Ollie had to swallow and then take a long breath. Anna's lips had closed around her fingers, ghosting over them as she snatched the mouthful. Anna sat back and put a hand to her lips, her cheeks flushed again, her gaze drifting to her plate. The act rested firmly on the borderline between innocence and something more. Where on the spectrum of affection it landed, Ollie wasn't sure.

I'm overreacting. It must be the food. She let the breath out slowly.

"Delicious," Anna said.

Thankfully, Anna used her fork to collect Ollie's repayment of food, and as Ollie took the food into her mouth, she bravely held Anna's gaze.

They finished the rest of their starters, which were small but wonderful, with more murmurs of enjoyment.

Ollie placed her cutlery neatly on her plate. Folding her hands in her lap, she looked around, taking in the lilt of the piano music over the stereo, the hum of the other customers, and the tinkling of glasses and cutlery.

"Tell me about places you've been," Anna said.

The change of subject surprised Ollie, and she parted her lips for a moment before answering. "I travelled a lot with the army. So holidays were usually in the UK." She smiled as she delved into one specific memory. "We did go to the south of France once, with the kids. When they were in junior school."

"Hotel, or self-catering?"

"Self-catering. We ate out a lot, though—wanted the kids to experience all the delights France had to offer." She laughed. "Kieran tried snails."

"Oh, I love escargot," Anna replied, her face bright. "I love French food. And Italian, Spanish, Indian. Any good food, really." She looked down at her plate, scraped clean with her fork. "Obviously."

"I don't get a lot of opportunity to go out for dinner." Ollie twisted her mouth, noting Anna's self-admonishing comment, perhaps about her own curvaceous body. *I think she looks amazing.* "What with the swimming lessons I teach, and the crochet classes. Whenever I'm off, I tend to spend it with Matthew, and he's happy with a takeaway." She shrugged. *I am definitely not telling her I have no other friends.*

"That's a shame," Anna said, a pout on her lips. "We shall have to make this a regular thing."

"I'd like that."

"That is..." Anna sucked her bottom lip into her mouth. "That is... you know, if neither of us ends up dating anyone."

Ollie took in her green eyes, her knitted-together eyebrows. *What do I say to that?* She blinked as the waiter arrived to clear their plates.

When he departed, Anna was still looking at Ollie, her gaze steady.

"Where did *you* visit?" she managed in the end. "On holiday, I mean?"

"We managed to take Bethany to various countries across the globe," Anna replied, her eyes flicking down to her napkin, which lay on her lap.

Why does that seem to make her uncomfortable?

"That's great," Ollie replied brightly. "She must have gained loads from experiencing different cultures."

"She did." Anna looked up again. "We took her to the US for a few weeks when she was five. Toured the whole of the West Coast. Took in the sites, all the usual places. We went to Bruges and Paris a few times. Rome. Mostly weekend breaks for the cities, just the three of us."

"Your ex-husband?"

Anna nodded. "In the days when he wasn't being a..." Anna cleared her throat. "Anyway. Once he was no longer part of our little excursions, Bethany and I visited Madrid, Athens. We did Dublin a few years ago; that was quite fun." She sighed. "So, since you've had the shop?" she asked, smiling at the waiter as he brought their main courses over and poured them some more wine.

Ollie nearly stopped him, nearly said she could do it, but it seemed like second nature to him, so she sat back. She held her glass once it was full and stared into the deep-red liquid.

"I haven't had a holiday," she replied, immediately sipping from her glass and very much *not* looking Anna in the eye.

"At all?"

Grimacing, Ollie shrugged. "No?"

"Well that's simply no good," Anna said, picking up her main-course fork, pushing a piece of ravioli across her plate before spearing it and slipping it into her mouth. She chewed and swallowed.

Figuring she was eventually going to get caught if she stared at Anna's mouth for much longer, Ollie picked up her own cutlery and begun dealing with her linguine.

Anna shook her head. "No, we shall have to do something about that."

"Oh? What do you suggest?"

"Well, perhaps on my next excursion away, you should come too." Somehow Ollie got the impression she didn't really have a choice in the matter.

"Wouldn't that…" Ollie swivelled a prawn to encase it in the flat pasta. The taste of it made her imagine sunset walks with Anna along an Italian street, cram-packed full of bustling restaurants. She cleared her throat. "Wouldn't that be a bit weird? You know?"

Small lines appeared between Anna's eyebrows. "Why?"

"Because…you know. Going on holiday with someone like me."

"Someone who's…," Anna looked at her with interest, "crafty?"

"No."

"Someone with a limp?"

There was a sparkle in Anna's eye. Ollie snorted. She should have known Anna was taking the mickey. "No. Although going through security is always fun. I have a lot of metalwork down there." She rubbed the side of her knee where the scars were hidden by her trousers.

Anna put her fork down and folded her arms, her gaze steady and demanding. "Are you saying I should be uncomfortable going on holiday with you because you're gay?"

Ollie's gaze flashed down into her linguine, and a sick feeling rolled through her stomach. *I hate that word so much.*

Anna frowned. "I'm sorry. Are you…" She cleared her throat. "Are you not?"

"No," Ollie said. "I mean yes. I am."

Fingers touched the edge of Ollie's plate. A forefinger lifted and gave Ollie a tiny persistent wave until Ollie finally looked up. *God*, Anna's eyes were so soft.

"I shouldn't have said that." Anna's hand moved back to her lap. "I was just teasing you."

"No, it's…it's okay," Ollie replied. "Matthew keeps telling me I should say it more often."

"Say what?"

There was a pause. "That I'm gay." Her gaze held Anna's. She swallowed and shivered.

It was a relief when Anna smiled broadly. *I made that happen, just by uttering three small words.*

"For the record," Anna said, "I wouldn't feel uncomfortable going on holiday with you, for any reason."

"Okay."

"I understand it must be difficult."

Ollie tilted her head to the side.

"You know, I…" Anna paused. Her gaze flicked back and forth as she seemed to be searching for words. "I once kissed a girl, when I was in college."

"Did you?" That was surprising. *Not that it's uncommon—loads of teenagers kiss their friends.*

"So, I mean I can't say I…" Anna seemed breathless, and she was looking into her ravioli as if it held the answers to all of the universe's questions. "I can't say I have had the same experience as you. But I think I understand how… how hard it can be."

"So…" Ollie picked up her wine and sipped to give herself a moment. "So, you're attracted to women?" *If she says no, that it was just a one-time thing when she was younger, I'll never be able to look at her again.*

Anna stared at her. "Maybe," she answered, her voice soft. She mimicked Ollie's motion with the wine glass. "Possibly. No. I think I am. It was just that once, but it awakened something in me, I suppose."

"Right." Ollie's heart rate sped up, and she tried to keep her jittery reaction hidden. *Oh my goodness.* "So, would you identify as…as bisexual?"

"I suppose I would," Anna said, frowning at her wine. As she dropped her gaze to her food, her expression softened into a smile. "This is good." Her voice was brighter, too, but she still appeared rather flustered.

Anna was bisexual. Ollie wondered how a single concept could make things so much more complicated. If she assumed Anna liked her like *that*, Anna would undoubtedly inform her that just because she was into women did not mean she was into *her*. Just because Anna found *some* women attractive did not mean she found every woman attractive. She should not expect anything because they were *just* friends. Any holiday together would probably mean Ollie seeing Anna in a swimsuit and trying not to look, but also trying to look a little bit, because she didn't want Anna to think she thought she was ugly and totally undesirable. The ridiculousness of that dual prospect already made her certain she would never go on a holiday with Anna. She would go crazy.

Ollie's gaze returned to her food, her mind whirring. When she realised she'd been staring at it for far too long, she wound pasta around a prawn and held it up to Anna.

There was a pause while Anna narrowed her eyes at the forkful, then she returned her gaze to Ollie. She nodded, however, and took the fork. Swishing the food around in her mouth, she closed her eyes in pleasure and handed the fork back. "Thank you. Also delicious."

"We'll have to come here again."

The change in topic was a relief.

"Once we've visited every other good restaurant in Nailsea." Anna scooped a piece of ravioli onto her fork, added a little sauce and held it out. Ollie took the fork and made sure their hands didn't brush. It felt like they were miles away from one another now, the table a playing field between them.

She handed Anna's fork back. They ate for a while in silence, both with their own thoughts.

Why couldn't Anna have simply kept quiet about it? Ollie had felt so much happier craving Anna when she knew she couldn't have her. But now? Her brain felt constricted and confused.

So Ollie drank her wine and finished her main course and watched as Anna finished her glass, too.

They both looked at the empty bottle and then simultaneously turned around to look for the waiter. They looked back at one another, smirking at their mirrored behaviour.

The waiter took their plates, and Anna ordered them a glass of wine each. *Good idea. I'd be drunk by the time we left if we shared another bottle.* This choice was not a Merlot, but it was red, at least, and Anna's choice.

"You know," Anna began, fingers toying with the stem of her glass, eyes very much trained away from Ollie's, "it's a shame you only have Sundays off." She locked Ollie's gaze with her own. "Have you never truly thought about employing a second in command at the shop? Or maybe stopping a few of the swimming lessons? Five in a week is a lot when you have a full-time job as well."

"I feel, I suppose…responsible," Ollie replied. "I spent all Maggie's money on…on getting my qualifications and buying the shop, and I'm not sure I could trust anyone else to keep it going one day a week."

"I do worry about you," Anna said, which caused Ollie's heart to pitter-patter. "I do worry that you work yourself ragged and don't allow yourself time to relax."

"I promise I do relax." Ollie reached across the table. When Anna looked down at Ollie's fingers, Ollie nearly pulled her hand back, but then Anna placed her hand over Ollie's. Her fingertips smoothed against the back of her hand.

"When?" she challenged.

Laughing, Ollie turned her hand over underneath Anna's and tickled her palm a little with her fingertips.

Anna inhaled audibly at the contact.

Well, things are looking up, aren't they? "I go out with Matthew at least once a week, usually on a Saturday. I only do classes on Tuesdays and Thursdays, and I teach swimming straight after I close up shop, and only for an hour. And I make sure Sunday is a proper day of rest." Ollie tilted her head a little to one side.

"Still," Anna said. "One day off a week can't be enough to really recharge?"

"I'm used to the army, I suppose." She looked out of the window beside them, into the dark street, falling into memory. But she kept her hand beneath Anna's, fingers still waving in a small tickle against Anna's palm.

The sensation kept her grounded. "Getting up at six, going to bed at eight," she continued. "And after my inconvenient accident, I was so miserable, just sitting around doing nothing that I swore if I ever got back properly on my feet I would never sit around again. I'd make the most of my life."

When Ollie looked back at Anna, Anna's eyes were a little wet. She was about to react, to grip her fingers and tell her it was okay, that she wasn't miserable anymore, when the waiter brought them their glasses of wine. Their hands pulled away from one another.

The candle flickered a little, and she marvelled at how the light from that one small flame made the skin of Anna's cheeks look golden. It lit up her eyes, too, small flecks of yellow shining out from the green.

"I still think you should get an assistant," Anna said.

"Are you offering?"

She laughed. "That wouldn't be very wise, would it?"

Ollie looked at her in confusion.

"My intentions are not completely selfless. I want to make sure if I'm busy on a Saturday night that I have an alternative so I can still take you out for dinner."

Ollie chuckled. "Ah, I see your game, Ms Rose."

Anna gave a little shrug that clearly said *what can I say?* before sipping at her wine. "Besides," she said, her eyes glinting over the rim at Ollie, "it must be lonely sitting in that shop all day, six days a week, with only a few customers to talk to."

"I'll have you know it can get very busy in my *meagre* shop."

"Oh, I didn't mean…" Anna looked suddenly appalled.

When Ollie shook her head and winked at her, Anna's mouth turned into a round O. Once she'd recovered, she leaned back in her seat, her chin jutting out. "I'm right, though." she said. "Admit it. You could use an assistant.

"It's not so bad," Ollie said, shuttering her eyes. "I feel like I'm helping people. Not in the same capacity as I used to, but when someone comes in with a pattern they can't quite work out, or a favourite jumper they want to repair, I'm there with my adequate knowledge. I usually manage to sort them out."

"Fine, I'll let you off. It's not like I have so much free time myself. I try so hard to spend time with my children that frivolous things like going out for dinner don't take priority."

The wine in their glasses dwindled. As Ollie finished hers, Anna twirled her empty one between her fingers, Ollie's heart sank. *She'll probably want to go home in a minute.* "It's been a lovely evening," she prompted Anna. She couldn't give her an easier opening than that if she wanted to end things there. She watched with a touch of sadness, though, when Anna took the bill from the waiter and flicked through a wad of notes in her purse. "It would be a shame to end it quite yet, though, don't you think?"

They split the bill in half and Ollie tucked an extra note underneath for the waiter.

"So, what do you suggest?" Anna asked, dropping her purse back into her bag and straightening up in her seat.

"We could find another place to sit?" Ollie suggested. "You could introduce me to another wine you like, and we can put the world to rights?"

Anna's face blossomed into a pleased smile, which gave Ollie that warm feeling in her stomach again.

"Let's do it." Anna stood and put on the coat the waiter handed her. "Where's good for solving the world's problems?"

She led Anna out into the dark night, and they stood close together for a minute, younger people milling around them, going from bar to bar. *Where to suggest?* Too intimate and it would be uncomfortable and too busy, and she wouldn't be able to hear anything Anna said. Her chest felt a little tight, and she tapped her foot. She didn't fancy taking Anna to the local; their evening had started out so decadently.

Luckily the decision was taken from her by a young man with a handful of fliers. Anna took one and smiled at him before he walked off towards someone else.

"Jazz night at The Cock and Duck," Anna said. "Sounds perfect."

It took a long moment for Ollie's heart to start beating again. "Oh, I'm..." She looked around, her foot continuing to tap. "I'm not sure you'd like it."

"Why not? I love jazz."

Anna honestly did seem clueless, and Ollie felt quite sorry for her. "It's a gay bar."

"And?" Anna's reply was immediate and without hesitation. Fitting her hand into Ollie's elbow like she had from the taxi, she looked up at her with wide green eyes. "Is it sleazy?"

"No." *There must be somewhere else that plays jazz in this bloody town.*

"Is it so loud we won't be able to talk?"

"Not on jazz night."

"No problem, then, is there?"

Ollie let out a defeated sigh.

The bar was quiet for once, the jazz night a little too niche for the regular customers, who were all about Matthew's age and would rather be bopping along to cheesy dance music than sitting quietly with a small jazz ensemble playing in the corner. The clientele appeared to be more Ollie's age. *Phew.* There were even a few straight couples dotted around.

I bet the bar is regretting their decision to host a jazz band on a Saturday. They've lost their usual heavy drinkers.

Anna's face had relaxed, and her cheek rested against Ollie's shoulder as they stood at the bar. The barman was busy taking payment for another customer's order, so she turned properly to Ollie.

"Good choice?" Ollie asked, one hand in the air to hail the bartender. She swiftly gave him a look that pleaded, *Don't you dare say a word.*

He smirked and looked between them but kept his mouth closed.

"Very good choice."

They ordered two glasses of wine at Anna's request and found a small booth with a low-hanging lampshade over the table.

Ollie slid into one side. Surprising her, Anna slipped in beside her on the bench, before stuffing her handbag next to her hip.

"Well, hello," Ollie said with an amused lilt in her voice.

They clinked their glasses together. "To setting the world to rights," Anna said just before taking a big gulp.

Ollie wondered why she always drank beer here when they clearly had such a good selection of wine. *I'd happily give up beer if it meant spending more time with Anna.*

After putting her glass on the table, Anna rummaged around in her handbag and pulled out the small bottle of hand cream Ollie had given her weeks ago in the greasy-spoon café. She held her hand out.

Ollie stared at the stern look Anna gave her.

"Whatever you say, I know your hands are sore."

Her cheeks burning, Ollie tried to hide her hands under her legs, but Anna caught one of them before she succeeded.

Lifting it to get a better look under the light of the low lamp, Anna squinted a little. "What have you been doing?"

"Cleaning." Ollie grimaced as Anna touched a particularly sore area at the base of her thumb.

"What with, white spirit?" Anna's voice was half-teasing, half-stern.

"Did the bathrooms this afternoon. And the kitchen."

"So, bleach," Anna said, and it wasn't a question, but Ollie nodded anyway. "Do you not have washing-up gloves, Sergeant Williams?"

"Was in a rush."

Anna uncapped the moisturiser, then smoothed some lotion onto her fingertips. "What are you?" she said archly, rubbing the moisturiser into the sore area on Ollie's thumb and then in a wider circle across the rest of her hand.

Despite wincing at how tender her skin was, she quickly discovered that Anna's chiding teacher tone—and her one hand cupping Ollie's and the other rubbing patterns into the muscles—made her lose her words. "An idiot?" she said eventually, very much feeling like one, and not simply because of her lack of personal protective equipment.

That earned her a brief nod. Anna traced her fingertips from Ollie's thumb into her palm, turning Ollie's hand over. "What else?" she asked, her voice low, rubbing the moisturiser into Ollie's palm and then into the fleshy bit where her fingers started.

"A twat?" Ollie tried, watching their hands.

Ollie's moisturised hand tingled between Anna's palms. Anna squeezed gently and then let go, reaching for Ollie's other hand and holding it against her knee. She shifted a bit closer. "So what do you need to do?" She squirted some more moisturiser into her palm and began rubbing.

"Wear gloves." *Please don't stop.* Was her voice trembling?

Ollie's right hand wasn't as sore as the left, no red patches, so Anna simply slithered her palms against Ollie's skin back and forth until Ollie strangely felt like she might fall asleep. The concoction of the alcohol and Anna's touch was causing her thoughts to run sluggishly. She rested her head sideways against the cushioned back of the bench, the wood where the cushion ended cool on her cheek. They'd drunk too much wine, way more than Ollie had intended. *Good job getting into Bethany's good books.* She now wished she'd drunk more of the table water Anna had ordered.

Anna's gaze seemed locked to their fingers now, and Ollie was surprised when Anna scissored their fingers loosely, palm to palm, the fingertips of her other hand snaking between the bones of her knuckles.

Pausing for a while, Anna then lifted Ollie's hand to her lips and pressing a kiss against her knuckles. They were so close. When Anna finally looked up into Ollie's eyes, she blinked a few times.

Ollie hadn't realised how close she'd shifted towards her. Their hands were still locked together, and now so were their gazes—only a few inches between them.

Jazz played softly around them. The yellow glow from the lamp was just bright enough to see by. Ollie studied Anna's face, the lines by her mouth and eyes, the glitter of the earrings just hidden beneath her hair, the gold-green flecks in Anna's irises as her pupils widened.

Anna leant forward.

Their lips met briefly, quickly. Ollie pulled back, her lips parting in amazement. She gazed into Anna's eyes, searching for something, some kind of indication of what Anna wanted. She hesitated once, twice, and then leant in, capturing Anna's lips again. She clutched at Anna's arms, and then Anna's fingers were at the back of her head, pulling her closer.

One of them moaned, Ollie wasn't sure who, and they parted their lips, tongues sweeping against one another. Ollie slid her hands up from Anna's shoulders, cupped her cheek in one, and threaded her fingers into the short hair at the back of Anna's head with the other.

Oh crumbs, I'm kissing Anna Rose. Something fluttered inside Ollie's gut, something confused but amazed and thrilled all at once. *She is attracted to me. She does like me in the same way I like her.*

Anna tugged at Ollie's neck and slipped her other hand around her back.

The kiss slowed to just a soft brushing of lips on lips. They stopped but didn't move away, noses snuggling against one another.

A wide smile expanded on Anna's face. Ollie let out a shaky breath, and Anna's forehead leant against Ollie's. She shuttered her eyes.

"Goodness," she breathed.

"Indeed," Ollie said, the back of her knuckles against Anna's cheek. "Was…was that all right?" Worry twisted Ollie's insides. She found herself squirming in her seat.

"I believe that *I* kissed *you*," Anna said, one eyebrow arched.

Squinting smugly, Ollie looked out into the bar, noting their seclusion, the booth almost completely hidden from the rest of the clientele. *Thank God, I'm not really into having an audience.*

She turned back to Anna and reached to take Anna's chin in her fingers. She stroked the freckles by Anna's jaw before guiding her in again and pressing their lips together.

This time, it was definitely Anna who moaned as their lips touched, her hands that pulled Ollie closer, and her head that tilted, giving Ollie better access.

One hand strayed down to rest against Anna's knee as Ollie kissed and kissed her, slowly and thoroughly. They kissed for a long while, and the whole bar disappeared. All Ollie could feel and hear was Anna.

Anna's phone rang noisily from her handbag. The room spun for a brief heartbeat, and then everything swam back into focus. The band had finished and a stereo was now playing something quieter.

After a small peck to Ollie's lips, Anna pulled away properly. She kept her thumb on Ollie's cheekbone, stroking there as though she didn't want to break the physical connection just yet. She reached to her handbag with her free hand with a huffed breath.

"Bethany," she said, holding the phone to her ear.

Ollie intended to slide out of the booth to give Anna some privacy to talk with her daughter, but Anna held her arm there and settled herself around a little. Ollie got the hint and slipped her hands around Anna's waist, letting them rest against her midriff, the thin folds of her wrap-around top under her fingers.

Anna flapped her hand as Ollie sank her face into Anna's hair, her nose beside her ear. "I'm sorry, darling I… We lost track of time and…"

It was obvious Bethany was giving Anna a hard time. Meekly, Anna allowed the concerned tirade.

"I'm sorry. I'll be home in around half an hour. You go to bed, don't wait up. I love you, darling." She hung up.

The spot behind Anna's ear smelled amazing, so Ollie kissed her there.

Anna's head dropped back a little and then turned towards Ollie's wandering lips. She slid her phone blindly onto the table. A visible shiver ran through her as Ollie's lips brushed her skin again.

Pleased with the effect she was having, Ollie decided it was safe to ask. "Are we in trouble, comrade?" She let her lips rest against Anna's skin.

"Mmm." A palm cupped Ollie's cheek. Their lips met again briefly. Anna sighed. "I should have told her we'd be out a little longer when we left Dulcie's."

"I should have reminded you."

She stroked Ollie's cheek. "It's all right." She shrugged. "Sorted now."

"Half an hour?" Ollie looked at her wristwatch.

Anna pulled a face. "I know. I would have loved to have spent longer, really, but she was quite upset and…" She shrugged again. "I think I should be getting home."

"Oh," Ollie said, her heart feeling like it was falling through her body. She looked at her hands as she heard Anna moving out of the booth and pulling on her coat. "'Course. Of course." *I suppose that's it, then.* She slipped out of the booth herself and pulled on her jacket as well.

They both stopped in their tracks as a tall man strode over to them, his face red and eyes blazing. *Did they kick him out of the theatre for being too drunk?*

At Anna's sharp intake of breath, Ollie frowned. She stepped in front of her, blocking Liam's access even as he reached out towards Anna. The veins on his hand were a thick, angry blue. His mother was sitting in a booth across the bar, her head in her hands. *Maybe we weren't so hidden from the rest of the crowd after all.*

"Replaced me already?" Liam shouted. "Wow." Ollie realised he was focusing in on her legs. "You so desperate to replace me that you're just settling for whatever's available?"

Ollie set her jaw. Anna was in front of her in a heartbeat. "How dare you?" she growled.

"She likes it, you know," Liam said to Ollie. "Someone to fix. That's why she likes that boy so much, lets him live with her."

A vibrating shudder went through Anna. Ollie grabbed hold of her arm to remind her she was there. Anna's jaw clenched and her eyes were blazing with emotion. She looked to Ollie like she was about to spontaneously combust.

"Makes her feel wanted," Liam continued with a wide smirk.

"Shut up," Anna hissed.

Ollie looked around. The entire bar was watching them.

"She doesn't like people to speak their minds." Liam's fists were white by his sides. "Terribly set in her ways."

"I happen to like her ways." She stepped forward to stand right beside Anna. The two of them made a formidable united front, ready for any battle. "And from what she's told me about you, and from what I've seen on our very *brief* encounters this evening, I'd say you're the one with something to fix."

He stared at her.

"You're a child who can't get over losing this wonderful woman's attention," she continued. "And you're a bigoted fool who can't be bothered to learn from his mistakes." Ollie lowered her voice and pursed her lips. "I used to be in the army," she said, her tone level and her words deliberate. "And while you are absolutely right that I have a leg injury, there are quite a few people I know from that time in my life who still owe me *favours*, if you catch my drift."

She tried not to laugh as he balked and stepped backwards, swaying a little.

"Now, can I suggest you leave us alone and go back to your mother? It's awfully kind of her to come out with you." Ollie smiled and forced cheerfulness into her tone, knowing she had won. She couldn't help one last dig, however. "It's not nice to leave your date waiting at the bar, is it?"

Ollie lifted a hand in greeting to Liam's mother. Anna took Ollie's free hand in her own and pulled her away. As they strode past the bar, Ollie caught the eye of a member of staff she recognised. She threw a meaningful gaze towards Liam, and the staff member nodded in understanding. *They'll chuck him out before he makes another scene.*

She let Anna pull her out onto the street, where a few people were still meandering around, their coats tightly around them in the December air. They rushed down the street while Anna rang for a taxi, her hands obviously trembling as she dialled. Ollie was surprised to hear her give the shop as the pickup address.

They walked towards the shop at a little distance from one another, Anna having dropped Ollie's hand once they were on the move. Ollie was too distracted by the anger bubbling in her throat to think much about what that meant. When they got to Ollie's side door, Anna turned to her and lifted a hand to stroke her cheek. Her hand still shook a bit.

Her stomach loosening, Ollie smiled at her, unsure but happy about the calmer look in Anna's eyes. "You all right?"

Anna nodded. "I'm so sorry about him." Her breath was spiralling up in a cloud of mist.

"Don't be, please."

Cold fingers traced Ollie's cheekbone. "God, I do wish he'd just leave me alone." Anna's eyes glistened with tears nearly formed.

Ollie slid her hand around Anna's waist over her coat and thumbed the wool. "Hope I wasn't too…" She bit her lip. "Forceful with the whole… army thing."

A smile pulled at Anna's lips. "I think it will do him good to know there are consequences to his actions."

"Good. Any more problems with him, please let me know. I wasn't kidding about having people who owe me."

"Okay."

Ollie leant forward a little, pausing when she was an inch away from Anna's lips.

Her smile widening, Anna tilted her chin up, sneaking her fingers beneath Ollie's jacket at the neck as they kissed, unhurriedly.

The sharp beep of a car horn broke them apart.

"I'll see you on Thursday." Anna stepped away, her arm stretching as she refused to take her hand away from Ollie's cheek until she absolutely had to.

Ollie watched her climb into the car and pull away from the kerb, red tail lights reflecting on the pavement. Her keys caught on the inside of her jacket pocket as she pulled them out, but she just stood there stock-still for a moment.

Her fingers touched her lips, and she was amazed at how they tingled. She disentangled her key from her pocket, before pushing her way inside her dark shop and closing the door firmly behind her.

Once inside, she had an overwhelming urge to tell someone what had happened. She didn't feel like texting Matthew, not until her brain had settled a bit. But she wanted to tell someone.

She leant against the wall in the unlit hallway and looked at her phone for a while. The light from it seemed very bright in the darkness, and she had to squint until her eyes adjusted. She scrolled through her text messages and opened the conversation with Kieran. Her finger hovered over the keyboard.

Evening. How are you doing? I finally found out how Anna feels about me. We kissed, and it's looking promising. Won't jump in with my eyes closed, I promise. So far so good, though. Mum x

She hoped it was okay that she spoke with her son about Anna, especially since he'd had such reservations when they'd spoken on the phone. A few minutes later, he replied.

Jackpot! Sending positive thoughts your way. I don't want details, but I truly am glad things are working out. Any problems, let me know. Kx

A warm flush swept through her.

Roger that. Same goes for you. If this accountant turns out to be a psychopath, send her my way. Mum's prerogative, you know. Mum x

She quickly started a new text and sent it.

Any word from Helen?

A few minutes passed, and she decided to make her way upstairs. The hallway was cold, and her knee was complaining. Even the memory of Anna's lips on hers wasn't helping the pain.

The reply came as she made it to the kettle.

Nothing much. She did ask how you were the other day but didn't say anything when I said you were okay. Sorry. Kx

Ollie sighed.

Maybe if she meets Anna, she'll be blown over by her charm. But first, she needs to actually contact me.

Cup of tea in hand, she carried it with her phone to the sofa for a bit of television before she'd be settled enough to be able to sleep.

Ollie spent Sunday agonising over whether to text Anna or not. Again. In the end, she figured she'd allow Anna to choose whether they had contact, and by eight in the evening she had resigned herself to the fact they wouldn't be exchanging texts anytime soon. *That's okay.* Anna was new to the whole 'dating-a-woman' thing, Ollie was not. Well, not that new.

For a few minutes, she allowed herself to dwell over the emotions that had surrounded her relationship with Zoe. The guilt about having cheated still made her stomach hurt. It had taken her a long while after her divorce to settle into the fact that relationships with women were okay to have.

After locking up the flat, she turned off the lights and settled down in her comfortable bed. She pulled her crocheted blanket up to cover the whole duvet and snuck her fingertips into the small holes between the sets of stitches. She allowed the edge of it to caress the skin of her cheek and closed her eyes. Her body hurt and her brain did too. *I need to doss down. I'm chin-strapped.*

Her phone, plugged in by her bed, buzzed. She took it from the bedside table, squinting in the darkness as she looked at the screen.

You up for a chat? x

Excitement rushed through her. Ollie swiped to Anna's number and held the phone to her ear. It rang only once before Anna picked up.

"Hi." The voice on the other end was soft.

A mixture of relief and worry flooded through her. "Hello," she replied, her voice a little cracked from settling down for sleep. She cleared her throat. "How was your day?"

"All right. I took Bethany out for a shopping excursion." A soft chuckle. "She wanted a coat to match her bloody hat and scarf."

Ollie snorted. "You're rubbing off on her, obviously." Shifting to her back, she stretched a bit before settling properly with the phone to her ear. "Impeccable sense of style."

"Thank you."

There was a pause, and Ollie braced herself for disappointment.

"Listen," Anna started but then went quiet.

Here it comes. Ollie gave her a moment to gather her thoughts.

"Last night."

"Last night," Ollie echoed, unsure how to feel about what was coming.

But then Anna let out a breath, and Ollie could hear the smile behind it.

"I'm sorry if I sort of...threw myself at you."

"You didn't," Ollie replied quickly but then huffed out a laugh. "Well, maybe you did, just a bit. But I'm not complaining."

"Good," Anna said. "It's just... It's all very new to me."

"I know."

"You're my..." There was another pause and Ollie's eyebrows furrowed a little. "I've never kissed a woman before. If I'm honest."

"What?" Ollie cleared her throat again. "What about your little moment in college?"

"Hmm." Another pause. "I wanted to tell you that I was attracted to you, but I suppose I just made up something silly to save me having to say it outright." Anna sighed.

Ollie slipped her fingertips into the crocheted throw again, comforted by the soft yarn.

"I'm sorry," Anna said.

"Forgiven." Ollie shrugged even though Anna couldn't see her.

"Thank you."

For a moment, they simply breathed together, and Ollie felt all warm and safe.

"So, do you have something you'd like to make on Thursday?" Ollie asked. *We didn't talk about crochet at all last night.* That made her feel warmer still, comfortable in the knowledge that her and Anna's relationship wasn't simply held together by craft activities.

"I have a loose idea."

"Am I allowed to know what?"

"I intend on finding a pattern by myself."

Ollie thought she could hear pride in Anna's voice. "Really?"

"Really."

"Don't need me anymore, hmm, comrade?"

"I wouldn't say that. I'm sure I'll make a right pig's ear of it before I get it right."

"You won't. Although I can't say I wouldn't miss you on a Thursday evening if you became too accomplished to need classes." She lay there in her bed with her mouth open and her heart thudding in her chest, waiting for some kind of confirmation, some kind of recognition that she wasn't the only one who felt like this.

"You can't get rid of me that easily."

Ollie's stomach unclenched. "Likewise." She caressed the soft wool-mix between her fingers. "If you stop coming I'll send out Matthew as a search party."

A giggle rumbled through Anna at the joke, which was interrupted by a large yawn that made Ollie smile. "Sorry."

"Better let you get to bed."

"I'm already in bed."

"Me too," Ollie said. Her stomach felt all tingly again. *I wonder what kind of pyjamas she wears.*

Anna made a little noise, like a small cat. "Merlot is sitting on my bedside table."

"Drinking so late at night?"

"Oh no. Merlot is what I've named my bunny."

"The one I made you?"

"You think I've been cheating on her with other bunnies?"

"You never know."

Another muffled yawn. "It's nice to talk to you." Anna's voice was quiet and her words slurred.

Ollie's eyes drooped, and she yawned herself, trying to cover the noise with her hand.

"Tired, Williams?"

"Yeah," Ollie said when she'd finished her yawn. "Someone kept me out until all hours last night."

"Oh dear," Anna replied. "We can't have that."

"It's okay." She swallowed and set her jaw. "It was worth it. She's pretty."

Anna's voice became soft but deep, like she'd held the phone close to her mouth. "Funny. I met with someone last night that I could use the exact same word to describe."

"What a coincidence." *I don't think anyone's ever called me pretty.*

"Goodnight, Ollie."

Ollie's eyes were already closed and her thumb was still rubbing the throw by her neck. "Goodnight, comrade."

They texted one another after the initial day-long silence. General things, how their days were going.

Anna had so much she wanted to tell Ollie, but it just didn't seem right, texting it all. And they didn't phone one another again but left it until Thursday. *I can't wait to see her in the flesh again. So much has happened, so much that I wanted to happen.* She continually found herself smirking. *My plan worked, well, for the most part.* While it hadn't been perfect, their dinner had, eventually, gone the way she had wanted.

Leaning in to kiss Ollie had been a huge leap. Anna had wondered how Ollie would react, whether she would pull away, for whatever reason, including not actually being attracted to her. *But she is. She kissed me back. And we kissed goodnight.* That had been her favourite kiss, all gentle and tender and… Anna shivered in delight at the memory.

And they had actually talked about it afterwards. The phone call had settled her worried brain. Even after their kisses, she had been anxious about what Ollie would say, whether Ollie would want to see her again. Whether she'd want to see her again in the way Anna wanted to see her.

On Thursday, Anna got home from work at four and was able to cook something from scratch for the kids and herself.

Bethany eyed her as she flitted around the kitchen. "Mum?" she asked after a few minutes.

"Yes, love?" Anna replied, laying Timothy's plate in front of him and touching his shoulder before he tucked into his dinner.

"You never told us how your dinner with Ollie went." Bethany's gaze on her was assertive.

Anna carried her own plate to the table and sat. She carefully picked up her knife and fork, cut up a piece of breaded fish, and popped into her mouth. She chewed as she thought about her answer. Communication was the key with teenagers, she knew. And honesty should be at the heart of every family. The ideals she had instilled in Bethany had proven, so far, helpful when the young woman was going through emotional upheaval with boyfriends or friends. They were a team, and they always tried to be honest with one another.

Anna stared at her plate. She looked up at the both of them, grimacing a little. *It's hard, but this thing is too huge for me to keep from them.* "We had a lovely evening," she began, easing herself in slowly.

"I want to meet Ollie," Timothy stated, entering into the conversation with his usual confidence.

"We um…" *God, how do I explain this?* She let out a huff, and Timothy frowned at her.

"You look tense," he observed, and she smiled at him.

"I feel a little tense, Timothy. But it's just because I have something to tell you and I'm a little anxious about how you'll react."

"You kissed, didn't you?" Bethany sipped from her glass of wine, watching her with curiosity.

Anna blinked. *What is she, a mind reader?* "What?"

"You and Ollie?" Bethany replied.

Is it common knowledge all of a sudden? "Well I…" Anna looked between them.

Timothy looked interested but not shocked or surprised.

Bethany just looked as though the food in front of her was more interesting than the conversation about her mother's sexuality.

"Yes," Anna said in the end, suddenly rather relieved she didn't have to say the actual words.

"Does that mean you're gay now?" Timothy asked, still apparently unfazed by the concept.

"I'm not sure," Anna replied. "I think I'm still attracted to men. So…"

"Bisexual, then."

Anna nodded. "Bisexual. I suppose."

"You mean you haven't talked about it? With Ollie?" Bethany asked, huffing in frustration.

"We have." Anna frowned to herself. *How much did we actually discuss?* "It's early days."

"You like her, though?" Bethany asked.

"Yes, I do."

"And she likes you?"

"I would hope so." The memory of the look in Ollie's eyes after she had kissed her sent a small thrill through Anna.

"Are you dating, then?" Timothy asked.

"I think we might be." Anna sucked on her bottom lip. "We talked about having more dinners out and… Well, like I said, it's early days."

"Keep us updated," Bethany said, her attention returning to her fish.

"I will." She turned to Timothy, who gave her his biggest grin. She squeezed his wrist.

They went back to their meals.

It wasn't the cold evening that made Anna shudder as she arrived at the side door of the shop. Her hands trembled as she knocked. One hand dropped to lie over her cloth bag, over the pattern she had found on the Internet. *The pattern is fine. Stop getting yourself into such a state.*

Ollie answered the door, and they exchanged a soft smile. Lowering her head, Ollie hid behind her hair. Stepping near to the doorway, Anna lifted a hand to brush it back.

"Nice to see you," Ollie said, her eyes shining.

Anna beamed and stepped into the dark hallway. They stood close together, and Anna was not really sure what to do, but she wanted to do something that would show a little of the affection she felt for Ollie.

Before she could decide what move to make, Matthew burst into the corridor from the classroom and went over to give Anna a hug. He seemed oblivious to the looks between them and ushered Anna into the classroom, eager to show her the brooch he had made for his mum.

Footsteps followed them in, and Ollie and Anna caught one another's gaze before Ollie gestured to Anna to continue with Matthew.

Anna nodded and sat with Matthew as he chatted away.

The room was packed that evening. Anna relaxed. The tension between them would have been far plainer to see if only been a few people had been there.

A couple of new people were introduced and a few more who hadn't been to the class for a while were welcomed back. Ollie held up a pattern for a shopping bag, covered in little crocheted flowers. Around half the room took one, but Anna shook her head. Ollie nodded and moved around the room.

After opening her trusty cloth bag, Anna pulled out a freshly printed pattern with small, brightly coloured pictures.

Matthew looked over. "Stars," he said. "They're nice. I was going to make my mum another brooch, the same as the one here." He indicated the bird-shaped brooch he had already fastened to a safety pin. "But I like that." He tapped the pictures. "May I?"

"Of course you may," Anna said. "It's good to share—so my mother always said."

"Mine says that too. Let's go and choose some yarn."

The pale blue yarn Anna had chosen had just a hint of sparkle. *I hope she likes it.*

Matthew had chosen a bright red and was making several stars to lay over one another in a sort of flower-petal arrangement.

Deciding to make several too, Anna fastened two of each of the points to one another so that they looked a little like paper dolls.

"So," Matthew began, hesitation in his voice, "we went to the cinema."

"I'm assuming you mean you and Harry?"

"And for a drink." A flush crept up Matthew's neck. "We nearly held hands."

"Nearly?"

"Very nearly. I sort of had my hand next to his and..." Matthew shrugged.

Anna reckoned the young man usually did more than hold hands with his dates. She was pleased he had found someone he felt comfortable going slowly with. *I've already done more than that with Ollie.* Her cheeks heated at the thought.

The lady with the huge throw came over to see what they were doing. "Harry told me you're a schoolteacher?"

Anna looked up from her stars, startled. "That's right. I teach English."

"Fantastic subject. My favourite at school, apart from music." She had long dark hair with streaks of white in it, tied up in a plat. She wore a long purple cardigan and large, dangly earrings.

Matthew sat back at the arrival of someone new. "This is Fiona. She used to play in a band."

"An orchestra, Matthew, love. Get it right."

He blushed. "Sorry."

"What did you play?" Anna asked, stilling her hands to give Fiona her full attention.

"French horn. All the brassy dramatic parts, you know. Good fun."

"Do you still play?"

"Not so much. Lungs gave out after a while. But my fingers are still as dexterous as they ever were."

"Perhaps someone could blow for you and you could do the fingering," Matthew said.

"Now there's an idea." She looked over to Ollie, and her whole body seemed to soften.

She can't do the thing she loves, either, just like Ollie.

Anna suddenly wanted to make a friend in the older lady. "I've been watching you make that enormous blanket for weeks," she said, amazement washing through her. "I've never seen anything so huge."

"Ollie inspired me. With all her talk of throws and things for the church hall. I decided to see how big a blanket I could make." She gestured over to her table, where the thick blanket sat bunched up. "So far, it touches the floor on each side of my king-sized bed, and then some. I reckon I'm doing all right."

"You going to make it any bigger, or is it done?"

Fiona shrugged and sighed happily. "I just enjoy the company, being able to do something with my hands, and the free tea on tap." She grinned over at Ollie. "That blonde doesn't half make a good brew."

"She does." Anna had to look away after a moment of catching Ollie's gaze. She felt like fondness was dripping from her own eyes. "And it's great you've found something you enjoy."

"Not just me. This group is full of people who've had broken hearts. But, hey, you just have to pick yourself up and pop your heart somewhere else. Find something different for it to focus on."

Anna hadn't thought of that, but she supposed Fiona was right.

"Hearts can be tricky things," Matthew murmured.

One of Fiona's large hands landed on his shoulder. "You, love, need to decide where your heart is supposed to be." Her gaze flicked towards Harry.

Matthew's cheeks reddened. "Already sorted." He smiled at Fiona. "We had a date."

After throwing her hands into the air, Fiona patted Matthew's shoulder. "Well, thank the Lord."

The laugh that bubbled up Anna's throat was affectionate, and so was the way she bumped Matthew's shoulder with her own.

Affectionate wrinkles appeared around Fiona's nose. "Matthew, it's been a pleasure. Anna, lovely to have finally met you." She winked. "I've been meaning to come over."

"Likewise."

Leaving them to their stars, Fiona went back to her table.

Ollie moved around the group, and Anna caught her gaze a few times when she glanced over at her and Matthew. She seemed far too busy with everyone else to allow her gaze to linger much, however.

It's all making sense now, the way I feel when she's close by.

Anna sipped her tea between working delicately on her stars. After making five, she looped them back around, attaching the first star to the last to make a ring. She put it on her own wrist and held it out to Matthew for inspection.

"That for Bethany?" he asked.

"No," Anna said. She didn't elaborate but did glance up at Ollie.

He must have noticed, because he smirked at her. "Well, whoever you give it to," he said, "I'm sure they'll like it."

"That would be my intention." She shook herself, took the bracelet off her own wrist, and tucked it into her pocket.

She wasn't sure what to do next. *I've still got almost three-quarters of a ball of wool left to use.* She made some normal granny squares, figuring she ought to spend the rest of the time in the class to full advantage. She'd been meaning to make some for the church hall anyway. There were seven in a pile on the table by the end of the class, and she slipped three of them into her cloth bag with the rest of her unused yarn and hooks. The remaining four she laid gently into the wicker basket, which was almost full to overflowing. She then caressed her pocket where the bracelet was hidden.

Matthew, who was dashing off to meet friends at the pub, threw her a wave.

As was not unusual, Anna was the last to stand from her chair, the last to bring her mug to the front and to remain after the final person had left.

Ollie leant against the counter, looking through the door into the corridor. Then she swung her smile to Anna. "You made me some squares."

"I did. I'm going to make myself something as well. But I've been thinking about contributing to the project for ages."

"And now you have." Ollie peered at the squares and nodded her approval. "They're great. Thank you, comrade."

Anna smiled back at her. "How are your hands?" Her gaze trailed down Ollie's long arm.

Both palms appeared obediently for inspection.

After taking each one in her own, Anna checked the front and back and ran a fingertip over Ollie's wrist. She looked up, found Ollie's eyes on hers, and blinked a little at the tenderness she saw within them.

Anna quickly slipped the bracelet over Ollie's fingers and pressed it as it hung on her wrist.

Ollie looked down and furrowed her eyebrows. "What's this?"

"A gift." Anna stepped back and dropped her trembling hands from Ollie's. "I don't know if you're a bracelet wearer usually or… You could put it around a mug in your flat or…a vase perhaps, or…"

A grin shone from Ollie's features and she gazed at the small sparkly stars, touching each with a gentle fingertip. "It's lovely. Thank you."

Anna breathed out a laugh.

After stepping up to her, Ollie wrapped the arm that wore the bracelet around her shoulder and pressed her cheek to Anna's in a small, one-armed hug.

A sigh rumbled through Anna at the contact, and she slipped her arms around Ollie to hold her close. She breathed in the feeling of Ollie's arms around her, of her face pressed close to her own. The familiar smell of Ollie's shampoo was heavenly.

When Ollie relaxed and made to let Anna go, Anna held on more tightly. She turned her head to press her lips against Ollie's cheek. "Just a minute longer," Anna said.

Ollie's hands dropped from her shoulders and lay flat against the small of her back, her fingers curling into the wool of her coat.

"Roger that," Ollie said, turning her head, too, snuggling her nose into Anna's neck.

Anna giggled as goose pimples rose across her skin. Her Anna's cloth bag, previously hanging from her shoulder, dropped down her arm and fell with a soft thud onto the floor.

Neither of them moved at the noise.

Anna trailed her fingertips up Ollie's spine in a slow caress.

As she burrowed further into her, Ollie's hands wandered, too, one smoothing over Anna's shoulder blade, the other around her waist.

Shivers flashed across Anna's skin at the way Ollie's touch made her feel suddenly too warm and rather swamped with emotion. She pulled away but caught Ollie's gaze as her hands fell to her sides.

Ollie pushed her eyebrows down as though she was afraid she'd done something wrong.

Quickly, Anna reached to brush the backs of her knuckles down Ollie's neck. When Ollie leant in, Anna took the hint, closing the distance between them.

There was a millimetre of space between them.

Ollie cupped Anna's jaw with her fingertips gently.

Closing her eyes, Anna shivered again. Their lips touched softly, barely brushing.

"Fancy a coffee?" Ollie asked breathily after they had broken the kiss.

Anna leant her head to one side, her pursed lips tingling. "That sounds wonderful. But…"

"But?"

Unable to make eye contact, Anna perused a small mark on the wallpaper. "I just feel a little… I'm still a tad overwhelmed by…" She spread her hands wide, attempting to indicate their situation.

Ollie nodded and took her hands in her own, squeezing them. "That's okay."

"Are you…are you sure?" Anna asked, her voice a little wobbly. "I feel like a proper prat."

"I don't mind waiting." Ollie rubbed her thumbs over the backs of Anna's hands. "And I'm aware it's only been… But perhaps we could do dinner again? Another night."

"And just take it from there."

Ollie smiled and nodded. "Spanish?"

"So long as they have a good wine list," Anna said, the wobbliness fading and her chin lifting.

"Goes without saying."

They grinned at one another again, their hands still joined between them.

After waiting a moment, Ollie pulled on Anna's hands gently.

Anna stepped forward and lifted her hands to Ollie's face, before resting her fingers by her ears and then pulling her in.

Another kiss so gentle that Anna hummed against Ollie's lips. Ollie's lips curled upwards too. When the kiss broke, they stayed close.

The hum turned into a girlish giggle. Anna laid her forehead against Ollie's as Ollie slid her arms around her waist. "I should go." She hoped the tickle of her fingertips against Ollie's neck expressed just how much she wanted to stay.

Ollie rubbed the dips of Anna's waist with her thumbs and nodded. "I wish you wouldn't."

"I know," Anna said but stepped away and bent down to pick up her bag where it had fallen to the floor. "But dinner. Definitely."

"Text me with your availability."

Anna nodded and then stepped out of the room. She walked out of the side door and onto the pavement. As her hand rested on her sternum, a flustered feeling began deep in her chest. She felt tingly and warm after kissing Ollie.

I haven't felt like this in years. She waited until the flustered feeling slowed and then dropped her hand, her whole body relaxing.

Nodding once to herself, she began the short journey through the cold winter's night to her car.

Chapter 9

Squares I Don't Need

Twenty-two days before the day, Bethany asked Anna what she would be getting Ollie for Christmas.

Anna shook her head and shrugged. "I've no idea." She wound the yarn she was making yet more granny squares with around her forefinger.

"Are you going to make her something?" Timothy asked from the armchair.

With her bottom lip between her teeth, Anna sighed. "I don't know."

"Is she the person you care most about?" Timothy asked. "Apart from Beth and I, of course."

"Different kind of 'care about'," Bethany said without looking up from her glossy magazine.

"I think so," Anna replied.

It was Friday, and Ollie was coming round to Anna's house for pizza and a film on Saturday night. It was all Anna could handle after spending two days on a school trip with sixty rambunctious pupils excited about seeing the plays they'd read in class come to life, but luckily Ollie had been game, because Anna had been up most of the night and had fallen into bed at eight that morning, before getting up at lunchtime. Her eyes were drooping, and her body felt heavy against the sofa cushions.

I've still got so much marking to do. Thank goodness I have today off.

Should she cancel her date with Ollie? Would she be in too much of a tired state tomorrow to be pleasant company? She felt woozy and bleary-eyed. She'd looked in her mirror and grimaced when she had seen the dark circles and the lines by her mouth. *I look so old.*

"You said you'd make something for one person," Timothy continued, snapping Anna out of her reverie. "And you should make it for the person you care about the most."

"I should," Anna said, putting her granny squares away and then shoving the top down on her cloth bag. For once she didn't want to look at crochet. *Squares and squares for no purpose, what's the point?*

"Be subtle, perhaps? Ask her about her favourite colour, if there's anything she's made for someone else but never for herself?" Bethany said, green eyes crinkling at her mother over her magazine.

Timothy, seemingly content that his questions had been answered, went back to watching his natural-history television programme.

"I suppose I could."

"When you see her tomorrow."

Anna nodded. She clambered dejectedly from the sofa and grabbed a large box full of folders. "Which reminds me," she said on her way to the study. "You'll be making yourself scarce, hmm?"

"I'll be at Adam's," Timothy said.

Anna chuckled and he grinned back. "Actually, my question was directed at my lovely daughter."

Bethany smirked over the sofa back. "Yes, Mum. Oh, and Jessica says 'thanks' for the pizza cash."

"That's my girl." Anna winked and hugged the damn files to her chest. She was not looking forward to the paperwork, but her stomach warmed at how much she loved her children. "I'll see you in the morning."

"Make sure you take breaks between marking," Bethany said, face back inside the pages of her magazine.

"I'll try, love." She closed the door to the study.

Anna worked solidly, desperate to get everything done before Saturday evening. She managed to crawl into bed at three. She slept until midday, then showered and fretted over her outfit for their official first date.

Ollie had impressed that she should feel comfortable—Anna had told her about the amount of work she'd completed, both on the school trip and at home. That quietened some of the butterflies that patted against Anna stomach. *She's very understanding, but I suppose she used to teach. She knows how tiring it can be.*

They were staying in, but Anna wanted to make an effort. She chose a deep green jumper and dark blue jeans and made sure she didn't smell like she'd been up all night, or in bed all day.

Ollie arrived right on time. Anna squinted at the taxi as it drove away. "Didn't you bring your car?" she asked as she ushered Ollie in.

Ollie shrugged her coat off, and Anna took it from her. "Actually, I have a confession." She toed the carpet with her boot. "I don't own one."

"You don't have a car?"

"Well, I couldn't physically drive for a few months when I got discharged," Ollie said, grimacing. "And once I'd spent all of Maggie's money on the shop…I didn't need a car. It felt frivolous to buy one."

Anna gazed gently at her. "Fair enough."

Ollie's shoulders relaxed.

"And hello," Anna said, her eyelashes dipping a little.

"Hi."

Once she'd wrapped her arms around her, Anna touched their cheeks together. She shivered at the contact and could feel Ollie smiling against her skin.

Ollie pulled back and her gaze flicked to Anna's lips. At the lift of Anna's chin, Ollie leant down to her, and when their lips met, it was soft.

The hair at the back of Ollie's neck was silky under Anna's fingers. Ollie didn't rush her, just maintained the contact, allowing the kiss to stay light.

Anna stepped back and held out her hand. "Let's look at the pizza menu."

"Tip-top idea," Ollie said.

Anna led her into the living room. She watched with interest as Ollie looked around.

A small smile pulled at her lips as she looked at the large television, the wide bay window, and the ornaments lined up neatly on the mantelpiece. *Oh, that's right, she hasn't been in here before.* A slight nod suggested Ollie was finished exploring at least the living room. They sat next to one another on the sofa and ordered the food.

Ollie indicated Anna's cloth bag, full to overflowing, leaning against the side of the sofa. "What're you making?"

Anna sighed and shook her head. "Just granny squares." The words tumbled from her lips bitterly.

"You don't like granny squares?"

"I feel like I've run out of ideas of things to make." She pressed her lips together. "I'm not sure what I'm making them for. I don't want to arrive with hundreds of boring squares for the project. Although I do intend on donating a few more."

Ollie tickled a fingertip against the back of her hand where it lay on the cushion between them. She traced a circle around one of Anna's knuckles.

Anna smiled, her skin tingling where Ollie touched her.

"You don't have to be constantly making things," Ollie said. "Feel free to have other hobbies in your life."

"Wine? Good food?"

They watched as their fingers interlaced.

Ollie squeezed Anna's hand warmly.

"I think I've hit a rut." Anna pouted. *I love crochet. I never thought I would, but I do. And I want to make things. But what?*

"What's all that, then?" Ollie asked, nodding towards the bag.

"I've just been sort of idly churning them out. Not sure what I'll do with them all." Anna twisted her lips in question. "Do you need all of these for the wall hanging?"

"No. You keep them for something you'd like to make." Ollie reached behind her to pull at a corner of the completed crocheted throw hung over the back of the sofa. "This one is lovely," she said, making happy stars burst in Anna's stomach. "What about a bed throw? Or a smaller one for the armchair?"

"A bed throw sounds nice." Anna took Ollie's hand back, missing how it felt in her own.

Ollie rested her cheek against the throw and closed her eyes. She looked like she'd sunk into a warm bath. "What colour's your bedroom?"

The question was perfectly innocent, but Anna couldn't let such a brilliant opportunity go. She rested her cheek on the sofa, too, her face close to Ollie's, and her eyes shuttered a little. Her thumb smoothed over the back of Ollie's hand. "Why don't you come and see?" Anna's voice was barely a whisper.

Ollie's throat worked audibly as she swallowed.

The doorbell rang.

"God, that was quick," Anna said, shooting up from the sofa. Ollie groaned as she stood to follow, and Anna tried not to grin. *She's right. The pizza bloke has terrible timing.*

They served up the pizza and the box of potato wedges in the kitchen. Anna pulled a bottle of wine, already open, from the counter and cocked an eyebrow.

"Yes, please," Ollie said.

Anna made sure she bent her neck and gave Ollie a good view as she poured them both a glass. The intake of breath from behind her meant she'd got what she wanted.

They sat across from one another at the table, eating with their fingers. They consumed the pizza quickly. *Did I miss breakfast* and *lunch when I slept in this morning?*

Ollie reached for a wedge, dipped it in the small pot of garlic mayonnaise, and lifted it to her mouth.

The way Ollie's fingers glistened with oil was mesmerising. Anna's heart sung as she realised she was allowed to look and allowed to feel desire for Ollie. Her stomach fluttered when Ollie sucked the tip of her thumb free from dip.

A flush crept up Ollie's cheeks, but she smiled and then reached across to tangle their sticky fingers together on the tabletop.

"How was your school trip?" Ollie asked.

As if on cue, Anna yawned. "So tiring, but great too. We saw some fabulous pieces of theatre." She paused with a potato wedge just by her mouth, relishing Ollie's further blush. She was watching her too. "Two of my Year 9s decided they were 'unfriending' each other or whatever the blasted phrase is. Big kerfuffle. Up until three in the morning with them both."

Ollie shot her a sympathetic look as she squeezed her fingers. "So that's why I woke up in the morning to a three a.m. text. I was wondering."

"Yes, sorry about that. It's just that you and I had been texting the whole trip, and I was just used to doing it whenever something occurred;

and I was so exhausted when I got done with those two girls, I wasn't thinking about the time before I hit Send."

"Have you had any sleep in the past two days?"

"Well, then I had an inconceivable amount of marking to do last night. I really..." Anna put a hand to her mouth as she yawned again. She hid behind her hand as her cheeks burned. "I'm so sorry."

"That's okay, comrade," Ollie said. "That's why I thought tonight it might be nice to stay in. No need to get dressed up or..." She shrugged.

Anna relaxed. "Thank you."

"You're welcome." Ollie sipped at her wine before reaching for another potato wedge. "Tell me about your favourite pupil."

"Miss working in the educational sector, do we?"

A smile made Ollie's face glow, and she shrugged again.

Anna drank a large gulp of wine before putting her chin in her hand and pondering Ollie's question. "I have this lad, Year 10, seems to be *not quite all there*, if you get my drift," she began, anticipating Ollie's reaction to the details of the story. "He was absolutely convinced that Willy Russell was a character from some Disney movie..." She poked towards Ollie with a potato wedge to emphasise. "Convinced."

"The playwright?" Ollie's face expressed how simultaneously delighted and appalled she was.

"Apparently," Anna continued, "he'd seen the cartoon at his friend's house."

"A likely story," Ollie said, laughter bubbling out of her.

"I wouldn't have been so bothered but *literally* the week before, we'd been studying *Our Day Out*," Anna said, chuckling too.

They reached for the last wedge at the same time. Anna simply broke it in half with oily fingers. "He says things like that all the time. Some kids absolutely baffle me."

"That's the brilliance of British kids, though," Ollie said. "You don't get that sort of consistent ignorance overseas. The kids in other countries tend to just sort of hang on your every word." Her hand rose flippantly into the air. "That, and getting into military gangs."

The room seemed to sink around Anna, but she tried to keep smiling. "That can't have been easy."

"It never was. All we could do was try and set them on a less...violent path again."

"Did it always work?" Anna asked, knowing what the answer would be.

"Not always." A dark shadow crossed Ollie's features, and she looked away.

Anna smoothed her fingertips over Ollie's hand. She then leaned back in her chair and sipped her wine.

Ollie looked a little disappointed but smiled anyhow.

"Mad, that. I can't believe that in this world of civilisation and intelligence, we still have kids going off with guns."

They were quiet for a while. Ollie must have seen some traumatic things in her line of work—Anna couldn't even imagine. The father of a pupil who had been in the army came to mind. He had come home a broken man, twitching at the faintest noise, traumatised by what he had experienced in the war zone.

Ollie drained her wine glass. "Let me guess," she said, lifting her empty glass to indicate it. "Merlot?"

Anna blinked rapidly and smiled, her sombre mood broken. "But of course. What else?"

"I like that you're predictable." They shared a look for a while. "Wish I'd been there. With your Disney kid. I'd probably have made the situation worse, though."

Anna grinned. "Bit of a terror with British classes, were we?"

"Back in the day," Ollie said, a flicker of sadness passing across her eyes.

Anna took her hand again.

"I would've probably gone along with it, made him describe the cartoon in intricate detail. Conned him into thinking he was right."

"Do you have any photos?" Anna asked. "Of your army days?"

"Hmm," Ollie said, reaching into her jeans pocket for her phone. "Fancy seeing me in uniform, eh?"

"I do," Anna said honestly.

Ollie shot her a raised eyebrow. "Got any pictures of you in a cap and gown?"

"No."

In an out-of-character gesture, Ollie poked out her bottom lip.

"We don't wear them at the school I work at. Schools these days don't. Private, maybe, but not local authority."

"I bet you looked lovely in them," Ollie said as she flicked through her phone. "Here." She held it out, turning it around so Anna could see the screen.

"I really don't—*oh*." Anna took in the photograph of Ollie in camouflage fatigues and a cap, her comrades gathered around her arm in arm. A few kids stood in front with dark skin and wide smiles. The girls wore head scarves. A brown-haired woman was next to Ollie, her gaze trained on her face. She wore an army uniform too. "You look like one big happy family," Anna said.

Ollie's smile was gentle. "We were."

"Do you keep in touch?"

Something dark trickled across Ollie's face. "Used to. Still email Richard regularly, but the rest..." She grimaced further. "I wasn't very nice to them w-when I was in-incapacitated."

Anna's hand was still in Ollie's, and she caressed her thumb gently over the back of it, rubbing the skin between her knuckles. "Is that...your ex?" Anna asked, pointing at the brunette.

Ollie looked up. "Zoe."

"She looks like she's very fond of you."

"D'you reckon?" Ollie asked, frowning.

To zoom in on the picture, Anna touched the screen and pinched her fingers outward. She turned the phone around so Ollie could see.

Ollie studied it, her eyes flicking back and forth. "I suppose you're right." She looked at the picture for a moment more, her eyes still. "I haven't looked at this picture in a very long time."

She looks like she could do with some time to think. Anna eventually squeezed her fingers, wanting to coax her out.

After swiftly locking her phone, Ollie shoved it back into her pocket. Her gaze lifted to Anna's, and her shoulders slumped.

"Must have been a difficult time for you," Anna said, slowly.

Ollie nodded. "Sorry," she said, voice a little stronger. "I didn't mean to get all maudlin. Stiff upper lip and all that."

"That's okay." Anna leant back but refused to let go of Ollie's hand. "Would you like some ice cream for pudding?" she asked, her gaze trailing over the empty plates in front of them.

"I'm full."

"Film, then?"

"Roger that."

They cleared away the plates. Ollie dried up while Anna washed. *No point in putting the dishwasher on for two plates.*

They refilled their glasses with more wine and sat next to one another on the sofa.

Anna felt Ollie's gaze on her as she used the various remote controls to turn everything on.

"Are you sure you don't have a picture of you in a cap and gown?"

"No, I don't," Anna said, laughing. "I only wore them for my graduation. And the sole photograph from that day remains hidden in my attic in a box."

"Shame."

Anna rolled her eyes and tore her gaze back to the television.

"Now, then. What would you like to watch?"

They settled on a comedy, something from the nineties that they'd both seen at the time but hadn't seen since.

Anna started the movie and settled back onto the sofa. She looked over at Ollie as the credits began and then looked around her living room. She got to her feet, drew the curtains, and then turned the standard lamp on in the corner and the main light off from above them. An affectionate smile and a touch to Ollie's shoulder would hopefully convey that she was trying to give them a more romantic atmosphere.

She snuggled up into her corner of the sofa again. "This all right?" she asked, fiddling with the stem of her glass.

"Lovely." Ollie stared at the space between them. "You're an awfully long way away, though, comrade."

"I...I wasn't sure if you..."

"Wanted to cuddle up?"

Anna nodded.

"I'd love to. If..." Ollie bit her lip. "Unless you don't want to?"

"No, I..." *Stop being so insecure.* "I do," Anna said after a pause.

Ollie held her arm out along the back of the sofa, her fingers wriggling in a gesture that clearly meant *come here, then.*

Sliding across the cushions, Anna pulled the television remote with her and then rested her body against Ollie's side. She kept her head raised for a moment and then tucked her hand around her waist.

The arm Ollie wrapped around her shoulders was warm, and she patted Anna to coax her down properly against her.

Laying her cheek against Ollie's collarbone, Anna closed her eyes for a moment. *Calm down, woman.* A shudder went through Anna when Ollie squeezed her. Her shoulder tingled as Ollie's fingertips trailed gently against the wool of her jumper.

"It's okay," Ollie whispered. "I promise I won't bite."

"Sorry." Anna forced her body to relax. *This is so different from sitting on the sofa with a man. Ollie's so warm and soft.*

Ollie shifted around and for a moment Anna thought she was uncomfortable, but she was just reaching to grab the throw from the back of the sofa. She pulled it around their waists, tucked her socked feet under it, and made sure it covered Anna's hip.

A sigh left Anna and she felt more relaxed. "Oh, that's a good idea."

"Full of them, me," Ollie said, her nose sinking into Anna's hair.

Anna lifted her head to look at her. The kiss Ollie gave her was quick before Ollie smiled and turned her head to watch the film.

After a few minutes, Anna found her body cooling down, so she pulled the throw up over her shoulder and breathed steadily against Ollie's warm front.

Ollie's hand was stationary on her hip, over her big woolly green jumper.

The pale pink jumper Ollie wore was terribly flattering. She looked pastel-coloured and gentle, and Anna's cheek was resting right where the jumper gave way to the cotton of her blue top underneath. A pale-skinned collarbone and a few freckles peeked out from beneath the top.

Thankful she had seen the film before, Anna relished the feeling of being in Ollie's arms. She was warm and smelled like lavender. Her eyes closed for a moment, and she subtly breathed in Ollie's perfume, something deep but spicy. It was pleasing that Ollie had felt the event was special enough to require perfume.

She turned her attention back to the film, and before she thought too hard about it snuggled deeper into the warm wool of Ollie's jumper. She inhaled sharply when Ollie's fingertips moved back and forth, stroking her hip and waist. She soon settled into the caress, her own thumb smoothing round Ollie's waist in a steady and slow rhythm. She made a soft noise in her throat, rubbed her cheek against Ollie's shoulder, and let her entire body sink into Ollie's embrace.

When Anna's caresses slowed and then stopped, with half an hour left to go of the film, Ollie carefully looked down to find her fast asleep.

Anna's lips were parted. Her breathing was steady and slow. Ollie took a minute to study her face, for the first time unobserved. *She's so beautiful.* Freckles dusted her nose and cheekbones, and the orange-red of her eyebrows was like cinnamon.

Ollie made sure the blanket was pulled up to Anna's chin and settled to watch the remainder of the film, Anna safely nestled in her arms.

When the credits rolled and Ollie's knee was complaining bitterly, disappointment flooded through her as she realised the peace between them would be broken. Anna had been so very tired. *But any longer without painkillers and I'll be an irritable mess.*

Deciding on a nice way to wake her, Ollie turned her head to kiss Anna's forehead, left her lips there for a moment, and then swept her palm up and down Anna's side. Anna shifted and stretched a little, her eyes blinking open in the faded light. She smiled, but then hastily pushed herself into a sitting position. "I'm sorry," she whispered, a hand to her lips. A blush swept across her cheeks.

"Don't be silly." Ollie lifted a hand to smooth down a bit of hair by Anna's ear that was stuck up.

Anna placed her palm over Ollie's against her face and blushed further. "Some company I am," she said, looking across at the television. Her hand dropped and so did Ollie's. She stood to turn the television off, collected her glass from the coffee table, and drank the small amount of wine left in it.

"Are you kidding?" Ollie said, hauling herself to her feet but hissing when her knee twinged. She desperately tried to keep her expression steady.

Anna frowned and stepped close to her, tilting her head in a way that told Ollie she'd been caught.

"My knee. Metalwork gets a bit cold sometimes. Aches."

"Oh," Anna said.

Her wine glass seemed to admonish her from the coffee table, reminding her how much wine she'd drunk. "Can't really have any of the good stuff. Got some ibuprofen in my bag, though."

Anna smirked and put a stern tone into her voice. "Go get it, then. Help yourself to a tumbler from the cabinet."

Ollie exhaled in a big rush, pleased Anna had resumed the teasing and hadn't made a big deal about it. At times like this she hated her leg. It was just something extra to spoil any lovely moments she experienced in life.

After limping away into the kitchen, she found a clean glass and swallowed the tablets with a grimace. When she shuffled back in, she wiggled the glass towards Anna. "It'll only take a few minutes to kick in." she said. She lowered her achy limbs onto the sofa. "Now, then, where were we?"

"I'm not sure we'd decided what to do after the film," Anna said, sitting next to Ollie, her wine glass between her hands. When Ollie trailed a hand over her back, Anna giggled shyly. She leant against Ollie's fingers when they moved up to her neck and then hesitantly across to her cheek.

"It's not that late," Ollie said, although when she looked at the clock, and discovered it was quarter to midnight, her heart sank. "Okay, I stand corrected."

"I've nothing to do tomorrow," Anna said, looking at Ollie with dark eyes.

Ollie narrowed her eyes in thought but was unable to keep up the facade, so she dropped her head. "I don't have anywhere to be either. Shop's closed tomorrow. I've got to do a stock take."

"I'd love for you to stay. But I'm…I'm sure you've got to get back."

"No, I don't need to start counting all my products until at least lunchtime." Ollie caught Anna's hand and looked up at her. Their fingers intertwined. "But…"

"But?"

"I think…" Ollie turned to look at Anna properly. She took the wine glass from her, placed it on the table, and then took her hands. Her lungs expanded wide as she took in a huge breath. "I think we should... I don't want to just fall into bed with you."

Anna lifted an eyebrow.

"No." Ollie's cheeks warmed, and she looked at their joined hands. "That's n-not what I mean. I do want to, of *course* I do, Anna, I just..."

"You want to take things slowly."

Ollie sighed at the understanding in Anna's eyes. "Do you think that's silly?"

"Not at all," Anna said, squeezing Ollie's hands in her own. "I think it's rather charming, actually."

"And a good idea?"

"Well so long as..." Anna lifted a hand to touch Ollie's cheek.

Ollie closed her eyes against the caress.

"...you don't make me wait too long," Anna finished.

"I won't."

"I'll be honest, I'm a little relieved." She flicked her eyes between Ollie and the floor. "First times and all that."

Ollie kissed her deeply.

Anna let out a little noise of surprise and amusement, which soon turned into delight as Ollie's arms wrapped around her, her fingertips skimming over her back. *I do love to kiss her.*

They kissed for a little while until Anna suddenly broke away. Her breathing was shaky and a bit fast. Ollie was relieved, given that she was having the same trouble.

Since when has a single kiss with a woman made you so...? The thought trailed away as she refused to even think the word to describe how she felt.

Anna stroked Ollie's cheek once before collecting the crumpled throw from the floor and pulling it over Ollie's legs to tuck it in round her right knee. "Save you getting cold," Anna said.

"I'm not an old lady yet, you know," Ollie said, and she caught herself, because she almost sounded offended. She tried to smile, sitting there with a crocheted throw around her legs.

To her relief, Anna's hands trailed up Ollie's arms, before coming to rest at either side of her neck. She rubbed lightly.

"We're the same age," Anna hissed into her ear.

Her tickling breath made Ollie shiver. "Mmhm."

They rested their foreheads against one another, their hands just sliding a little.

Ollie sighed. Her whole body felt like it was made of cotton wool. *Meds must be kicking in.*

"Would you like to stay, though?" Anna chewed her bottom lip.

Ollie realised she hadn't really answered. "If that's okay with you."

Anna nodded swiftly.

"I um…I don't have any pyjamas or…"

"You weren't a Girl Guide?" Anna asked. "You surprise me."

"I like to think I'm not presumptuous," Ollie replied and lifted her chin.

With a chuckle, Anna leant sideways against the back of the sofa, pulling Ollie with her. "I'm sure I can find something," she said, their noses almost touching. "Might be a bit baggy…"

Lips caught lips, and Ollie wasn't sure who'd started the kiss; didn't care really. They continued to kiss for several minutes, and Ollie enjoyed the quiet and the togetherness. Anna held Ollie's face, her fingertips digging into her scalp. A surge of something impassioned overcame Ollie, and she pressed Anna firmly against the back of the sofa, leaning on her good hip, and sliding her bad knee over Anna's. She couldn't kneel up properly, but Anna didn't seem to mind as her hands drifted down to Ollie's waist to sneak under her jumper and top.

Those fingertips touched her skin, and Ollie hummed her appreciation against Anna's lips.

The kiss deepened, tongues battling, occasional small moans emanating from both of them.

A slow heat crept between Ollie's thighs. *Uh-oh. I need a breather.* She broke the kiss but brushed her lips down Anna's neck, then to the collar of her big jumper.

Anna's hands lay flat against her back, stroking rhythmically up and down. It was a soothing gesture, and Ollie was thankful for it. Her heart slowed, allowing her brain to take charge of her libido.

Ollie buried her nose into the woolly material, snuggled in, her hand behind Anna's shoulder, caressing the soft yarn with her thumb. "I like your jumper," she murmured into it, turning her head to lay her cheek against the softness.

Anna stroked her cheek. "Specially picked out." Her other hand trailed down Ollie's thigh, before rubbing the side of her knee through the blanket.

The gesture was so tender that tears threatened behind Ollie's eyes. Burrowing in further, she felt like she wanted to burrow in all the way. She could smell something apple-like, and figured it was Anna's shampoo.

Anna squeezed her. "Feeling better?"

"Immensely," Ollie said.

Anna yawned and put a hand to her mouth. "Oh, I'm so…"

"Shhh," Ollie said, her fringe all over her face, and pressed a fingertip to Anna's lips. "You're chin-strapped. Let's go to bed."

"Thought you'd never ask."

Ollie climbed off Anna's lap, where she'd basically been sprawled, undignified but ever so comfortable, and held out a hand to pull Anna up too. Ollie combed her fingers through her own hair, trying to tame it back behind her ears. They folded the blanket, took their glasses into the kitchen, and Ollie locked Anna's front door. She could hear Anna clanking around in the kitchen.

Then Anna emerged, a soft smile on her face, and kissed Ollie lightly on the cheek, tugging on her hand to lead her upstairs.

Ollie wasn't sure what she expected when she entered Anna's bedroom—maybe she wasn't expecting anything specific. Style, certainly. Warmth, definitely.

The room was chocolate and cream with accents here and there of a colour she could only describe as *Merlot*. The bunny was perched proudly on the bedside table next to what Ollie assumed was Anna's side of the bed. Reading glasses and a coaster sat there too.

Anna moved into the room and turned on both lamps, one on either side of the bed, and then pulled the curtains. Stooping down by her drawers, she pulled hard and one opened with a light squeak. She fumbled around a little.

Her hands clasped, Ollie waited, trying to look more comfortable than she felt.

When Anna stood, she was holding a grey top and some tartan pyjama trousers. She tilted her head.

Ollie nodded and reached out for them.

They stood before one another, Ollie with a wad of clothes in one hand, Anna breathing rather deeply and sucking her bottom lip into her mouth.

Stop it. Ollie lifted a hand to lay it on Anna's shoulder. "I could go in the spare if you like?"

"I don't have one," Anna said. "Three-bedroomed house."

"Oh, okay."

Her gaze was trained on the carpet, but when she lifted it to Ollie's, her voice was quiet but confident. "I want you to sleep in here with me."

Ollie nodded.

After pointing into the en suite, Anna collected her own pyjamas and headed in.

A moment of shock kept Ollie attached to the ground for a minute more, and then she sprang into action. The last thing she wanted was for Anna to finish and find Ollie struggling into the pyjamas. Getting dressed was never a dignified occurrence for her.

She wobbled as she pulled her clothes off and then stepped into the slightly roomy pyjamas bottoms, before tying the drawstring so they didn't fall down. The long-sleeved cotton top felt so soft against her skin. The entire outfit smelled of apples, and Ollie hugged her arms around herself, allowing the scent to wash over her.

She folded her clothes, mindful of how neat and tidy Anna's bedroom was, and sat on the foot of the bed with her socks still on. She fiddled with her fingers as she listened to the sounds of Anna in the bathroom.

She had a further look around the bedroom to distract herself from her fluttering heart rate. The curtains were cream with a burgundy stripe along the bottom. The carpet was beige, and the rug at the bottom of the bed that lovely deep-red colour. She scrunched her toes into the rug, enjoying how squishy it was, even through her socks. It was a stark contrast to her threadbare one at home, the one that lay in front of her wood burner. *Maybe I'll buy a new rug.*

The furniture was solid oak, she could tell. Not like the mismatched assortment in her own flat. *Anna's so grown-up.*

With her hair a little fluffy at the front where she had washed her face and a little toothpaste at the corner of her lips, Anna returned to the bedroom. Ollie stood quickly and strode across to kiss it away before she could stop herself. When she pulled back again, Anna smiled, catching Ollie's jaw, and just looking at her.

"You look lovely in my clothes. I've left you a new toothbrush." Her thumb brushed Ollie's cheek.

"What service." Ollie went into the bathroom and closed the door behind her.

Anna folded her clothes, put the relevant items in the hamper, and settled under the covers. She turned off her bedside lamp, leaving the one on Ollie's side of the bed glowing dimly. *Does she like to cuddle in bed or would she prefer some space? Does she sleep well? Does she get up in the night like I usually do? Does she snore?* She smirked at that last thought.

She checked her phone and found a text from Bethany, wishing her a nice evening, with a wink emoji at the end. Anna rolled her eyes and sent her a brief but informative text back.

Hobbling back into the bedroom, Ollie fiddled with her fingers.

Anna held the duvet open for her. "I don't mind switching sides if you prefer."

"No, that's fine. This is fine." Ollie sat and turned off the lamp by her side of the bed before awkwardly swinging her legs in. Anna tried not to show the sympathy she felt, but Ollie must have noticed, even in the dim light from the streetlamps outside. "It's fine," she said. "Almost doesn't hurt."

"Does it stop you doing things?" Anna asked and then felt her cheeks burn when Ollie smirked and she realised the innuendo within the question.

Ollie lay down next to her. Anna could thankfully make out her features in the low light.

Curling her hands by her face on the pillow, Ollie shrugged. "I used to run a lot; can't do that anymore. Using the pool at the leisure centre is fine, although the adult pool can get a bit cold. I prefer teaching the smaller kids. We get to go in the baby pool, and it's much warmer."

"I never used to do any exercise, but I started going for regular walks recently, of an evening. When I can." Anna shifted to face Ollie, bending her knees up under the covers. She snuck a hand under her own head and blinked at Ollie in the darkness. "I've not been swimming for years."

"You should come with me when I go just for a regular swim. I really enjoy it."

Anna arched an eyebrow. *I'd like to see her in a swimming costume.*

Ollie blinked once, and Anna was sure she was having the same thought. "If you like."

A wave of tiredness flooded through Anna and she nodded. She pulled the duvet more firmly over her shoulder, tucking it in by her own neck. A shiver flew through her body, making her teeth rattle. Her bones stung with the cold, like it had seeped inside them and turned them to ice. "Don't know what on earth is going on with my heating tonight," she said, huffing. "Although damn, actually," she said, and then bit her lip, "it goes off at midnight. I'm usually fast asleep by now."

The mattress bounced as Ollie shifted closer, tickling her fingers by Anna's neck. "Are you a cuddler, Ms Rose?"

Relief washed through her and pulled a laugh from deep inside her belly. "I was going to ask you that," Anna said. "I do like a cuddle in bed, yes." She smiled wryly. "And I'm sure I'd appreciate a bit of shared body heat tonight."

"Come here, then, comrade."

Anna moved across the bed and shifted to lie against Ollie's shoulder, mirroring how they had cuddled together on the sofa. It was approximately a hundred times more comfortable, however, with all the space around them on Anna's big bed and the duvet wrapped around them like a cocoon. She slid a hand slowly across Ollie's flat stomach and felt the soft brushed cotton and the dip where her belly button was. She leant her chin against Ollie's shoulder and pressed her lips to her collarbone, now exposed by the slightly low cut of the pyjama top.

The skin beneath her lips puckered in goose pimples, but Ollie didn't complain, and Anna figured it probably wasn't the cold.

Anna's hand stilled, and she found herself taking pity on the lithe woman beneath her, supposing the effects she was having on Ollie were similar to those Ollie was having on her.

Ollie slipped her hand up around Anna's shoulders, her fingers curling between her shoulder blades. Her other hand reached across her own middle and slid over Anna's hand, cupped her elbow, and pulled so she rolled closer. She sighed deeply and comfortably.

Resting her knees against Ollie's thigh, Anna hummed at the warmth now spreading through her tired bones. The icy feeling was melting away.

"Goodnight, gorgeous," Ollie said. As soon as it left her mouth, her whole body tensed.

A happy-sounding noise vibrated in Anna's throat, and she pressed a kiss against Ollie's neck, and then another under her jaw.

The body beneath her relaxed. Ollie dropped her chin and they kissed gently. Her hand strayed to Anna's hip, her thumb rubbing the material of her pyjamas in time with the movements of their kiss.

Anna giggled against Ollie and grasped her fingers, holding them still. Her eyes flickered open, and she found Ollie staring at her, looking guilty. "Ollie," she growled, putting on a pout.

"Sorry," Ollie whispered, balling her fists for a beat before stilling her hands to hold Anna close.

It felt natural to tuck her fingertips under Ollie's back, and Anna snuggled against her shoulder.

"Warmer now?"

"Yes." Anna yawned widely and closed her eyes again.

"Hope you sleep well."

"I'm so comfortable," Anna said. "How could I not?"

"D'you snore?"

Anna chuckled deep in her chest. "I don't think so." *It's like she can read my mind.*

"Good."

"Night." Anna felt sleep drawing her down, like being pulled into a dark but safe ocean. Her body felt so heavy against Ollie's, but the shared warmth caressed her all around.

"Goodnight," Ollie said.

Chapter 10

The Tea Cosy

They had woken in one another's arms, slowly and tentatively, and then kissed with horrible morning breath that probably neither of them cared about. Anna certainly didn't.

They had shared touches and glances in bed before coffee and breakfast had called them downstairs. Ollie had ducked out of their comfortable pyjama-clad little world to retreat back to her own flat. Their goodbye kiss had not been short.

Their wonderful sleep together the previous night had convinced Anna—she *would* make Ollie something for Christmas. A teapot cosy seemed the thing after remembering a teapot in Ollie's flat, stored on a high shelf with a layer of dust covering it. Ollie obviously didn't have many people round, and certainly not many who would share a pot of tea with her.

Tea was delicious. Sometimes Anna drank more than one cup after another. She fully intended on suggesting they have a pot next time she went to visit. *It's silly for her to own something she never uses.* And with a cosy, it wouldn't get cold if they were otherwise occupied and left it for, say, half an hour. *An hour, maybe*, she thought wistfully.

She had seen Ollie's flat and knew the shades of her décor but was unsure whether the paint and paper were of Ollie's choosing. Anna wanted to know her favourite colour, or at least the one she would like for a pot-adorning crocheted item.

Asking Ollie directly would ruin the surprise. So, after discussion with her daughter, who had a more devious mind than Anna had realised, she texted Ollie, a plan ready.

Could I ask for Matthew's number? Beth has a friend who's gay; he'd really appreciate some support? Xxx

She added an extra *X* as Bethany clomped up the stairs to her university work. Hopefully Ollie would notice and take it as a direct result of their night together.

I spent the night with Ollie. Her stomach quivered at the thought, and she trailed the tips of her fingers over her neck, causing goose bumps. A few minutes later, she got a reply.

I'm sure he'd be happy to help, here it is. Xxx

The contact pinged to her phone a few seconds after Ollie's text. She sent a brief text of thanks back before pressing the number and calling Matthew.

He answered after a few rings. "Hello?"

"Matthew? Hi, it's Anna." There was a pause. *That's thrown him.* "Bit out of the blue, I know. Ollie gave me your number."

"Oh, okay," he said, and she heard a rustle, then silence; perhaps he had sat down. "What can I do for you?"

"I'll get straight to the point. I've obtained your number under false pretences, I'm afraid. Ollie is under the impression I'm going to give your number to Bethany."

"Not my type," he said without missing a beat.

"I know. I've told Ollie she has a friend who's gay and that her friend wants some support. She said you'd probably be happy to help, so here we are."

"Right. But that's not why you've got my number?"

"No," Anna said. "I…Matthew, I want to make Ollie a tea cosy. For Christmas. A little twee, I'm aware, but she seems to have everything else, and I do so want to make her something lovely."

I hope my voice doesn't display how eager I am, like some lovesick adolescent. She put her fingers to her forehead.

"She's a modest kind of person," he said. "Don't stress yourself out over making something too complicated. She'd be happy with anything you made her. Perhaps another bracelet?"

Ollie had shown him the bracelet. *How sweet.* "Ah, yes," Anna agreed. "But I would like to make her something special."

"She got that pot from Maggie. You know, the old lady who taught her to crochet." He sounded slightly wary.

"Oh." Anna's heart dropped. "Would she not want a cosy for it? I could make something else."

He paused and made a long noise, as if he were thinking. "Actually, I think a cosy would be a great idea."

"Do—do you?"

"Yep. Why not? She never uses that thing."

"I noticed. Okay." Anna set her jaw. "What colours do you think she'd like? I know her flat is mostly blue and grey. And green, isn't it?" *I wish I'd paid more attention to her décor.*

"Have you got a pattern?"

"I have," Anna said. "It's got flowers and leaves and a little butterfly on it."

"I'd say two different tones of blue flower, dark green leaves, and…" He made the thinking noise again. "Maybe pale yellow as the main cosy."

"And the butterfly?"

"Burgundy. That way there's a bit of you in there too."

He really was a sensitive lad. "Thank you. I knew you'd be the perfect person to ask."

"Because I'm an avid follower of Dorothy?" he asked, adding a mock-offended tone.

"No," she said, amused. "Because you know her much better than I do."

There was a pause. She wanted to ask Matthew if Ollie had mentioned her. *Maybe they're not the kind of friends to talk about their love lives.*

"Did you have a nice time last night?" He broke the silence.

"Um…yes. Yes, it was lovely, thank you."

"She slept over?" he asked, brazen as could be.

"Did she say she was going to?" *Maybe I can wheedle something out of him after all.*

"No, I just figured, dinner, movie—maybe she'd end up staying."

"Well, she did, if you must know." She paused for effect. "And that's all I'm saying."

He groaned, and she found herself laughing at the young man. "So unfair. The one time she has a date and I can't get any sordid details."

"I'll let Ollie tell you herself next time you see her."

He huffed and groaned again.

"And, speaking of Ollie, not a word about the cosy, okay?"

"Mum's the word."

"Good. Thank you ever so much for your help, Matthew."

"You're very welcome. Have a nice afternoon."

"You too."

Twenty days until Christmas. Ollie was speaking with a customer about buttons. She was trying desperately to listen, but her mind kept flicking back to how Anna had felt in her arms, the apple scent of her hair, and the warmth of her body.

The customer left the shop with a tinkle of the bell. Ollie nearly fell from her chair when Anna stepped out from around the corner, a hand up in greeting and her arms full of balls of yarn.

She smiled at Ollie from under her eyelashes, and Ollie nearly tripped over the corner of the desk to get to her. Anna stuck out her free arm and laughed as Ollie took the support with good grace.

"You prat," Anna said.

"Do excuse the clumsiness. Someone seems to make me fall over my own feet when they're around." She lifted a hand to cup Anna's cheek and then pressed a kiss of greeting to her lips.

They were careful, didn't want to get carried away in case someone came in. But the smouldering look on Anna's face was plain to see as the kiss broke.

"I should have said I was coming." Anna held out her chosen balls and then dropped them onto the desk.

Ollie rang up her purchases, knocking off twenty percent. She hoped Anna didn't notice. "I would have closed the shop for a few minutes," she said. "Made you a cup of tea."

Her cheekbones tinged with red, Anna stood fiddling with the strap of her handbag. *Why does she look nervous?*

"No need." Anna shoved the balls of wool into her cloth bag as if she wanted to get them out of sight as quickly as possible.

Ollie watched her curiously.

"I'm sorry to say I can't stay. Things to do."

Ollie's stomach fell as Anna looked over her shoulder at the door to the shop and then stepped around the desk to Ollie's side. Gathering her off the chair, she kissed her hungrily.

Responding in kind, Ollie moved her hands around Anna's waist to the small of her back and curled into her red coat. *I wish I could lift her up onto the desk.* Her body hummed. She settled for dipping her tongue into Anna's mouth and pressing her against the desk, relishing the little noises Anna made.

The simultaneous noises of Anna's handbag clunking to the floor and the little bell at the door ringing broke them apart. To Ollie's amusement, they were both panting.

Anna wiped her mouth and ducked away as Ollie smiled at the customer, who, thankfully, was Sarah. With her eyebrows raised, Sarah looked from one to the other and strode out of their line of sight with the pretence of looking at yarn.

Unable to stop the grin that made her cheeks ache, Ollie caught Anna's hand and kissed her knuckles. "I'll see you on Thursday?" she asked.

It seemed to snap Anna out of her embarrassment. She scampered away.

Ollie had nowhere to run, however, when Sarah sidled up to her. Anna's red coat disappeared out the door, and Ollie blinked at the snow starting to fall.

"So you finally got around to asking her out?" Sarah brought a couple of balls of yarn to the desk. She held them back, however, implying she wouldn't hand them over until Ollie answered.

"Sort of." Ollie held out her hand, her other arm folded across her front.

Sarah rolled her eyes. Ollie rung up her purchases.

I've known Sarah for years; I should be able to tell her things. "We had our first official date at the weekend."

A high-pitched squeal made Ollie's ears hurt, and Sarah grabbed Ollie's hands before pulling her half over the desk. A squeak of shock to nearly compete with Sarah's excitement ripped from Ollie's throat as she nearly fell forward, having to brace her hips against the desk. She stumbled and yanked her hands from Sarah's.

"Double date, then? With me and Christian?"

Ollie looked at Sarah in horror until Sarah's face broke into a grin. *Oh, she's joking.* "I think we'll pass."

After a strenuous day at the shop, Ollie relaxed on her sofa with a big mug of hot chocolate, sufficiently dosed up with painkillers. *I need to start planning my gift for Anna, at least get an idea what she'd like.*

She decided the best person to ask about this would be a family member. She had access to a certain daughter, however roundabout her way of contacting her might be.

She found Matthew's number in her phone and hit Call.

"Hello?" he said, stretching out the end of the word.

"Hey, Matthew. How are you?"

"About to fall head over heels for Noah Wyle in hospital scrubs."

She snorted. "Have you still not watched that *ER* box set?"

"I'm just doing it now."

"Say hi to Abby Lockhart for me when you get to season six."

He groaned. "I'll be asleep by then. Mashed into a vodka-induced stupor on my sofa."

"Living the life, soldier." Ollie paused as she took a mouthful of hot chocolate, allowing the sweetness to fill her senses.

"What can I do for you, anyway?"

"Oh, right." Ollie's voice was hoarse, so she cleared her throat. *This is so inappropriate, but I've got to ask.* "Um. Yeah. I was wondering if I could have Bethany Rose's number?"

He paused. "Oh. What for?"

"I want to get Anna something for Christmas, and I've no idea what to get her, and you know how I'm no good at subtlety."

He let out a seemingly involuntary 'ha'.

"Yes, all right. I was going to text her and ask what her mother would like."

"I don't have it anymore," Matthew said. "Deleted it once her friend texted me."

She stared into the dark depths of her drink. "Oh. Well, do you have her friend's number? Maybe you could ask him?" A pause. "Her?"

"It was a him," Matthew said, his voice a little strained. "And…I deleted it as well."

"Already?"

"It was brief. I put him onto the local LGBT support network. Sorry."

"You don't have it…written down or…?"

"No."

"Right. Tip-top." She tried to hide her disappointment. "Never mind, then."

"Were you going to make something…or…?" He left the question hanging.

"I don't know." *Dammit. Unless I actually go round when she's not there, I'm never going to get to talk to the kid.* "Anyway, thanks." She felt dejected.

"Sorry I couldn't help more."

"No problem."

"Bye, then." The line went dead.

What was that about? Matthew had sounded like he was making excuses, but he and Ollie didn't have the kind of relationship where you questioned things like that. *I'll just have to make a wild guess and hope she likes whatever I've made her. Damn!*

Ollie's phone rang a few minutes later. She stared at it and emotion bubbled within her. Helen's number flashed on the screen. *She's calling me. Finally, she's calling me.*

Answering the call, Ollie pressed her mobile to her ear. "Helen."

"Hello, Mum."

There was a pause. Ollie felt like she should say something, but Helen had called her, not the other way around.

"Um. Sorry. Should have maybe texted… Are you busy?"

"Not at all. Just sitting down with a hot chocolate."

"Yum."

Ollie pulled the drink towards her nose, hoping the sweet smell would comfort her racing heartbeat.

"So, anyway. Sorry." Helen seemed to be tripping over her words. Ollie gave her plenty of time. "Kieran said you have a new partner."

"That's right."

"I'm assuming she's a she."

Ollie swallowed. "She is a she, yes."

Silence. Then a noise of frustration. "Fine. Whatever. Just thought we should probably meet her."

"Meet her?"

"Kieran suggested it, but he wouldn't agree to it unless I was on board. And I am. Let's meet this woman." Her words were clipped, but Ollie was happy they were even conversing.

"Um...o-okay. Yeah, sure. Let's do it."

"Coffee? In that horrible place you chose last time?"

"You think it's horrible?"

Helen laughed. "It's not exactly top-notch dining, is it?"

"You wouldn't know. You left before you could properly taste their products."

"Hmm. Point taken."

"Anyway, Nailsea's selection of eateries is pretty sparse for a relaxed coffee out. Unless you want to do a pub?"

"I'm not going to a gay bar with you, Mum."

Ollie bit her tongue. *Sometimes she's just so cantankerous. She always was as a little girl.* "Okay. Have you got any suggestions?"

Helen sighed. "The greasy spoon will be fine."

Was she trying to be difficult or testing me? Ollie decided to let it go. "Okay. When, where?"

"Text me when you know when this woman is free."

"Her name is Anna."

"Okay. Whatever. Text me. And text Kieran too. I don't have time to be your go-between." Helen hung up without saying goodbye.

Ollie slumped back into her sofa and turned her head so her cheek snuggled into the throw spread over the back. *At least we're talking.*

Eighteen days before Christmas, Anna arrived on time to the crochet group, her cloth bag full of granny squares. She rocked back and forth on her feet, and tapped the cloth bag. *It feels like it's been ages since I've seen her.*

The smile Ollie greeted her with made her feel all toasty, as did the way Ollie reached out to catch her by the waist.

"Ladies," a voice sang behind them. Matthew popped his head around them in the doorway.

Ollie dropped her hands to her sides, and Anna bit back a groan of annoyance. *I'm going to have to have a word with that boy. Seems he is the king of inappropriate timing.*

Matthew looked between them and then rolled his eyes in something like frustration. "Honestly." He walked around them and disappeared into the dark corridor, then the classroom.

"No need to be discrete with Matthew, I suppose," Anna said.

"I suppose not." Ollie pulled her close. "Good evening, comrade."

"Good evening."

Ollie cupped the back of Anna's head gently in both hands and turned her smiling face upwards.

Anna looped her arms around Ollie's neck. They kissed briefly, and Anna felt light, as if her whole body were made of dust. *Those eyes, that hair.*

Lowering herself shakily into her usual chair next to Matthew and trying to ignore the smirk that seemed plastered to his features, Anna pulled out her squares. She joined two together, then two more, building the blanket slowly. The squares littered the table, a mass of blue, pink, yellow, and cream. She smiled in satisfaction—it looked like a cottage garden in summer.

My bedroom throw can be as girly as I like. I really don't plan on having a man in there anytime soon.

Ollie walked past a few times, and they shared a smile or two from across the room.

Anna made sure she touched Ollie's fingers when she handed her a cup of tea, which made her skin warm as Ollie moved away.

Anna worked solidly, sipping her tea between squares. She'd managed to make forty-eight, and a rectangle of eight squares long that draped over her lap and the table in front of her.

The room was bustling, everyone excited about their approaching family gatherings. She and Matthew didn't talk much, but they exchanged the occasional smile when another conversation drifted over concerning Christmas, or a funny anecdote was recalled. Fiona had brought in mince pies. Matthew and Anna both took one gratefully. They were good—sweet and spicy, with buttery pastry. Anna relished the lovely taste and texture with closed eyes.

Harry came over a couple of times, and Anna clocked the new additions of small touches and glinting eyes between him and Matthew. Matthew showed Harry a granny square he'd made with the pattern Harry had allowed him to borrow.

"That's fab, Matthew."

Matthew beamed at the praise. Their gazes locked, and for a moment Anna felt like she ought to leave them to their tiny, warm, private world.

His smile faded as he watched Harry go.

"Don't worry. I'm sure he'll be back in a while." Anna rubbed his arm.

"Hmm? Oh no. It's not that."

"What is it?" Anna slipped into a role she was used to. It was a role she used both at home with her children and at work, when a pupil was upset—half teacher, half mother. It seemed to work well in both cases, and Matthew's eyes were a little watery as he considered her question.

"He's just… I feel like a child when I'm with him. He's so sorted, and I'm…"

"You don't seem like a child to me. And believe me, I would know. I spend all day with them."

He breathed out a laugh. "Yeah. True." He finally smiled again, but then held his hand out towards the granny square he had brought. "I just… Look at this. It took me ages, and while I was making it, all I wanted to do was just make a simple, plain thing and then get on with something more fun."

"You don't find crochet fun?" Anna blinked in surprise.

"I do. Of course. No, I just don't see the point in making something really complex if all it's doing is hanging on a silly wall in the church hall."

"So why make the squares you've made at all?" The teacher in her was taking over from the parent.

"Because..." Matthew glanced over to Harry. "Harry was so pleased when he let me have the pattern. I wanted to him to think I wasn't some frivolous person that only does things if they're easy."

"Well, you're not. You made the square."

"But what about him? He's so...meticulous. The blooming horse is the most exciting thing he's ever done, and he researched the thing for months. I throw caution to the wind all the time and do stupid things because of it. I'm a child."

"You're really not. You have a good job, don't you?"

"I work in a solicitor's."

"Okay. And you have a place to live, and you don't get rip-roaring drunk every night. And you pay your bills and, I assume, aren't in reams of debt?"

"Just my student loan. To be fair, I've nearly paid that off."

"Good for you. See?" Anna patted his hand where it clutched his hook. "You're not a child. I think people are just different, but it doesn't mean they can't get along." Her gaze drifted to Ollie, who was bent over Amy's table. "Ollie and I are very different..." Ollie gave Amy a thumbs up, causing the young woman to smile.

When the two hours were up and everyone else had left, Ollie came to perch on Anna's table, the side of her thigh touching Anna's. Matthew seemed to have taken what Anna had said on board and caught up with Harry before he left.

Anna finished folding the completed blanket and then threaded her hands with Ollie's. They just gazed at one another for a while.

"Oh, I forgot to ask." Ollie looked down at her hands and fiddled with her fingers. "My daughter phoned me the other day. She wants—well they both want...to meet you."

"Oh." *So soon?*

"Yeah. I know. Bit out of the blue."

"That's great, though." Anna touched Ollie's arm. "I know you've been hoping they'll get in touch."

"Hmm. Yeah, I'm not sure how it will go. Just to warn you. Kieran will probably be fine, but Helen... I think she still hates me."

"She's eighteen, isn't she?"

"Just started uni, yep."

"How do you feel about them meeting me?"

Ollie looked a bit pale. "Terrified."

Affection surged inside Anna. "I'm not surprised."

"Do you mind? I mean, would you mind?"

"Not at all. If it's important to you."

Ollie nodded. "It is."

"Did they tell you when?"

"I'm supposed to get your availability."

"Well, I'm free Tuesdays from three, as I have a free period."

Ollie nodded, took out her phone, and wrote a text to both her children with the proposed date. She stared at her phone for a while, perhaps hoping for a reply, and then put it away. "I'll…I'll let you know."

"Okay."

Ollie blinked a few times and then looked down. Anna wanted to cuddle her close and keep her safe. *She must be so worried. What if her children don't like me?*

"This is beautiful." Ollie indicated the blanket on the table next to her, the ends neatly sewn in.

"Thank you." She kept her voice quiet.

Ollie cleared her throat. "A beautiful throw for… um… a-a beautiful woman." Ollie held her gaze as Anna's cheeks heated up.

"Well, you've been in my bed late at night. You know how cold it gets in my house." *Are we flirting? Properly flirting, with the actual intention to flirt?*

"Next time, feel free to stay round mine," Ollie offered. "I have a wood burner."

Anna groaned in something between excitement and pleasure. "You do? Why didn't I see that?"

"Too busy gazing at me, comrade?" Ollie's lips were pursed and her chin high.

"I think I'd quite like that. A picnic on your rug, in front of the fire."

The way Ollie brushed her fingertips up Anna's arm made Anna shiver. "Whatever the lady wants," she whispered, cupping her jaw.

Anna tugged her downwards and captured her lips. She kept her own hands in Ollie's one, and gasped as the fingertips of Ollie's other hand tickled the back of her neck. The angle was delicious, having Ollie leaning down to her, while she was seated in an old classroom chair. *Isn't this the ultimate teacher/pupil fantasy?* Anna tugged further, an overwhelming desire to have Ollie in her lap taking her over momentarily.

The kiss broke too early and Ollie pulled away, looking down at where Anna wanted her. Anna thought she could see an apology and sadness in her eyes. Ollie's lips twisted and she shrugged.

Oh. "Don't worry," Anna whispered. "It's okay, I understand. How about we swap?"

Ollie smiled. "I'm not sure I'd b-be able to restrain myself."

Anna's whole body flushed. She tugged Ollie towards the hallway, grabbing her bags and coat from her chair on the way.

"How about we plan our next dinner out, then?" Anna said, smoothing her hands around Ollie's neck. "Spanish? Day after tomorrow? I won't keep you out late."

"Sounds wonderful."

They moved together, lips brushing. Anna sighed contentedly. The sound seemed to spark something in Ollie, because she caught Anna's lips properly, kissing her with a swooping hunger. Ollie wrapped her arms around her, parting her lips over Anna's. Anna forced her hands into Ollie's hair, her fingers scratching a little at her scalp. The resulting moan from Ollie's chest made Anna laugh in delight against her lips.

When they broke apart, they were both grinning like idiots.

"I like kissing you," Ollie said, her gaze very obviously on Anna's lips.

"I like kissing you too." Anna stroked Ollie's cheek and waited a few moments before going back in for another kiss, softer this time. *I could kiss her forever.*

They eventually said goodbye, and Ollie locked up before walking up the stairs on shaky legs. She stumbled on the top step and shook her head. *I'm going to end up flat on my face one of these days.*

She turned the temperature on the shower down to cool, hoping it would calm her raging hormones. The spray made her already-oversensitive skin tingle, and when the water ghosted over her hard nipples, she arched her back, shaking. *Which stupid person told me cold showers dampen one's libido?*

She got out and dried off, every brush of the towel against her skin feeling like electricity. Images of kissing toothpaste from Anna's mouth flickered into her mind as she brushed her teeth. Ollie groaned and shook her head.

She lay in bed for a while, trying to think of anything at all that would distract her from the ache between her legs. *She's such a good kisser.* She screwed her eyes up. *Her lips are so soft.* Folding her arms across her chest, she breathed out a sigh. Her eyes slipped closed and her body sank into the mattress. *Maybe I'll just drop off to sleep.*

Half an hour later, this seemed like an impossible dream.

Anna seemed to have lit a fire inside her, more so than anyone before. Just a couple of kisses and she was soaked. The moans Anna had made, the way she had pressed her body close and clutched at Ollie's hair as they kissed all made her sure about one thing: *Anna wants me. And I want her too.*

This realisation allowed her to think of Anna's red hair while she caressed her clit, while she smoothed her other hand over her breast in the same rhythm. For the first time ever, she thought about another actual woman as she circled faster and faster over that bundle of nerves, against that place she had always thought of as something pure but tainted at the same time. The place a few women had touched her, the place she wanted Anna to touch, the place she wanted to touch on Anna.

When she came, it washed over her like a tickling tide and she moaned out loud, immediately smacking a hand over her mouth. Her back arched against the bed, her shoulders pushing downwards. As she relaxed down from it, her knee throbbed painfully. Her hand was warm as she rubbed at the offending joint—her whole body still shaking—and she turned onto her side. The pillow from the other side of the bed was comfortable as she rested her knee over it. She breathed for a while, allowing her heart to slow. Then she stretched her limbs out and pulled the pillow more comfortably between her legs. The whoosh of a sigh escaped her lips.

Her phone buzzed, and she smiled as she saw the goodnight text from Anna, only a hint of embarrassment swishing through her stomach. *It's okay. She doesn't know what you did. And even if she did, I don't think she'd judge you.*

She replied in kind, feeling only affection for Anna in her post-orgasmic state, reminding herself Anna had texted her before going to sleep and that this was positive. *She's thinking about me too.* Her phone buzzed again—a picture message, the new throw in situ on Anna's bed, a black-and-white cat curled up in the middle of it.

I'd forgotten she had a cat. Ollie wondered where he had scarpered off to when she'd stayed over. *I hope he's not jealous of Anna's new sleeping companion.*

Ollie snuggled into her duvet, comforted by the memories of being so very warm in the middle of December with Anna curled up around her.

She fell asleep and dreamed about baking warm apple pies on a frosty morning.

Chapter 11

Snow

They met outside the Spanish restaurant on Saturday. It was dark already; snow was drifting around them and had started to settle. It definitely felt like two weeks left until Christmas.

Anna stepped up in front of Ollie and placed her hands on Ollie's hips. Ollie thought Anna looked ethereal, her eyes deep and shining with affection, her woolly hat touched here and there with snowflakes. She leant down to brush their lips together.

The pain in Ollie's knee and back ebbed away. *She's better than paracetamol.* She pressed their lips together again. When they broke apart, they were both grinning, cheeks tinged pink from the cold.

"Come on, you." Anna put a hand against the small of Ollie's back. "Let's get you inside."

Ollie could hardly argue. They shrugged their coats, hats, and scarves off in the foyer and allowed the waiter to hang them up close to the radiator. Anna wore a deep-red dress, and Ollie could barely keep her gaze from the dipped neckline and gathered-in waist.

"What are you trying to do?" Ollie whispered close to her ear, caressing the back of her fingers across Anna's waist. "Kill me?"

Anna fumbled at her pendant, which only made Ollie's gaze shift to a sight even more alluring. The waiter led Anna to their table. Ollie trailed behind.

Am I dressed okay? Ollie hastened a glance down at her outfit. Patent leather shoes with laces, black slim-fitting trousers, and a black satin collarless blouse. A thin chain with a tiny heart nestled in the hollow of her throat. She had actually even brushed her hair and used a little mousse to keep it tamed. She was also wearing the crocheted star bracelet Anna had made for her. She wanted her to see it again, so she pulled back her sleeve.

Anna scoffed at it, blushing profusely. "You don't have to wear that thing, you know."

Shame coiled in Ollie's stomach. "But I like it." *Oh God, is it not posh enough? This restaurant is so fancy.*

A twinkling smile pulled at Anna's lips, though, and she touched the stars around Ollie's wrist. "I can hardly argue with that, can I?" When she brushed Ollie's skin, Ollie felt the tiny hairs stand up.

Anna's elegant bracelet sparkled; a chain with three delicate charms hanging from it. *Now that's posh. Oh well, I suppose if she's happy, I'm happy.* Taking a chance, noting the earliness of the evening, but also her own need to continue the contact, Ollie turned her hand over, palm up.

Anna accepted her offer and slid their fingers together. It made Ollie's shoulders relax.

The menu, however, caused her to squint and lower her head. "It's all in Spanish," she said quietly.

"It's okay, the English is underneath." Anna didn't seem bothered by the mistake. "Fancy sharing a mixed tapas to start? The *banderillas* look fantastic."

At the way Anna's lips caressed the word, Ollie's mouth watered so much she had to swallow. She didn't even glance at the English translation, didn't even care what it said. She nodded. Anna's smirk suggested she knew what was going through Ollie's mind.

They chose their main courses, and Ollie ordered a bottle of red for them to share. She was pleased when Anna squinted and smiled.

"We *can* have something else, you know," Anna said when the waiter left the table. "I do drink other things."

"But you really like Merlot." Ollie ran her thumb over the back of Anna's hand. "And these days I find I like it too." Their eyes locked, and Ollie wondered how she'd ever got through a day without seeing Anna smile. "You look stunning tonight, by the way." Her heart was pounding. Ollie would have not dared say that on a date with someone before. *She makes me feel so brave.*

As she tucked a curl behind her ear, Anna lifted her hand as though she was going to touch her face. Her fingers hovered for a moment, then fell, and red tinged her cheeks.

"So do you," Anna replied, tilting her head to one side, her earrings twinkling from below her hair. "That blouse is very flattering."

"I…I went shopping." Ollie dropped her gaze to her empty place setting.

"Did you?" Anna said. "Well, what a good choice. You have great taste."

Their wine arrived, and after Anna tasted it, she lifted her glass in salute. "Great taste in wine too."

Ollie clinked her glass against Anna's. "Thank you."

"So," Anna began, her eyelashes lowered, "I was going to ask. What are your plans for Christmas?"

Ollie grimaced and then chewed her lip.

Anna squeezed Ollie's fingers. Ollie wished she could take back the grimace and hoped Anna didn't feel sorry for her.

"Nothing," Ollie replied, her free hand idly poking at the base of her wine glass. "I tend to get a ready meal in. Lazy, I know, but I really can't be bothered when it's just me by myself. The kids always go to their dad's. Matthew and I usually have a drink Christmas Eve…" She gave Anna an apologetic look. "I suppose you're spending Christmas Day with a huge family sat around your big table, a massive spread—"

"Actually," Anna said and Ollie looked up at her, "Timothy and his friend Adam are spending Christmas watching old *Doctor Who* episodes at Adam's house, Beth is going to her father's mother's for Christmas dinner, and I will be all alone with Arthur for the day."

Who on earth is that? Does she have a new boyfriend already? "Arthur?"

"My cat."

"I keep forgetting you have a cat."

"Not a very sociable one, going by your recent visit." Anna rolled her eyes. "After you'd left, I found him in the study, curled up under the radiator."

Ollie figured she probably wouldn't have noticed the cat unless he'd landed on her with his claws spread. *That green jumper held my attention rather well.*

"I'll hunt for him next time you're over." Anna caressed the back of her hand again, which made Ollie smile. "Make sure he comes to say hello."

"There'll be a next time?"

"Of course," Anna said. "You have yet to meet Timothy, and you've barely met Bethany. They'd like to get to know you."

Meeting the kids, that'll be a first. Ollie thought back to all her other relationships. Either there was so much secrecy Ollie had never met her partner's...anything. Or the relationship had been so brief, amounting to a quick fumble in the back of pub. *Anna's meeting my kids in a few days.* That thought made her stomach clench, but she forced herself to focus back on her date and her lovely red dress.

Their sharing platter arrived, and they spent many moments feeding one another oily olives, tasty ham, and skewers with tart, pickled items on them. Ollie found it half-sexy, and half-comical in the end, especially when she dripped oil down Anna's chin, apologised profusely, and nearly set fire to the napkin as she reached over with it to help. The oil dripped down Anna's front, and she took the napkin from Ollie with a smirk. The addition of a gleam in Anna's eyes made Ollie press her thighs together and look away for a self-preserving minute.

There was rustling as Anna dabbed at her cleavage. "Sorry," she said, but when Ollie looked back at her, she looked anything but.

Their starters were cleared away and their mains brought to them before Anna seemed to realise their conversation hadn't exactly concluded. "Oh, so I was going to see whether... I'm not sure if this is... As you're all by yourself for Christmas, and so am I, I wondered whether..."

The way she fumbled over her words was endearing. *She's usually so confident. At least I have an effect on her too.* "I ought to invite you round to mine," Ollie said eventually, taking pity on her. "You fed me already. And I'm sure I remember you saying something about a picnic in front of my log burner."

A thankful look flooded Anna's features. She reached across the table to take Ollie's hand from where it rested on her fork. "A picnic on Christmas Day?"

Ollie nodded but then thought about it more as she detected an unsure tone in Anna's voice. *Does it sound childish? What if she doesn't want that?*

"What could be more romantic?" Anna tickled her fingers against Ollie's.

Thank God. "I'd book a string quartet and half a tonne of rose petals, but I don't think they'd all fit in my flat."

The tension eased considerably after that. Anna chuckled and squeezed Ollie's fingers before letting her go. She cut into the deep-coloured venison with relish.

They ate for a minute or two, but it wasn't long before Ollie's self-doubt began to niggle again at her insides. She needed confirmation. "So… so would you like to come round? If you don't, that's fine. We can have a picnic another day."

"I'd love to," Anna said. "Would you like me to bring anything?"

"No that's…that's okay. Um…" She speared a potato on her fork and looked at the perfect little chargrilled lines on it and wished she could produce something as decadent from her kitchen. "Is there anything you don't like?"

"No," Anna said, grinning with something that looked like pride in her eyes.

What do I make us, then? They could hardly have a full Christmas dinner on Ollie's rug. Maybe she could seek help from somewhere? Matthew was even worse at this stuff, though. His idea of a posh meal was to decant the takeaway food into ceramic dishes rather than eating it out of the plastic containers it arrived in.

Her worry must have shown on her face, because Anna's hand was covering hers again.

"Ollie," she said, and Ollie looked up. "Anything you make will be lovely. And just spending time with you at Christmas will be wonderful enough."

"All right." The rushing sound in her ears quietened. Her chest ached for a moment, and she pressed her hand against her sternum, waiting for it to ease. She looked up and saw Anna's little smile directed her way, and that was all it took: the ache dissolved into the warmth and the candlelight between them. She was here now in this beautiful restaurant, with this beautiful woman, and she felt good, confident, and safe.

After deciding against dessert, they gathered their coats, hats, and scarves around them and made their way out into the snow. Anna caught

Ollie's hand in her own and stuffed them both, joined, into the pocket of her big red coat. Her grey handmade scarf was tucked into the front, and Ollie hoped it was stopping the light but icy breeze from shooting down the front of her coat. Anna tugged on Ollie to indicate they walk in the opposite direction to Ollie's flat.

"Let's go for a walk? It's so gorgeous out tonight."

Ollie nodded, and they moved through the orange-tinged snowfall, their boots crunching in the lightly settled snow. Flakes fell all around them.

"My teaching assistant, Rachael," Anna began with a small smile, "she told me today that she's never seen real snow."

"How old is she?"

"Twenty-five."

"Wow." Ollie's breath spiralled upwards.

"I know," Anna said. "It used to snow every year, didn't it? Without fail. But now, not so much." She shrugged. "Kids these days."

"I remember getting snowed in when we lived in Strensall. I think I must have been eleven, maybe twelve. And then it rained all spring, and our barracks flooded."

"Barracks?"

"My father was in the army too. Infantry officer. He trained the new recruits to shoot guns."

Their boots crunched along the pavement. "Did you move around a lot?"

"Some," Ollie said, snowflakes dusting her fringe where it poked out of her bobble hat. The streetlights shimmered across her vision, the light split by the snowflakes on her eyelashes, and she blinked rapidly to remove them. "Not as much as some of the kids we hung around with."

"We travelled a great deal too." Anna's fingers scissored inside her pocket between Ollie's. "Mostly with my mother's job."

"Siblings?"

"Nope. You?"

"Three brothers."

"Are you in contact with them?"

A particularly strong gust of wind blew towards them from down an alleyway and Anna cuddled up closer to Ollie's side for a moment. Ollie thought she would step away once the chill was gone, but she continued walking close to her, their shoulders touching.

"Not anymore." An ache, a different one than before, began to winch itself around in Ollie's stomach. *Not a part of my life I'm particularly proud of.*

But Anna just smiled and pulled her close. She coaxed Ollie down to rest her cheek on her shoulder as they held one another, hands still bundled up snugly in Anna's pocket.

"They're devout Catholics," Ollie said. "We were in touch before all the mess with my ex-husband. He decided it would be appropriate to tell my entire family what I had done, so…it's been a few years since I've been on their Christmas card lists."

Anna rubbed Ollie's back through her coat and pressed her cool lips against her cheek. Ollie closed her eyes into the kiss and found that Anna was moving them towards the shadowy gateway of a house, between two tall hedges. She pulled back and took her hand out of her pocket, then untangled their fingers. Bare fingertips smoothed Ollie's cheeks and Anna let her thumbs linger on Ollie's cheekbones. When Ollie could concentrate again, Anna's eyes were wet.

A lump formed in Ollie's throat. She tried to duck away, but Anna's hands on her cheeks meant there was no hiding the single tear Ollie felt rolling down her cheek. She closed her eyes in embarrassment. But Anna seemed not to care. She leant forward, touched her lips to the place on Ollie's cheek where the tear had trickled, and kissed it away. Then she pressed gentle, slow kisses all over Ollie's cheek, down to her jaw, around and over her chin, and across the other cheek.

Ollie opened her eyes, staring in wonder at the glorious woman kissing her. She sprang into action, caught Anna's lips with her own, and wrapped her arms around her.

The ache in her stomach faded.

A bitter wind whipped her face and swept Anna's scarf to one side. Ollie pulled it back gently around Anna's neck and dropped a last kiss to her lips. "Let's go back. I'm about to start shivering."

Anna gazed up at her with wide shining eyes and then brushed her cheek with the backs of her fingers. "Your brothers are idiots."

Ollie snorted.

"I'm serious," Anna insisted. "You're kind and beautiful and talented and strong and fantastic." She shrugged. "Why on earth would anyone want to cut you out from their lives?"

"Some people just can't deal with it." Ollie traced little circles behind Anna's ear.

Anna placed her hand atop Ollie's. "Some people need to get a life. There are worse things in the world, surely, than two women being together?"

They stepped out onto the street again, hands joined and back in Anna's pocket. Anna leant her head against Ollie's shoulder as they walked back the way they had come. Her hat was soft under Ollie's cheek. "I just think anyone would be crazy to not want you in their life."

"I don't mind how many people are in my life," Ollie said as they walked along, feeling inordinately brave, "so long as one of the people is you."

Warm fingers squeezed Ollie's hand. "I feel the same."

They walked together to Ollie's door. Ollie shifted so Anna was in front of her and slipped her hand into Anna's other coat pocket, making Anna giggle, slide close to her, and look upwards towards the window to Ollie's apartment.

"Do you have your decorations up yet?" she asked.

"Yep. A plastic tree covered in little crocheted snowmen and reindeer."

"Do I get to see?"

Anna's voice had dropped about an octave, and Ollie bit her lip. She was sure she looked hesitant.

Anna stroked her thumb over the back of Ollie's hand and her gaze seemed to be searching Ollie's expression. "But you know what? I can wait until Christmas Day."

"Probably best," Ollie said. *I don't want to rush it. I don't feel ready just yet. I want it to be special.* She shifted on the concrete, her knee screaming at her. *It's truly beautiful out here, and I really do not want the night to end.*

Anna squeezed both her hands. "Perhaps we should just wait inside while I call a taxi?" she asked. "I promise I'll keep my hands to myself."

"Roger that," Ollie said, taking her hands out of Anna's pockets and pulling her keys from her own. She unlocked the door as Anna took out her phone, pulled the door closed behind them, and stood against the radiator.

"Oh, for goodness sakes," Anna said, huffing and staring at her phone, the screen glowing blue and lighting up her face.

Ollie frowned. "What?"

Anna huffed again, dropping the hand holding her phone. "Liam. He's been texting me, begging for my forgiveness. I suppose he's had too much whisky."

Ollie's jaw stiffened and she folded her arms, shaking her head. "No. That's not okay." Her tone came out low, and she felt some of the strength from her army days collecting in her muscles.

Anna looked up at her, eyebrows rising. A smile pulled at her lips. "It's nothing, really. He's just all 'why can't we work it out' and 'I'm so much better for you than that…'" Anna sucked at her lip. "You get the idea."

Ollie stood with her fingers touching her chin for a moment. "Have you asked him not to text you?"

"About six times, if I'm not mistaken."

Ollie spoke slowly. "If you've asked him not to contact you and he *is* contacting you, that's harassment."

Anna cocked an eyebrow, reached to rub Ollie's arm. "I do know that."

"So, call the police," Ollie said with a shrug.

There was a pause as Anna rubbed at her forehead. "I don't know. He might react rather unpleasantly, and I'd rather not have to deal with that." She looked around her, head lowered. "He knows where I live, and where I work."

Not wanting Anna to think she was unable to keep her anger in check, Ollie forced herself to relax. *She can take care of herself.* "Maybe give him an ultimatum?" Anna's hand was still on Ollie's arm, and Ollie laid her palm over it.

Her lips twisting this way and that, Anna re-examined her phone.

"Tell him if he doesn't leave you alone, you'll report him to the police?" Ollie took in a big breath. "I don't like to see you all…" She shrugged.

Sparkling eyes smiled up at her. "You're very sweet." Anna sighed and stared at her phone, her face creasing in a frown.

Redirecting her emotion to try to soothe Anna, Ollie caressed her knuckles and gave her a moment.

"You could always block him," Ollie said. "He won't even know you did it if you don't tell him."

"Block?" Anna looked up from her phone with a frown.

"You know." Ollie turned so they could both look at Anna's phone. "Block his number. He can send all the messages he wants, but they won't get through to you. You won't have to see them."

Anna's eyes were wide. "You can do that?"

Ollie leant to kiss her cheek and felt Anna shaking with laughter against her. "Yes, you can do that, comrade."

The little screen was bright in Ollie's hallway. They worked together to write and send a text, stating clearly what Anna wanted, and what was going to happen if he didn't follow her instructions. Then, with a flourish, Ollie scrolled down to his contact, and pressed Block.

"Let's hope he doesn't decide to turn up at my door." Anna stared at her phone, then turned back towards Ollie.

"If he does you really can call the police. You've made it very clear what you want."

All the frustration seemed to float from Anna as she nodded in agreement. "Thank you."

Ollie smiled. *She's happy, that's all I care about.* Stepping away so Anna could talk to the taxi company, Ollie rubbed her hands together and blew into them.

"Ten minutes," Anna said as she hung up.

Ollie held an arm out to her and pulled her around the waist so they were flush against one another and could feel the heat from the radiator. Anna unbuttoned her coat and wrapped the sides around them both. The warm air filtered inside it. Ollie snuck her hands under Anna's coat and held her sides, rubbing the undersides of Anna's ribs.

"Now who can't keep their hands to themselves?" Anna asked, cocking an eyebrow at her.

"Just trying to keep you warm, comrade."

"Your hands are cold," Anna said, pouting.

"My mother always taught me it's friendly to share." They were very close, so close Ollie could feel Anna's breath on her face.

Anna's eyes closed like a cat's, and she leaned her head a little to the side. She tilted her chin up.

Unable to keep her gaze from Anna, Ollie just looked at her. She pretended to not know what Anna wanted.

Anna tilted her chin more and then pinched Ollie's side, causing her to squeak. "Would you just kiss me, please?"

A laugh later, Ollie had pressed their lips together.

I feel like we're the only ones in the world. She held Anna close, their shared body heat mingling between them. When headlights flashed outside and Anna's phone bleeped with a text from the taxi company, they broke apart.

"Until Tuesday?" Ollie asked, feeling like it was a terribly long time until then.

"Yes. I'm glad we could arrange a time when we're all free."

"And then Thursday. Three times in seven days. I do feel special."

"Oh, um, actually." Anna sucked at her lip. "I can't make it to the crochet group this week."

"Oh," Ollie replied, her voice small. She made an attempt at a brave face. "Okay."

"Sorry," Anna said, her gaze sliding sideways. "It's not because I don't want to come, it's just...I have things to do." She shrugged. "Christmas, you know."

"Okay."

Anna smiled and pulled Ollie down to her, before kissing her firmly on the lips. "But I'll text you, and we'll see each other on Tuesday."

"You might have to save me from my children." She let Anna go, waited for her to button her coat up and pull her hat down over her ears, and then opened the door for her.

"Text me when you get home."

"Of course." She stepped down from the side door and strode over to the taxi. Ollie watched her sit inside and wiggle her fingers in a little wave as it drove away.

Delightful tingles spread through her as she locked the door and went up into the flat to make herself a hot cocoa and a hot water bottle. *Coffee on Tuesday is good. And I suppose her not being there means I can focus on the other members of the crochet group for once.*

Ollie worried about the meeting with her children all of Sunday, all of Monday, and all day Tuesday. At five to four, Ollie locked up the shop and limped down the street, her coat and scarf pulled tightly around her. She was sweating, even though it was freezing cold.

Anna was already in the café when she arrived. Ollie went to her and kissed her hard on the lips, her insides fluttering. When they pulled back, Anna stroked her cheek. "It's all right. I'm here too."

"Any minute now," Ollie said, her gaze trained on the door.

Kieran and Helen arrived on time and together.

"Hi, guys." Kieran breezed through the door. Confidence shone from him as he held out his hand to shake Anna's. "So nice to meet you, finally."

Anna beamed at him and shook his hand warmly. Then she turned to Helen. "Hi. I'm Anna."

The same hardness radiated from Helen that Ollie had been privy to when they'd met up a few weeks before.

"Hi." Helen narrowed her eyes at Anna and moved around the table to sit before Anna could offer her a hand to shake.

Kieran patted Ollie on the back and sat too. Ollie tripped over her chair as she rounded it to go to the counter.

"Cake, kids?"

"No thanks, Mum." Kieran gave her another smile.

Helen shook her head. "Just tea."

Kieran winked at Ollie. Ollie leant heavily against the counter.

"Mum says you teach English," Kieran said.

"That's right." To Ollie's pleased surprise, Anna sounded tentative but confident.

"You like it?"

"Yes, I love it. Perhaps a bit too much sometimes." It was meant as a joke, and Kieran laughed.

"So you're a workaholic?" Helen asked.

"I used to be," Anna said, her voice level. "Recently, though, I've relinquished some of my responsibilities."

"You're part-time now?" Kieran asked, his tone intrigued.

"Nope. Still do a full week. But I used to run book clubs at lunchtimes and after school. And I do that less now."

Throughout their conversation about the clubs, Ollie noticed that Helen remained, on the whole, fairly quiet. *She's also not making nasty remarks, so I suppose that's good.*

The swirling sensations that had buzzed around her stomach since she'd arranged the meeting were beginning to calm. She slid into the chair next to Anna and they exchanged a smile.

"We've both given up a few things, haven't we?" Anna said, moving her hand across Ollie's thigh for a brief moment before she removed it.

Ollie nodded. "I'm thinking about only doing two swim lessons a week instead of five. And I'm looking into getting an assistant for the shop."

"That's great." Kieran seemed genuinely pleased.

"Yeah," Helen agreed, although there was a spark of derision in her eyes.

Ollie allowed her children to quiz Anna about her life. She supposed it was only natural. *I'd be like that with anyone they brought to meet me.* It struck her how grown-up they were becoming, bringing up topics like work and family. She'd had outdated expectations of them, talking about television and the latest music craze when they were children.

Their drinks arrived a moment later, and Helen actually drank her tea, although her attitude wasn't much improved. *Never mind. Perhaps she just needs more time.*

Once Kieran and Anna had discussed things like the finer points of growing dahlias and various novels they had both read, Helen folded her arms. The whole of Ollie's body tensed.

"You seem lovely," Helen said to Anna, "but I'm sorry. I don't like this. I don't want you dating my mother."

Ollie's heart dropped. She closed her eyes briefly.

Keeping Helen's gaze steadily, Anna nodded. "Is there anything specific you feel especially strongly about?"

Helen blinked as if she hadn't expected Anna to be interested in why she felt the way she did. "Um. Yeah. The gay thing."

"'The gay thing'?" Anna asked gently. Ollie marvelled at how natural the word sounded on her tongue.

"Yeah. It's gross. And unnatural."

Kieran stared at his sister in disbelief. "Really?"

Helen nodded once. "Really. I disapprove." Her knuckles were white as they gripped her forearms. "So, there you go. I don't like it."

"What's it really about?" Anna asked. "From what I've heard about you, and Ollie does talk about you a lot, you haven't been brought up as someone that would have an issue with it."

Helen's mouth opened and she seemed stuck, like a fish in glue.

"You're not a homophobe," Kieran said with a similar expression.

"I know I'm not." Helen unwound her arms to poke at the handle on her teacup. "I just don't want my mother dating a woman. It's gross."

Ollie sighed. So that was it. *She's being a stroppy teenager and going with her gut rather than thinking about it rationally. Fine. That I can deal with.* She thought back to her time in classrooms in England before she was sent to various countries with the army and the fantastic but difficult kids she'd taught back then. She'd had her share of stroppy, malicious teens out for a fight.

"Helen, listen. I know you hate me, or at least what I did." Ollie felt Anna's hand back on her leg, but low down, next to her knee, a source of comfort she drew strength from. She took a deep breath. "Whomever I date—and I am allowed that privilege, you know—I'm a human being. Whomever I date, you won't be happy. I'm…I'm g-gay, and that's not going to change."

Helen rolled her eyes and refolded her arms. She glanced behind her towards the door.

"Don't even think about running off before I've finished." Ollie leant her elbows against the table and focused solely on her. "You do not get to say your piece and then dash off before you hear what I have to say."

"I'm your ride, anyway," Kieran muttered.

"Helen, I'm not going to stay single and lonely just because you're under some illusion that you have a say in what I do or who I spend time with. You're my daughter. I take your views very seriously, but you're still punishing me for something I can't take back. And I won't take your views seriously if they're just irrational."

Helen looked down at her hands.

"I like Anna, and I'm going to date her. How you feel about that doesn't influence my choices."

The gaze that drifted to the ceiling truly did remind Ollie of her old days teaching. "Fine. Whatever. Do what you want, Mum."

She didn't leave, though. She slowly lifted her cup and sipped her tea.

Anna's hand squeezed Ollie's leg. Her eyes held affection and encouragement.

They drank their teas, and eventually Kieran started up a conversation about plants again. *My son the horticulturist. Who'd have thought?*

He and Anna talked for another half an hour, and they all had another cup of tea. Helen stared into her drink moodily, and Ollie wondered whether she was looking for more arguments in the steam. But she didn't talk again. She also didn't leave until Kieran announced he needed to get back.

Helen stepped into Ollie's arms and gave her a wooden hug. Ollie rested her cheek against Helen's hair and said, "I'll see you very soon."

Thursday was odd. Ollie was so used to Anna's presence at the crochet group that she was disappointed about the empty chair next to Matthew once everyone had arrived.

Sarah and Christian had come, dressed in their matching accessories. Matthew's eyes were full of something Ollie identified as gentle understanding as he watched her move around the room. She made everyone a drink and fingered the mug with blue flowers on it. *Anna's mug.* She put it back in the cupboard.

She's phoning you later. Stop being a lovesick wimp. Ollie set her jaw. She forced herself to make the evening an enjoyable one for all in attendance. An extra bounce flooded her step. She couldn't help but tease Sarah and Christian as they gazed lovingly at one another. She gave Matthew a hug when he told her that he and Harry had made it official. He was all smiles.

Good. He needs some stability and happiness in his life.

Now she had something she could relay to Anna later, a piece of gossip that would make her smile.

Ollie washed up the mugs after everyone had left, making sure to wear her washing-up gloves. *Although, perhaps Anna would give me another massage if my hands became sore.* She shook her head, her mouth tugging into another grin. Anna's good books were a lovely place to be, as nice as a massage sounded. She ought to do what she was told. She blinked. *This is very unlike me—what happened to the Ollie that ignored the order to run and stayed to protect her class from a raid?*

She was just popping the last mug away when her phone rang. "Good evening," she said, leaning back against the work surface.

"What're you wearing?"

"My usual crochet-group attire." Ollie shrugged. "You know, thigh-high PVC boots, my string vest."

"Nothing else?" Anna was laughing.

"Nothing else."

Anna's laughter was infectious. "How was your day?"

"Okay, thanks, comrade. Yours?"

"Busy," Anna sighed but sounded fulfilled and happy. "My hands are killing me."

"Been writing end-of-term reports?" Ollie idly scuffed the toe of her boot against the carpet. "I remember those well from when I started teaching."

"Nail on the head."

"Working late, then?"

"You could say that."

There was a pause. Ollie chewed her lip. "Want to hear some gossip?"

"Always."

Ollie chuckled at the relief in Anna's voice. "Matthew and Harry are together."

"Finally." Rustling on the other end of the phone made Ollie imagine Anna settling down. Anna's breath echoed cavernously in the bowl of what Ollie was sure was her wine glass as she took a sip. "How did they manage that?"

"Matthew said you had a serious talk with him last week."

"Ah, yes."

Ollie chuckled. "What did you say to him? Must have been very persuasive."

"I might have gone a bit 'strict teacher' on him, I'm afraid. Told him it was all okay and that just because he and Harry are different people doesn't mean they won't work as a couple."

"I've been telling him that for ages." Ollie's mouth opened in mock dismay. "That boy never listens to me."

"I obviously have some kind of charm that gay men fall for."

Ollie laughed. "Not just gay men, you know."

"No?"

A pause while they both hummed happily over that fact.

"I suppose Sarah and Christian were there tonight?" Anna asked.

"They were," Ollie said. "Matching outfits and all."

Anna made a gagging noise and Ollie laughed.

"Don't take the mickey. Apparently we're just as bad."

"Who told you that?" Anna asked, sounding mock offended.

"Matthew."

"We'd better get some truly sickening outfits, then. I'm thinking jogging suits in pink and blue."

"Disgusting," Ollie said. "However, I'm not sure I mind being disgusting with you." There was a pause. She hoped she hadn't said the wrong thing.

"In that case, we shall just have to be disgusting together."

Ollie smiled and relaxed, moving over to the door. She turned out the lights before locking the side door and shuffling in the dark towards her stairs.

"How's your knee today?" Anna's voice made Ollie feel very comforted, without a single hint of irritation sparked by Anna's concern.

She huffed, however, and leant heavily on the banister. A deep breath filled her lungs and the dusty smell of the staircase made her grimace. "I hate the winter," she grumbled.

Anna made a tiny sympathetic noise. "I can imagine." The care in her voice made Ollie's irritation at her own inadequacies ease a bit.

"I'll take some ibuprofen when I reach the top of my stairs." Ollie groaned and gripped the banister as a particularly strong pain squeezed her knee. "Give me an hour."

"Oh, love," Anna said, and Ollie was hit by the word, the ominous four-letter word neither of them had spoken to one another yet. She tapped the banister with her fingers to rid herself of the anxiety that word evoked before she hauled her mangled body up the last step.

"I've reached the summit."

That made Anna giggle, which made Ollie smile despite the pain. "To the medicine cabinet with you."

"Yes, love," Ollie replied, forcing herself to echo the word. *Relax. It's important to say it back.*

"So your day was okay?"

Ollie filled a glass with water and popped two tablets into her hand. "Everyone's winding down now for Christmas," she said with a sigh.

"Pretty quiet, then?"

"Yep. Very boring."

"Anything from your kids?"

"A couple of texts. Kieran thanked me for cups of tea and the chat. He seems to like you, so that's something. Helen actually said we should meet up again after Christmas. She didn't specify whether she meant you as well, though."

"I don't mind. Must be really confusing for her. Having her mother be with someone else, someone who isn't her dad."

"She's had five years to get used to it."

A hum vibrated in Ollie's ear. "Found yourself an assistant yet?"

"I put an advert out in the local paper, I'll have you know."

"Really?"

"Yes." She took a deep breath. "One day a week at first. Then perhaps stretching to two if I feel it's working out. And the swimming lessons? I've made it official. I've asked the leisure centre to reduce my classes to two a week. Five is too many."

"Good."

"I must confess, though," she said before swallowing the tablets with a gulp of water. "I feel quite uneasy about it. Having so much time on my hands. And relinquishing control of my shop to someone else. What if they do something I'm not happy with?"

"If you want any help interviewing," Anna said, "I'm quite used to that."

"Head of department?"

"Used to be. Gave the job to Jack when Timothy moved in. More important things, you know?"

"Senior management, hmm?" Ollie leant against her kitchen counter, her fingers at her chin. "I find that quite sexy."

"Do you?"

"I expect you've told a lot of people off in your time. Adults, I mean."

"I've done my fair share of supervision and appraisals."

Ollie moved towards her sofa and snuggled her shoulders back into the cushions. "Me too, although not for a long while."

"Try not to be too 'army sergeant' when you're showing whoever the new person is the ropes."

"Like I said, it's been a long time since I've held any authority over anyone except myself."

"Because...you know..." Anna's voice had dropped in tone as well as volume. "If anyone gets to see that side of you...it should be me."

That made Ollie start. "Unexpected."

Anna laughed. *She sounds nervous.*

"Not unwelcome," Ollie said.

An exhalation of air. "Okay."

Warmth settled around her. "Anyway. What about you? All those book clubs you do? Why don't you give some to...Jack, is it?"

"He is keen, I'll admit. But I do love them. And I'm not sure I'd be able to explain what I do, to him."

"He runs them too, doesn't he?"

"Only a couple a week."

"He's qualified. I'm sure he'd be fine."

"I wouldn't want to let anyone down."

"I don't think you would be."

"It feels like I've been working so hard for so long, I'll end up just sitting with too much time to think."

"I know that feeling. I did that a lot when I came out of hospital."

"But you threw yourself into crochet, didn't you?"

Ollie nodded. "This is true." She glanced down at her watch. "You're working tomorrow."

Anna hummed affectionately. "I am."

"I'll let you get some sleep."

"What makes you think I'm not already in bed?" There was a depth and softness to Anna's words, and Ollie had to physically hold back from jumping in a taxi to Anna's house and hopping into her bed with her.

"Drinking wine in bed?"

"How on earth did you know that? Anyway, I'm all on my own. Need some kind of company, don't I?"

"Tease." Ollie relaxed a little.

"Goodnight, love," Anna whispered.

"Goodnight, Anna."

They met for coffee a few more times at the small café they had begun to call their own. The coffee was good and the cakes spectacular. The staff automatically provided them with two forks when they bought a slice now. Anna liked the cosiness there, the gentle ambient music, and the way Ollie looked at her over the shiny, varnished table.

I still don't like having a secret from her. The secret of the tea cosy had been more difficult to contain than she had expected. The hours of working on the little blue flowers, the leaves, the tiny red butterfly, and then the yellow body of the thing had left her with dark lines under her eyes and achy hands. *I'm never making one of these again.*

She considered whether making one for someone she didn't hold in such high regard would be quite so stressful. Her brain ached when she thought about getting the cosy right because it was for Ollie and because it was for Christmas.

Timothy came with them for coffee one afternoon on his day off between work at the school shop and *Countdown* marathons. The atmosphere had begun thick with nerves, although Timothy had seemed far less tense than Ollie. He eventually made Ollie laugh, and then they seemed to get on like a house on fire. Ollie was so interested—or at least behaved as if she was—in Timothy, in the way he saw the world, and this meant for flowing conversation. Anna simply sat back and sipped her coffee, unable to keep her relief under wraps.

When they left, Timothy asked for Ollie's email address. They agreed to swap research into social conventions. Timothy liked to research pretty much everything that came up in conversation, including conversation itself, which Ollie seemed to find truly fascinating.

When they got home from that particular lunchtime out, Anna patted Timothy's shoulder.

With a grin, Timothy held his arms out, an unusual thing for him to do, with his aversion to touching others.

He towered over her as she leaned into his embrace and closed her eyes. "So, you like Ollie, then?"

"I do."

Anna relaxed—he was no good at lying and therefore rarely did so. "I'm very glad." Pulling back as she felt him get to the end of the counting that meant the finish of any hug he gave, she patted his shoulder again.

"Ollie is intelligent, says kind things, doesn't hate *Countdown*, and is not averse to communicating in a way that I understand."

"I think there should be more people like you." The love she had for the young man flowed out of her in glowing waves. "I think the world would be an amazing place if people just said how they felt."

"If everyone was like me, you and Ollie would have said you liked one another about three weeks before you actually did anything about it."

Anna stared at him for a minute. *He really does know what he's talking about sometimes.*

He stared back, and Anna assumed he was unsure about why she was staring at him.

"Talk to me about your girlfriend, Timothy," she said, tilting her head to one side. "How did you two manage to get together?"

"I walked up to her, after careful consideration of the consequences of my words, and told her she had an asymmetrical face," he stated, his chin lifted high.

A strangled but joyful laugh flew from Anna's throat. She slapped a hand over her mouth. "Apologies." The grin remained plastered over his face. She realised he understood that this would not be neurotypical behaviour, but that he didn't mind that it wasn't. He also didn't mind that she had laughed, it seemed. "Is that a...did she take that as a compliment?"

"I have researched extensively my own attraction to asymmetric faces. I find them more attractive than those faces that display complete symmetry."

"Really?"

"Is it so difficult to understand?"

"I don't think I've ever thought about it."

"Ollie has a mole on her cheekbone. But only one cheekbone. And one of her ears is higher than the other. Would she look as attractive to you if these things were the same on both sides?"

Anna smiled, shook her head. "I have no idea."

"I have, and I think not." Timothy smiled, and went over to the kettle. "I think Ollie is attractive, otherwise you wouldn't have kissed her." He eyed her from across the kitchen. "You seem to think she's attractive."

"Do I?" Although she'd said the words out loud to him, told him she thought Ollie was pretty, he'd used the word "*seem*," which meant he had observed and taken mental notes.

"When she looks at you, and you look at her, your pupils dilate. You smile about fifty percent more. You get red in your neck and face when she speaks to you." He patted where he meant on himself.

The kettle clicked, and he prepared their drinks. "I'm sure other changes happen in your body also, but I believe it would be inappropriate for me to comment."

Anna laughed. "I dare say you're right."

"You're going to hers at Christmas."

"I am."

"Will you be sleeping over?"

She paused and looked away from him for a moment. The feeling between Ollie and her when they spoke about Christmas was something hot and buzzing, like they were behind a rocket about to launch. Sometimes it was so hot, the world shimmered about her and she had to blink hard.

Hadn't they waited long enough? *I want to sleep with her. I want to make love with her.*

She gave Timothy a steady and honest look. "I think so."

"Please text me, let me know when you decide what you're doing."

She nodded immediately, taking the cup of tea he offered to her.

"That way I know where you are. And I can watch *Doctor Who* in peace."

"Of course. You'll know as soon as I know."

Ollie had spent hours sewing hundreds of granny squares together. The wall hanging reached down to the floor as she sat at her till, so she moved onto the sofa and rolled the throw when it got long enough to become a trip hazard for her customers.

Matthew and Harry arrived on Saturday afternoon, their hands joined.

Ollie was covered in granny squares and was starting to feel the effects in her knuckles of constantly sewing. *Could really do with a hand massage from a certain redhead.* She shook her head to push away the tingly thoughts and smiled at the couple as they approached.

"Wow," Harry said, leaning his backside against the arm of the sofa. "That's amazing, Ollie." He pulled Matthew close to him, and Matthew shyly slid up to his side and rested his chin on Harry's head.

"Yep. It's massive. And I'm taking it to the hall tomorrow. So please don't distract me for too long." She tried to make her words light, but the change in their expressions told her she'd failed.

"Don't get stressed," Matthew said, concern flooding his features. He moved away from Harry's side and pushed it out of the way before sitting next to Ollie. "Give me a darning needle and let me help?"

Ollie stared at him and tears pricked her eyes. Matthew had never offered to help her with anything.

Harry, for his part, picked up the other side of it and slid onto the sofa too. "And don't think I'm above giving you a hand either." He pointed to Ollie's sewing kit, and Matthew took the hint, standing and grabbing the things they needed.

They worked in companionable quiet only punctuated by the occasional exclamation of how beautiful a particular square was. Warmth washed over her as she sat between them, working busily. *I'm going to make the deadline. And my hands aren't going to give up before I do.*

Matthew leant against her side at one point, and they exchanged a comfortable look. "This was such a good idea. It's really given the whole group a purpose and a sense of community."

"Do you think so, soldier?" Ollie asked, her gaze flicking almost imperceptibly in Harry's direction. Matthew got it, though, and hid a smirk just behind his eyes.

"Oh, definitely." Harry's gaze was trained on his hands, but the glint in his eyes was evident nonetheless in the way he spoke. "When I joined, I thought you'd all known one another for years."

Ollie laughed in delight. "Well, I'm glad we've provided you with a safe place to come once a week."

Something passed across Harry's face, but it was too buried and she didn't feel comfortable asking about it. Whatever it was, Matthew reached around Ollie's back and rubbed the back of Harry's neck, and Harry relaxed. Ollie caught the sad smile he flashed at Matthew for a second, though.

When Ollie raised an eyebrow in Matthew's direction, Matthew shook his head and returned to his work. Yes, she supposed it wasn't really her business.

Two hours later, they'd finished. The thing was huge. It took all three of them to fold it up, the resulting shape a good four feet wide and two feet thick. Matthew danced on slightly nervous but excited feet.

Harry touched his chin and took a few steps back to look at their work, which Ollie had managed to lift in both arms. "It's perfect."

"I hope Sandra thinks so."

"Want a lift to the church hall?" Matthew asked.

Another offer of help? He must be getting soft in his old age. Ollie decided not to comment but nodded gratefully. *This thing is heavy. I'd never make it all the way without my knee screaming at me.*

When they arrived, a small group of children were gathered around a piano, singing carols. Ollie struggled with the heavy, awkward hanging. Harry immediately grabbed one side to help, and Matthew followed suit on the other.

Sandra, a middle-aged woman with curly grey hair, sat in a small office to one side of the hall. She stood and held her arms out as the three brought in the mammoth item. "Oh, you darlings. Look at it."

Ollie laughed uncomfortably and pulled her two helpers over to an empty table. They lay the mammoth blanket onto it and stepped back. Ollie thought she detected an air of accomplishment from the two lads that matched her own.

"We shall get the boys to put it up tomorrow. Thank you for dropping it off early," Sandra said. "And, again, thank you so much."

"Send us pictures?" Matthew asked, waggling his mobile phone.

"Of course, of course. Let's have your number, darling."

They exchanged numbers, and Matthew assured Ollie he would send her any pictures he received. Ollie absolutely intended to forward any photos straight to Anna. She caught sight of one square, sat neatly on a corner of the throw.

Anna made that. She helped too. They all did.

Chapter 12

The Shawl

On Christmas Day, the Rose Family opened their presents early, and for the first time in years Anna felt like her children were happily children again. Bethany sat on the floor and immediately pulled a Santa hat onto her head, proclaiming herself "Christmas elf" for the morning and therefore in charge of giving out presents. Timothy commented she was too tall for an elf, or too short, depending on her interpretation—traditional or Tolkien—but that he would let it lie just this once as it was Christmas.

Bethany had bought her mother a new pair of slippers, fluffy boot-type ones, in red and white. Timothy had bought her an expensive fountain pen and had explained that one should always have a nice pen in case one had to write to an important person. Anna gave him an impromptu hug, which he allowed with his classic wide grin. Beth clambered next to her on the sofa and kissed all over her cheeks when she'd opened the vouchers for a restaurant and clothing store she liked. Timothy beamed when he opened the new tie and cufflinks Anna had bought him.

"In case you take your girlfriend on a posh date," she explained.

They loved their crocheted presents as well, holding them up and taking pictures on their phones before posting them on social media immediately. Anna felt simultaneously proud and terribly nervous—the whole world would see the things she had made, and they had both named her as the creator of the items.

Oh well. This is what people do these days.

She saw her children off to their respective events, told Bethany to text her if she needed to, and hoped Timothy had a lovely time with Adam.

Her house was empty apart from Arthur, who was playing excitedly with his present: a small ball of wool Anna had wrapped an elastic band around, leaving a tail to trail about as he batted it. It bounced across the tiles in the kitchen and he hunkered down, his backside in the air and his tail flicking from side to side, until he pounced and the ball continued its escape. She watched him until the nervous fluttering in her stomach became too much.

Anna paced around the house, packaging up the mince pies she had made into a box. She slid the bottle of wine into a bag. She'd been told to bring only herself but decided disobeying just this once would be okay. She eyed the neatly wrapped package that contained Ollie's gift, hesitated, and then held it for a moment. *I'm not as skilled as she is. I hope she likes it anyway.*

She forced her shoulders down and rubbed at her stomach. *You made it. So she'll love it.*

Once everything was packed into the car, she went to change. She had chosen—with much help from Bethany and Timothy—a low-cut black blouse without a vest top underneath, something she'd never dare do at school. Grey trousers. A horrible jumper with a reindeer on. She packed her new slippers and some new pyjamas Patricia had bought her into a shoulder bag, climbed into her car, and set off.

A glance at her watch when she arrived confirmed she was right on time, exactly two in the afternoon. The door opened, and a mess of blond hair and shining eyes greeted her. Anna took in Ollie's outfit with a short, sharp, pleased breath.

She had exchanged her usual skinny jeans for a pair of grey leggings and a tunic in navy blue. It had a wide neck, which showed off her collarbones, long sleeves, and an owl detail at the hip.

I've never seen her looking so feminine.

Anna's mouth watered, and Ollie must have noticed her looking, because her cheekbones turned pink. Anna allowed her to take the shopping bag.

"Merry Christmas," Anna finally said, her throat gravelly as she walked inside.

A smile shone from Ollie's features. "Merry Christmas, comrade."

Anna made the first move towards her, caught her jaw, and kissed her. Lavender swirled around them, and Ollie broke away briefly, her free hand at Anna's waist.

"You look adorable," she said, pointing at the reindeer jumper.

That made Anna laugh. "Well, I'm not allowed to wear it any other day of the year."

Ollie lifted the bag. "I said you shouldn't bring anything."

"I know," Anna replied, her bottom lip in her mouth. "I find I simply cannot arrive at someone's home for dinner without gifts. Whatever I am told." Another kiss and Anna didn't care that she'd disobeyed.

"I'll have to forgive you, I suppose." A teasing sparkle shone from Ollie's eyes.

"Lead the way, soldier."

Ollie strode up the stairs, her fist white with exertion on the banister. The image of that made Anna's stomach swirl in sympathy.

The flat was decorated for Christmas. Pastel crocheted rings adorned the curtain rails and hung from some of the light fittings, like paper chains but made out of yarn. A plastic but stylish tree stood to the left of the wood burner with those snowmen and reindeer and fairy lights Ollie had described slowly blinking. The wood burner was already lit, and although it hadn't warmed the room quite yet, it was crackling away and glowing yellow with flames.

There was a thick, new-looking rug by the wood burner, and Ollie had arranged cushions and crocheted throws around it like a nest. A small tray stood to one side and held a plate with small pieces of bread, cubes of cheese, and a pot of pickle. Two wine glasses stood on the tiled hearth, an open bottle of red wine beside them.

The setup made Anna's breathing hitch while Ollie moved into the kitchen area with the bags. Her laughter rang through the kitchen, breaking Anna's reverie.

Ollie was holding up the bottle of the same brand of red wine. "Great minds," she said.

"Crumbs." Anna went to stand with Ollie by the counter so she could have something to hold on to while she pulled her slippers out of the bag and tugged them onto her feet.

Ollie chuckled at her.

"We really are disgusting, aren't we?" Anna smirked.

"Honestly." Ollie shuffled the bottles and box to the back of the counter. "Matching outfits. Got to be done."

Anna's attention was drawn back into the living area. "Ollie, this is just…" *There isn't a word for how lovely this all is.* She splayed her fingers in a gesture of huge proportions and took Ollie's waist to pull her around to face her.

Ollie took the hint, sliding her hands to either side of Anna's neck, her thumbs caressing her ears. She mirrored the look Anna gave her with a soft, twinkly one of her own, her smile widening when Anna sighed into the caresses. She leant forward to nuzzle her nose against Anna's. "Wanted it to be special."

"It is." Their lips were so close she could feel Ollie's breath against her face. "It's amazing."

Anna wrapped her arms around Ollie but allowed the kiss to remain soft and tender.

"I've missed you," Ollie breathed against Anna's lips, teasing her bottom lip with both her own, making Anna sigh.

"Missed you too." *It's been three days! But I have.*

Anna's stomach interrupted them with a huge growl. Ollie chuckled and then kissed her swiftly.

After rubbing her inconvenient stomach, Anna looked around the flat. "So, what other culinary delights have you prepared?"

Ollie chivalrously insisted that Anna sit in the prepared nest and wait for her to bring in their dinner. She flicked on the stereo, which already had a CD inside—Anna recognised it as Dean Martin and Friends. The music was soft and flowed around the room, making Anna's limbs feel pleasantly heavy.

Ollie laid the tray down and dropped one hand to the floor at her hip before lowering herself onto the rug. She grimaced as she did it, but Anna got the impression she did it all the time and so refrained from reaching out to help her.

The tray held small pieces of turkey coated in a crimson-coloured sauce, small potato wedges, sprouts that smelled vinegary, and pastry parcels containing a green-looking stuffing. This, in addition to the bread and cheese and pickle, felt like a feast. "This looks delicious."

"I didn't make it all from scratch," Ollie replied, sitting by her side but facing her and stretching her legs out by Anna's hip.

"You didn't have to make any of it from scratch." Anna took one of the small plates by their wine glasses, and a napkin.

Ollie fingered the sleeve of Anna's Christmas jumper. "This really is gorgeous, by the way."

"Not silly?"

Ollie shrugged. "More gorgeous than silly."

"I insist on my family wearing at least one item of Christmas clothing on the actual day. I can hardly argue that I mustn't wear one myself."

"Rose family tradition?" Ollie asked.

Anna nodded, directing her hand to a parcel and feeling the crisp edges of the pastry with her fingertips. "These are fantastic," she said with her mouth full.

Following Anna's example, they ate with their hands. Anna's fingers became sticky with the cranberry sauce covering the turkey. They quickly polished off the main course between them. Ollie seemed to be enjoying the food, too, and kept shooting Anna surprised and pleased expressions, even though she was the one who had provided it all.

They'd kept their hands to themselves, mostly because Anna couldn't bring herself to share any of the mouthfuls she lifted to her lips.

Once the turkey and trimmings disappeared, Ollie spread some pickle into a piece of crusty bread and then topped it with a cube of cheese. She held it out, and Anna carefully took it from her with her mouth. When Ollie leaned in to kiss some pickle from Anna's lips, Anna pulled her in with a sticky hand and they ended up kissing properly, open-mouthed. They had to force themselves apart, but Anna was delighted to see a dark longing in Ollie's eyes.

While Ollie poured them some wine, she poked the two wrapped gifts she'd apparently just noticed nestled underneath it. She gave Anna the glass and a squinty smile. "Looks like Saint Nick has been."

"Must have," Anna replied into her wine glass before she sipped. *Perfect.* "You do have a chimney, after all." She suddenly felt the urge to take Ollie's hand. "Let's finish eating first," she whispered.

"Roger that."

Once the cheese and bread and chutney were gone, Anna left their little nest and returned with one large bowl containing four mince pies she'd heated in the microwave briefly. She laid the bowl between them and then poured cream into it. Her backside snuggled into the nest again as she sat properly, her thigh resting against the side of Ollie's thigh, the bowl now in her own lap. She used the spoon to break off a little pie, dipped it in cream, and held it to Ollie's lips.

Ollie took the spoonful slowly, her tongue working to roll the dried fruit, the sugar, the buttery pastry, and the subtle cream around her mouth. She closed her eyes for a moment.

Mesmerised, Anna suddenly realised she was holding the spoon in the air near Ollie's lips. She knew her own face was flushed. An ache had begun in her stomach and lower. Her ribs expanded and contracted as she breathed deeply. *How am I turned on simply by Ollie eating a mince pie? I need to get some control.*

Dark eyes opened, and Ollie brushed Anna's cheek with her thumb and then took the spoon from her. "Homemade?"

"Apart from the cream," Anna replied and had to clear her throat when her words came out stilted.

"Mmm," Ollie scooped up some more pie and cream, lifting it to Anna's lips.

Anna held Ollie's gaze as she took the spoon into her mouth.

A trembling hand crept around Anna's waist as the spoon clattered into the bowl, and they leaned their foreheads against one another.

Anna chewed as quickly as she could, everything tingling despite the warmth from the wood burner. "Ollie." Anna's heart pounded in her chest, and her whole body shook.

"Food is a serious problem for us, isn't it?" Ollie said, an eyebrow raised.

"Good food, certainly," Anna replied, her voice a little stronger.

Ollie touched her face. "Next time we'll have something less delicious."

Shaking her head, Anna placed a hand over her sternum. "It's just…you affect me." Anxiety fluttered through her. *I don't think I've ever told anyone that. Not in fifty-two years.*

With insistence, Ollie nodded. "You affect me too." Her palm smoothed soothingly back and forth around Anna's waist.

The caress was calming, and it steadied Anna's racing heart slightly. She took a slow, measured breath. "Maybe we should just eat the rest like normal people?" She gently poked Ollie's side.

Ollie chuckled. "That's a tip-top idea. As much as I'd like to feed you every remaining piece of food on offer…"

"It's barely three o'clock."

They nodded once, simultaneously, the decision made.

Anna shuffled back a little, plumped a couple of cushions behind her, and rested against the sofa. "You all right over there?"

"Very comfy, thank you," Ollie replied. They continued to eat the pies and cream, handing the bowl back and forth.

"Honestly, Ollie, this was so lovely," Anna said after all the food was gone and Ollie had rested down on her side with her head in her hand.

"I'm going to have to agree with you," Ollie said, then seemed to take it back. "The turkey was good."

"Where did you purchase our Christmas picnic from, anyway?"

"Local butcher does a pack of various things, including potatoes and a seasoning mix. I just figured wedges would be more finger-friendly than roasties."

"The parcels, though," Anna said, before her tongue darted out to lick her lips.

Ollie fiddled with the napkin between her fingers. The knuckles of her other hand were tense in her hair.

"Kudos to your culinary skills."

"I don't cook a lot."

When Anna reached out and rubbed her forearm, Ollie stopped pulling at the napkin. The log burner had quietened somewhat. It was simply glowing embers now and had made the flat fairly warm. The present Anna had brought appeared in Ollie's lap. Then Ollie turned back to the tree and threw up her hands in mock surprise.

"But what have we got here?" she said in a high-pitched, overdone voice.

Anna laughed and took the larger parcel from Ollie. The fluttering started again in her belly. Ollie nodded once, an affirmation, and they both ripped into the presents.

A grin spread across Ollie's face as she got hers open first. She held it up, turned it over, and put one hand inside to hold it up. She immediately hauled herself to her feet, groaning as she did, but her expression was like a kid's with a new toy. She hopped into the kitchen and brought her teapot and the cosy back to their colourful nest. She sat and dusted the top with her sleeve until it shone. Then she carefully pulled the cosy onto the pot, guiding the spout and handle through the holes.

All the breath seemed trapped in Anna's lungs as Ollie turned it back and forth.

"It's beautiful, Anna." She examined every side of the tea cosy, fingering the flowers, the leaves, and the butterfly. "Absolutely beautiful."

"I wasn't..." Anna cleared her throat as her stomach fizzed. "I wasn't sure if it would fit or...or if you'd like it." She fiddled with the edge of the paper in her lap, her present not yet revealed.

Ollie shuffled over and pressed a kiss to Anna's forehead, her fingers gentle on her cheek. "I love it. It's perfect." She pulled away and focused back on the cosy.

"I have a confession to make." Anna bit her lip. "When I asked for Matthew's number weeks ago, it wasn't for Beth. It was for me." She tried to gauge Ollie's reaction. "I wanted to ask for his opinion. For colours and... and the style."

"I did wonder," Ollie said, still grinning. "Is that why you haven't been to the class for a couple of weeks?"

"That's right." Anna put a hand to her own hot cheek. "I wanted to work on it, make it perfect."

"And look how well it fits," Ollie said, holding up the pot again.

Anna dropped her hand to her lap. "I'm so glad you like it."

"Of course I do."

Her stomach settled. She genuinely liked it.

Ollie sat back and stroked the flowers on the tea cosy for a while with absentminded movements. Then she dipped her head towards Anna's present. "Come on. Now you."

Whatever was underneath the paper of Anna's present was squishy. She ripped it open and allowed the contents inside to fall onto her knee. A burgundy shawl, made using incredibly fine yarn, soft as rabbit fur, sat in her hands, its tiny shell-shaped rows lining the edges. Anna gazed at it, motionless, and then lifted a finger to one of the shells. She traced each stitch, tinier than she'd ever seen, intricate patterns swirling round and around. She couldn't work out the individual stitches, could only see the finished piece. So much work must have gone into it.

"Wow," she said, her voice breathy.

Ollie watched her, a soft smile on her face.

"God." Anna's palm covered her cheek in wonder.

"I prefer 'Ollie'." Her lips twisted with amusement.

Anna finally tore her gaze from the shawl and looked at the woman sat in front of her, whose foot was bouncing up and down. "It's just..." She struggled to form words, let alone full sentences. Dropping her gaze back to her lap, she swiftly crossed her hands over her front and pulled off the silly Christmas jumper. The shawl was cosy when she slid it around her shoulders, the soft yarn pressing snugly against her cheek. She closed her eyes.

She felt Ollie take one corner of the shawl and tuck it across the other side of her neck. Fingertips brushed over Anna's exposed collarbone. She opened her eyes and grabbed for Ollie, holding her cheeks in both hands, kissing her full on the mouth.

A moan escaped from her as Ollie fell awkwardly against her, but she didn't care in the slightest. Ollie settled next to her on one hip, and they kissed and kissed, tongues sweeping and touching in mid-air.

Anna trailed her hands down, one at Ollie's neck, the other around her waist. *I think I love her. I think that's what this feeling is.*

Ollie broke the kiss, started to move back, but Anna leant up and captured her lips again, drawing her back down. Ollie hummed against her, one hand clutching at her hip, the other disappearing behind Anna's head. Then she pulled her lips from Anna's but stayed close, touching her face with a fingertip.

"I'm guessing from that rather...exuberant reaction..." She was panting a little, Anna realised. "...that you like the shawl?"

"I love it," Anna replied and reached up to tuck a piece of hair behind Ollie's ear.

Ollie sat back and grimaced. Her knee was obviously complaining.

"I'm sorry," Anna said, kneeling up and putting a hand to Ollie's thigh, her bad one. "I shouldn't have..."

"Thrown yourself at me?" Ollie asked, a glint in her eye.

"I was trying to convey a sentiment."

Ollie smiled. "Sentiment understood."

A wave of heat rolled over Anna, so she shrugged off the shawl and folded it back up. She flapped a hand in front of her face.

"This will be perfect for keeping me warm," she said. "But your log burner and my hormones are doing rather a good job of that right this second, so…" She placed the shawl away from the fire, on top of the wrapping paper it came in. "Thank you."

"You're welcome."

Anna looked around at their empty plates and trays. "Maybe we should get this cleared up."

"Did you…um." Ollie clambered to her feet and followed Anna into the kitchen area, arms full of their dinner things. "Would you like to watch a film in a bit?"

Anna started to fill the basin full of warm soapy water and took Ollie's washing-up gloves from the little hook by the window. "That sounds lovely. So long as we can make use of the picnic area. That is, if you're comfortable down there."

They washed up and cleared away. Ollie went to rearrange the cushions so they would cradle them against the sofa, then went to her DVD collection and chose one. She held it up and Anna nodded. "It's the recent one, you know with the little girl who played Matilda?"

"That's fine. I always preferred that one anyway. Richard Attenborough."

"The music is more festive too."

The folded-up shawl was soft under her fingers as Anna sat against the cushions.

Ollie smiled at her careful touch and pulled up the thick pair of white socks she wore over her leggings. She stepped around the room, lighting a few candles and adding another small log to the fire. She turned off the main light, leaving the room lit only by the fire and candles and the television. She dropped down next to Anna, and Anna held her arm up in silent invitation. Ollie crawled to snuggle underneath it, resting her head on Anna's shoulder. She smelled apples and sighed. *She always smells so good.* Anna pressed a kiss against her forehead as the film started.

A few minutes of fidgeting meant Ollie found a position she was comfortable with—on her side, with her bad leg bent up over Anna's knee and her arm around Anna's waist. Anna caressed her shoulder when Ollie shifted around, as though to tell her wordlessly that her fidgeting was okay. The fire crackled next to them, and the candles spluttered on occasion.

There's that safe feeling again. Ollie closed her eyes for a moment as she allowed the feeling to spread through her.

Drawn into the film's touching story, after several minutes Ollie barely noticed when Anna's fingers started a gentle circling on her neck, and her own fingers started a similar caress in response on Anna's waist. But when Anna's hand slid up into the short hair at the base of Ollie's neck, Ollie couldn't miss that. The caress sent shivers all down her torso.

Anna's hand went still. "Sorry," she whispered.

"Don't stop," Ollie whispered back.

There was a pause, and then Anna's fingertips began to caress Ollie's neck again. Ollie snuggled further in. She carefully and slowly swirled her own fingers in little circles against the dip of Anna's waist, gentle enough for it not to tickle but firm enough for Anna to know it wasn't accidental. The circles got bigger, and Ollie's fingertips slipped under the hem of Anna's blouse to touch her soft skin.

Anna stretched a little, but she burrowed her own nose further in Ollie's hair so Ollie didn't stop. They went on like this for a while, slowly and gently touching one another's skin, in no hurry to go anywhere with it. Ollie then took a chance and moved her fingertips upwards. She touched the side of Anna's bra, pushing her blouse up a little in the process. The cup was warm and contained a wire. Anna's breath hitched.

She brought her fingers down again and trailed circles against her waist. Starting a rhythm, up and down, she smoothed them against Anna's pliant skin; it reminded her that Anna was curvy, so unlike her own wiry and skinny frame. When Anna's breath deepened, Ollie's fingers moved down her spine and curled around Anna's waist. It was an opportunity to slide her fingers around to Anna's belly, to touch at the waistband of her grey trousers, and she took it gently, gradually, respectfully. She tickled upwards, undoing the bottom button of Anna's blouse with one hand. With a glance upwards, she noticed that Anna's attention still appeared to be on the film, but she had a small smile on her face. Ollie sat up a little to look at her properly.

"May I?" Ollie's fingers stilled at Anna's second button.

Anna turned away from the television and treated Ollie to that toothy, wide smile of hers. She nodded.

She kept Anna's gaze as she unbuttoned the next three, slowly, all the while with Anna's arm around her. Ollie's hand at her waist kept tracing patterns on little bits of exposed skin.

Eventually, Anna turned around to fully face her and gathered Ollie's tunic above her hip, her intention shy but clear. She touched Ollie's bare skin, making Ollie sigh and dip her head forward. They kissed gently. Ollie continued to undo Anna's blouse buttons until she had completed her task. Breaking the kiss, she looked into Anna's eyes and found they had gone a deep green.

Ollie traced a wandering line down Anna's front, over the middle of her bra and down to her navel. She then went back up the same path, pushing away one side then the other of the blouse, exposing Anna's black bra. Ollie looked down, and Anna cupped her cheek as Ollie just stared at her for a long moment. Finally Ollie lowered her head to press a small kiss against Anna's neck.

Breathing out a very quiet moan, Anna held Ollie against her as she kissed down her neck, her lips teasing the skin at the hollow of her throat. She tugged Ollie back up, then threaded her fingers into her hair and pulled her back to her lips.

As they kissed, Ollie slid her hand up to cup her breast through her bra. Anna moaned a little more loudly when Ollie's fingers touched through the satin, found her nipple and caressed it. Her chest rose and fell, her lips parted in a smile.

She does want me. Ollie's nerve endings were on fire. *She really does want me.*

Anna felt like she was being worshipped, the way Ollie was touching her, kissing her, so slowly and so tenderly. Ollie's fingers against her suddenly hard nipple sent jolts of pleasure straight between her legs. New pleasure erupted as Ollie's hand moved to the other side, her fingertips trailing over her other breast as well.

Her fingers curled into Ollie's tunic. "Come on," she said, and Ollie sat up straight. Anna looked down at her own open shirt and flushed chest. "Now, it's only fair, isn't it?"

After shuffling so she could pull the tunic above both her hips, Ollie slipped it over her head. Anna took in the grey leggings and black bra. *Look at her. I'd never be able to wear leggings with no top to cover them. They'd cut into my squishy belly.* She pulled a couple of the cushions into place to cocoon them.

Ollie sat with her bad leg stretched out, the other bent in front of her. She reached for Anna, pushing the blouse from her shoulders and allowing it to drop. The sound of the credits rolling made them both stop and turn to look at the television. Ollie grabbed the remote controls from the floor and switched both television and DVD player off.

"You okay?" she asked, touching Anna's cheek.

Anna nodded and slipped her hands around Ollie's bare waist. "You?"

"Yep."

She looks so happy. Anna shifted up close to Ollie and sat in the little space provided by her encircling leg. They were face-to-face.

Ollie reached down to smooth Anna's thigh and tugged it upwards over her hip. Anna's foot sank into the throw behind Ollie. She took in their position, one leg each around the other's waist and sitting close together amid all the throws and cushions. *This is so lovely, and so intimate.*

"You let me know, okay?" Anna shifted into a less awkward position, and Ollie's waist was warm on the inside of her thigh. "If at any point you want to move to more comfortable quarters."

"Roger that." Ollie's gaze flicked across Anna's exposed skin. She gathered the throws around their waists, covering their legs, and then bent down again to kiss her neck.

Anna looped her arms around Ollie's shoulders and sighed. As Ollie's lips trailed downwards, Anna felt her hands at her back, fumbling a little, before she felt something give and her bra fell away. "Done this before, Williams?"

Ollie gave a quick kiss to the slope of one breast. "Not for a long time."

"Still, more practice than me." Anna looked away.

Ollie reached behind herself, unhooked her own bra, and allowed Anna to pull it off. Anna threw her own bra across the room. They both watched it go, sniggering.

Anna allowed her gaze to trail over Ollie's torso. She looked at her small breasts, the nipples standing out despite the warmth from the fire. She let out a breath and then framed Ollie's face with her hands before drawing them down over her neck, her shoulders, her collarbones, and then down to her breasts.

Beautiful. Anna cupped Ollie's breasts, smoothed her palms against them, the hard peaks of her nipples catching a bit against her skin. At the contact, Ollie inhaled deeply. Anna smiled up at her and did it again, delighting in the soft gasp it caused.

They kissed again. Ollie moved her hands up from where they rested on Anna's hips and moved them to the underside of Anna's breasts, lifting them. It made Anna shiver. She moved closer still and kicked her slippers off and away under the blankets. The throws she kept in place around their hips. She then wrapped her leg more snugly around Ollie's waist. They resumed kissing, Anna's hands hungrily against Ollie's skin.

She pulled back to check that Ollie was okay and found her eyes dark, her pupils wide. Encouraged, she dropped her lips to Ollie's shoulder and sucked a kiss to her skin. She trailed more kisses downwards until Ollie was shifting around. Anna's lips encircled her nipple. *Wow. She tastes good and feels even better.*

Anna sucked gently, then flicked her tongue against the very tip. In response, Ollie put a palm on the floor behind herself, as if she couldn't trust her own balance under Anna's quiet ministrations. She arched her back. After a moment's thought, Anna slipped her hands around to tickle against the small of Ollie's back and help her remain sitting upright. She then got down to touching Ollie once more. Anna lapped at her nipple with strong but slow sweeps of her tongue until the bud was pink and swollen. Then she moved to the other side, leaving a tender kiss between Ollie's breasts on the way. The other nipple received the same attention. She splayed her hands against Ollie's back, took some of her weight, and dipped her fingertips below the waistband of her leggings.

A sudden urge to feel Ollie against her swept through Anna's body. She sat up, pressed as much of their fronts together as she could, and kissed Ollie's parted lips. *She feels amazing.*

As for Ollie, she moaned quietly against the kiss, her arms wrapping Anna up in an embrace and her palms leaving hot trails against Anna's naked skin.

I want her hands on me. I want it so much.

She shifted backwards out of Ollie's arms, and Ollie looked as if someone had died. Anna smiled and touched her cheek. "Just think we're wearing far too many clothes."

The frown on Ollie's face soon turned into a smile. "Are you sure?" Her voice was a whisper.

Anna hooked her fingers into the top of those soft leggings. She pulled them down to Ollie's knees along with her briefs.

Ollie raised an eyebrow.

"Definitely sure," Anna answered. She pulled Ollie's leggings and underwear completely off and then stood to remove her own trousers and knickers. Kneeling down in front of her again, she noticed Ollie had wrapped one of the crocheted throws around her waist, covering her legs. The look of apology in Ollie's eyes made it clear she knew Anna had noticed.

If she needs to hide her injured leg for a while, that's okay with me. It must be weird having it on display. She sat back down and traced the line of Ollie's jaw as she smiled at her. "You're beautiful," she said, taking in again the way Ollie's eyes were so dark. *I did that.*

"You're the gorgeous one," Ollie replied, smoothing her hands around Anna's waist, just sitting and holding her, smiling as they looked into one another's eyes. "I'm all…broken and imperfect and…"

"Oh be quiet." Anna pressed a kiss against Ollie's temple. "I think you're perfect."

"I'm covered in scars and metalwork," Ollie said quietly, clearly taking in the newly exposed parts of Anna's body. "I'm broken and battered and…"

"I don't care," Anna said, her thumb brushing Ollie's cheekbone. They both blushed. Anna's heart had been racing, but now she felt calmer and more grounded. A heavy feeling had settled between her legs, but it wasn't uncomfortable. "I'm covered in stretch marks from Beth, and look…" She pulled down her shoulder to show Ollie her upper back, where small, thin white lines decorated the skin of her shoulders. "When Timothy first moved in, he was so anxious. Sometimes I had to hold him close to stop him hurting himself. He scratched me when I did that, didn't like being touched."

Ollie trailed a fingertip over one particularly deep scar and then leant down to kiss it.

Anna shivered and lifted her head to look at Ollie.

"I suppose nobody's perfect," Ollie said.

Anna nodded slowly, the smile slipping back onto her face. "Would you…" she asked, her eyes lowering to the throw over Ollie's legs, "…let me see you?" Anna rolled her eyes. "In all your glory?"

Ollie nodded.

The look in her eyes was so trusting, it made Anna's heart swell.

A couple of cushions got pushed to the side of their little nest that was furthest from the sofa. Ollie lay back on them, her knees tenting the blankets. Firstly sinking down onto her side next to Ollie, Anna pressed her lips to Ollie's and then her cheek. Then she pulled back and took Ollie's hand from where it clutched the blanket.

Ollie took in a deep breath and let it out slowly.

Pulling back the blankets inch by inch, Anna exposed Ollie's hips and legs. She could see Ollie's stomach muscles twitching, and she laid her palm over her navel. Their gazes locked, and Ollie sighed, her stomach going soft under Anna's hand. Anna shifted down a little, left a chaste kiss next to her hand and then pulled the blankets completely off her.

Ollie's knee, the bad one, the one closest to her, was mottled with scar tissue. The lines reminded Anna of the underground in London, some angular, some jagged. The flesh between was bumpy and disfigured. Anna studied her knee carefully before smoothing her palm warmly over it. *It's not disgusting. I was so worried about that.* She left a kiss against the white lines and swept her hand down Ollie's shin, to her ankle and then back up.

She gave Ollie's other leg the same attention. She tried to convey with her caresses that she wasn't bothered about the scars or Ollie's limp, or her inability to run. She wanted to show Ollie she could imagine and understand how hard it must be for her to expose this part of herself, when the place she had come from had known her as nothing but strong and indestructible.

With her cheek resting gently against Ollie's scarred knee, Anna smiled up at her where she had nestled back in the cushions.

The smile Ollie returned was still shy. "Told you," Ollie said, touching the lines by Anna's mouth with her thumb. "Bit of a mess."

"I still think you're beautiful," Anna whispered like it was a secret only the two of them knew.

Something passed between them, an understanding and a peace.

Anna's gaze lowered. She looked further up from Ollie's knee, at her thighs, the muscles of the right slightly less defined than the left. *If I hadn't known she'd been injured, I would never have noticed the difference.* Her thighs seemed strong, however, and Anna remembered Ollie regularly went swimming. Her lip snuck into her mouth as she tracked the line of Ollie's thighs to the neat hair between them.

Not a natural blonde, then. Anna smiled a little more and exhaled deeply. *I can't believe I'm allowed to look.* She snuggled her cheek into the side of Ollie's knee, making sure to be gentle. Her hand trailed idly up the outside of her thigh, fingers curling around Ollie's hip.

When she looked back up, she was greeting by Ollie smiling down at her with a raised eyebrow. "Are you done?" she asked, wiggling her feet in the blankets.

Anna took pity on her and slid up her body to settle down beside her again. "Sorry," she said, but continued to smile. "Feel free to…you know…take a look." She indicated with a random gesture down her own body, and Ollie shrugged.

"Well, I suppose it's only fair," she said and hauled herself into a sitting position.

Anna laughed and settled back into the cushions as Ollie had done, bending one knee up and resting her forearms protectively around her stomach. *I'm naked. I barely noticed that happen.*

Ollie's hand on Anna's hip was warm, and, in contrast, her thumb swept her skin, causing tiny goose bumps to rise halfway down her leg. Anna shuttered her eyes, wiggling her hips anxiously. Ollie removed her hand and touched Anna's arms where they lay across her belly. Anna fidgeted some more and pursed her lips.

"It's okay," Ollie said.

But Anna's bravado of a minute ago disappeared under Ollie's focused inspection. Anna bit her lip before dropping her hands down into the blankets. *I hate my belly.* She shut her eyes tight and turned her head to one side. When she looked back, she found Ollie's smile and dark eyes looking into her own.

"I'm all…chubby," Anna said. "I mean, goodness, look at you, and look at me."

With a shake of her head, Ollie traced a finger around her navel. Then Ollie looked further downwards, eyebrows lifting as her gaze settled between Anna's legs.

Butterflies swarmed inside Anna's chest.

Ollie grinned and flicked her eyebrows up twice.

The tension inside Anna finally eased as laughter bubbled up and out of her. "Yes, I'm a natural redhead." *Why do people always find that amusing?* Anna made a motion down Ollie's body. "I do not dye my hair. Unlike someone."

Ollie chuckled, too, dropped a kiss to Anna's raised knee, and hugged it to her.

"Don't blondes have more fun, though?" Ollie asked.

Laughter is great for breaking tension, isn't it? At least my insecurities haven't spoiled the moment. But she didn't have time to think more about it because Ollie was pressing kisses down her calf, making her squirm deliciously.

She giggled. "Okay, that's enough." She pulled Ollie back up by the hand. The mood quietened, but their smiles didn't fade. "Come on, I want to feel you against me."

Ollie pouted but shifted back up anyhow. She dropped to one elbow and resumed the position they had adopted while they watched the film, but this time with far fewer clothes.

They moved close and kissed, hands cupping each other's cheeks.

Oh God, we're actually doing this. The thought made Anna tingle all over, made her deepen the kiss and press her tongue into Ollie's mouth. Something caught her up in a flood of want, and her fingers trailed down Ollie's side, tugging at her hip, wanting her on top of her.

But then Ollie tensed, pulled back, and looked away.

Hoping to comfort, Anna tickled her knuckles against Ollie's cheek.

Tears gathered in Ollie's eyes. "I can't."

Anna pushed herself quickly to sit up, guided Ollie down onto her back again—nestling her head in a flat pillow—and leant over her. *Whichever way works. I want to lie with her against me.*

"All right?"

"I'm sorry," Ollie said.

"Shhh," Anna replied, a finger going to Ollie's lips before trailing down her chin, her neck, and the space between her breasts.

Ollie's hands smoothed against Anna's waist. Anna rested on one knee, her elbows on either side of Ollie's head. She snuck the other knee between Ollie's legs as she rested her weight against her. "Still all right?"

Those strong hands pulled her down. They kissed again. The feeling of skin upon skin, of being so close, caused a groan to rumble inside Anna. *God, my thigh is right there. Her thigh is right there.*

They kissed for a long time, and Anna's body warmed up, the space between her legs starting to thrum. Their hands swept backs and sides and cheeks, fingers tangling in hair.

Shifting slightly, Ollie lifted her good foot to place it on the blanket, her bad leg between Anna's.

Oh that's good.

Heat touched her hip, combined with a little wetness. Anna pressed her hips down, and Ollie wrapped her leg around Anna's waist, gasping into Anna's mouth. Anna felt the throws under her knees, her forearms, all of it a delicious friction that only heightened as they began moving against one another a little, their breaths becoming deeper, faster. *Oh goodness, this is amazing. But I'm not sure I want our first time to be like this.*

Ollie gripped her around her back, and Anna's thigh rubbed between Ollie's legs. Ollie arched her back and groaned. *Was that pain?* Anna eased up a little. The flush all down Ollie's chest and the smile on her face made her relax; however, she didn't begin moving again.

A palm smoothed against Anna's hip before rounding the swell of her backside. The touch was accompanied by Ollie squinting up at her in question. Anna rolled from her, settling down by her side again.

"Are you okay?" Ollie asked, frowning.

Anna trailed the back of her fingers up Ollie's tummy. Goose bumps followed her touch and Ollie stretched back. Anna paused with her hand between Ollie's breasts. Then she looked up into her eyes. "As wonderful as it was...," Anna said slowly, her lips pursed. "I want to touch you." Anna continued to suck her lip. "Is...is that all right?"

A whoosh of breath left Ollie's lips. "Of course it is." She settled back into the cushions while Anna's fingertips trailed across her skin. Ollie shivered, however, and wrapped her arms around her own shoulders. "I don't want to hide from you again," Ollie whispered, prompting Anna to lift her head from Ollie's shoulder. "But I'm cold."

"I'll get it," Anna said and pulled one of the throws over them, tucking it around Ollie's side and under her back.

Ollie sighed, her arm around Anna's shoulders and the hand of the other just resting against her hip. Anna's hand began a meandering journey down her body. "Much better."

"Your skin is so soft," Anna said.

"So is yours." Ollie trailed her fingertips against Anna's shoulder.

Her thudding heart was almost a distraction as Anna slipped her fingers down, the very tips of them brushing Ollie's mons. *Her hair is softer than mine.* She curled her hand between Ollie's legs and swallowed. *What do I like? Surely we can't be that different?*

Fingers slipped between Ollie's outer lips but stayed outside her inner ones. Ollie lifted her good foot to rest it on the blankets and dropped her bad knee outwards. Anna kissed her, catching the next moan she created by sliding her fingers downwards and then back up. She was amazed at how wet Ollie was, how warm.

I did that. The thought sent a rush of wetness flooding between her own legs.

Experimentation was the key, she supposed, so Anna slid her fingers back and forth, avoiding Ollie's clit as much as she could. *She feels familiar, yet different. Will she like what I like?* She pressed her fingertips just to Ollie's entrance, the flesh there swollen and soft, and slipped inside a little. Ollie's breathing stuttered. She slid further inside and curled her fingers, watching as Ollie stretched back, her wrist over her forehead.

They kissed again, and Anna thrust gently inside her, in and out, a slow rhythm, until Ollie was thrusting with her, her breathing ragged.

Anna wanted to ask her how she was doing but wasn't sure what phrase to use. Ollie must have noticed the insecure look in her eyes, because she reached down to lay her hand over Anna's. She grasped her wrist gently and pulled, so she withdrew and moved her upwards and forward so her fingertips rested on Ollie's clit.

Anna waited until Ollie's hand was back above her head before she started to circle, a jolt of warmth flicking through her whole body as Ollie groaned low in her throat.

Their gazes locked and Anna felt something connect between them. She started to circle faster, feeling Ollie's entire sex, how distended it was. *I've never felt anything so sexy in my whole life.* The little stifled moans Ollie made caused her own sex to ache.

Ollie's hips began to move, to thrust against her hand under the blanket. She could smell the evidence of Ollie's arousal, too, a sweet scent mingled with sweat and lavender.

Anna sped up again and increased the pressure, figuring that, at least, was universal, that everyone, surely, wanted more and more the closer they got. She studied Ollie's face, the darkness of her eyes, and the furrow in her brow. *She's going to come. I can't believe I'm going to make her come.* "Please don't hold back," she said.

Ollie simply moaned in response, the lines in her face deepening, her lips parting, the breath rushing from them as her whole body tensed.

"Oh God," the words jumped out of her. *She's so beautiful.*

A flushed Ollie thrust her hips in a slow rhythm, her ribs expanding over and over as she panted.

It occurred to Anna to change her plan: she stopped circling and simply began rubbing back and forth over Ollie's swollen, wet centre. It turned to be absolutely the right thing to do, because suddenly Ollie was gripping Anna tightly and arching her back, her body tensing more and more until she squeezed her eyes shut and Anna could feel the waves of it through her sex—the twitching, the spasms of impending release. Ollie shuddered hard, her hair wild on the cushions.

Then she was pulling Anna's hand away from touching her any further, her moans filling the room as her whole body vibrated with her orgasm.

Anna gazed down at her, tears in her eyes, watching as Ollie rocked and twitched, the waves slowly subsiding. When Ollie could eventually open her eyes again, her pupils were huge; her hips were still jolting with tiny aftershocks.

"Oh Anna." Ollie reached to gather her up in her arms and settled Anna's head against her shoulder.

"I'm so very sorry. I'm not usually one to blubber." Anna wiped at her eyes with her dry hand. "You just looked so beautiful." She didn't cry, she simply screwed her eyes shut tight and held on to Ollie for a while.

I don't know what has come over me, how embarrassing. As the tension from her own body fell away and Ollie let her go, she rested her head in her hand and looked down at Ollie, who had beads of perspiration between her breasts and in her hairline.

Still in that languid, post-orgasmic state, Ollie looked away for a moment, but Anna could see how red her cheeks were. She leant in to kiss Ollie, who rolled over onto her side at the touch of Anna's lips to her cheek. She wrapped an arm around Anna's waist.

"It's me that should be crying, surely?" Her eyelashes tickled Anna's shoulder as they fluttered closed.

"I'm barely crying, really." Anna stroked Ollie's face.

"That was amazing," Ollie whispered, then drew back to press a kiss to Anna's lips. "You're amazing." She kissed her again.

They kissed a little longer, and the ache between Anna's legs throbbed. She pressed against Ollie, rolled her hips, and clutched her fingertips against Ollie's shoulder blades. She whimpered and felt Ollie's hand sliding downwards.

When Ollie's fingers touched her, Anna's entire body jolted. Ollie pulled at Anna's knee, allowed her to bend it to rest against Ollie's hip, then pulled back to look into her eyes. Anna's breathing was laboured.

God, I want her to touch me. She shivered, her gaze shifting away.

Ollie cupped her cheek. "What is it, love?"

Anna swallowed, Ollie's fingers stationary against her sex, barely touching her. "I'm fine."

"No." Ollie removed her hand and Anna nearly cried. "Come on."

Anna looked away.

"You can talk to me about anything."

"I..." Anna swallowed thickly again, her hands up in Ollie's hair, teasing the blond curls between her fingers. "I just...I'm worried I'll...come right away and...and that would be a shame."

"It's all right," Ollie said, her thumb brushing Anna's cheekbone. "I don't mind at all."

"You've just got me so…turned on." Anna said the last two words with a grimace. She'd never been the type of person to say things like that. "I don't want to disappoint you."

"All I want is to make you feel good."

Anna let out a breath, and Ollie smiled at her.

"And if that takes one hour, or one whole minute, I don't care, so long as you enjoy yourself."

They stared at one another for a moment, and then Anna gave a swift nod. Ollie's smile widened.

"All right, then." Ollie leant forward to kiss Anna.

A whimper sprang forth from Anna's lips. *God, I don't think I've ever been so turned on.* Ollie just kissed her for a while, her hand on her cheek, the other on her waist. The hand on her waist moved away, and Ollie's fingertips ever so gently nestled between her legs. Anna tried to relax into her touch, but then she broke the kiss. She wanted to see Ollie's face.

When Ollie's fingers found Anna's wetness, a small narrowing of her eyes displayed her surprise. She gave Anna a gentle smile and kissed her forehead. Her fingers started to brush Anna's clit, which brought forth a grateful moan. Anna canted her hips forward and rolled them back. They found a rhythm together, and Anna was shaking within minutes, so Ollie slowed down a little, caressed her cheek, and kissed her hair.

"It's all right," Ollie told her. "If you want it, you should go get it."

Anna gazed into Ollie's eyes, pushed the crocheted blanket away from her damp skin so it pooled around her hips, and gripped Ollie's shoulders. Her nails dug into the skin at Ollie's neck, and she pushed and pushed and groaned with each thrust of her hips. It was too much, the pleasure, what Ollie was doing to her, touching her so perfectly, and her eyes fell closed.

"Ollie, Ollie," she breathed. "*Ollie.*" Anna's voice became more determined. The name was a mantra, a pledge sworn over and over until suddenly her entire body went still, tense beyond belief on the cusp of maddening pleasure…

Oh God.

It lasted awhile, the orgasm a sea of brilliance washing over her entire body. Once the feeling receded, Anna opened her eyes, her skin prickling where the perspiration was evaporating.

I feel a mess.

She was still twitching, her insides clenching and releasing with aftershocks. Her pulse and breath sounded loud in her ears. The heat from the log burner was thankfully waning, the wood finally glowing simply as embers. She pushed the blanket from her entire body and just breathed, her eyes half-closed, but her gaze locked with Ollie's.

Ollie was positively beaming, her hand still between Anna's legs, like she didn't want to leave. She flexed her fingers after a while, once Anna's breathing had slowed, and at Anna's breathy giggle she withdrew them.

"Amazing," Ollie whispered, pressing her lips to Anna's forehead.

Anna smiled, squeezed Ollie around the shoulders, then stretched her leg back out and rolled her eyes at the crack of her knee, then her hip. She shifted onto her back, stretched everything out, and snorted at the continued pops of all her joints. *I'm too old to be having sex on the floor, however many cushions we're lying on.* She snuggled up beside Ollie, who pressed her lips to Anna's cheek. Anna leant into the kiss and pulled Ollie's arm around her.

"I'm aware we'll be moving to a more comfortable location in due course." Anna's voice cracked, and she cleared her throat. "But, just for the moment, we'll have to remain here on your living room floor."

"Roger that," Ollie said against her neck.

Anna giggled again. "I don't think I can move my legs, let alone walk anywhere," she hissed.

Ollie squeezed her around her hip. "Glad you enjoyed yourself."

"Oh, I did." She squeezed her back on the arm with tired fingers. "I really did." A lump bubbled up in her throat as the wash of emotion swept over her. She stared at Ollie.

"What?" Ollie asked.

Anna continued unabashed. "I love you," she said quietly.

"*Oh.*" Ollie blinked and touched Anna's cheek with the back of her knuckles, then gazed at her for a moment. "I love you too, comrade."

Anna's face broke into a smile so wide, she could feel it. In fact, her face hurt. Ollie snuggled into her neck and laughed, and soon the two of them were laughing into the quiet of the living room, prone on the floor, damp and naked, lying amongst crocheted blankets and cushions, candlelight flickering all around them.

Chapter 13

A Different Kind of Silence

Ice clinked in the glasses Kieran carried through as Helen followed him with a plate of cupcakes.

Anna sat back in her plastic chair, the sun wonderfully warm against her cheeks. "Thank you, team."

Kieran handed Bethany and Timothy their drinks and sat in his own chair. The feet of the chair sunk a little into the damp earth, but Anna chose not to say anything. Maybe it was too early in the year to sit outside, but the sun was bright, and no one seemed to be complaining.

"It's s-so lovely you're here," Ollie said to her children, her fingers firmly scissored between Anna's. Her eyes were soft, and her skin was bright in the sun.

She's so beautiful, even when she's nervous.

When Anna thought about it, it was amazing that both Kieran and Helen were here, visiting the both of them for a springtime drink in her garden. They had come such a long way, especially Helen, the more reserved of the two. But she seemed to understand Timothy more than the flippant Kieran did, and for that alone, Anna would have liked her, despite Helen's hostility at the beginning. Helen was quietly spoken and frank, and Anna could appreciate that. And Timothy seemed to like her, which was always a good sign.

Kieran, nice-looking and kind to Ollie, had been easier to like from the beginning. And Bethany seemed to agree, Anna thought with bemusement.

"Happy Easter," Bethany said loudly, holding up her glass, which contained some kind of fruit cocktail Kieran had assured her she'd love.

Anna raised an eyebrow. Bethany was quite giggly around the new young man in their lives, but Anna was determined to keep them separate, at least until they'd known one another longer than two weeks. Five years was a bit too much of an age difference for her liking. *He's got a beard, for goodness sakes.*

They all cheered, clinking glasses with those people they could reach. Bethany hummed with approval as she sipped her cocktail and gave Kieran a pleased look. Anna rolled her eyes.

Feeling Ollie squeeze her fingers, Anna reached out with a lifted finger from her glass to push that shaggy fringe away from Ollie's eyes. *She still needs a bloody haircut.*

Ollie just smiled more, her eyes crinkling.

"Did you tell Dad yet?" Helen's voice was slow and monotone and her gaze flickered between them both.

Lines appeared between Ollie's eyebrows. "Of course I told him."

Helen just stared at her.

After throwing Anna a "help me" kind of look, Ollie looked back at her daughter. "I think it's been long enough that we're allowed to be with other people now."

"Did you meet his new girlfriend?" Kieran asked, before biting into a cupcake. He didn't seem at all bothered about whether his mother and father communicated about their love lives.

Helen kicked him, not very subtly, and he nearly choked, the cupcake wrapper over his mouth.

"I did." Ollie turned to Anna, who nodded. "We both did."

"She's not as pretty as you," Helen said, her arms folding.

Anna tried not to smile too much. "It's funny, isn't it?" She smiled at Ollie. "I thought the same thing."

"Biased," Bethany mumbled into her drink, but her eyes shone with humour over the rim.

"I think everybody should date people at least as attractive as themselves," Timothy said, his hands clasped around his glass. His expression was very serious and thoughtful.

Bethany laughed, but she nodded, quite used to her brother's strange way of expressing an opinion.

Helen's eyes were a little round, but Kieran turned and smiled at Timothy.

"I think you're right, Timmo," he said.

Timothy frowned. Kieran looked like he'd been kicked again.

"Sorry," he said eventually.

"My name is Timothy. It's on my birth certificate." Timothy's face became bright, as though he was explaining a very simple maths problem to a very slow child. "I like to be called Timothy."

"It's not like he hasn't told you that before," Bethany said, rolling her eyes.

So we don't like him enough not to stand up for our brother.

"I don't mind repeating myself," Timothy said.

"Mum's name isn't the same as on her birth certificate," Kieran said, a grin splitting his face.

A snort sprang forth from Anna, and Timothy turned his full attention to Ollie.

Ollie's eyes went large. She flapped a hand at her son. "Don't you dare, soldier." Her voice became a growl.

Kieran seemed cowed for a moment but then said with a shrug, "Olive."

Blond curls fell over Ollie's hands as she hid her face. Bethany laughed, and Timothy looked back and forth between Kieran and Ollie.

"That's an old lady's name," he said.

"Which is exactly why everyone calls me 'Ollie'." When she lifted her head, her cheeks were bright red. She let her hair hang down to obscure her eyes.

"That's brilliant," Timothy said and joined in with the laughter.

As an attempt to make Ollie feel better, Anna squeezed Ollie's fingers. While the children chatted and continued to tease Ollie about her birth name, Anna looked around the garden. Arthur was trying to catch a butterfly, unsuccessfully by the look of things.

Relinquishing her hand, Ollie leant forward and pulled her hand gently away from Anna's. She made a clicking noise with her tongue and then rubbed her finger and thumb together down by her own ankle.

Arthur's head rose, his eyes squinted in a cat smile. He padded over the soft grass towards Ollie, who looked honoured. The kids were quiet for a moment.

"Hey, Arthur," Ollie said as he rubbed his face across her fingers. She ruffled his ears. He purred so loudly everyone heard it.

"I like your cat," Helen said, watching. "Mum never let us have one."

"Erm, excuse me," Ollie said, smiling at her daughter. "I was all for it, if I remember rightly. It was your father who was adamant a cat was a bad idea."

"He just figured he'd have to look after the thing when you went on tour," Kieran said but visibly swallowed when Ollie looked at him. "That's just what he said."

"Can't say he wouldn't have been right." Ollie shrugged, turned her attention back to Arthur, and smoothed his back gently.

Anna watched Ollie lean down to stroke the cat. The sight made her stomach was warm. She lifted her hand and rubbed soothing circles across Ollie's shoulders.

"He's a bit of a grumpy sod, our Arthur," Anna explained to Kieran and Helen. "Doesn't let just anyone fuss over him."

"Ollie's got the touch," Bethany said, her voice warm.

Anna winked at her daughter and their gazes locked.

With a nod, Bethany went back to her drink, and to her surreptitious observation of Kieran.

"Did you see the wall hanging Mum and Ollie made?" Beth asked.

"It wasn't only us," Anna reminded her. "The whole group helped. Everyone made at least a dozen squares each."

"We heard about it," Helen said.

"Wasn't it like a mile wide or something insane?" Kieran asked.

"That would be almost impossible," Timothy answered. "A mile is one thousand six-hundred and nine metres and thirty-four centimetres. Each square averaged about twenty centimetres."

Everyone looked at him wide-eyed, but he continued. Anna wasn't sure if he had noticed their shock or if he was simply ignoring it, anxious to get out his calculations. "That means a blanket of a mile wide would need at least eighty-one squares. And that would just be one row. If it was two metres tall, say, you'd need eight-hundred squares." He turned to Ollie. "How long would it take the group to make eight-hundred squares, Ollie?"

"The mind boggles, Timothy, it really does."

Anna gazed at Ollie with affection tingling in her belly, and Ollie shot her a wink.

Apparently satisfied he was better at maths than Ollie, Timothy continued. "A long time. A very long time. Did you see the photos?"

Kieran and Helen got up and came over to Timothy so he could show them the photos Sandra had sent Ollie. Anna glanced over. The hanging reached the ceiling and nearly covered half of the window next to the space for which it was intended. Pride spread through her stomach.

Arthur was rubbing his spine along Ollie's shin when another butterfly appeared into his field of vision and he pounced off in search of a chase and a tasty snack.

They all laughed, watching his small feet and skinny tail bobbing around.

Ollie sat back again, pushed her hair from her face, and slid her fingers back between Anna's.

"How are things going with your assistant?" Helen asked, going back to her chair. Kieran followed her.

"It's...not awful," Ollie replied.

Anna nudged her and she rubbed at the back of her neck.

"Good. You needed someone to help you out," Kieran said.

"I've been telling her that since the day we met," Anna said, brushing Ollie's cheek briefly with a fingertip.

There was another lull in the conversation.

"Plans to move in?" Kieran asked, and from the look between him and Helen, Anna could tell it was something they both wondered.

"Not just yet," she said, her attention on Ollie.

Ollie shook her head. "It's early days." She squeezed Anna's fingers.

"I can't count the number of kids in my classes who talk about *Jacob's mum* and how *Jacob's mum* has shacked up with some bloke after knowing him for three weeks. And five minutes later they've broken up, and I have to deal with the subsequent '*Jacob's mum's a slag*' comments."

"Why pick up the pace?" Bethany said, and Anna's cheeks burned. "It took you so long to get together."

"Slow and steady wins the girl. No sense in marching on ahead," Ollie said so quietly that Anna wasn't sure if any of the children heard.

The sun seemed to shine just a little bit more brightly as she looked down at their joined hands. She wanted to lift Ollie's fingers to her lips, but she wasn't sure. She was anxious about doing anything that would irritate or anger Ollie's children. To be fair to them, they had been through a lot. It couldn't have been easy finding out your mum had cheated on your dad with a woman while she worked away. And Ollie was just getting to know them again.

Ollie looked right at her, however, and lifted Anna's fingers and kissed her knuckles. She was looking at Anna as though they were alone, like the kids weren't there watching them.

Anna's anxiety floated away with the spring breeze. She laughed. Ollie smiled back at her, the silence between them comfortable and gentle. Anna caught the morning scent of first-mown lawns, the sweet smell of flowers starting to open. She watched the butterflies and bees and Arthur scrabbling for a spider in the grass. She sighed happily and looked around at their strange but mostly happy family gathered all around. The trees rustled, the sunlight flickering between the leaves. It dappled across Ollie's face.

Wanting to hold on to that perfect image, Anna closed her eyes, content to sip at her fruit cocktail and hold hands with the one person she cared about the most in the world.

About Jenn Matthews

Jenn Matthews lives in England's South West with her wife, dog, and cat. When not working full-time as a health-care assistant at a mental health rehab unit, she can be found avidly gardening, crocheting, writing, or visiting National Trust properties.

Inspired by life's lessons and experiences, Jenn is a passionate advocate of people on the fringe of society. She hopes to explore and represent other "invisible people" with her upcoming novels.

CONNECT WITH JENN

Website: www.jennmatthews.com

Twitter: @whispersmummy

E-Mail: jenn@jennmatthews.com

Other Books from Ylva Publishing

www.ylva-publishing.com

Lost for Words

Andrea Bramhall

ISBN: 978-3-96324-062-1
Length: 300 pages (104,000 words)

Massage therapist Sasha's meddlesome mother and best friend conspire to shake up her mundane existence by entering her into a scriptwriting contest. She's not entirely sure how she feels about the life-upending chaos that ensues, which includes meeting an attractive, perfectionist film producer. A bittersweet lesbian romantic comedy about the fun of never knowing what life will bring.

In Fashion

Jody Klaire

ISBN: 978-3-96324-090-4
Length: 220 pages (68,000 words)

Celebrity Darcy knows all about perfection. She's famous for stripping bare and restyling women on her UK TV show, Style Surgeon. Fans hang off her #EmbraceDesigner tweets and there's no challenge she can't meet. That is, until security guard Kate struts into her changing room. Suddenly Darcy's the one who feels exposed. A lesbian romance about facing and embracing your own unique design.

Heartwood

Catherine Lane

ISBN: 978-3-95533-674-5
Length: 311 pages (86,000 words)

When the law firm she works for sends Nikka to the Springs, home of lesbian author Beth Walker, she is determined to prove herself to her boss, Lea.

But nothing is as it seems. Beth is hiding her past with a film star. Lea may be keeping Beth prisoner in her own home. The only person who knows the truth is adorably impulsive Maggie.

Will Nikka dare look into the mystery—and into her own heart?

Party Wall

Cheyenne Blue

ISBN: 978-3-95533-886-2
Length: 223 pages (63,000 words)

The moment Freya looks at the new sex shop, she knows it will clash with her new-age store next door. She's right. Outgoing newcomer Lily begins to intrude on Freya's ordered life. The woman stands for everything Freya has lost—playfulness, spontaneity—even sex. But does Lily have more in common with Freya than the wall that divides them? A lesbian romance about crossing lines that hold us back.

Hooked on You

ISBN: 978-3-96324-133-8

Also available as e-book.

Published by Ylva Publishing, legal entity of Ylva Verlag, e.Kfr.

Ylva Verlag, e.Kfr.
Owner: Astrid Ohletz
Am Kirschgarten 2
65830 Kriftel
Germany

www.ylva-publishing.com

First edition: 2019

Credits
Edited by Michelle Aguilar and JoSelle
Cover Design and Print Layout by Streetlight Graphics

Made in the USA
Coppell, TX
12 April 2022

76411381R00173